I0606734

The lead detective said the case was cold, no new leads, but she didn't buy it. This was one case she was determined to solve…

Sam scanned the office. Nothing great. A bland doctor's office in a hospital. Sterile. White walls. His diplomas hung on a wall opposite his colonial, dark wood desk. No pictures on the wall. Either he wasn't a showy kind of guy, or he didn't feel that this place was his milieu.

She deduced that it was both. If she was going to help him find his wife's killers, she'd have to know him and, so far, this hunk hadn't let out a clue to his emotionality. Everything she needed to know about him was hidden behind his even temper and soothing, deep voice. She had to make a connection with him, even on a primal level.

"Is this your private office?"

"Yeah. I insisted they get me something where I could write out my reports in private. Hate doing them at the nurse's station. Way too busy for me."

She removed a huge file from her bag and put it on his desk, looking for the slightest reaction. Nothing.

Frank didn't pay attention at first. He didn't seem to be in a hurry. She couldn't believe that it didn't affect him anymore. That surprised her and worried her at the same time. He had probably been through Jen's folders more than a million times and didn't expect anything different from these new ones. Discouraged and pained would describe how he probably felt. It had been over two years. It was considered a cold case now. She agreed with the lieutenant on reopening it. Never give up on a colleague's case, no matter how long. There's no statute of limitations on a murder case, so she'd do what she had to, even wake up the dead.

Lying. Deception. Cover-ups. Anger. Revenge. Death. That's what happens when an Aries-obsessed killer combines black magick rituals, knives…and murder.

Samantha Wright, a rookie NYPD detective, gets her first case, a big one, by stumbling over the body while jogging in the park. Sam has a lot to prove, both to herself and to her new precinct, on this serial murder case involving fashion icons in New York City. Together with a rough around the edges BJJ fighter, forensic psychiatrist, Frank Khaos, Sam chases down leads through the five boroughs of NYC. As the bodies pile up, sparks fly and Sam and Frank, polar opposites, go from their dislike of each other to setting the sheets on fire. But their main suspect is hooked up to an IV in a hospital bed, so how has she pulled off five murders in seven days? And can Sam and Frank stop her before more innocent lives are lost?

KUDOS for *Aries*

In *Aries* by Ronnie Allen, Samantha Wright is a brand new detective, out to prove herself on a high-profile murder case. Her precinct calls in Dr. Frank Khaos, forensic psychiatrist, to profile the killer of a high-fashion designer. When a second designer turns up dead, Frank and Sam are confused because their main suspect is in the hospital and was there under guard when the second murder took place. Still, Sam is convinced the woman is guilty. Now all she has to do is prove it. Like the first book in the series, *Gemini, Aries* is a solid psychological thriller, but this time with a twist in the form of a BDSM romance between the two main characters. Makes it all that much more appealing. ~ Taylor Jones, Reviewer

Aries, The Sign Behind the Crime ~ Book 2 by Ronnie Allen is another first class thriller by an obviously talented author. Our heroine Sam Wright is a newly promoted detective, starting at a new precinct in New York City. Her first day on the job, she is running in the park before going into work and stumbles over a body. The case turns out to be big, really big, and Sam has her hands full, not only with solving the case, which turns out to be a serial killer, but also with the handsome, rough-around-the-edges shrink the precinct calls in to help her find the killer. Allen has crafted another page turner, this time adding a hot and heavy romance with some bondage and domination elements that give the story a unique twist. If you like romance, along with edge-of-your-seat tension, you'll love Aries. ~ *Regan Murphy, Reviewer*

ACKNOWLEDGEMENTS

I love writing the acknowledgements for my novels. It gives me the chance to thank people who helped me along my journey to publication. For *Aries: The Sign Behind The Crime, Book 2,* there were many.

I'd like to thank my critique partners, Mikki Cober and Judith Kammeraad, and my beta readers, Darlene Cochran and Sherry Wilson. Without these gals, I couldn't be confident that Aries was ready for submission.

An important aspect for crime-based thrillers is to have accuracy in police procedure. So, when you know how it really works, you can then stretch protocols for the sake of fiction, which I did. Any misinterpretation of the facts is on me. Thank you, Ralph Bud Brumley, FBI retired; John Ciuffo, NYPD retired; and Butchy Lyon, Rikers retired. These men told me how cops roll, about intra department cooperation, ranks, what it's like on the inside, gang relationships, weaponry, forensics, and a lot more. Also, Fiona Quinn, the creative force behind ThrillWriting—the blog that helped me with all things crime and forensic.

A fun part of writing Aries was delving into a field I do not know anything about from my own experience. That was BJJ, Brazilian Jiu Jitsu, the ground-fighting component of Mixed Martial Arts, and Muay Thai, stand up, kicking and punching, fighting. Even though mixed martial arts, MMA, matches are not allowed in New York State, training gyms are. There are many gyms in the Tri-State area. Thank you to Brian American, BJJ Black Belt from Team Link Mixed Martial Arts in Connecticut, who let me use his gym rules. And thank you to Christopher Lyon, BJJ fighter, who told me about gym set up and what a gym looks like, weight classes, workouts, how to use the heavy bag, attitude in the gym, and much more.

I'd also like to thank my editors at Black Opal Books, Lauri and Faith, for bringing Aries to fruition, and Jack in the art department for my awesome cover.

And of course my husband of forty-two years, Bob, who continues to allow me to spend more time in my characters' heads than with him.

I hope you enjoy this romantic thriller and the wild ride it'll take you on through the five boroughs of NYC.

ARIES

The Sign Behind the Crime
Book 2

Ronnie Allen

A Black Opal Books Publication

DEDICATION

To survivors of life's greatest challenges,
who picked themselves up and flourished.

CHAPTER 1

Eyes cemented shut in deep concentration, palms placed upon her midriff, she felt the power she craved being directed straight into her core by Tuesday's new moon, as if a cord attached the moon to her solar plexus. She interpreted the moon's personal signal as something she'd better heed. The charts she referred to told her tonight marked the night—perfect for an Aries to invoke her deepest desires. Nothing else mattered now.

Opening her eyes, she checked the light-resistant blinds on the window facing Garfield Place, leveling the way they fell on the sill. She pulled them tightly to make sure they shut out any reflections from the streetlights. The last thing she wanted was someone taking a glance in her direction, intruding on her peace.

She needed to remain low profile now. Everyone had told her that she'd been and would be "low profile" her entire life. She hadn't realize how important those two words would become. Low profile—low, unsuccessful, pitiful, minuscule, never good enough. From the time she entered school, those words had drilled apart her soul.

Even at night, this upper crust Park Slope neighborhood didn't sleep. Her tree-lined street was residential, but an avenue away the new age shops, restaurants, cafes, bakeries, and fresh-food markets all hopped until midnight. The aromas of fresh baked bread and European cuisine found their way into her windows, especially now, in late fall when Brooklyn had cooled from the hot summer.

The residents, though, minded their own business, so she could do what she wanted, when she wanted. In fact, they ignored her. She'd been living in this northern part of Brooklyn eight months and not once had any one of them asked her how she could afford it. They just gave her dirty looks, as if she didn't belong. She assumed that's what they were thinking. They had no idea if she rented or owned. These yuppies were too busy climbing their own ladders in the arts to be bothered with a nobody like herself. But she'd show them. All of them. Soon she'd be at the top, looking down on exactly the right people.

She stood facing her altar in the dark basement with her arms up in the air, spread apart, palms facing each other. Under her black ritual robe, she felt the heat swell within her, rising up from her core to the top of her crown. She was ready.

"Oh, Goddesses of the Dark, and Aradia, the Devine Queen of Witches, hear my call tonight," she whispered. "In the light of the moon in the Mars hour, I, BlackRam, High Priestess of the Covenant of Lasting Darkness, hereby summon every deity in my circle to come to me now. As I use my wand to consecrate the four directions in your honor, I vow to you my complete devotion."

BlackRam glanced at the clock on the wall behind the altar. Nine p.m. She nodded. She had marked off this hour as the moon in Mars conjunct, perfect for plotting an evil deed. And, yes, she was evil, down to her demon soul. She faced east, held her right arm out in front of her, and, with her selenite wand grasped in her hand, encased herself with spiraling motions. First, her aura in front of her, then above her head, and lastly behind her back—all the while, making sure that she stayed within a two-foot circumference. "I invoke, from the Dark Goddesses, commitment to my beliefs." Then she turned south and repeated the same movements with the selenite wand. "I invoke, from the Dark Goddesses, success and strength." Then she faced west. After repeating the movements with the selenite wand, "I invoke, from the Dark Goddesses, a flexible nature." She turned to face north. The selenite wand whisked through the air. "I invoke, from the Dark Goddesses, accomplishment." Now facing the altar, she continued the invocation.

"Oh, Goddesses of the Dark, I have proved my devotion to you. My triple-beholden will require your strength to walk the left-hand path. As I gaze into your light, bestow upon me the power and energy to command my triple-beholden, BlackMoon, BlackFlower, and BlackCloud, to carry out my deeds. Command them to worship me, obey me, without fault or hesitation. Make their obedience unfaltering, no matter the difficulty, complications, or forces by others to disobey. I'm tingling with ripples of warm energy running from head to toe. I feel my body swaying forward and back in rhythm to your burning flames. Your dancing light empowers me to accomplish the tasks at hand. Oh, Goddesses of the Dark, I am indebted to you. Thank you, Goddesses. I will make you proud. This spell will not place any curse upon me. As I proclaim in Hecate's name, my beholden and I shall remain Dark Souls Forever."

She bowed her head for a moment, giving thanks, then stepped back to admire the altar. The black and white paisley silk cloth lay neatly, covering the mahogany bar in the basement of her brownstone. She concentrated for a moment, remembering Hecate's favorite oils, then chose from her assortment the small bottle of Death Commanding Oil from a shelf, standing on the left side of the bar. She tilted it to let a droplet touch the middle finger of her left hand. Her right middle finger met with the left. Gently she tapped the sides of the black, seven knobbed candle from bottom to top. As the candle released the aromas of jasmine, basil, and pennyroyal, its flame, dancing high and strong, gave her the affirmation that her deities surrounded her. Forming a circle around this candle, she placed five more. Three black, two red—five, seven knobbed candles. One knob for each day. One week was all they had. Five candles for five deaths. Five deaths in seven days. Then she and her beholden could disappear.

No. She could disappear.

Her beholden would be dead.

BlackRam picked up her lighter. The flame ascended with a pop. She held the wide sleeve of her robe close to her right arm as she lit the other five candles and then stepped back to the left side of the altar. Everything was in place. Chunks of black tourmaline and logs of kyanite lay interspersed between the candles. The blues and the silver tones in the kyanite balanced her chakras and deflected negativity from her, as did the tourmaline. She released a prolonged breath.

She'd need as much protection as she could muster. A wooden pentagram, six inches in diameter, lay in front of the candles closest to her. She worshipped this five-pointed amulet, never performing a ritual without it. She lifted it off its programming bed of clear quartz crystals, brought it to her heart with her palms crossed over it, and then replaced it on the mantle.

As she adjusted the hood of her robe on her head to conceal

her hair, she bent her head down toward her chest. She inhaled deeply as the scent of lavender whiffed across her nose, remnants from her cleansing bath to prepare for tonight. She reminded herself she had to clean the tub. This time she had remembered to put in the plug so the carnations wouldn't clog the drain again. Boy, were they hard to get this time of year. She had finally found a florist in Carroll Gardens that had them preserved in silica in the fridge. She bought the entire stock. Five bags of petals cost her over a hundred dollars, but it was so well worth it. There was nothing like her cleansing bath, soaking in a tub, and rubbing her body down with carnation petals until they crumbled in the rose water that was sprinkled with lavender oil. She inhaled deeply to bring the scent within her memory into her nostrils.

Everything had to be perfect. Her gaze traveled the circumference of the magick circle she had created on the rose-colored tile floor. Not one grain of salt was out of place. Only a small path remained without the marking. She checked the mahogany bench that hugged two walls. Each of her beholden had her favorite cushion. Affirmed. They were in place. The mahogany panelled walls, bookcases, and ceiling still radiated the scent of the lemon cleansing oil she had used earlier today. There was not one atom of negativity from the outside to impede their ritual tonight.

Contented, BlackRam turned her attention to the bolline on the altar. Lifting it, she gazed at the pentagram on its white marbleized handle. With her fingernail, she scraped the remnants of wax from her previous ritual off the curved blade. She'd use it tonight when carving amulets for her beholden from the candle wax drippings. They loved her amulets. They felt protected. Little did they know when the amulets were in their pockets, they would be commanded to commit murder.

ↄ☙ↄ

They dragged the naked body, trudging backward into the dense foliage in the park on the outskirts of Chelsea, in the lower west side of Manhattan, with a flashlight app on their smartphones guiding the way. Two women with latex-gloved hands held him, while the third kept lookout, and lifted his feet to help, but she grimaced and had to let go. The two pulling him couldn't ignore the foul odors of his discharge upon death, either. Most of it remained in his GT-R coupe and on his Armani suit, which he wouldn't miss. With his butt scraping against the ground, more fecal matter would be removed from his body.

BlackFlower knew they'd have to cover those tracks. She wondered what it would take to clean that one-hundred-twenty-grand ride but, just for a moment, to re-think if they had left any evidence behind. She checked their left wrists. Good. The white band with the letters DSF in black, honoring their sisterhood, remained in place. On the three of them.

She had a job to do. It had to be done. Now. A few more weeks and the trees would be barren. The only ones that heard the rustling of bushes were the birds that were up at four-thirty in the morning. Not even joggers passed through here at this hour. They'd made sure of that. Planning had taken months—the park, their prey, everything, down to the hour, the Mars hour. The kill took place at four a.m. She had only another half hour to execute the commands.

"Damn! This guy is heavier than he looks. This place is good. You two leave. This was my kill, and I've still got lots to do. Gimme that, Cloud," BlackFlower barked as she grabbed the knapsack Cloud had slung over her shoulder.

BlackFlower hated that, using a shortened name, but when they addressed each other, BlackRam insisted they drop the "Black." It was just too cumbersome to say, especially when she chastised them. BlackRam granted permission to use their formal Wiccan names when they performed ceremonies, and only then. To BlackFlower that was demoralizing, demeaning, and childish. However, it was her job to obey.

Flower saw Cloud and Moon shine their lights over the path made by the dead man. *Good*, she thought. *At least they're being useful*. She reached into the knapsack and handed them fresh disposable gloves. After they put them on, she handed each of them a small rake with an expandable handle and a black garbage bag. Moon pulled the handle up. Flower knew Moon would know what to do. This wasn't her first time disposing of evidence. Actually, Flower had to admit that this wasn't the first time for any of them. Aside from their own indiscretions, if Ram had her way, and Flower knew she would, this week wouldn't be the last, either.

The two women knew their assignment. Whatever leaves, branches, and dirt they or this man had touched on the path coming in was to be raked up, put in a bag, and dumped in the river on the east side. That included every item of their clothing except their wristbands. Wouldn't find evidence so easily across the borough. That would give them more time without interference from the cops. Flower studied them as they retreated. They packed so much into the bags, Flower doubted that any evidence would remain. Lastly, she'd have to clean up after herself. It was part of the plan. Faltering equaled punishment. At one time or another over the last couple of years since they formed Dark Souls Forever, each one of them had succumbed to Ram's wrath. One time was all it took.

Flower crouched down on her knees on a bed of leaves by the body of the man who weighed about one sixty at five feet, nine. He appeared to be in good shape for a guy in his fifties. She poked at his ribs and waist with her index finger. No fat. Not good. That would add some complications.

She pulled a ponytail band out of her jeans pocket and picked up her mid-back-length cornbraids, tying them back. Some strands of her coarse black hair stuck to her latex glove. She moaned a sigh of relief, glad she noticed, but annoyed at the same time that she'd wasted precious moments. She pulled the strands off the gloves, rubbed them between her fingers to make a ball, and stuck it into the zipped compartment inside the knapsack. She put on another pair of gloves just in case the first became torn.

From inside the knapsack she retrieved a plastic surgical cover-up, placed it around her neck, and tied it behind her, covering her T-shirt and jeans. Good thing she was wasn't overweight. She could wrap it around her. Next, she slipped on plastic arm covers, to protect her still open, self-inflicted wounds from splatter and transference. Yeah. Bandages covered them, but you never knew, and they oozed. Besides, they hurt like hell. She dug two fingers into her jeans pocket and pried out a thirty-mg Blue. She popped it into her mouth and dry swallowed, giving a non-verbal thank you to her street pharmacist for her supply of oxycodone. She retrieved a new plastic mat, removed its Saran protective sheath, and placed it on top of leaves next to her. Everything was brand new. It had to be done right—no, more than right. This was by far the most important kill to date. She removed her tools from the knapsack.

Two paring knives and a machete.

CHAPTER 2

The phone ringing at six a.m. made her stomach queasy. She stretched, rolled over in bed, picked up the handset, and glanced at the caller ID. *Shit, what could have possibly happened now?*

She sat up, leaned against her light wood headboard, and paused before answering. Stalling, she adjusted her pillow behind her back in the hopes they would hang up. No such luck.

"Hi, Mom, what's going on?"

"Nothing, Sam. Just wanted to hear how my darling daughter is feeling about going into work today."

Sam rolled her eyes and pushed the comforter down to her thighs. "Mom, I'm fine."

"Well, it's not every day you move up a rank. And Daddy and I…well, you know, are just a little concerned."

"Mom, you've been telling me this for four years now. It's getting old."

"Yes, but, every day you seem to be going deeper into the trenches."

"Mom, the only difference between today and yesterday is my uniform. I'm in plain clothes now."

"That doesn't mean you'll be behind a desk more, does it? I hope."

"Not exactly, but I'll never be alone either. Please stop worrying. You're putting undue stress on me, not to mention yourselves." Sam glanced at the clock embedded in a floral vase on her night table. "Okay, Mom, I've got to get ready. Love you."

"Love you too, baby."

Sam looked at the handset. *Yeah right, baby. I'm thirty-seven and a detective.*

Pulling the covers off her, the excitement hit! She'd made it. The rank she'd been aiming for—detective in Manhattan Midtown South.

Nothing would be as memorable as her first day.

She sat on the edge of the bed with her feet dangling, looking around at all she'd accomplished. She had finally saved enough to purchase, and furnish, her own house, in her own style, contemporary. She stared at the faux painted wall that was behind her dresser. Wow, she had fallen in love with that muted-line design the moment she had seen it in the book. She nodded. Yes. It definitely looked better close up and personal in her own shades of teals, blues, and greens. She still couldn't believe the hassle she had, finding a painter. Finally, one of the girls at her gym had told her about this guy in the East Village. He ripped her off, though, charging a lot more for him having to schlep to Brooklyn. She'd never tell him, but his fee was so well worth it. Still, the inside didn't reflect the frame of the house built in the 1930s. She'd get to the outside in due time.

She had five hours to get to her new assignment, so she figured she'd get in a run. Showered, dressed in sweats and a T, she almost made it out the door, but the ringing phone forced her to stop. Looking at the handset, she answered the call with a sense of dread. "What's up, Loo?"

"Sam, I know you're not mine anymore, but I really need you on this one. Cleared it with your new captain. Domestic disturbance. Not far from you. I'll text you the details. Get there ASAP. Don't even bother to change."

She glanced down at her sweats.

How in hell did he know that?

෫෨෫

She stopped at the base of the stoop and checked her Glock 19. Ready to go, she replaced it in her waist holster covered by her T-shirt. Walking up the stairs to the front porch of the attached, two-family home on the tree lined block in Sheepshead Bay, Brooklyn, she heard the commotion from inside the house—a woman and child, screaming. Her first instinct was to call for backup, but it arrived, as if on cue. She abruptly turned and faced him, as he walked up the stoop.

He leaned against the wrought iron banister that outlined the perimeter of the porch, his arms crossed over his chest. "Nick Valatutti, your new partner. Some way to get acquainted, huh?"

"A detective from Manhattan South in Brooklyn? How you'd manage that?"

"Captain to captain deal. No time for that now. It's your lead."

Sam got the impression, on the spot, that this was a test. She sneered at the suited man twice her size, her intense glare sending him a message that she got it, and turned her attention to listen to the noises coming from inside the house.

She knew better than to bust in. Last time cops did that, a teenage girl was shot and killed. This was no time to be a maverick. This was the time for her to use her strongest weapon, her training. She knocked on the door.

"Who's there?" yelled the gruff, angry voice.

"It's Officer Samantha Wright, Mr. Holden. I was called because of the disturbance inside."

"There's no disturbance. Go away."

"I'm sorry, Mr. Holden, I can't do that just yet. Is it okay if I call you Mr. Holden?"

"Yeah, but nobody calls me mister. Yeah, okay, you can. Ah am Mr. Holden. Just go away."

Sam smiled. She made a positive dent in his self-esteem. "I'm sorry again, Mr. Holden. I can't do that just yet."

"Why not?"

"Well, I heard a child screaming in there, sir."

"That ain't your business."

She leaned her head closer to the door. "Yes, sir, it is. Can you tell me what's going on, Mr. Holden?"

"I'm not talking to no cops."

Sam paused before speaking, her eyes widening. "Had some bad experiences?"

"Some."

Good, he's talking. She nodded, different thoughts running through her mind. "In New York?"

"Yeah, and back home, in Alabama."

Nick got on his smartphone and made contact with his office for info on this guy. In a few minutes, a rap sheet came up. *David Holden. Forty-two. Three arrests for aggravated spousal abuse with those charges dropped by his wife, two arrests for petty larceny, and one arrest for prescription drug trafficking with fire-*

arms, for which he spent a dime in federal lockup in Alabama, 1999-2009.

"Okay," Sam whispered after reading the sheet. "Plans may be changing." She turned her attention to the door. "Mr. Holden, how long have you lived in Sheepshead Bay?"

"Why?"

"Well, we just like to get to know the people we're talking with, you know? Just to make conversation."

"Three months, but ah can't get this bitch here to move back to Mobile with me."

"Oh, that's too bad. Why doesn't she want to go?"

"Doesn't want to leave her dang family. An' ain't leaving this bastard kid."

"It sounded like a little girl. Is she your daughter?"

"Yeah."

"How old is she?"

"Three, almost four."

"Oh, that's such a sweet age. I don't have any children yet, but I'd love a little girl. So what's the problem, then?"

"Ah'm not letting them leave. That's what the old lady is bawlin' about."

"Oh, so you're holding them against their will?"

"I don't like the sound of that, Officer…what did you say your name was?"

"Samantha Wright. Yeah, well, you're not allowed to do that, Mr. Holden."

Nick got on the phone and called in a hostage situation. Sam glared at him. "I got this."

"Not taking any chances. Go on."

Is he my partner or my boss?

"Mr. Holden, may I please come in, so we can relax and talk about this? I'm getting tired, standing here."

"You wanna come in? Hah! Just so ya know, I got firepower in here."

"Oh, what do you carry?"

Nick shook his head. "You're staying out."

She mouthed "Shut up" to him. "Mr. Holden, out of curiosity, what do you have?"

"A couple automatics, an' ah ain't afraid to use them."

"I believe you, Mr. Holden, but why would you want to?"

"This bitch is annoyin' me."

"Have you been married a long time?"

"We ain't married. Just met her when I got out of lockup, and she had this brat."

"You don't sound like you love them, so why are you preventing them from leaving?"

There was a tension-filled minute of silence. Sam glanced at Nick who already had his SIG P226 held down at his side.

"Ah do love them, I think."

"Well, if you love them, why do you want to hurt them with guns and all?"

There was another long minute of silence. She'd made him think. Good. Nick nodded. She read his body language. So far, he approved.

"I dunno."

"You know, Mr. Holden, I'd really like to sit down and talk to you. So we can help fix this. And no one is hurt yet, right?"

"No, no one ain't hurt."

"Okay, that's good. Very good. So why don't you let your precious little girl—you do think she's precious, right?"

"Yeah, she's precious."

"Okay, so why don't you let your precious little girl and girlfriend out, and you and I can talk?"

After what seemed to be an hour to Sam, the door crept open, and she saw the brownest little eyes looking up at her with tears streaming down her face. She looked angelic with about twenty barrettes in her braided hair. Her pink dress was tattered and looked about two sizes too small for her already petite frame.

"Hi, sweetheart. Is Daddy letting you come out?"

After receiving a meek nod and sniffles, Sam glanced over the little girl's head to view the inside of the living room. She saw Mr. Holden seated on a couch, holding a Luger 9 mm to his girlfriend's chest. He had pinned her next to him with his right arm around her shoulder.

With caution, Sam took the little girl's hand in hers and escorted her out of the house, onto the porch. Nick scooped her up in both arms, holding her against his chest for a moment. He then handed her over to a female officer right behind him, who ran with her to a squad car.

Sam watched for a moment as squad cars and an ambulance got in place. Officers cordoned off the narrow one-way street to keep bystanders from coming close. Two detectives exited a car and started to approach. Nick gave them a hand signal to back off. Um…he was actually letting her continue?

Sam turned her attention back to the open door and slid it open a sliver wider. As she stood in the entryway, she didn't see a hardened criminal. She didn't see a man who wanted to do harm. She saw a man who looked more weathered than forty-two, balding, and who looked tired of the lifestyle. He looked plain exhausted, with bags under his eyes, a paunchy stomach, and soiled white undershirt. The tattoos on his now undefined biceps had faded from their original reds and greens. Some looked like gang tats. "Mr. Holden, may I come in?"

"What did you go ahead and do? Call all the cops in the city?"

"It's standard practice when someone tells us they have weapons and are holding someone against their will, sir. I'm just following the rules." Sam crept in to the entry hall and leaned against the doorframe. Her gaze scanned the room—sparse, only the couch against the pale blue wall with a chipped glass coffee table in front of it.

"He's threatening to kill me," cried the thirty-something woman. She wrung her hands together on her lap as she kept her gaze peeled on the gun.

"What's your name, hon?"

She swallowed and made eye contact with Sam for the first time. "Carmen, Carmen Rivera."

"Mr. Holden, you do see how frightened Miss Rivera is, don't you?"

He gave a pitiful laugh. "Yeah."

"Come on, Mr. Holden. What do you expect to accomplish?"

"What do ya mean?"

"You expect a woman to want to be with you when you hold her and her child at gunpoint? That's not what love is about, and you did say you loved them, right?"

Carmen's hand tenderly touched his. "And I love him too, most of the time. Most times, he's sweet and kind to me. I just don't know what ticked him off. Where's my baby?"

"She's safe outside, Miss Rivera. I'd like to know what ticked him off too, so why don't you tell us, Mr. Holden? What really got you ticked off today?"

He lowered his gun and let it fall between his knees, though his finger remained on the trigger, then lowered his head as if ashamed. "They're after me again."

"Who?"

He kept his gaze down on the floor. "Some dudes I used to run with in the hood back in the day. Who ah went to prison for."

"So why take it out on Miss Rivera and your daughter?"

"Ah thought that if I got arrested again, I could get protection. Know what ah mean?"

"Yes, I do. We could have protected you without you having to resort to this. So how about it? Let Miss Rivera go and we can talk about it."

He paused. "Okay." He shoved the woman off the couch. She ran out of the house without looking back.

"Mr. Holden, slide your weapon across the floor over to me, please." He slid the gun around the coffee table. "Good, now get down on your knees, please, with your fingers interlaced on top of your head. You'll talk to us down at the precinct."

He came out from behind the table, knelt beside it, and three uniformed officers rushed in to take over. She had reached her goal of no shots fired.

Sam bent over, her hands on her knees, and let out a deep sigh of relief as Nick approached her. "Nice job."

She looked up at his stoic face. "Thanks. And thanks for letting me run with it, without letting them interfere."

Nick didn't respond to her last comment, but nodded. "Just remember, you won't get praise easily from me, or often. See you at the precinct." He turned to walk down the steps.

"Hey, Valatutti. You're not my supervisor, remember that."

He paused for a moment but didn't turn around. With his back toward her, he retorted, "And you're a detective now. Get used to using the title. Remember that."

She looked after her training partner as he skipped down the steps. What a bastard! A handsome one, but a bastard, nonetheless. Tall, long straight dark hair covering his shirt collar, hazel eyes, clean-shaven rugged facial features, looked muscular under the suit. She couldn't help but notice his wide marriage band on his left hand. He was definitely off limits. Okay, he was one man whom she could count on to be safe.

She walked to her Murano and slipped into the driver's seat. She retrieved the recording device from inside her bra and turned it off. Transcribing her report, which Nick had to review, would be much easier this way, and would fairly determine Mr. Holden's fate. That was what she would tell them, anyway. In reality, she didn't remember what she had said. In times like this, her Spirit Guide, Dara, took over.

It looked like she had just opened another case for this Brooklyn precinct. But to be honest with herself, she was glad she wasn't a part of it anymore. Everyone would get her DD5, in the meticulous way she had always written them, and her part would be over. Yay!

Now, she needed that run. She'd be able to get it in before heading to her new precinct. She'd shower and change into a suit when she got there. With her hands on the steering wheel, she sat for a few moments, reflecting on the past few days. She spent quite a bit of time choosing her outfit once she got notice. Everything planned down to the smallest detail. Something that would scream professionalism, yet display her femininity. Something that would make the men and women in this Manhattan division respect her, even though she was the newbie.

She looked out the car window. Clouds formed, predicting rain. That was okay with her. When starting a new venture, rain was an omen of good luck. With a new partner like Nick, she'd need as much luck as she could conjure up.

ↄﬞↄ

She loved this park in the outskirts of Chelsea. It was always clean. The residents here didn't litter. The dense foliage bordering the jogging track was trimmed and unobtrusive. Orange, yellow, and red leaves, shed from the trees and bushes, padded the ground. Caretakers did their best to blow the leaves off the track, but their efforts were short lived. She felt as if she'd escaped to the country, if only for an hour. If she took pics of this quadrant of the park, without buildings to intrude, no one would know this was lower Manhattan.

The rain hit just as she reached a half mile. Just a drizzle, not nearly enough to stop her. She made another half mile with her heartbeat not even reaching her optimum. One thing that served her well in the academy was her strong physicality.

Then the thunder boomed and jolted her but, with no lightning, she continued. Rain poured without warning a moment later. Okay, there were warnings. She chose not to heed them. She found herself splashing in the puddles on the track. This wasn't one of her smartest moves, but she needed to release the tension from this morning. Her light gray sweats were drenched and stuck to her. Her T-shirt clung to her breasts. Oh God, she'd have to sneak into the back entrance of the precinct looking like this.

And I wanted to be taken seriously?

With her jogging attire adhering to her body like saran wrap, she felt she looked like a pin up in a porn magazine. She could have been one, too. Hadn't she refused a couple of years ago, less than politely? She wrung out her ponytail while she stopped under a tree for shelter. Her white sneakers, saturated with rainwater, had turned red. Red? She looked at her legs and red water splattered up both, to her crotch. This wasn't red water.

This was blood.

She ventured into the dense foliage, following the flow of the darkest red. She spread her feet to walk beyond the outline of the stream, pushing aside dangling branches with her forearms, careful not to touch the branches with her hands.

She stumbled upon the dead man.

Literally.

She twisted her body like a contortionist, so she'd land on her butt, not flat on her face when she fell over his blackened toes. Sitting up with her hands in the air palms facing out she stared at the mutilated dead man fed upon by vultures. Damn it!

She recognized him.

CHAPTER 3

With headphones on, bobbing his head to the beat of the rap on the YouTube video, Frank Khaos sat pensively at his desk in the back office of his gym, tapping a pencil on a folder while analyzing the thought processes of his new charge. The beat was typical to a 2K14 rap, steady rhyme scheme—fourteen syllables a line, sixteen bars long, fast tempo.

Frank sighed. *Okay, the kid could follow a pattern. Good. Could pay attention. Think logically? Maybe. Depressed. Telling the story of his life. The story of his gangbanging life. The story of his years upstate in a New York prison.*

The kid had posted this—Frank checked the date of the YouTube video—last week when he got out. What wasn't included, which didn't surprise him, were any aspirations for the future. Nothing to say what excited him. Without a passion, he knew this kid, this gang fringe member, would be heading right back to the Harlem gang that initiated his incarceration.

Okay, first job. Find out what gets this kid up in the morning.

Opening the kid's jacket, he peered into the cold, heartless eyes of a nineteen-year-old's mug shot. His face was expressionless. His Afro looked filthy with specks of cotton, most likely from his sweatshirt. Acne raged on his forehead and chin. His oval shaped face was clean-shaven. Both parents were African American from his facial features.

Frank knew those eyes wouldn't have changed, even though the kid was now twenty-four. The kid had gotten five years for possession of one firearm and three glassines of heroin. Guess he didn't hit the square. Yeah. Definitely. A gang initiation gone bad.

He was supposed to sell the glassines to a customer who

turned out to be an undercover DEA agent. The gang denied knowing him. No one came forth to say that he could have been set up. Frank shook his head. *That's the way it is in gang related cases. No one to talk to. No one gave a damn. Witnesses disappear.* The notes in the file indicated that he wouldn't rat. *Good thing. He'd be dead by now if he had.*

A knock at the door brought Frank back to the present. He closed the folder, slipped it into his middle desk drawer with his headphones. He turned in his swivel chair to face the door. "Come in."

The door opened. "Doc, Jarvis McKinley is here."

"Thanks, Dale. Come on in, Jarvis." He looked up into the cold dark eyes he expected. The teenage acne was gone. "Have a seat." He pointed to a club chair opposite his desk.

Jarvis came into the office, looked around at the furnishings, his eyes smug, and his lips pursed together.

Frank had made it a point to decorate in plain woods in his desk and wall cabinets that hugged muted beige walls. The carpeting was a brown tweed that pulled together the light brown tones in the upholstery in the couch and club chairs. It was nothing to intimidate or tempt for burglary or vandalism.

Jarvis sneered and sucked his teeth at Doc as he sat down in the chair. As he leaned back with resentment on his face, he rubbed his hands over the scotch guarded fabric armrests. "My name is Pitbull. Don't fly by Jarvis."

Frank smiled, knowing he'd knock that smug look off his face. In time. "In here, you do. How did Pitbull come about?"

"My mama named me that when I was a kid. Said I'd attack like a pit with no reason. Sorta stuck. An' I do." He leaned forward and stared straight into Doc's eyes.

Frank assumed Jarvis didn't see anything through that stare. "Why are you here, Jarvis?" He relaxed, leaned back in his chair, his arms on the armrests, open and ready to handle the anger that he had trained himself to repel and make slide off him like warm butter.

"Don't you know? You get all my homies in here."

"I want to hear it from you. What do you want to gain from being here?"

Jarvis emitted a sadistic laugh, shaking his head. "I've been warned about you. You like to get inside everybody's head. Well, White Boy, you ain't gettin' inside of mine."

Frank didn't flinch a muscle. He'd never back a kid into a corner, not unless he wanted to be bit by a venomous snake. "White Boy, huh? How'd that work on the inside if you called someone that?"

"I had my share of bein' in the box, not for long, or maybe longer. Don't remember." He shrugged. "Those correction officers, they messed with any of us from the hood they could get their hands on. But I don't care, I'm good at fightin'."

"Tell me, how many times were you put into solitary?"

"A couple months at a time. Maybe three, no, four."

"That probably delayed your release. Did you know that?"

"Yeah. I had no place to go, anyways. An' fightin' is the only thing I'm good at." The smug expression hadn't left his face. The expression deepened. Pride.

"Well, in case you haven't thought about it, so am I, Jarvis."

"Oh yeah? Let's go, anytime, anywhere." He perked up ready to strike.

Here comes the venomous snake.

Frank had gotten the response he wanted. He was little unorthodox in his methods, but they worked. He didn't crack a smile, knowing it was a sure sign of disrespect to laugh at the comment. "Not so fast, Jarvis. We will." He settled on a deliberate pause. "In the cage, when you're ready."

Jarvis' eyes lit up for the first time. "You're shitten me."

Yeah, Frank got the response he wanted, again. Jarvis became interested and engaged. "Nope. But first, see the rules up on the chart on the wall?" Doc pointed and Jarvis nodded. "What's the first one?"

"Khaos Rules." Jarvis read it but squinted as if confused.

"That's the name of the gym. Look at the twenty items below that."

"Check your ego and your bad day at the door."

"What does that mean?"

"Don't know what ego is." Jarvis glanced away.

Okay. He's embarrassed. Let it go. "Attitude, thinking you can take on anyone," Frank responded casually. "If you're pissed at someone from something that happened earlier in the day, you don't bring it in here."

"Uh, that's gonna be a problem. The COs upstate told me all the time that I got that problem. I don't forget. In lockup, you couldn't forget. Had to watch yo back all the time."

"Well, here you'll learn how. Before you leave here today, you'll read the other nineteen and remember them."

"Yeah sure," Jarvis said.

Frank shot him a glare.

"I meant, the first rule will be hard for me, an' I'll read the rest of 'em. But I gotta tell ya, I'm not good at followin' rules."

"Think that's why you've gotten into so much trouble?"

"Probably."

"Even your gang has rules. Follow them?"

"Yeah, too good."

Frank nodded. *The kid's getting it. Hopefully, the five years did him some good.*

"Hey, what do I call you, anyways?"

"Definitely not White Boy. Khaos, Doc, Frank. Sometimes, I even get called Dad. Whatever comes out of your mouth that's appropriate." He gave it a moment to sink in. "Got your med clearance?"

"Yeah." Jarvis tugged it out of his baggy jeans pocket. He handed Frank a crumpled piece of paper.

Frank handed it back. "Un-crumple it. That's an official document."

Jarvis tried to smooth out the wrinkled paper, rubbing his hand over it, on his knee. He handed it back.

Frank nodded, his lips curling up in approval. "You're five ten, one sixty, you look like you're in shape. Work out in the gym much?"

"Every day, upstate. Pretty big gym, too."

"What did you do?"

"Weights when we were cleared for it, cardio, they had us run track. It was way better than working out in a homie's basement. We couldn't afford to go to a real gym."

"Very good. In here, you're in welterweight. You'll learn the weight classes for matches. Just to give you a comparison, I'm six four, two seventy, which puts me in super heavyweight. If you were participating in a United Fighting Championship regulated match, we call it UFC, you'd have to fight someone exactly your weight, but here, in training, we mix it up. Okay, right now you're clean. Plan to stay that way?"

"Yeah. I do. The junk they caught me with wasn't mine. It was for a sale. I don't shoot."

Frank looked at him long and hard. "What did you do?"

"Barbs. They detoxed me at Rikers. Been clean five years. I could have gotten shit any time, but us with drug offenses, they searched our cells and lockers at random, strip-searched too, and they didn't hesitate to go in. You're gonna read it anyway in my file. The first time a CO did that to me, he went in deep. He pulled an' it hurt, man. I had nothin', no drugs inside of me, but I shitted on his fingers on purpose. The food was givin' me cramps an' I let it all out. Man, they were pissed. That earned me a beat down by three COs an' four months in the box. Couldn't help it. I had to let them know they were hurting me. But I'm not usin' now."

"Okay. Good. Just so you know, as a condition of your probation, you'll have mandatory drug testing."

"Yeah. I know. My probation officer told me."

"Good. He'll call me if anything comes up, even performance enhancing stuff from a health food store. You do not want that. Not only will you be bounced from here, you'll go back upstate. That wasn't your first arrest. Got it?"

"Yeah."

"And I have to let you know what we talk about in here, stays in here. Nothing's recorded."

"You expect me to buy that?"

"Yes. You have doctor-patient privilege."

"I know you're a shrink, but that even goes in a gym?"

"Yes, I hate that term, though. I'd hate to think I shrank anyone. But yes, I'm a psychiatrist. The only time I have to report something to the police, immediately, is if you tell me a crime is about to go down. No matter how small, no matter to whom. Understand that?"

"Yeah, that outreach lady who comes to speak with my mama told me the same thing."

"You mentioned your mom twice, so are you close with her?"

"Yeah. Very. When I went away the first time I was sixteen and only for ten months. That almost killed her. An' this time, I was sure it would put her into her grave. I can't hurt her no more. I gotta stay clean an' get my act together."

Frank was getting closer to finding out what he needed to know. His starting point. "What have you thought about doing to make that happen?"

"Don't know yet. Upstate I got my GED an' I got trained for electrician. Got a certificate. But I was talking to my PO. I still got a lot of 'anger issues,' he called it. Thought comin' here would help me deal with it, an' I like fightin'. I busted up some gangbangers real good."

"Okay. Come on, I'll show you around." Frank got up, flexing his muscles, stretching every part of his torso. His T-shirt clung to his defined mass.

Jarvis got up and stared at him with his gaze following the outlines of Frank's chest and settling on the tats that covered his arms. He backed away a bit, licked his lips, and swallowed.

Good, got the intimidation across.

Intimidation was big in gangs. Physicality ruled. The bigger, the better, equaled more respect. So did weapons. The bigger the better. Frank felt his Glock 19, NYPD issue, in his ankle holster rub his leg as he started to walk. It wasn't the biggest, but one of the few in this building. No need for Jarvis to know about that.

"You wear the name of the gym on your T-shirt?" Jarvis asked.

"Yeah. Good advertising. Everyone in here wears it. Everyone—cleaning people, trainers, and all the guys who work out here. In this gym we're all equals. Uh, except for me. My word is final."

"Uh?"

"Know the difference between a noun and a verb?"

"Uh, no."

"A noun is a thing, a verb, action. It's both with me. My rules, the noun, and I rule, the verb. What I say goes in here. Got it?"

"Yeah, but I gotta say, Doc, that maybe you should look at the first rule."

All right, he could dish it out and take it as well. "Okay, Jarvis, well done. As long as you said that respectfully, I'll let it slide. Are you ready for a workout?"

"Yeah!"

"Let's get your gear."

Frank opened the door to the office and walked with Jarvis down a hallway into the main part of the gym. He stood for a moment for Jarvis to take it in. It was a *lot* to take in, over seventy-five hundred square feet of the best mixed martial arts equipment as could be found in any upscale MMA Manhattan gym.

But this one was in Central Harlem, in the poorest area, and it was free.

"Can anybody come in here?"

"Only if they're in a New York City gang. If they're referred by their probation officer, lockup, outreach, or if I recruit them."

Frank counted his blessings every day that he had this gym and was able to give back. He mouthed a big "thank you" to his parents in the sky, who, by adopting him at ten and getting him out of the group home, had prevented him from becoming prey for his neighborhood gang.

He glanced at Jarvis who probably had a similar childhood to his own.

Man, could things have turned out differently.

Dale approached and handed Jarvis his workout gear. A black Khaos Rules T-shirt with the letters in a white Gothic font with a white leaf pattern forming a rectangle border, black cotton pocket-less workout pants, a protective cup, white crew socks, fingerless black leather gloves, and low top, solid white sneakers.

"Thanks, how did ya know my size?"

"Everything's in your file. The locker room is through there. Pick a locker, make sure you remember the four digit code you type in. Put everything in there. Even your phone. No phones in the gym. Don't want any calls or texts interrupting a workout." Frank looked at his wrist. "Leave your ID band in there, too. And make sure to wear those gloves at all times in here."

"Why the band and gloves? Maybe I'll meet one of my homies in here that joined when I was away."

"Exactly. No flagging. No gang affiliation IDs in here. No one knows who's in what gang. All equal. Clean slate. Can't hustle anyone if you don't know who's who and you can't judge them either."

"But even in lockup we had our tats showin' on our hands so people could see our set. So people outta our crew knew better than to mess with us."

"Okay. I'll address that. Been asked before. First, this isn't prison. This is real life, a real gym. Guys in here want to leave the gangbanger lifestyle. Don't want temptation. And we want to encourage communication, not keep people away. Even in training, guys won't want to fight if they think you have a gang to back you up when you go out the front door. Besides, it's how you make out in the cage that forms who you are, not the gang. Got it?"

Jarvis nodded. The light bulb went on. "Thanks." He headed to the locker room.

Dale stood with his hands on his waist. "Okay, Frank, how did it go?"

Frank smiled at his best friend. "He'll be fine. He's a good kid. I think I can save this one."

"Why would I expect you to say anything different, bro? Where do you want to start him, any idea? We have a spot in the beginner wrestling group."

"No, no groups yet for this kid. Individual training first. I get the impression he isn't a team player just yet. Oh, while I've got you here." He pointed to the back end of the space with the mirrored wall. "I noticed some of the vinyl tiling around the treadmills and step machines aren't lying flat. Get some of the kids to snap them back into place."

"Will do."

❦

As Jarvis looked around in awe at the massive area, Frank saw him relaxing. The kid looked limber, eyes less rigid, facial muscles less taut. He relaxed in the gym, too. It was his protective environment. Jarvis nearly tripped over his own feet, as his attention was glued to the cage, when they walked past.

He looked excited and scared at the same time. "When are we goin' in there?"

"It will be a while. But it will happen." *If you stick around long enough.*

He led Jarvis to a punching bag in the corner where the balls were kept: stability balls, resistance bands and tubing, medicine balls, balance trainer.

"What's all that stuff?"

"We'll get to everything Jarvis, not all today, but we'll get to it. Today we're working with this. Have you ever used one?"

"They had smaller ones, narrower ones. This one's a wide sucker."

"Yes. This one is for full body contact. It's a one hundred fifty pounder. Called the heavy bag. Use it for Muay Thai. Stand up fighting. Striking. Kicking."

"Yeah, that's what I'm good at."

"Good. That's why we're starting here."

"Okay, cool."

Frank handed him ten-ounce black boxing gloves from a

hanger on the wall. "First, I want you to get a feeling of the floor underneath you. It's anti-slip, vinyl. If you guys spill anything, even bottled water, you're expected to clean it up."

"Got it."

"Jog in place for a few minutes. Let me know if you can feel it move with you."

"Yeah, I can."

"Good that's for shock absorption. Less injury if someone falls. All right, in the gym upstate, what did you do to warm up?"

"They only had a trainer in there with us, once in a while. Usually we just went to the weights."

"Uh-huh, not here. We do a full body warm up before we touch a piece of equipment. Show me how you'd stretch out and limber up. Do you know the proper names of movements?" Jarvis gave him a distant stare. "Okay, if I told you to do a lunge, would you know what that is?"

Jarvis gave him an offhanded smile. "Oh, stuff like that, yeah, sure."

I'll take care of that cockiness. "Awesome. Give me ten lunges, each leg, twenty squats, twenty swings, then get into a plank position, hold for twenty seconds, and give me twenty push-ups."

Jarvis, stood with mouth gaping. "Uh?"

"Well?"

"Hang on, Doc. I never did it like that!"

"Okay, help me understand. And I need you to be honest. Is it the sequence that you have a problem with, or remembering them, or the number of reps?"

"Everythin'!"

"All right. Let's do this." Frank started off slowly, showing Jarvis the right form for each exercise.

Jarvis paid attention to everything, working along with Frank, performing the movements with him as Frank modeled them. Good, the kid really wanted to do this. After getting him up to half the number of reps, one round, Frank knew he had to reward the effort with the heavy bag. In between exercises, while catching his breath, Jarvis hadn't taken his gaze off it.

"All right, Jarvis, ten minutes on the bag. Give it all you got. Full body. Go."

Jarvis slammed the bag with the agility of a street fighter, not with the skill or form of an MMA trainee. *In time*, Frank thought, as he analyzed and noted Jarvis's style on his clipboard. After three minutes, Jarvis stopped dead. Sweat poured down and out of every pore in his body. He couldn't catch his breath. He bent over.

Frank handed him a bottle of water. "That was only three minutes."

Still not catching his breath, Jarvis had a hard time getting the words out. "I—can't do—no more."

"Okay. For today. Your first goal will be five minutes, then up to ten. Then up to an hour. Hit the showers. You're responsible for your own laundry."

"How often can I come here?" Jarvis asked with still-labored breathing.

"Every day if you want and you can stay as long as you want."

The kid grinned from ear to ear for the first time. "Thanks, Doc."

❦

Frank heard the heavy click of the bolt as he locked the door behind him. Back in his office, he slumped in his chair for a moment and closed his eyes.

He wasn't any closer to coming to grips with his wife's murder after two years, one month, six days, and fifty-three minutes. He swallowed hard.

Opening his desk drawer on the bottom right, he hesitated this time and exhaled a prolonged breath. He needed courage every time he did this. He lifted the sterling silver frame that laid face down. Turning the frame over, he gazed into loving eyes.

Oh, man, Jen, I sure miss you. Frankie misses you. Every day I tell him how special you are. How his mommy is watching over us from heaven. How his mommy sees everything we do. I have to tell ya, Jen, though I'm sure you already know. Frankie got a little rambunctious the other day. I took him in my arms and patted his behind, love pats.

He laughed, but I know you wouldn't have approved. Then I grounded him. Two days, no cartoons. Then he stopped laughing. We agreed upon it, Jen. Zero tolerance for disrespect.

Tears trickled from the corner of his eyes, audible whimpers from his mouth. Good thing his office was soundproofed.

Jen, I swear I'll find out who did this to you. I'll find the bangers who mowed you down, just to get even with me. I promise, princess. I promise.

CHAPTER 4

Nick grimaced at the remnants of paint odors from last week's renovation as he sat at his desk, involved in preparing his report from this morning that he knew he had to send to Brooklyn, ASAP. His cell rang. "Valatutti."

The last thing he expected was a call from his new partner. She still had an hour before her shift began.

"Nick, Sam. I need a team here, now. Off the Tenth Avenue and Twenty-Second Street entrance to the park. Mutilated body. Male. Bring me sweats and sweat shirt, and towels. I'm a mess. I put in a 911 call a minute ago."

"On it." Nick surveyed the office to see who was available. He shouted out to Dingo Withers, lead homicide detective, who was at the other end of the open space, chatting with a few uniformed cops. Vacant desks in quadrants in the space between them caused his already baritone voice to echo. "Get a team, guys, now! Body in the park." He went back to the call. "Why are you in the park when it's teeming out?" Nick was up, weapons holstered, and out the door as he continued talking.

"Needed a run. Never mind that. Look at it this way, I landed my first case."

"Your case?"

"Yep. I'm declaring it as mine."

"We'll talk about that, Wright."

"Just get your ass here. I need sneakers, too. My clothes are evidence."

"Stay put and don't touch anything."

"Nick, don't insult me. I know the drill." She disconnected before he could respond.

Ass? She told me to get my ass, here? And hung up on me?

Oh, man, she's going to be a picnic to work with. First job— knock her down a peg or two.

As he was racing to his SUV parked in the precinct's outdoor lot, Withers caught up to him.

"What have ya got, so far?"

"Not much. Male and mutilated, and she's wet. What were you doing out of your office? Don't have enough homicides on your plate?"

"I had to speak to Loo about something. He told me to tag along. What do you mean, she's wet?"

"That's all I got. She hung up on me."

"Hung up on you? Not even one-step into the building and your new little partner hung up on you? Oh boy. Glad I ain't you. You're going to have your hands full with this one. Looks like she needs to be taught how we roll."

Nick could swear Withers's baldhead had reddened, and that would be nearly impossible with his dark brown skin. "I realize that. Hate to say it, but she did great this morning."

Withers rubbed his nose with his index finger and smoothed out his mustache at the same time. "Yeah, she's got a good rep in juvie cases. But as a detective? It's coming down the pipeline that she isn't going to make it here."

❧

The rain tapered off by the time Nick arrived at the scene and got out of the car. He didn't neglect to notice Sam's perfect body through her clingy sweats and T, even though she was covered in mud and blood. Her ponytail hung loose. Straggling wisps of hair stuck to her face. He smiled for the first time. His wife was never going to meet this one. Blonde and blue eyed with the perfect nose and full lips, to boot. Nope, his wife was never going to meet her.

Sam approached the other suited man who also towered over her. "Hi, I'm Sam Wright."

It was all Nick could do, not to laugh. He knew Dingo well enough to know what went through his mind.

"Dingo Withers, lead homicide expert from Homicide Investigative Unit. What have we got here?"

Nick couldn't mistake his curt attitude and, he assumed, neither could Sam.

"What are you doing here?"

"You lucked out, rookie. My unit is housed in your precinct. I'll be busting your ass."

"Okay, Withers. I see this as a test, right?"

He didn't crack a smile. "I said I'd be busting your ass, but no. It's the job of a first responder, and you, Detective Wright, happen to be that person."

"I was the first on scene, yes. No one has gone into these woods since I've been here. No civilians to interview. The scene is safe. No assailant. On first look, I saw blood still oozing from wounds. So they're somewhat fresh. The rain wasn't pouring down so forcefully when I was under the shelter of the trees near the body. It's a lot of cuts, more than ten at first glance. I got up after I fell. So you'll have my DNA evidence that was transferred because my arms touched the branches, yeah Locard's Exchange Principle, and there'll be wet origin footprints. Didn't notice any other footprints going to or away from body. Ooh, ooh, ooh. There's more!"

Oh, man. How old is she?

Nick bit the inside of his cheek to keep from laughing.

"I knew I shouldn't have taken the direct path to the body because that's probably what the assailant did. But I had no choice. The bushes on either side are so dense. See them over there? So there was no other way to get through. I did, though, try not to tread in the water. Didn't stick around to make exact count of cuts. Kept my arms straight down at my sides when I ran out and my eyes on the ground. Didn't see any weapons or possible tools. Noticed the puddle water was red, right over there where I was standing when you pulled up. Splattered up on me as I jogged through it. I haven't gone back to the body, but looked at it through this path.

"While I was waiting for you, I took pics on my phone of my shoe prints, the soles of my shoes, which have mud embedded in them now, the splatter on my clothes, and I documented the time, and conditions with my ID. I also noted the exact time the rain started. Also made videos of the flow of the water from every angle, except directly from the body. As I said, I didn't go in there again. In one of the videos when I replayed it, I found…"

She set the video to pause on an object deep within a bush low to the ground and gave him the phone. "This oval white thing. Looks like a band of some kind. I didn't touch the bush, or try to retrieve it. May have some blood residue, but I'm not sure. It's down deep enough, so I can't tell how much rain hit it. We actually shouldn't even be standing here. It's within three hundred feet of the scene. The body is less than twenty feet in. I'm thinking that the killer or killers wanted the body found. They could have taken it deeper into the woods. I did see some indentations in the ground that indicated a path. Took pics of that, too. Maybe they dragged the body. But they also raked up leaves and debris, and removed them, leaving a muddy path around the body. I fell butt down into that mud." She twisted around to show them.

Nick couldn't help but look at her perfectly rounded bottom. He had to turn away to conceal his burning cheeks. He saw Withers do the same.

"Maybe trying to outsmart us by removing what they considered to be evidence, so what we see on the surface may not be what really is. In removing stuff, they actually told us a lot. I'm getting the impression that because of this, the murder was premeditated, carefully planned, and not random. As I'm thinking, it could be a woman. Maybe she wasn't strong enough to pull him farther, or it was more than one woman. Can't tell if the wounds were post mortem and I definitely couldn't see the COD. And it stinks. Had a full meal before he was offed, otherwise he wouldn't have released fecal matter. I know it's not dog poop, stepped in enough of that while jogging. Nope, this isn't dog poop on my sneakers."

She raised her foot to show Withers. He just stared at her with his eyes widened and his mouth slacked open.

"I stepped in it next to the body. Oh, and he was laid on his back, hands down at his sides, arms and legs intact, cuts on torso, eyes open, and—"

Withers cut her off. "Are you finished rambling? How in the hell are you going to remember what you just said? I don't see your brown book. And I need your notes, Detective."

"Oh." Sam plucked her recording device from inside her bra. "Always have this with me. I turned it on when I came across the body. I also recorded my prelim before you got here."

Withers blew out a breath. "You mean to tell me, rookie, you recorded what you saw and then proceeded to give me this long-winded ramble? So now I have to go through two fucking tapes? And your complaint form?"

Sam shrugged her shoulders as Nick tried to conceal his

laugh, again. He nodded in approval at her recount and still couldn't take his eyes off her. A uniformed patrol officer brought over a duffle with fresh clothes and towels. He couldn't help but check her up and down, either. He shot Nick a you're-a-lucky-bastard look. Nick grinned back.

Withers retrieved evidence and garbage bags from the trunk of the SUV. "Here, Valatutti, hold up a towel for your partner so she can change. Put each item of your clothes into a different bag. I'll see that it gets processed in less than two hours. Everything, including underwear and socks, sneakers. Go."

"Change right here?"

Nick glared at her. "Suck it up, Detective."

"You better not drop that towel, Detective."

Nick held up the towel spread out by both hands. The garbage bags hung from his wrists by their ties. Sam pulled off her T-shirt and deposited it into a bag. All the while, Nick looked up at the sky. He would have loved to peek, but how professional would that be? In his fifteen-year career as a detective, he was respected for his integrity when working with partners. The only reason he was assigned to be Sam's partner was because Carol Hubbard, his former partner was home, recouping from a bullet she took trying to thwart a grocery store heist when she was off duty. He loved working with Carol. He thought about the rapport he had built with her over six years and how it would be unparalleled. He knew they could depend on each other to cover their backs. They were at the point where they completed each other's sentences.

He had trained Carol, quite successfully, he thought, so when she took that bullet, he blamed himself. He thanked God every day that she had recovered. So it was a natural and timely fit that Sam would be assigned to him, and it was Carol's injury that opened the position for Sam. His rotten luck, this little big mouth was next in line. Nick had asked the captain not to assign another rookie to him, but his asking wasn't strong enough, and he wasn't the type to beg. Even as a detective second grade, in New York City precincts, he didn't have his way with assignments. The job demanded he follow orders, promptly.

Sam tugging at the drawstrings of the garbage bags forced his attention back to the matter at hand. She had changed quickly. Nick had never known a woman who could get dressed that fast. She handed the bags to a patrol officer.

Nick stared at her. "Guess they misjudged your size."

Sam pulled the two-sizes-too-big sweatshirt out from her body and laughed. "You think? At least it's big enough to hide my boobs. They didn't send a bra."

Nick chuckled.

"Okay, I see you're short in the smile department, Valatutti."

"Yup. Deal with it."

Withers had called Crime Scene and the coroner's office. He paused for a moment. "Officer, get that to the lab, ASAP. Process immediately. Can't have this wet crap forming mold. Detective Wright, give me your phone. See if we can zoom into that white band."

He held up the camera, cut, and cropped an image. "Three letters, numbers, can't make them out. But we'll get it."

Crime Scene arrived in about forty minutes. Now time would stand still. These guys didn't rush. They had one opportunity to catch every bit of evidence. Immediately, the two-man team in personal protective equipment jump suits, PPE, approached Withers.

He gave them the initial report. One of them got out cotton swabs and took DNA from each of them, from the inside of their cheeks in order to distinguish them from any other persons that came up in the evidence.

Sam didn't take her gaze off the investigator, as he wrapped the cotton swabs in white paper, using the pharmaceutical fold method to keep them from falling out, put them into separate manila envelopes, and marked them with his ID number, name, location, time, and conditions.

Nick observed her the entire time. Her intent seemed flawless. To him, it looked like she had a photographic memory, calculating each step. Then he remembered what she'd told him. 'I declare this case as mine.' That meant it would be his, as well.

The investigators unloaded their van. Out came tables, tents, lighting apparatus, generators, physical and trace evidence manila bags with retrieving implements, garbage bags for wet items, laptops, cameras, powders, gelatin lifters, fuming glues, brushes, chemicals, tarps, and white boards to lay the victim on. Nick knew the process of set up would take at least an hour and a half, with only two guys, before they could start processing the scene. This was going to be a long day and more rain was in the forecast.

He called to the investigator putting out the crime scene tape. "When can we get in to see the body?"

"Hold on, Detective. The body's never processed first. In the middle, maybe, probably at the end. We gotta examine the path to the body first. And in this place, do you realize how much evidence we need to collect?"

Sam chimed right in. "Yup. Impressions, fingerprints, biologicals, serology patterns, entomologicals, botanicals, trace—macros and micros."

Nick shuddered and looked up at the sky.

Oh, man. This one could annoy the fleas off a dog.

"And don't forget about me. Transfer," Sam added.

"Just the three of you don't move. We'll get working on your shoes when we can," the investigator retorted with a smirk.

"Hey, rookie. Let's get something straight. Right now."

She looked up at Withers with a solemn expression.

He waved his index finger at her face. "No one here, and I mean no one, is impressed with what you know. So put a plug on the Samantha-knows-it-all-hose and stop spraying us. It doesn't matter what you fucking know. What does matter is how you put everything together. And so far, you haven't showed me squat. Capiche?"

"I most certainly did in my prelim."

"No. You formed a hypothesis, based on what, I do not know. Not on facts, for sure. We don't have any facts yet, other than it's a dead man. You better not form theories on what this case is about based on your hypothesis."

Nick saw the disappointment on her face. Okay, she did need to be knocked down a peg. He could always depend on Withers to be the bad guy.

Another hour passed until an investigator came over, camera ready. He directed each of them to raise their feet, one at a time until he shot about twenty pics from every conceivable angle. Foot molds were taken, so their footprints would be compared to others at the scene.

Nick watched Sam's reactions. That was his job. To assess her every move. She still looked mesmerized by everything. He thought she looked like a little kid in a museum for the first time, learning, being the sponge, soaking up every detail. She appeared to be a quick learner. Good. He could live with that. Overall, he was impressed with his new, big-mouthed partner.

The investigators put white raised boards from where the three detectives stood to the crime scene near the body. In addition to the time that they had already spent, it took them another half hour to board the twenty-five feet. The detectives' shoes were taken, packed separately in garbage bags, and they were given replacements covered with surgical booties. They were getting closer to seeing the body.

"Oooh. Oooh. I almost forgot." Sam jumped up and down like a little kid.

Withers had lost patience. He bellowed. "What?"

"I know him."

Even Nick had lost patience with her now. "You know him? You know the victim?"

"Not personally. I mean I recognized him. Steven Larcon, Larcon Fashions. I love his evening wear."

Lava from the top of Withers's head erupted. "You mean to tell me that you IDd the victim and you're telling me now? Three hours into being here? Three hours that was wasted! Three hours that the media could have gotten hold of this? Do you realize how traumatic it would be for the family to have found out about this from Facebook and Twitter first, before we notified them? This is going to cost you, Wright. And send you right back to your fifth grade classroom in Brooklyn, where you belong."

"Withers, take it easy." Nick tried to lead him away. "She did good. Saved us the ID."

An investigator interrupted them and signaled. Withers trekked to the body with Nick and Sam following.

Nick stared at a half-eaten man with pus formed and coming out of about twenty cuts from a small blade, from his neck to groin. He closed his eyes and turned away, not only because of the flies he had to swat, but because, even he, with fifteen years investigating homicides, never had gotten used to scenes like this. But it was the job so his turning away was just a momentary lapse. Then he refocused. At scenes like this, he acknowledged first, that this was his job, and second, that people depended upon him to cope. That was his motivation. Next, he always thanked God, that it was no one he personally knew.

Sam stared at the mutilated man and her complexion turned ghostlike. Nick grabbed onto her arm as she bent over and turned away. After a moment, she composed herself and pointed. Nick followed her finger to about ten feet away. He became dizzy, too.

He grabbed an investigator who joined them with an it's-nothing-out-of-the-ordinary stare. He marked the foot-path, took about twenty photos—including of the bushes surrounding the object—and positioned cone markers to note the path. Then he waited.

"Hey, Barry, he's been chopped."

"Got it!" With gloved hands, Barry bent down and picked up the man's genitals, scrotum attached. He wrapped it in white paper and deposited it into a manila evidence bag, marked it with his ID, time, date, location, and weather conditions. "Just another day at the office, Detectives."

"When can we get the body to the ME?" Nick asked.

Barry glared at him. "Are you kidding me, Valatutti? We haven't even fully set up yet. Just doing this to accommodate you big-wigs. Got at least twenty hours here. And I'll have to call in more crew. Just keep the family away."

"Okay. But it looks like a lot of anger taken out on this one. I'll call Doctor Trenton," Withers said.

"You can't, Dingo. He's in Florida, the lucky bastard, recouping from a bullet he took in his last case."

"Ah. Knew he was shot, but didn't know he hadn't come back yet."

"Yeah. He almost got himself wacked on the Montgomery case. A few times. All right. I know who I'll call. Khaos, Frank Khaos."

Withers squirmed. "That MMA guy?"

"You got a problem with him?" Nick asked.

"Yeah. But I'll deal with it." Withers looked like his mind had taken a spaceship away from the scene.

CHAPTER 5

Get yourself into the lieutenant's office, now, Wright!" Dingo Withers hadn't stopped chewing her out, the entire ride from the crime scene to their precinct. His voice stretched beyond raspy. He led the way down a hall with Sam and Nick following. Sam observed Nick avoiding eye contact with anyone in the office, as he walked, eyes down, scrutinizing the new flooring. Guess she had embarrassed him, too.

She hadn't said a word to Withers during his tirade. He wasn't worth the effort. All she knew was that he'd have a stroke if he continued and smoking had taken its toll on him. He had had at least three at the crime scene. Good thing he put his butts into a bag, not dropped them in the water. At least, he hadn't contaminated the scene more than she had. Damn him for making fun of her report. She could tell it was a female killer. But he was right. She'd have to prove it.

Some of the other men and women in uniform, working at their desks or standing at the water cooler, rolled their eyes when they heard him bellowing. She wasn't the only target of his aggression. Okay, he had a rep. Nothing personal. This guy was limited on people skills. She hoped he wouldn't be the one to make the family notification.

There didn't seem to be a warm bone in his body. He didn't flinch when he saw the dead guy. Not even when he realized the guy was missing his family jewels. Most men she knew would grab onto theirs as an automatic protective response or, at least, make a hand motion toward their groin. All right, this guy was less than human.

She made a pact with herself, right there, that she'd never become so heartless.

She'd do her best not to work with him. He was toxic and she'd do all she could to prevent his energy from penetrating her. She'd had the experience of negative energy traveling into her and digging in like vermin, and she had to protect her own energy field at all costs. She had gotten rid of all the toxic people in her life by distancing herself and breaking ties. Usually, that was all it took. That was, along with her secret methods. If this Withers had to be in close proximity to her, she'd no longer be able to stay in the closet. She would have to blatantly show these men what she could do.

Yes, Dara. You'll be working overtime here with me.

And her partner, Nick. He must be the strong, silent type. He did react at the gruesome scene, just for a moment, but it was a humane reaction, nonetheless. They hadn't had a moment to talk to get to know each other, or for him to tell her the ropes. She did see him pull Withers over at the scene to tell him to lighten up, but it fell on deaf ears. In the car, Nick did nothing to shut him up, either. You couldn't talk rationally to an irrational person, at least not at that moment. *Guess Nick felt that way, too.*

Right now her mind was reeling between of the hostage situation first thing in the morning and the gruesome murder a little while later. She hadn't even met her new loo yet.

What kind of an impression was she going to make with her hair full of mud, wearing a sweat suit two sizes too big, with no underwear?

Oh yeah, nothing would be as memorable as this first day.

Withers knocked at the lieutenant's office door. "Come in, Withers. Heard you down the hall. Who pissed you off, now?"

Withers opened the door and practically shoved Sam in, landing her right in front of the lieutenant's desk. She read his nameplate facing her, *Lt. Miguel Rojas.* The lieutenant stared at her, his gaze traveled from her head down her legs. He removed his glasses, placed them on his desk, and stood up.

Oh my God! What does this precinct have, all the handsome men?

She stood there examining the dark Latino man with the mustache, extended soul patch, and largest round brown eyes she had ever seen on a man. His full head of wavy jet black hair made those eyes seem even bigger. Oh God, how would she be able to focus on what this man was saying?

Dara, help!

"Who the hell are you?" His sharp tone straightened her to attention.

"Uh, Detective Samantha Wright, Lieutenant."

"You look more like the suspect, than one of my detectives."

"Sorry, sir, we came here right from the crime scene. And I was off duty then."

The lieutenant shot both Nick and Withers disdainful looks. "And neither of you thought to let Detective Wright get herself presentable before dragging her into my office, for our first meeting? Don't say a word. I'll deal with you, two, after, but I damn know well who the instigator is." He glanced at Withers. "What have you done to get Detective Withers so pissed off?"

"I don't know, sir. I gave him a recount of the scene as any first responder would."

"You're leaving two important things out, Wright. Own up to it."

"I IDd the body, Lieutenant, but in the moment, I forgot to tell that first. I didn't mention it until Crime Scene arrived."

"And what else, rookie?"

Sam didn't know what else. Her stomach fluttered. She was at a loss for words. Never had that happened to her. She had to get over this brain freeze. She glanced up at Withers and swallowed.

"You told your new partner here, that you landed your first case? And with the victim making it high profile? I don't think so. You come in here with the audacity to take charge. Well, rookie, standing there in your two-sizes-too-big sweat-shirt-and-pants, try to convince the lieutenant now that it should be your case."

"This is your case? Okay Withers, point well taken. Why should it be your case, Detective? And I use that term very loosely now, since you are not coming across as one."

This isn't fair, but homicide isn't fair. Saying that would definitely not fly. Come on, Dara, if it was any time I needed you, I need you now to fill in the blanks.

"Okay, Lieutenant, I'll tell you why. Number one, I discovered the body. Fell into it, no, over it, actually. I was there as the first responder. Number two, you'd need a detective on this case, anyway. I made a full recording of a prelim and I recorded everything I told Detectives Withers and Valatutti about the scene. Three. I have a photographic memory, Lieutenant. That will definitely serve me well. I can add to whatever the investigators collects on this case. Four. I'm excellent at talking to families, did lots of that in children's crimes in Brooklyn. Five. Detective Valatutti is my training partner, so he could oversee everything I do. Six. Detective Withers is right in this building. Ordinarily, he'd get the high-profile cases, anyway, and because he's so close, he could supervise me, along with Detective Valatutti. Shall I go on?"

"What you will do, is march yourself out of my office and sit on the bench to the right, until I call you back in."

"Yes, sir." Sam turned to walk out, thinking this wasn't going well at all.

What else could happen?

She closed the door on her way out.

❦❦❦

Rojas sat down, not at all amused, and he was not afraid to show it. "Have a seat, Detectives."

The tension in his face was deliberate. His work, cleaning up this precinct had just begun, two months ago. They had called him in from the Bronx to stiffen up some of the laxness in their paper work and follow-ups. And damn it, he was going to do it. The detectives here did great work.

They just needed a tougher leader with tougher expectations, and Withers wasn't cutting it. Rojas had a lot of bones to pick with Withers and, if he didn't succeed, he'd make sure that Withers was bounced. He couldn't care less about his great rep. Withers had failed in the most important case as far as he was concerned.

Nick and Withers sat in arm-chairs opposite the lieutenant's desk.

Rojas leaned back in his chair with his hand under his chin, pen in hand. "All right, Nick. What's your initial assessment?"

"Very bright, observant, detailed, a little flighty, rambles—not necessarily in order. She did great with the family this morning. Really thoughtful, developed a rapport with the HT."

"Who was the hostage taker? Nah, never mind. It's Brooklyn's case. How did she react when she saw the body?"

"A little squeamish when she saw the body, chopped. But she held it together. I like her smarts, even though she is a little over zealous. I can live with it."

"Her file indicates she's interested in forensics. Does that threaten you, Withers?"

"I could have guessed that. But you're kiddin' me, Loo, right?"

Rojas didn't respond right away, just shot him a hard look. "Do I look like I'm kidding?"

"No, I'm not threatened by her. We could use her skills in recording the scene. She didn't miss a beat, but I won't tell her that. Had some thoughts that I may not agree with. Don't know how she'll put it all together."

Rojas nodded. "While you were in transit, I did get positive ID of the victim. She was right. Steven Larcon of Larcon Fashions. Has a wife, three adult kids, an older daughter, and twins, a boy and a girl. Close knit family. No one notified them yet. We need Frank on this one."

"Yeah. Nick mentioned him. Isn't there anyone else?"

"No. He isn't a fan of yours, either, Withers. Hey, Nick, now would be a good time for you to catch up on paperwork."

"Sure, Loo." Nick got up, pushed the chair in.

"Don't stop and talk to her. I want to see how she handles this."

"Yes, sir." He nodded and walked out of the office.

Withers waited until the door shut. "Hey, it's been two years. Evidence gets cold, Loo."

"It was his wife, for Christ sake. You are the most experienced lead homicide detective in the city. And you came up with nothing. He's one of ours, Dingo! Unlike the former lieutenant who sat in this chair, I expected you to still be working on it. And from your response, I can tell you're not. I want you to go over every single file. I don't care if there's ten boxes in cold storage. You better get your unit working on this. Am I making myself clear?"

"Crystal."

"Better yet. Get little miss photographic memory, there, to go over it all with you." Rojas spoke into the intercom. "Jessica, get me Doctor Khaos on the phone, please." In less than ten seconds the connection was made. "Hey, Frank, it's Lieutenant Rojas. We need you here. High-profile case. The family needs to be notified and we need you to profile."

"I'm in the downtown area now. I was heading home but I can be there in fifteen."

"When you get here make contact with Detective Sam Wright."

"Will do."

Disconnecting the phone, the lieutenant got a look of surprise from Dingo. "You think you two are the only ones testing out the rookie? Let's see how she handles the tattooed behemoth."

"So you are giving her the lead on this case?"

"Sure am. You two are going to be real close on this one with Valatutti and Khaos looking over both your shoulders. You better take off now. Khaos sees you, you're a dead man. Until he learns you're back on the case. And he'll want proof of that."

"Then how in hell am I supposed to work this case with him, if I'm not here?"

"You're a veteran detective. Figure it out."

⌘⌘⌘

Sam sat on the bench like a little girl reprimanded by the principal. Her head bent down, she wondered what could happen next. It had seemed like she had waited for over an hour. No one had come over to introduce themselves, or to make her feel welcome.

Okay, this must be an ego-oriented bunch just like the other New York City precincts.

Every cop was in competition for cases, and here she comes in on her first day, demanding a high-profile one.

There you go again Sam, with your delusions of grandeur.

She did have to pat herself on the back, though. She knew she did great today. Her self-confidence was something no one would succeed in taking away.

She didn't have her watch. Withers had taken her phone to download her pics and recordings for Crime Scene. There was no clock on the wall. She looked up when she heard heavy footsteps. And had to look way up.

The man looked around. "Hey, know where I can find Sam Wright?"

To her, with his deep voice, his tats covering both arms, his muscles bulging through his T-shirt and skinny jeans, his olive complexion, this looked like one unsavory character. "Who wants to know?"

"Khaos."

She couldn't tell his expression through his dark shades, but she needed to get rid of him. "No, thank you. I have enough chaos in my own life right now." She turned away, grimacing at his appearance, while sliding to the other end of the bench.

"Excuse me? No. I'm Khaos, Frank Khaos. It's a metaphor for my life, too." He removed his shades and hung them on the nape of his T-shirt. He sat on the bench, spread his legs, and bending over with his arms on this thighs, folded his hands between them. His massive frame took up most of the bench.

Sam didn't know what to focus on first. The smirk on his rugged face, his clean-shaven head, or the red crossbow skull on his T-shirt that reminded her of all the blood she witnessed today. She looked into his dark oval eyes. "You're the psychiatrist?"

He frowned. "Yeah, forensic. And you are?"

"Detective Sam Wright."

He looked her up and down and didn't hide his facetious laugh. "Didn't think this precinct had dress down Wednesday. Man, and they scowl at me in my T and skinny jeans."

Um, a smartass tough guy. And the tats. Eww. "Well, I was off duty and found myself at a crime scene. They took my clothes and brought me this. It's my first day. So what's your excuse?"

He ignored the comment. Damn him. She'd love to blow off steam right about now, and this guy looked like he could take it. But what he could do to her would be another story.

"This is your first day? As a detective?" She nodded. "And you're still sitting here?" He smiled and shook his head. "Oh, man, they're getting you but good."

"What do you mean?"

"Welcome to the big-boy fraternity, Detective Wright. You're getting hazed."

"No." Her eyes widened. "Seriously?"

"Who's your partner?"

"Nick Valatutti."

"Was he at the scene with you?"

"Yes."

"Have you asked to go home to get cleaned up and changed?"

"No. Loo told me to wait here until he calls me back in."

"Wait here." He got up and walked to the corner to Loo's office.

Sam looked after him. At his butt. *Oh my God. That swagger. This guy has a bigger ego than all of them put together.*

One thing, though, that had hit her immediately—his energy. Clean, pure, positive, and protective.

A few minutes later Frank returned. "Got clothes to change into?"

"Yes. Everything."

"Good. Go do it."

Then it hit her. "Oh my God, I can't!"

"Why not?"

"Please don't think I'm an idiot. My car is at the crime scene."

"How in hell could you forget your car? You sure you're a detective?" He bellowed out laughter, a deep laugh that emanated from his diaphragm. "Oh, man."

"I'm glad I'm the butt of your humor, Doctor Khaos. It's not funny. Withers was so busy yelling at me, and I was trying to block him out. He forced me into his SUV with them, and my car slipped my mind."

"Withers? Dingo Withers? He's on this case?"

"Yes."

"That's going to be a problem. Let's go." She stood up and he frowned. "How short are you?"

"I'm five-six," she retorted with pride.

"You're not five-six. That's here on me." He leveled his hand on his pecs. "You're barely five-five. Come on." He patted her back. Then stopped dead. "They didn't bring you a bra?"

"Nope. Nor panties."

He stared at her with a closed-lip smirk. "TMI. You don't censor anything you say, do you?"

"Nope. What's on my mind is on my tongue, most of the time."

"That's going to be a problem, too. Come on. We'll drop you at your car and Valatutti and I are going to notify the family. You'll meet us back here."

"I wanted to go."

"No time."

Sam opened her mouth, but he cut her off before any words came out. "Hey, when I'm in the house, Khaos rules."

CHAPTER 6

Frank and Nick stared up at the massive home of Steven Larcon in the historic district of Central Park West, as they sat in Nick's car with the dossier. The Gothic columns that stood on the landing shouted prominence, as if a warning that nothing could penetrate the power within.

Nick laughed. "Not in my lifetime."

Frank shook his head, almost in distain at the symbol of wealth. "Nothing I'd want. Okay, let's do this."

They sprinted up the twenty-step path to the wooden door. The oval door-knocker, hanging out of a lion's mouth, looked recently polished. It reflected the setting sun so glaringly that Nick had to squint to find the doorbell. They had taken a chance to come over without calling first, so after a few minutes of waiting, they were about to turn around. The housekeeper—who looked like she came right out of a historical novel, right down to the ruffles on her apron—opened the door.

"How can I help you gentlemen?"

"I'm Detective Nick Valatutti and this is Doctor Frank Khaos. Is Mrs. Larcon home?"

"Yes. Oh dear. What did one of those trouble maker kids of hers do now?"

Frank shot a quick glance in Nick's direction. "Nothing that we need you to know about at the moment, but we may have to speak to you at another time."

"Well, come on in then." She led them through a massive center room with beige marble floors, crystal chandeliers, and original works of art from Renaissance painters adoring the non-mirrored walls. Sparse in furniture. Indicative of the style. "Wait here please."

Frank took in the home that wasn't much different from the one he had been raised in after he hit ten years old. He stood in the center of the hall, staring into space. He never could get used to so much openness. He compared himself to a cave animal, who preferred warm and cozy to cold and massive. He shuddered, even with a leather jacket on.

After his mom died, he couldn't wait to dispose of the house. She had passed away, five months after his dad, when Frank was thirty-seven. He stood still with his hand over his mouth. He missed them so much. They had turned his life around. They had taught him how to love. They had taught him how to love Jen, the woman of his dreams. Jen didn't want to live in their house either. He and Jen had been in sync on every level. At least his parents had gotten to meet her, and Frankie. They had lived for their only grandson.

He told Frankie about Grandma and Grandpa every night when he read a story to him at bedtime. How they were together with Mommy in heaven. Sometimes Frankie just wanted to read the helicopter book, the one that Frank was in, jumping out of an army copter with his medic gear on his back. He was glad he was stateside, but those two tours in Special Forces in Iraq, were the best thing he had done in his life, next to marrying Jen. They had met in Iraq. She was the nurse who had worked side by side with him. Those years as a medic formed his future to go to college, become a trauma doctor, and then gave him the launch into psychiatry. Wanting to give back for the privileged life his adoptive parents afforded him had catapulted him into forensics.

The psychiatrist, his parents had spent a fortune on when he was a kid, told them they needed to get him into a gym to release his aggression. Just like the housekeeper, before Tae Kwan Do, his parents, with every phone call, would wonder if it was from school, telling them he was in trouble. The gym changed his life. So, by the time he had turned eighteen, not knowing what he wanted to do with his life, he joined the military, already holding a Black Belt in Tae Kwan Do.

The housekeeper returned, jolting him. "This way, please." She led them into a sitting room where Mrs. Larcon sat on a Mediterranean-style couch.

Nick sat on a club chair opposite her, holding his note pad and pen. Frank approached her. "May I?"

"Yes. Please."

He sat down next to her on the couch, unbuttoning his jacket.

"I'm assuming this isn't a good news visit, but Clara told me it wasn't about one of my children."

Frank looked at the woman whose green eyes were as glittery as the house. Her flattened, shoulder length salon-done, dark-red hair, looked as if she might have been napping, and dressed hurriedly for them, forgetting to fluff up her tresses. Even her attire, a blouse and designer jeans, were as ostentatious as he would have expected. She even remembered her jewelry.

"Mrs. Larcon. When was the last time you saw your husband?"

"Steven?"

"Yes."

"Oh my God. What did you say your name was?"

"Doctor Frank Khaos."

"With a C?"

"With a K. My adoptive parents had Greek heritage."

"Oh. I saw Steve yesterday afternoon. He told me he was working late with his team of designers at his Chelsea office. But, to him, that would be around midnight, or later."

Frank shot her a suspicious look.

She understood the need to explain. "When Steven had a deadline to meet with one of his manufacturers, he worked till all hours. He paid his team double for working after five. My husband is a very generous man."

"Where would he go after that?" he asked. She swallowed and looked away. "Mrs. Larcon, would he come home?"

"Sometimes, but not usually."

"Where would he go?"

"Uh, we had an open marriage, Doctor. Usually he'd go to a club in Chelsea, rather a little south of Chelsea. He never told me the name and, frankly, I didn't care enough to ask."

Okay, this won't be too hard then. Frank looked straight into her eyes. "Mrs. Larcon, I'm sorry to have to tell you, your husband was murdered last night."

No shock. No surprise. No tears. Almost catatonic.

He reached out to touch her hand, but she jerked it away before he made contact. "Mrs. Larcon, shall we call someone for you? Your children?"

She kept her gaze straight ahead, not focusing on any object in particular. "Where was he found?"

"The investigators are still at the scene, so I can't divulge the exact location to you now."

"How did he die?"

"I can tell you there were knife wounds, but the exact cause of death, we don't know. And he was found naked. At this point, we don't know if he was murdered at this location, or moved. We'll need to speak with your children."

"They're in their own little worlds, Doctor, which fortunately doesn't include us."

Frank looked at her startled. *Where did the 'close-knit' family idea originate?*

"I might as well be blunt, Doctor Khaos. There was no love lost between any of our children and us. I know you look at the immediate family first, but I can assure you, it was none of us. For several reasons. One, they don't have the guts. Second, if there were cuts, there was blood. And I can assure you, none of my children, nor I, like to get dirty. Even the thought of gardening, sickens us."

"Interesting analogy." Nick put an asterisk next to her last comment in his notes. "Did your husband have any enemies?"

"Want the list?"

"A list? That many?"

"Yes. The fashion industry is fraught with jealousy."

"Well, Detective Valatutti is ready to take notes, so please, go on, Mrs. Larcon."

ↄﬁↄ

Sam couldn't wait to get the grime and blood out of her hair, and off her body. It had taken her over an hour to get home in the rush hour traffic. As soon as she opened her door, she bolted up the stairs to her bedroom. She stripped off her clothes, threw everything into the hamper, and started the shower.

This would be more than just a shower to get rid of grime. She'd make the most of it to cleanse and consecrate her body, and to add the protection she'd need against those testosterone-driven men at the precinct. Nick was off limits. Thank God. The lieutenant and Withers, too. Marriage bands on both. And ugh, Withers. She detested the man and she'd just met him. The tension in his aura was so thick she'd need her athame to cut through it.

What is his wife like?

He probably ran his household with an iron fist. Their poor children, if they had any.

And then there was Frank Khaos. Ugh. Why a man would want to desecrate his body with tattoos befuddled her. This was definitely not the man she'd dare bring home to meet Mommy and Daddy. The imaginary scenario made her laugh out loud.

Oh, Frank, meet my dad, the neurosurgeon and my mom, the pediatrician.

Her dad would want to perform brain surgery on him, giving him a lobotomy, and her mom would want to call child protective services if he had any kids. Nope. To her parents, who based everything on first impressions, this wouldn't work at all. She sneered, acknowledging that was why she was still single. They had chased away any man she had dated. No one was good enough for their princess.

She was pissed that she couldn't go with Nick and Doctor Khaos. The initial interview with the family was so important. She hoped Nick would take great notes and be willing to share. *Wait a minute. I'm his partner, he has to share.* But Khaos. The nerve of him to tell her that when he was in the house, he ruled. She had stopped herself from laughing right in his face when he retorted with that. But making two enemies in one day was enough.

She retrieved her big pot from her closet, small bottles of sandalwood and lavender oils from a shelf, put them outside the shower door, and stepped into the shower. The warm water running over her head and down her body felt so good. She used double the amount as usual of her lavender shampoo and saw remnants of blood go down the drain. She shampooed twice until the water ran clear. Then she used her lavender shower gel to cleanse her body. First to cleanse, next to protect. She washed her body from neck down to her toes with her purple mesh sponge, waiting in the shower until every drop of water went down the drain.

Opening the door, she brought the pot and oils in with her. She put a few drops of each oil in the pot and filled it with water. Holding the pot in both hands at midriff level, she began her invocation, after inhaling through her nose and exhaling through her mouth several times to ground herself and give her focus.

I need to do a fast one now so, Dara, help me out, please. Oh my deities, Isis, the Goddess of Healing, and Artemis, the Goddess of the Wilderness and of the Moon and the Hunt, come into my energy field now, so I can manifest my desires. Let these lavender and sandalwood oils cleanse and protect my aura, so I do not absorb any negativity from anyone in my new precinct, or from this crime. I need to stay healthy and strong to compete with these people and solve this case. My future as a detective depends upon this.

She poured the water and oil mixture from the pot over her head with her eyes closed, absorbing the protective energy of the oils.

I acknowledge I need to do this three times, but I just don't have the time now. Forgive me, Isis and Artemis, for working in haste. My protection is complete. Dara, I need you to make contact with Nick and Khaos. Thank you, Dara.

Sam shut off the water, dried herself quickly, and blow-dried her hair, while mumbling over why it had to be so thick. At least it was fairly straight. She dressed in a navy blue pants suit with a white silk blouse, just low enough to show some sex appeal and, at the same time, be professional.

Looking in her closet, she selected a pair of navy heels. The arrogance of that psychiatrist to say she was short. Humph. She was the height of the average American woman. Okay, these would add three inches. And her sneakers were in her bag, in case she had to dart out in them.

When she finished dressing, she pulled a pendant from her top drawer after surveying her copious collection.

Um, that's it.

The three-inch sugilite petal pendant, topped with three oval moldavite stones in 14-K, held on a twenty-four-inch solid-gold chain was slipped over her head. She tucked it under her blouse. There was no need for them to see the pendant that had kept her safe and multiplied her abilities over the last couple of years. Then she lifted the cover to a box on her dresser and removed two healing stones to slip into her right pocket—rhodochrosite and kunzite, both to relieve stress and enhance calmness, and two healing stones to slip into her left pocket—black tourmaline and rutiliated quartz to give her the confidence to assert herself and reflect the negativity from those men.

ଓଓଓ

Getting up from the sofa, Frank gave Mrs. Larcon a sincere smile. "Mrs. Larcon, we need to speak with your children tomorrow. I know this will be a hard time for you, but we need as much information as we can get to help us find your husband's killer. Can you come to the precinct in Chelsea tomorrow morning around ten?"

"I don't know if I can lasso all three of them together at one time Doctor. They're all in the city, but so busy, doing who knows what."

He sat down again guessing this would be a long explanation. "Okay, tell me what they do."

"Well, Valerie, the oldest, is on Steven's design team. She's the only one worth a damn. Very talented, but she did have her stint in rehab several years ago. They all had their time in rehab, the twins, multiple times. And to tell you a secret, please don't judge me, Doctor Khaos, I've had mine, too. Multiple times. I just got out, actually. From a wonderful place in Suffolk County. They bled us, but pampered me, knowing I'd be back. Alcohol is my drug of choice, as it is with Valerie. The twins, Adam and AriellaRose, are into the party drugs, cocaine, barbiturates. And AriellaRose, oxycodone. Don't know why she chose that one. She couldn't possibly have any pain. She never did anything strenuous in her life.

"They don't relate to us at all. The only time they come running to us is for money. Then they are the sweet children every parent wants. Then we pay off the drug dealers who are after them, and they disappear again. For weeks at a time. Even when we talk to them on the phone, Steven can tell that Adam and AriellaRose are high on something."

Frank listened to everything Mrs. Larcon recounted without moving a muscle or making any judgmental expression. He exhaled deeply before he spoke. "Mrs. Larcon, do any of your children have a record?"

"A police record? Meaning were they ever arrested? Oh, no, no, no. Thank God. They don't do any drug dealing themselves. Everything is for their personal use." She nodded, as if that made it all right.

"Is there a drug dealer you know of who might be upset with your husband for not paying him or her fast enough?"

"I don't know any of them personally, by their name, or what they look like. When they send a courier to the house to get payment—in cash, of course—they don't tell us their name either. And, to be honest, we don't ask."

"Just how many times did you pay off these people?"

"A few, for each twin. Different dealers, each time."

"How did you feel when you had to do this?"

"Horrible, as any parent would, but even though I didn't approve, I didn't want to see any of my children maimed by these bastards."

Frank shook his head. "I'm going out on a limb here, Mrs. Larcon. But what would have AriellaRose or Adam done, if you and your husband said 'no'?"

"An all-out tantrum. And we couldn't bear that. So we just sighed, after all the yelling and screaming, and gave in."

Frank cleared his throat. "All right, Mrs. Larcon. Let me have your children's cell numbers, and Detective Valatutti will call them. Coming from our department, they'll be more cooperative as we won't allow them not to show. You've been through enough. Can we get you something, or answer any questions?"

"Thank you, Doctor Khaos, you are very kind. Clara will call Valerie. She's the only one who will come over."

"One more thing. You said Valerie was on your husband's design team?"

"Yes."

"Was she with him Tuesday?"

"No. This Tuesday, he worked with the eveningwear team. Valerie works with him on lingerie. Larcon Fashions has many divisions."

"Thank you, Mrs. Larcon. We can show ourselves out."

CHAPTER 7

Frank, Nick, and Lieutenant Rojas looked at the life of Steven Larcon in a file they had printed in triplicate. Their eyes scanned the minimal pages thus far. Just identifying info, basics—name, address, phone, businesses, along with a retouched photo of him from *Money Magazine*. Frank's back had been facing the door. The Loo, taking off his glasses and staring at Sam when she had entered, triggered Frank's brain to pay attention.

"Now, that's much better, Detective."

"Thank you, Lieutenant."

When Frank heard her voice, he looked up. He swiveled around to face her and was taken aback. He didn't expect this vision, this Venus, who responded to his hungry gaze with an offhanded smile. *Oh crap, she cleaned up good.* "About time. You look great. Pull up a seat."

She sat next to him. "Thanks."

The lieutenant slid over his file to her. She nodded.

"All right," he said. "I'll be in my office. You'll catch me up to speed later. Behave yourselves, both of you."

"Sure, Loo." Nick smiled.

"Hey, Loo. You expect me to work with this homecoming queen? No, make that homecoming princess." Frank's gaze traveled over her long blonde hair, flowing to mid-back, and up then to her sparkling blue eyes. That navy suit accentuated the specks of gray that popped within her iris. And her body. Oh, man. She had the perfect figure. Just a hint of cleavage. So this woman knew how to tease. Or she covered herself because she wasn't really interested.

"Yes, Doc. I do."

Sam laughed.

Frank laughed too, realizing she had assumed the comment about behaving themselves meant the way they treated her. She'd been right.

After the lieutenant closed the door, she blurted it out. "You mean to tell me you went to make a family notification, dressed like that? With a skull on your T-shirt?"

Nick came to his defense. "No, he dressed for the occasion."

"He doesn't approve of my style, either. Mr. Conservative."

"Oh, so you put on a solid T and leather jacket."

Frank interpreted that her statement was meant to be snide, not a question. He and Nick exchanged looks. "How did you know?"

"I just figured it was your style."

Frank smirked. He leaned over to her a bit to get a whiff of her fragrance. "What are you wearing?"

"Lavender and sandalwood."

Frank nodded. "Nice. Like it."

"Oh, thanks. Okay, so how did you make out?"

"Wife not all broken up."

"No, I wouldn't assume so. She has an alcohol addiction." After they moved in toward the table to pay attention, she went on. "I follow him on Twitter. He complains about it, a lot."

Frank frowned and narrowed his eyes. "He talks about his wife's addictions on social media? That's quite passive aggressive of him. What kinds of things does he say?"

"In several tweets last month, he complained about how much money it's costing him. He even tore into the rehab. Wilbur Resort in the Hamptons. They're initiating a law suit against him for slander."

"That's significant. He doesn't seem to object to paying off his kid's drug dealers, to protect them. Any tweets about them?" Frank intended to pay attention to her every word.

"No."

"Okay, she also told us he had a lot of enemies," Frank said.

Sam bit her lip. "Um, um."

"Twitter again?"

"Yes, a lot of bickering. For long periods of time. He has a habit of airing the dirtiest of laundry."

"Okay, here are some names." Nick read from his list. "Meghan Mason."

"Yes, designer jeans. Very glitzy, stones, glitter, floral designs. Very expensive. Two to three hundred bucks a pair. But she'll only go up to size twelve. Most women in the United States are over size fourteen. She'll blatantly call them bimbos, or America's fatties on social media. Actually, she's my favorite designer."

Frank cocked his head and studied her. *How can she afford two hundred bucks for a pair of jeans on a cop's salary?* "Hold on. Mrs. Larcon wore jeans fitting that description. We'll ask her." He noted the file.

Nick laughed. "How do you know so much?"

She grinned. "I love, love, love fashion. It's one of my downfalls."

Nick went to the next one. "Okay, Fashionista. Lacy Lust. But I can guess that one."

"Yes. Erotic lingerie. Very minimal and very expensive. The strippers in the clubs in this area wear her stuff."

Frank held in a grin. "You know that, how?" His mind traveled to seeing her in the sweats, sans under garments. She'd look damn awesome in something minimal.

"One of them posted on Facebook that the fortune she spent on her outfit wasn't worth it. The crotch split when she was performing a lap dance."

"Sorry, I asked."

"Larcon does lingerie, too. Competition?" Nick asked.

"His is more conservative. Much more. More like bride on wedding night, not hooker."

"Slim difference there," Nick admitted.

"Who else?"

Nick's finger trailed down the page. "Jaye Manning."

"He designs conservative men's suits and accessories. He does have an arrangement with Larcon. He makes ties and handkerchiefs to match Larcon's gowns, in the same fabrics. Gorgeous. Next?"

"That's all she knew of," Frank said.

"Don't believe her. There's tons more. We'll subpoena his social media accounts. He's on all of them, and a lot. Don't think he uses an auto program because he responds within minutes. He seems mean spirited and negative about everything."

"Okay. Good info. His kids all have drug problems. Anything about them?" Frank asked.

"No. Only bad things about his wife. He doesn't post pics of any of his children either. We should get their social media accounts, as well."

"Okay. Let's see what we've got. A guy who has enemies and a dysfunctional family. The same as every murder victim in New York. So far, we have nothing." Frank slumped in his chair and blew out a breath. "This superficial bullshit isn't cutting it. Get me more to work with."

"Hold on. I called the kids. They're coming in tomorrow. Sam, you and I will interview them, as Frank—"

Frank's cell rang, interrupting Nick. He looked at the ID. It was a Facetime call from Frankie. He answered it, without excusing himself, and smiled at the oval faced little boy with the squared chin, the brown oval eyes, and military haircut, who was a replica of himself, thirty-seven years ago. This time, those eyes were reddened from profuse tears.

"Frankie, what's the matter?"

His lower lip quivered, as he tried to contain himself. "I'm in big trouble, Dad."

"What kind of trouble?"

"I had a fight in school and it was bad." His sobbing increased. "I—was—just protecting—Jessie."

"Who's Jessie?"

Frankie sniffled and swallowed before he answered his father. "My girlfriend."

Frank put his lips together to avoid smiling. "Your girlfriend? You're seven."

"I know."

"How come I don't know about your—" He stressed the word. "—*girlfriend*?"

"I'm keeping her a secret."

Nick covered his mouth, with a smile underneath.

Okay, he has sons, Frank decided. *Sam has that "how sweet" look on her face. Okay, she has that maternal instinct.* He stifled a chuckle. "You're not supposed to keep any secret from me. But what happened?"

The crying intensified. "Chubbs started up with her, pulling her hair. And he's so much bigger than us."

"It's not nice to make fun of someone's weight, Frankie. You know that."

"No, Dad, that's his name. Charlie Chubbs. Anyway, he

wouldn't leave her alone, and I told him to stop. Then he pushed me."

"There was no teacher around?"

"They were busy talking and getting classes on line."

"Then what happened?"

"I told him to get away from me. Dad, he's in fifth grade. Then he said something that really got me upset."

"What did he say?"

"He said—" The sobbing increased. "That—I—didn't even—have a Mommy—to come up to school—to protect me."

Frank saw Sam's expression change from nurturing to grim. Apparently, she hadn't known.

"Dad, I got so upset—and I didn't—want him to see that—so I pushed him hard and put my leg around his—and I got him on the ground in a submission hold, and I punched him bad—a lot—and I busted open his lip, and the security guards broke us up, and carried me into Doctor Cohen's office, and he told me I was suspended." Frankie sniffled and wiped his nose on the back of his sleeve. "He said there's zero tolerance for fighting in his school."

"Suspended. Okay. For how long?" Frank had had his share of suspensions for fighting when he was Frankie's age, but their circumstances were way different.

"Two days." His sobbing became whimpering, but then Frankie went silent for a minute. "I'm in big trouble, aren't I?"

"You think? We'll talk about this when I get home in a couple of hours. Right now, just stay in your room. No TV, no computer games. Got that?"

"Yes."

Frank remained stoic. "Good." He disconnected the phone, sat back in the seat, and heaved a sigh. Resting his elbow on the armrest, he covered his mouth with his fingers spread apart.

"Frank. He's seven and it's a sensitive issue for him. He had to protect himself."

"Believe me, Nick, I know. I know exactly what he's going through, but I had hoped he'd learned how to process it better than me."

"I'm sorry about your wife, Frank," Sam said.

He barely looked up.

"What's with the submission hold? Who taught him that?" she asked.

Frank stared at her, stunned. "You're kidding me, right?"

"No. I am not."

Nick snorted. "This guy, here, is an MMA champion, third degree BJJ Black Belt."

"You're kidding me?" she snapped, throwing his words back at him.

"You're familiar?" Frank asked.

"I know what MMA is. The academy brought those guys in to teach us self-defense. But the specifics, I don't."

"BJJ is Brazilian Jiu Jitsu. It's a form of ground fighting. Submission holds."

Sam looked bewildered. Frank was almost at a loss for words. He shook his head in disbelief. "Ever watch wrestling on TV?"

"Eww, no! The thought of gross tattooed men, throwing each other around a wrestling ring, is not exactly my idea of sexy."

Frank laughed. "She doesn't censor anything that comes out of her mouth, by the way." *I'll have to change her mind on that one.* "Millions of women would beg to differ with you on that."

"Good for them."

Oh, man. She is one opinionated princess. Frank just laughed and shook his head. "Hey, you look like you're in shape. Where do you work out?"

"A gym near me in Brooklyn."

Frank liked that. "I live in Brooklyn, too. Mill Basin. Where are you?"

"Madison," Sam said.

"I know the area."

"Good. Very good. I'm finally learning some things about you. They just threw us together today. Where do you work out?"

"With Frankie in Brooklyn. But, for me, in my gym in Manhattan. Harlem."

Her eyes widened. "Harlem? Why would you go there?"

"Because it's my gym."

"Yeah. I live in Brooklyn and my gym is there."

"No, princess. My gym as in I own it."

"Why would you own a gym in Harlem? Can the residents there afford it?"

"It's free," he told her.

"Excuse me? You own a gym and you let people come for free?"

"Yes."

Her eyes begged him for an explanation.

"Okay. I won't let you suffer anymore. I rehab New York City gang members, just released from prison."

"Who pays for this?"

"My parents adopted me at ten and left me a shitload of dough. I wanted to give back and—"

Interrupting his explanation, Dingo Withers entered the room and slapped a file down on the table in front of him. Looking up, seeing Withers, Frank didn't hide his disgust, even though the man looked exhausted. The bags under his eyes had puffed up more than usual, his fingertips yellowed from his nicotine habit. Frank could have sworn that his wrinkles had deepened since last time he had seen him, a few weeks ago. "What's this?"

"The latest on Jen's investigation. Not much has happened, but there have been many more gang related killings since hers, with similar MOs, so we're picking it up again. I'll be getting all the crime scene reports, and as per Loo's order, little Miss Photographic Memory here, has been assigned to assist. We'll get them, Frank. I know we will."

Frank sat solemn and didn't respond right away. He felt like doing what Frankie did. He was seething inside. But he, unlike Frankie, couldn't show it. A psychiatrist assaulting a detective first grade wouldn't fly, and he'd lose his license, to boot. But he sure as hell would take it out on the heavy bag for an hour tomorrow.

"Okay, Withers, we'll see. I won't hold my breath. What have you got so far on the Larcon case?" Frank's fingers involuntarily tapped on the folder Withers had placed in front of him, but he knew his head should be in the job now. He picked up the folder and placed it on a ledge behind him. This was one folder he wouldn't forget and leave there.

"I brought this over. It's the only bit of evidence they'd let me take. It's what this rookie found." He removed a manila envelope from his attaché. He put on gloves and handed Nick, Frank, and Sam a pair. After tearing the seal on the envelope, he retrieved a clear baggie, further protecting the white band that Sam had filmed in the bush. The band had snapped on a branch, but the letters on it were visible now. He handed it to Frank. "Recognize it at all?"

"Could be a gang band. They wear them in all colors. DSF? I don't know of any gang in New York City with these initials.

And I've been in contact with every one over the last five years. There are smears on here. I'm assuming they took blood samples and fingerprints, already."

Withers nodded in the affirmative.

"If you put the ends together we could see it's smallish. More a woman's size than man's. That goes along with what I said at the scene. Might be women."

"However, this may not even be from said crime. We can't jump to conclusions that it is, rookie, until we get serology and DNA back. Rule number one. Don't form a judgment without the science to back it up."

"You're right, Withers. You're right."

"What else did you say at the scene?" Frank's curiosity was on a professional level. She had impressed him with her knowledge about Larcon. Maybe she could help them find Jen's killers.

Withers handed Sam back her phone. "She made two recordings. Knock yourself out, Frank." He handed the flash drives to him.

"Okay. What else did they come up with?" Frank stared hard at Withers who sat at the end of the table.

"The ME figured the time of death was between four and five a.m. It was deduced from the path, the body transport, and the state of the body. Then they recovered his car in a parking lot of a strip club. Meat packing district. Close to the water. The owner of the club called 911 and the precinct closest to it went. They called me, knowing it's your case," he said to Nick and Sam. "Crime Scene sent a team to the parking lot. So, you two, have a lot to start with. This case is going to be so big, rookie, I have a feeling you're going to regret taking it on."

"No. I won't. Let's go, Nick."

"You want to go to the club now, don't you?"

"Yes. Come on."

"You forgot to ask a crucial question, rookie."

"Oh." She grimaced. "Who owns the club?"

"Carlo Philetano."

Frank stopped dead. "The Philetano? The Staten Island Mob family?"

Withers shot him a snide grin, while Frank's mind floated to Jen. If this was a Mob hit, they wouldn't need him, and he could focus on Jen's case. He said a silent prayer.

After they left, Frank played the two recordings, taking over an hour to go through them. He realized she had a lot of knowledge. But did she have the ability to process her knowledge into forming theories, and applying them into practical uses for them? A lot remained to be seen, with this princess.

CHAPTER 8

Nick split his vision between the driveway and the investigators on the scene, and maneuvered his SUV into a spot outside the perimeter of the cordoned-off area, as directed by a patrol officer. They had marked off three hundred feet around Larcon's sports car, not nearly one third of the strip club's lot. The lot stood at the back of the renovated warehouse, overlooking a pier. They had completed their set up—tables and laptops were in place, cameras were on tripods, they had pulled down fire escapes, the photographing was completed, cone markings were in place, debris had been picked up and packed, and now they were working on the car itself.

Sam had left the driving to him and kept her gaze on the team. Nick assumed she was soaking it all in, again.

The three-story brick building had been servicing New York City execs who'd craved escapes into paradise for ten years. The owner, Carlo Philetano, paced around the perimeter of the lot while on his cell, yelling at a person on the other end of the line. He disconnected when he saw Nick's SUV pull into the spot.

The chill in the late-fall dusk air was warmer than the reception he gave Nick. Carlo's gaze darted to each side entrance of the gated lot, before he focused on him. "Hey, Detective. When are they getting this ride outta here? They won't tell me anything. They won't give me the time of day."

"They're not supposed to. We need to talk to you. Calm down, Carlo. Why so edgy?"

"Yeah. Sure, Valatutti. My pop's carrying on like a lunatic. Yelling that this could look like it came from us. Edgy? That doesn't explain it, pal. He's not gettin' any younger, ya know? We gotta treat him with kid gloves."

Sam exited the car and, immediately, Nick noticed a change in Carlo's attitude.

"Hello, Mr. Philetano. I'm Detective Samantha Wright. You obviously know my partner." She walked toward him with a smile as bright as the summer sun as she spoke. "First, I want to thank you for calling this in. It's much appreciated."

Carlo grinned from ear to ear. Nick could have sworn he saw sparkles in his eyes and a bulge by his zipper.

"Yeah. Sure. I'm talking to her, Valatutti. You can take a hike." He winked at Sam.

Nick laughed. *Whatever it takes.* "You can talk to her, Carlo, but I'm staying right here."

Carlo changed his tough guy intonation to warm and mellow. "Suit yourself. Now, Detective Wright, what do you need to know?" Carlo's gaze traveled down her body and landed tight on her breasts. He put his arm around her shoulder to walk her over to an area hidden to any passersby. She gently removed his arm, but continued to walk with him. He grimaced at the stale urine odors that assaulted his nose. "Damn these guys. We have gorgeous bathrooms and they choose to piss here. Ah, maybe it's bums who can't afford to get in. Caught a few of them. Okay, Detective, back to your questions."

"Oh, thank you, Mr. Philetano. Do you know who owns this car?"

"Yes, and you know I do. I told the 911 op. Steven Larcon."

"Great. We didn't get their tape yet." Sam looked at Nick.

He had sensed the same thing. Withers didn't tell them everything.

"Do you know Mr. Larcon personally?" she continued.

"As far as being a customer, yeah. My wife wears his gowns. And the bastard doesn't even give her a discount. I stopped giving him drinks on the house, too, after the last time. She spent five thou on two…maxis? I think that's what you dames call them. Yeah, maxi dresses."

"Yes. That's what we call them." She reciprocated with a warm smile. "What time did he come in last night?"

He unbuttoned his jacket. "About one."

"Was he with anyone?"

"Yeah, his son, Adam. Always with his son. Maybe he's teaching him about women." He laughed. "But I have a feeling this kid already knows a lot."

"How so?"

"He's a good-looking kid. Tall, blond, dark blue eyes. He and his twin, those eyes. If I was describing a woman, I'd call them exotic. Well built. Into the gym, a lot. He models for a men's line. I'm sure the women are already lined up."

Sam smiled. "Did they come in together?"

"They walked in together. But the kid left earlier. I think Dad's supporting him or something. He always gives him a big wad of cash. It's almost as if this place is their meet. I don't mind. If it were two strangers exchanging dough, they'd be bounced outta here. My guys follow my rules."

Nick's mind wrapped around what Mrs. Larcon told him and Frank. Totally different perspective. That was major.

Sam nodded. "How often do they come in?"

"Every Wednesday and Friday, one a.m., like clockwork."

"Have any idea what time they left?"

"Didn't watch them. But I close at six. I went out to check the lot. Had to see what mess my cleaning crew would have to deal with. Liquor bottles, condoms, these odors to disinfect, the usual crap. And I spotted his car. At first, I thought he may have gone with his son. Drives a Jag. Then I saw a shoe by the door. I went over and saw the mess."

"What mess?

"The door was open slightly, and his clothing was inside, bloodied. Whoever did this, Detective, is a sicko."

Nick wanted to get it straight. "What are you saying, Carlo?"

"You know what I mean, Detective. This was no Mob hit. They would have taken him in his clothes, or left him there. In plain sight. Body in bloodied clothing sends a stronger message. A hell of a lot more threatening."

Sam nodded, again. "Thank you, Mr. Philetano. I couldn't help notice your suit. Nice. I love the linen fabric. The blue herringbone looks like a Jaye Manning shade."

Nick suddenly became self-conscious and put his hand into the pocket of his suit, even though he thought he looked great in it, and his wife loved it. A thousand bucks on a suit, he couldn't spend. Three hundred was more than enough and that put a dent in their monthly budget. Good thing his wife was an elementary school principal. If it were only his income, they couldn't do even that.

Carlo shot Nick a grin. "You know designers of men's wear?" he asked Sam.

"Yes. We were talking in the office. Manning's an associate of Mr. Larcon's. You obviously cater to a higher echelon clientele here, so I thought I'd mention it."

"Yeah, I do know him."

"And? I have the feeling you want to tell me more, Mr. Philetano." She gave him an innocent-little-girl pout.

Wow, she really knows how to play a man. But a pout? She's kidding me, right? Nick put it on his agenda, right there, to make this princess grow up.

"Carlo, please. You're too much, ya know that, Detective? Associates? I'd use that term loosely. They were both in here last Friday and had an all-out pissing match. Neither one of them have the balls to throw a punch. Adam got in the middle. He models for Manning. I saw them from the balcony. Couldn't hear a thing over the house music. But I doubt if they're getting along."

"Do you have security cameras inside?"

"No. And that's an exaggerated 'no.' My clientele come to Constellations for a private getaway. No consummate sex, but for a sexy time. All in the fantasy. Their future is in the stars. Or at least, they hope it is. Larcon was the look-no-touch type. Never asked for a lap dance. Never so much as even patted a bottom. Still devoted to his wife, I guess." Sam arched an eyebrow. Carlo shrugged. "More like, he wants to show his son, he's still devoted."

Sam arched the other eyebrow. "Oh, you think he's not, devoted to his wife?"

"No definitive proof. But if you dig deep enough, I'm sure you'll find something."

She compressed her lips. "So why don't you save us some time, Mr. Philetano, and give us a clue as to what you're thinking? The quicker we find who did this, the faster your family's involvement won't be an issue."

Carlo smiled then swallowed. "She's good, Nick, where did you find her? Okay. He digs younger women, adult, but half his age. One of my bouncers is going out with one of the girls, and she told him that her friend, not one of my girls, saw him for a time."

"So your assumptions are from third party info, not personal."

"Yeah."

"Okay, Thank you, Mr. Philetano." Sam handed him her card. "If anything else comes to mind, please call."

"Sure will." He shot Nick a *you're-a-lucky-bastard* look. Nick nodded. He'd have to get used to that look. This time, made it twice, in one day.

Once inside the SUV, Sam blurted out what was on her mind. "Nick, you're on a first name basis with him?"

"Yeah. His brother, Doctor Paulie Philetano, delivered my three kids."

❧❧❧

As soon as he got home, without even talking to his in-laws who babysat, Frank sprinted up the steps to his son's bedroom right at the top of the landing. He stood at the open doorway, looking around, surprised that everything had been put away. Frankie must have straightened up his room, waiting for the wrath of his dad to impale him, attempting to lessen the blow. Laundry in the hamper, check. Transformers, lined up on his bookshelf, check. Lego blocks in their container, check. Tae Kwon Do gi hung on a rack with his boxing and baseball glove, check. Homework was out on his desk in a neat pile, waiting for Dad to go over it, check.

He grimaced at a light beige blotch on the brown and tan sports wallpaper near the baseboard, where there had been scuff-marks, yesterday. Frankie must have used some detergent to clean it up, but he erased a couple of the baseball player's heads, along with a hockey goalie, in the process.

Crap. The paper was less than a year old and it was supposed to be washable.

What in the heck did he use to create that much friction?

Frankie had decided he didn't like the spaceship themed wallpaper anymore. Jen's parents—whom Frank considered his, they were that close—convinced him to give into Frankie when he wanted his room redone. Now Frank shuddered, looking at the six inch in diameter oval on the wall. Okay, no worries. There was room to move his desk and bookshelves over it. He let out a deep breath to calm down and took a few moments for deep breathing. His gaze went to Frankie, in baseball pj's on his bed, reading.

When Frankie saw his dad focus on him, he threw off the matching covers and started crying. "Dad."

Frank sat down on the bed and Frankie jumped into his arms, sat on his lap, and clutched him around the neck, holding on for dear life.

"Dad, I'm sorry."

"All right, okay, champ." He rubbed Frankie's back to calm him down. Closing his eyes, he counted his blessings he had Frankie in his life. The boy was the reason Frank had gone on living after Jen's death. He breathed the air on this Earth for him. It devastated him to see his son so upset. Frankie had punished himself more than Frank would have punished him. The poor kid. He knew right from wrong. Frank would do what he had to now to stop his son's seven-year-old-body from quivering. "Okay, tell me about Jessie."

With his head buried in his father's neck, he sniffled as he got the words out. "She's pretty."

"Oh yeah? What does she look like?"

Frankie sat up and swallowed his tears. "She's got long orange hair."

"Orange?"

"Yes. Like a carrot. And she has green eyes."

"Ah, okay. Girls call that color strawberry blonde. Do you see her every day?" Frank couldn't believe he was having this discussion with him, already.

"Yes, Dad. She's in my class. We sit next to each other."

"Does your teacher know you like each other?"

"Yes, Dad. Everybody knows."

"Really? How come I didn't know?"

Frankie looked away and down. "Well, Dad, I felt bad for you."

"Felt bad for me, why?" Frank didn't have a clue as to what would come out of his son's mouth.

"I have a girlfriend and you don't."

"Oh, man. That's okay." Crap. It was a father's duty to feel bad for his child, not the other way around. The universe sent him a jolt of humility with this one.

"No. It's not. You're not doing anything to get me a new mommy."

Shocked couldn't explain how Frank felt. "Oh, man. I'm not ready to find a new mommy."

"There's gotta be ladies where you work, right?"

"A couple, but they're married."

"There's gotta be one. Come on, Dad!"

Frank laughed at his persistence. "Well, there was a new one who started today, in fact."

Frankie giggled. "What does she look like?"

"She's got long blonde hair, and blue-gray eyes, and a perfect Grecian nose."

"What's a Grecian nose?"

"Straight, with no bumps."

"Eww. What else?"

"Come to think of it, she resembles Mommy."

Frankie opened his eyes wide and blinked a few times. He put his index finger over his mouth before he spoke. "Hmm, maybe, just maybe, this lady—maybe Mommy sent her down from heaven for us."

Frank didn't know what to say. Even the psychiatrist in him froze. He took Frankie back into his arms and squeezed him tight. "Wow," he whispered. "Wow." His voice became lower each time. "Okay, champ, bed now. We'll talk about this tomorrow." He tucked Frankie back under the covers and kissed him.

Wow. Just wow.

In the shower, Frank let the warm water cascade down his frame. He'd had to raise the showerhead to give him a good seven inches above his head. They had bought the two-story house built in the eighties, but gutted the interior, renovating completely. To him, the decor was a bit too feminine. He always let Jen have her way regarding the decorating. He really disliked the mauve tiling and shower curtain. Jen had been torn between the trend of almond-themed décor, and the mauve for the bathrooms. So their master bedroom settled with the mauve, and the two other guest bathrooms in the house went with the almond. Even after Jen's death, he wouldn't have changed it for anything. Jen was in every tile, every wallpaper design, every picture, every appliance, every bit of furniture in the ten rooms, every crevice, every atom in this house. He would never change anything, nor leave it.

Frankie's words boomeranged in his brain. Frank had to relax. He stood still after washing himself down and just did deep breathing. His neck was tight. He'd have to schedule a massage from his guy at the gym.

After he dried off, he trudged into the attached master bedroom. Plopping down on his bed, nude, he laid his hand on Jen's side. That was the only way he'd fall asleep. In the military, he had been trained to fall asleep in two minutes. Since Jen was murdered, he was lucky if it only took him two hours.

He stared up at his and Jen's wedding picture that was on the wall facing him. The hand painted mauve and burgundy floral design on a cream background paper accentuated the sterling silver frame, perfectly. He had to admit, he looked great in that ivory single-button tux with a cummerbund, though he'd never put on another one, ever. He couldn't believe he had actually let Jen talk him into it. But whatever Jen wanted, Jen got. His mission was to make her happy. That would have been his only mission in life. To make Jen happy.

Damn the bastard who took that away from me.

So now his mission was Frankie. To make him a happy, healthy, successful person with a good heart, so he could find his own Jen. Frank just hoped, this wasn't Jessie, yet. He pulled Jen's pillow onto his chest, as tears trickled from the corners of his eyes. He'd never bring another woman into this bed. Whenever he indulged for a release, but never a relationship, it was in the woman's home or in his secret place.

He stared up at the wedding picture again. Jen was gorgeous in her off-white Victorian gown, with an off the shoulder line, long sleeves with ruffles at the waist, tightly cascading down her perfect body, ending in a trumpet swing. Trumpet? How in heck did he remember that? Oh, man. He missed her.

He swallowed hard, holding back the tears. "Okay, Jen. Tell me, princess. Are you telling me it's time? Did you send Samantha into our lives?"

CHAPTER 9

Frank entered the conference room, feeling unsettled from his son's comment last night. '*Maybe Mommy sent her down from heaven for us,*' kept reverberating in his brain, like a tune one repeatedly heard and couldn't get rid of. No matter how hard one would try, that tune would overtake their day, their consciousness. Sometimes for weeks at a time. He hoped this wouldn't be the case. He massaged his forehead, as if that would help him stop the voice. It didn't. He would have trouble focusing on the case today. No. He had to force himself. That was his personal ultimatum.

He wasn't one to accept messages from the universe. He'd never gotten them before. Yeah, he was intuitive, but that came from his psychology and psychiatry training, and listening to his body came through MMA. He did believe in the mind-body connection but the universe had never spoken to him personally before. Or he hadn't opened himself up to being receptive to messages, was more like it.

Ah, forget about it.

Sam wasn't for him. She cringed at his tattoos. She was just too flighty and high strung for him. He needed a woman like Jen, who could control her enthusiasm. Except in the bedroom. Then all hell broke loose. Sam. She looked like she'd be hot, but she hadn't connected with him at all.

This was the first time he had been in the war room since the renovation. He scanned the room—sky-blue painted walls, rewired for new computers, navy blue upholstered seating, light toned wood rectangular conference table. Nice. He put his lips together and nodded in approval. He would feel comfortable meeting with the multi-task force agencies in here. Up to date,

like the ones in other states with more modern precincts. All
right. New York City was finally entering the modern age.

Sam was the first person he laid eyes on. She was wearing, he
guessed, a Meghan Mason beige denim pants suit. The oval studs
running up the sides of her thighs, accentuated her legs perfectly,
even sitting down. The jacket had the same stud pattern on the
back.

Highlighted blonde hair flowed mid back, her beige eye shad-
ow making those blue eyes pop, and pale pink lipstick that coor-
dinated with her blush. Minimal.

Gorgeous. Spectacular.

Those were the only two words he could think of to describe
her.

"You okay?"

He knew the words hadn't come from Sam and he knew the
voice. He just hadn't seen Nick yet.

"Yeah, I'm fine. Good morning." He pulled a chair out from
the table next to Sam, sat down, and sank into the chair. His body
weight pushed the seat down, close to the ground. He laughed
and shook his head, using the lever on the underside to raise him
up to an appropriate level. It took him a few tries to get it right.
"This chair is mine. I'm not going through this crap every time."

Sam laughed and waited to greet him until he settled down.
"Good morning." Her cheerful tone changed when she turned her
eyes to scrutinize his attire.

"What?" He furrowed his eyebrows in a dare. He could guess
what would be coming out of her mouth, next.

"A Khaos Rules T-shirt? Skinny jeans? For a formal interview?"

"Hey! What you see is what you get, princess. Deal with it.
I'm the behind-the-scenes guy. You two are conducting the interviews. If I see you floundering, or going in the wrong direction,
I'll type questions for you to ask. So keep glancing at the computer screen. What happened at the club?"

"Carlo gave a different picture of the relationship between
Adam and the vic. Dad gives him lots of cash." Nick scanned his
brown book. "And get this. There's friction between the vic and
Jaye Manning. Adam is one of his models."

"Okay, so Mom doesn't know her children. How are you
breaking this up?" Frank asked.

"We'll see them together, first. Then I'll lead in the interview with Adam and Valerie. Sam will take Mom and AriellaRose. One thing, Sam—"

She cut him off. "I know, don't leave off the Rose."

Frank frowned. "How did you know that? And don't tell me a little birdie told you."

"You're really out of sorts this morning, aren't you, Doctor Khaos? How's your son?"

"Fine. More upset than I am. Shows he has a conscience. And it's Frank. I'm an informal guy, in case you couldn't guess. Now, how did you know?"

"Um, I just thought, with a high-profile family, they might like things more formal. You know, use complete names, not nick names. That sort of thing."

He stared at her for a moment. "Okay. Good assessment. What time are they coming in?"

"Around eleven. I did get back some reports." Nick referred to the file. "The ME said the cause of death was a small knife in his jugular. He bled out in the car. What was seen on the body were remnants of dried blood, made fluid by the rain. No DNA yet. That could take a couple of weeks. Don't know if all the blood belongs to the vic. Maybe we'll get lucky."

"Along with the cuts on the body, I think that might put a hole in your theory that it was a woman. Female killers don't like to get dirty. They'd use poisons or suffocation. Rarely do they touch their victims, and as far as the cuts on his body, they usually don't torture or bind them. Afraid of getting hurt in the process and hate the blood, especially on themselves." Frank sat thoughtfully for a moment before he continued. "Females usually target the elderly and defenseless. Larcon was neither of those. A lot of them are nurses and caregivers. Easy access to their prey." He folded his hands in his lap, sat back awaiting Sam's retort. He knew she'd have one.

She cocked her head. "Okay, I knew that, as a doctor, you'd have your research down. But what if—just, what if—this person, this killer was the exception and knew the research? Their clean up shows they know some forensics. What if they wanted to throw this investigation, off? If the white band is from a gang, or supposed to make us think it's from a gang, that could be to throw us off. They already wanted us to question the Mob's involvement with the very location of the murder. And I researched the Philetano family last night. A general Google search. Carlo, who owns this club, as well as an Italian restaurant in Staten Island, has never so much as had a parking ticket. He's thirty-eight, married. Wife looks lovely from the internet pics, four kids. The father Paulo has many legit businesses. He's been on the FBI watch list for years, but nothing. They're watching him because of ties his extended family has to the Mob. The middle son, Stephano, is a criminal defense attorney. The youngest, Leonardo, has a car repair shop on Staten Island, and the eldest son, Doctor Paulie Philetano, Nick knows. He's an OB/GYN on Staten Island."

"I know him, too. He delivered Frankie."

"Oh, so you know this family? So why don't you tell me?"

Nick sighed. "First. They're not off the hook, Sam. We can't do anything till we get all of the reports, and that can be several days. We start with the family. And I'm going to tell you now. I expect you to be hard on them. No little girl pout."

Frank smiled, arms on armrests, wanting to hear about this. "Little girl pout?"

"What?" She glanced at Frank, who sat with a closed-lip smile. "And you! Stop calling me, princess. Only my dad calls me that." She turned her attention toward her partner. "First, I was getting info from him, wasn't I? He was willing to talk to me, wasn't he? So don't question my approach, if I get the job done."

"Well, unfortunately, Loo put me in the position of correcting your protocol since I'm so good at it."

"Um—that, I'll have to wait and see, since we never did get a chance yesterday to get acquainted, so you could teach me the protocol." Her tone matched his, obnoxious.

Before an all-out pissing match ensued, which Frank knew would fall upon him to neutralize, the conference room door opened. "Detectives, Doctor Khaos, the Larcon family is here." Lieutenant Rojas stopped dead when Sam stood up. He stared at her, shaking his head.

Frank didn't get the message. 'What, Loo?"

The lieutenant opened the door wider. "In here, to start, please."

In walked Mrs. Larcon, wearing the exact Meghan Mason suit as Sam, and Valerie, the same suit in lavender. Everyone stood still. Mrs. Larcon turned up her nose, scrutinizing Sam. She didn't hide her disgust. This would be some interview, one that

Frank was glad that he'd be in another room for. Even their short-sleeved tops were the same, in a gold Lurex for her and Sam, and the same in lavender for Valerie. Profiling Sam, he deducted she was a loner. She must have spent her entire salary on clothes. Nothing left to spend on entertainment. Not on a cop's income.

Good. Just like me, except for the money.

"And who might you be, dear? I've met these two gentlemen." Mrs. Larcon gave Frank what appeared to be a condescending look of disdain. He just let it roll off his back.

"I'm Detective Samantha Wright. I'll be speaking with you today. Come, please sit down."

"Very well. Oh, this is Adam and AriellaRose. She's fat because she's on prednisone."

Time stood still. No one spoke. They were at a loss for words. Sam and Nick both had the same solemn expression on their faces—one that mirrored his own, Frank was sure—of deep concern for AriellaRose and immediate dislike for Mommy Dearest. Adam seemed to be a mere oversight in his mother's eyes. *No judgments, Frank*, he reminded himself.

As they took seats around the table, Frank peered into AriellaRose's soul, seeing a tormented young woman, who probably hadn't received a smile from her mother in years. She wore black oversized sweat pants and sweatshirt, most likely to conceal her weight.

What a demented thing to say about your daughter in an introduction to strangers.

Yeah, he couldn't prevent himself from judging. AriellaRose hadn't flinched, or paled, or let out any sign of disapproval with her mother. Her rounded face—broadened from prednisone use, he assumed, the moon face as doctors called it—hung down low, without making eye contact with any of them. When he did get a glimpse of them, her eyes, unlike Valerie's, had no sign of tears.

"I think I'm going to participate in this interview, Detectives, if you don't mind."

"Not at all, Doctor Khaos." Sam's and Nick's voices trampled over each other's.

"We're sorry for your loss." Nick began. "I know it's a difficult time for all of you."

Adam looked up at the recording strobe in the corner of the room and rolled his eyes.

"What's going on, Adam?"

He sneered at Nick. "I don't know why we're here. You spoke with my mom yesterday. We hardly talk to each other, so if you expect me to grieve, forget it. And what kind of a doctor is he, with his name on his T-shirt? I have a meeting to get to and this is a waste of my time." Staring at Frank, Adam flicked some specks of lint off his denim sports jacket. He straightened the front of his jacket and smiled at his own attire, conveying a denigrating message.

Um, not so much different from my gang kids, just richer. "Forensic psychiatrist. You know? Everyone shows grief, disappointment in different ways." The only person at the table who showed any movement was AriellaRose. He noticed her already labored breathing, becoming tighter. Her hand moved up to her throat and wheezing became more audible. "AriellaRose, how are you feeling?"

She held her head down, merely tilting her eyes up for a split second.

"Oh, she's just bringing on an attack for attention," Mrs. Larcon chirped. "She couldn't care less about how I'm going to get along now, being a widow. She'll do anything to get the attention on her. Pay her no mind, Doctor Khaos."

"I'm talking to AriellaRose, Mrs. Larcon. She's an adult and can speak for herself."

AriellaRose snapped her tongue over her teeth, but that was the only response he had gotten.

Okay, she heard.

"Detectives, I think we need to go into different meeting rooms, now. I'll stay in here with AriellaRose."

Valerie waved a hand. "Why? We're a close family, Doctor Khaos. We can talk freely together. Plus, we have so much to do to plan my father's funeral. When do you think we can get custody of his body?"

Adam rolled his eyes. "Valerie, cut the bullshit. The lollipop act is getting old. These douche bags can see right through you."

Nick sat straight up, leaned in toward Adam. "Adam, do I have to remind you you're in a police precinct? Control your language." He stared into the kid's cold eyes, sending the message there was a decorum to be followed in here.

Frank had worked with Nick long enough to read his body language. Most of the time there had been a positive effect on the recipient.

However, to Adam, that didn't register. "That's how I talk. You don't like it, fuck off." He stared at his Rolex.

"What time is your appointment, Adam?"

"None of your business, but I can't be late."

"You're right, Doctor Khaos. Time to separate. Come on, Adam. We're going to talk privately. Now. Let's go." Nick got up while Adam didn't move. "For a guy who has an appointment and wants to get out of here, you're awfully slow."

Adam sneered at him, but got up, and rammed the chair into the table.

This kid needs a few rounds with me in the cage. Frank contemplated how he could arrange that. "Yes, Detective Valatutti, as much as I'd like to hear more obscenities from Adam, I think you'll convey how we roll. Detective Wright, why don't you speak with Valerie? Mrs. Larcon, please wait in the waiting area. One of us will get to you when we're done."

"I can see this will turn out to be an all-day affair. This won't do at all."

"Mrs. Larcon, deal with it." Frank dealt her his favorite curt response.

"Well, I don't like the way I'm being treated.

"Sorry you feel that way. In here, everyone is treated equally. Now, I'd like to speak with AriellaRose."

He stood up exerting his power—straight, tall, and foreboding—through his intimidating physicality. Adam stared at him, wide eyed. Valerie's mouth went into an O, then her gaze settled on his crotch. Mrs. Larcon backed off and headed to the door, after checking out his tattooed arms. Yeah, he had chased away some parents back in the day. And Sam. Hers was the response he wanted to observe. She put her lips together and then bit her lower lip.

Crap. Jen used to do that.

Frankie's voice reverberated in his mind again.

Nick escorted them out of the room, leaving Frank sitting opposite AriellaRose at the table. He focused on her breathing that seemed to have eased up when her mother left the room, but her wheezing intensified. He picked up the intercom. "Susan, please bring me my bag from my office." He disconnected without waiting for a response. "AriellaRose, have you seen your doctor?"

"I'm okay. I'm always like this." She coughed the words out.

"Always this congested?" There was a knock at the door. He

got up, opened it slightly, and retrieved his medical satchel. Putting it on the table, he opened it and pulled out his stethoscope. He approached AriellaRose, but was met with a palm up, facing him. "I just want to check your lungs."

"No." She put her head down again, fiddling with her fingers in her lap.

He leaned against the table with his arms folded against his chest. Calm and compassionate, his way, he looked at her with a relaxed, unthreatening expression. "Why not?"

She didn't respond.

"AriellaRose look at me." His voice sounded so peaceful it wouldn't wake a sleeping baby. She glanced up at him, for a moment. "I'm not going to hurt you. How long have you had this congestion?"

"My whole life."

"You've had asthma your whole life." She nodded. "But how long have you had this episode?"

"About a month."

"What medications are you taking?"

"My usual."

"Which is?"

"A couple of inhalers, the nebulizer machine, prednisone."

"How much prednisone are you on?"

"Twenty, thirty, ten milligrams. It varies."

His focus intensified. He felt the change in his face, destroying his preferred relaxed composure. "It *varies*?"

"Depending upon how many I pop into my mouth that day."

He moistened his lips before he spoke. "Does your doctor know this protocol you're on?"

"He told me I could take my asthma meds as needed."

"Don't think he meant the prednisone. That has to be regulated carefully."

"Oops. So shoot me." She put her head down again.

He smiled. "That's not the solution, AriellaRose. You know? I do see your face is puffy from the pred, but for someone on a large doses, you're not as fidgety as I would expect."

She shrugged her shoulders.

"What do you take to calm yourself down?"

She looked up and, for the first time, Frank saw worry in her eyes. Then she blinked and completely shut down. Almost a catatonic gaze. Eyes blank. Face stoic. Pale.

Okay, forget the interview.

He approached her with the stethoscope. Putting the earpieces in place, he rubbed the metal base with his palm, slipped it under her sweatshirt, all the while without a response. It was as if AriellaRose had left the Earth plane.

That she can do this in an asthmatic episode is unusual, if not impossible. This young woman has a lot more pharmaceuticals than just asthma meds in her body. "Calling EMS, AriellaRose. I don't like what I hear in your lower right lung."

No response.

Frank put in a call to 911.

⧫⧫⧫

Nick sat opposite Adam in a smaller but updated conference room. Adam sat back, looking at a crease in his jeans as his right leg lay over his left thigh. The only info Adam had given in the hour, was his home address on the upper west side of Manhattan and where he worked as a model for Jaye Manning. It was what Nick had already known from his file. Most of the hour had been spent with Adam and Nick having staring contests. Nick had won all of them, forcing Adam to emote a few words.

"We've been sitting here an hour, Detective. I'm not telling you squat."

"I'm a very patient man. I told you I need some answers."

"I have to get outta here by two thirty."

"What time is your appointment?"

"Three."

"Don't think you'll make it." Nick would do the necessary to make sure he didn't make it.

CHAPTER 10

After buttoning her black, double-breasted denim jacket, raising the collar to cover her neck, and pulling her long hair back into a ponytail with a scrunchie, Meghan Mason strutted out of Bistro Alexander on Broadway. She didn't pay attention to the passersby or the chilly wind, as she rummaged through her tote for her phone. She pushed her way through the crowds of executive men and woman, who were immersed in their own little worlds, chatting on cell phones as they trudged to their destination on Broadway. This was New York City, the world of the workaholic. Glancing up occasionally, so she wouldn't crash into a lamp pole or garbage bin, she recognized some of her designs on the women who smiled at her as they passed. She offhandedly waved in response. She had hoped to make it home to Yonkers before rush hour, leaving her office for a late lunch at the Bistro as she did every Thursday.

She loved their gluten-free menu—actually, starchy carb-free menu. She was obsessive about her weight, after having lost a hundred pounds in her thirties, right before she began her fashion line. She had turned her life around after her doctor had given her an ultimatum. Lose weight or fall victim to innumerable illnesses her doctor had listed nonchalantly. None of them appealed to her. Not after all the work she had put into going to the top design college in Manhattan, getting her degree, all the while raising her daughters, as a single parent. The only ones who were more proud of her than herself were her girls, whom she worshipped. They had survived despite their childhood full of angst.

The same motivation and mindset she used to get through those four years of college after a messy divorce from an abusive husband, she just transferred to weight loss. *Lose it or die, just like you almost did so many times from that bastard.* She had finally made it. The fashion line she had created was one she could actually wear. Now a size eight, she'd never allow herself to gain that weight back. She had become the role model to her daughters, that she had hoped to be for so many years. She gave herself an imaginary pat on the back as she did every day when she left work. Yes! She had made it to Broadway, in New York City, the fashion mecca of the world.

The crowds of people rushed in all directions toward their destinations, consuming the streets. It was a tsunami of people flooding Broadway and Fifty-Ninth. She slipped the phone back in her tote. She couldn't make her call now with all this noise. To top it off, an ambulance siren blared right next to her on the other side of the steel barricade, and none of the cars moved. They couldn't in the bumper-to-bumper traffic. She glanced at the ambulance.

That poor soul.

She literally didn't have the room to move closer to the display windows of the high-end boutiques to avoid to traffic and intoxicating fumes from car and truck exhausts.

Then she saw them. The life size gorilla, tigers, leopards, and elephant costumes. They had taken over Broadway, their heights, alone, overwhelming the pedestrians. She laughed out loud, mesmerized by the natural colors in their faux fur and skin. The newspaper article in yesterday's paper came to reality. The Maxwell Gallery on Seventy-Ninth and Broadway was introducing the work of new painter, Hans Witier, a South African who celebrated endangered species in their natural habitat in his works. They had done so much promotion for the event that these lifelike creatures had consumed social media for the past few months. She stared at the leopard, recognizing the brand of faux fur, from some wisps moving in the wind. Her friend used the same material in her faux fur coats. As they walked by, people petted them, smiled as the creatures waved. Some people stopped in the middle of the street to take pics with them. It was a fun time, the hour before rush hour. It was a fun time for her. For others, annoyance at the intrusions was apparent as they pushed the animations aside.

She rummaged in her tote again and pulled up her smartphone. Her mail lit up from industry colleagues. She did a double take and stopped dead. People bumped into her from all sides at her unexpected halt. Fright steeled her body. She didn't budge.

No. Can't be. Steven Larcon has been murdered?

Frantically, she checked her Facebook. The news had spread into every post.

Why in hell didn't someone in my office bust in to tell me?

Maybe because she threatened to fire them if they disturbed her. When she was on a deadline, like for next week, nothing mattered but that deadline. The articles said there were no suspects yet. She froze.

Should I come forward and give them the list? Oh my God! He was one of her closest friends and supporters when she was up and coming. Steven was the one who convinced her to leave the bastard after she showed up in his office with a black eye and swollen cheek. No amount of makeup hid it. Steven saw through the dark shades she wore. He had said, 'You'd never cover up those gorgeous blues, so what did he do now?' Tears flowed. She'd lost her main supporter, confidant, mentor, and friend. Poor Steven. The articles said he had been killed, but not how, or where.

She knew his family wouldn't be all that broken up. He had confided in her as well. His wife was an ice cube, so he did have to look elsewhere. She closed her eyes in appreciation. Not once had he come onto her. He respected their industry relationship. Her mind wandered to his many flings. Most of them had been with single women. He wasn't the type to break up a happy marriage. But there were those two. She nodded at the possibility.

Should I?

She'd sleep on it.

Then there was the drug trafficker on Staten Island, to whom he still owed money for his son Adam's habit. She had discussed him with Steven. Even though he withheld payment, Steven didn't think these guys would hurt him or Adam, because of their celebrity status. Who knew? Then there was the guy who had pirated Steven's designs. A Canadian who had hacked his computer. Steven tracked him with his own resources, sent him a rather explicit cease and desist order, and threatened him with a formal law suit for noncompliance. The guy laughed in his face. That had really pissed off Steven, and that was just a couple of days ago.

Then there was the guy that Steven had fired for incompetence. He'd screw up orders time and time again. Her mind went to all of the employees he'd let go. He had discussed all of them with her. It tormented him to end someone's livelihood. But he had to do what was best for his company.

Then it hit her. *Oh my God! The affair with Calinda. Oh, no! That was it.*

☙❦❧

BlackCloud sat at a bar stool at the window in a cafe on Broadway and Sixtieth. She had just dived into her cranberry-vanilla muffin when Meghan stopped dead to look at her smartphone. She couldn't tell what Meghan was reading, but she bet it had something to do with Steven Larcon. Seeing Meghan just standing there, in a cocoon of airspace, annoyed the heck out of her. People just walked around her as Meghan kept her gaze on her smartphone.

Shit. That woman's in la-la land.

Cloud double-checked her appearance in the reflection of the cafe window, inhaling her double chocolate latte through a wide straw. Yes, that gooey makeup she put on covered her freckles. *How in the hell do women feel good wearing this crap? Fuck it. This better be over real quick.*

She put on the thin leather gloves and zipped up the thousand-dollar black-leather jacket that Ram had bought for her for the occasion. The navy, wide-bottomed pants also fit her damned good. She had to admit it. She looked good. She nodded at her reflection in the mirror. Five feet ten and stunning. For the first time in her life, she was pleased with her height. She even looked great in those hazel contact lenses and short blonde doo that Ram insisted she get. Too bad this look would be short-lived.

She put her hand into the vertical zipped compartment in the back of the designer tote. The Ruger was ready to go, silencer and all.

What a shame to waste a six thousand dollar handbag just to hold a weapon. What the fuck? It isn't my money.

She slipped off the stool and exited the café, just as Meghan began walking, hunched over as if in tears. Cloud glanced at her watch then pulled the wide cuffs of the jacket down to cover her hands.

Damn it! Two-fifty.

Just ten more minutes and it must be done. If she missed the moon in Mars conjunct hour, she'd be dealt with. Harshly.

∽∻∾

Sam and Mrs. Larcon sat at a conference table in the rear of the precinct. "Mrs. Larcon, I see that you're nervous and fidgeting."

She ignored Sam and continued to focus on her cuticles with her hands in her lap.

"AriellaRose is in the ER," Sam continued. "Doctor Khaos went there to see she gets immediate attention. Do you want to go and we could continue this later?"

Good test, Sam. See what kind of mom she is.

"That's perfectly all right, dear." Mrs. Larcon made eye contact with Sam. "My daughter—" She swallowed as if she had a bitter lemon stuck between her teeth. "My daughter has never wanted my company, even when she was ill. And she gets ill a lot. The poor thing."

"Tell me about that, Mrs. Larcon." Sam folded her hands in front of her on the desk and gazed with intent at Mrs. Larcon.

Mommy Dearest relaxed.

"She couldn't care less about taking care of herself. Just look at her. She eats what she wants, despite doctors telling her she's allergic. She hasn't ever stepped foot into a gym. Me. I couldn't go without my aerobics and Zumba. Steven insisted upon it. If I didn't look the part of a fashion icon's wife, he'd tear me apart. And I mean that literally. Mr. Fusspot, I'd call him. God forbid my scarf had one shade in it that conflicted with the rest of my attire. Whenever we were getting dressed for an event, he would come into my dressing room and make me model. Thank God, I still have my figure. I'm fifty but I still look damned good. Would you believe that Steven would even come to the salon with me? He would drive my stylist crazy! He would bring his own swatches that he made up for her to copy. Some for the reds he loved, and some he warned her against even trying. That poor woman. But I have to admit. This shade of dark auburn I love. And my eyes, green? Not mine, dear. Mine are blue-gray, almost like yours. At least, now, I can get rid of these painful lenses." Sam glared at her. "Yes, Detective. That's very shallow of me."

"So you didn't have too much independence then?"

"None. Nada. Steven was involved in every part of my life. Even my volunteer work."

"That's wonderful. What do you do?"

"Larcon Cosmetics. We create a line for women who have gone through cancer, burn traumas from abuse, disabled veterans who are scarred. We give them the makeup and teach them how to use it. When the makeup is applied, all scarring is hidden. Some women use it to even hide something as adorable as freckles. But if a woman is unhappy, we will help them."

"How long have you been doing this? I haven't heard of your cosmetics division before."

"Going on nine years. We keep a low profile. Women are recommended by their physicians and come from the Tri-State area. We don't even have a website, and never do that social media rant. Women in these situations want privacy, and we respect that. But their end result is life changing. We respect that, too."

"Very nice, Mrs. Larcon. Do any of your children work with you on this?"

"Valerie, a little. What I mean by a little is less than one hour a month. So a minuscule amount is more like it. Adam and AriellaRose, they do nothing to give back. Adam models for Steven's dear friend, Jaye Manning."

"Jaye Manning?" Sam feigned scanning the file. "Um, didn't you tell Detective Valatutti and Doctor Khaos there was friction between them?"

"My dear. Whenever you have two brilliant men working on the same project, using the same fabrics, there's bound to be friction. Just a battle of egos. But their end results brought in millions for both sides. Men and women love wearing the same look when going to affairs. Photographs come out stunning. So any arguments were petty and definitely not life altering."

Okay. Jaye Manning might be lower on the suspect list. "Mrs. Larcon, tell me about AriellaRose. You mentioned her ill health."

♥♥♥

BlackCloud followed behind Meghan. She nodded as her cohorts, BlackFlower and BlackMoon came up on either side of her. They had followed Megan's path for over a month. That woman was predictable. Every Thursday, at one thirty, she left her office on Broadway and fifty-Eighth, had lunch at the Bistro, and by two-thirty she made the three-block walk south to the out-door parking lot. She wanted to make it home to take her daughters to gymnastics. That irked Ram to no end.

Cloud scrutinized her friends' attire. Dressed up in pants suits, conforming to the outfits of the pedestrians around them, so they'd fit in, she was pleased at the results. They had a couple of blocks to go, so she let her mind wander to their preparation. Ordinarily, right before her job, she'd pay full attention. This was her responsibility, and she'd relish the credit for this one. Just like Flower had the credit for the Steven kill. This would really put her in Ram's good graces. Now Cloud had to prove she deserved that, too. Her friends wore the outfits Ram had selected for them. They must have just come from the Brooklyn brownstone. Ram spent a fortune on their clothes and made a closet on the upper level of the house. Ram had tons of clothes, none of which she'd ever wear. Cloud had taken her outfit home yesterday.

She thought about why they couldn't reach Ram. Good thing they knew where she kept the spare key. Cloud wasn't worried. Just curious. Ram would disappear for days. Most likely with her boyfriend. She'd come home happy. Probably from fabulous sex.

Cloud was the tallest of the trio, but not the most shapely, so she felt great getting smiles of approval from her friends. Wow. Their outfits were different from the Larcon kill. That guy was so trusting, so receptive, that they were able to get close. He had actually believed them when they approached him for money, looking like homeless women. When they walked up to him—wheeling the grocery wagon they borrowed from the store down the street, with tattered clothes, hair a mess—he'd opened his wallet to take out cash without hesitation.

That dick. Didn't he know that, in New York City, you can't trust anyone? Three women approaching him at once?

There wasn't a suspicious bone in his body. Ram had been right. She had told them all about him. Little did he realize that the wagon held supplies they needed to cover up the murder. His murder.

Forget about him. Gotta do this now.

They continued to follow Meghan across the street into a bubble of yuppies. The Express Bus pulled up, and a torrent of clock punchers ran toward the curb. Cloud pulled her Ruger from the compartment on the bag, her right index finger on the side of the weapon. She edged herself so close to Meghan, no one could get in between them with Flower and Moon on each side. Meghan was still oblivious—lost in sorrow, Cloud guessed. She moved a little to the left of Meghan. Aiming so the .380 would enter her from the rear but go sideways through her torso, Cloud pulled the trigger as fire engine sirens blared. That wasn't by coincidence. Sirens blared every few minutes. Cloud had waited for one.

With the suppressor and environmental noise, the hollow point bullet would do its job without drawing any undue attention. The gun made it back into her handbag as Meghan fell straight down. The assassins continued walking, as did everyone on the street.

Okay, Meghan, guess your daughters will have to make it to gymnastics on their own.

CHAPTER 11

Frank entered AriellaRose's hospital room wearing a long white lab coat over a light blue button-down shirt. He'd even put on a tie. In this Manhattan hospital, they had insisted he conform. So he did. With a new patient. Tomorrow he'd be back in his T and skinny jeans. He adjusted the obligatory stethoscope hung around his neck. He hated that symbolism. He wasn't any better than anyone else.

She appeared to be dozing, lying on her back with her upper body raised to almost a sitting position. After reviewing her prelim blood work, he ordered an IV with fluids combined with an antibiotic and Solu-Medrol. He was glad he was able to secure a private room. With her father's murder, and the media wanting to swarm her, this was actually the best place she could be. He approached her slowly and put his hand around her wrist, his fingers on the pulse point. Moderate. She turned wearily and looked up at him.

He needed to confront her about the oxycodone use that her mother had reported, and she certainly appeared to be using. Head nodding, dilated pupils, but he'd wait for the right moment. "How are you doing?"

"Okay."

"Your chest X-ray says otherwise."

"What?"

"You have pneumonia."

"No, I don't."

An argument with a patient never made it onto his agenda. "AriellaRose, that's a beautiful name."

She gave him a doubtful glance. "That's where it ends."

"Come on. What do you mean?"

"Don't bullshit me, Doctor Khaos. Look at me. I'm five feet, one hundred sixty pounds. I have scars from chickenpox, my—"

He cut her off. "AriellaRose, Come on. Now's not the time to be hard on yourself. You need to relax. We have to talk about something."

She rolled her eyes. "What?"

He pulled up an armchair to the right of the bed, sat, and leaned in toward her with his hands folded in his lap. She looked down with half-closed eyes.

"Spoke with your pulmonary doctor," he said. "The one you listed with the intake nurse. Luckily, he has affiliation with this hospital as well as your local one, so he'll be seeing you. But he did tell me he hadn't seen you in over nine months. At first, he told me he wasn't your physician anymore. Thought you went to someone else."

"Why would he think that?"

"Because he had only given you prescriptions for three months." He waited for her response. None. "He found your blood glucose level to be very high. In the diabetic range. Did he ever discuss that with you?" She swallowed and rolled over on her side with her back toward him. He sighed. "AriellaRose, come on, turn around. I'm not going anywhere."

"I'm tired. Go away."

"Nope. Where are you getting your medications?" He leaned back in the chair and waited. And waited.

Her breathing relaxed. She had fallen asleep.

How in the hell can someone with strained respiration fall asleep in a millisecond?

There were definitely more pharmaceuticals in her blood stream than even Blue and asthma meds. And it would be imperative to address the diabetes. He'd have to wait at least another hour for her toxicology report.

⁓⁓⁓

Sam stared at her smartphone after she received the call from Withers. Damn it. Another fashion industry murder. Her favorite designer, Meghan Mason, had been shot in plain sight in daylight on Broadway and Sixtieth Street.

What the hell?

She had just let Mrs. Larcon go on a potty break. There was

so much more she needed to know. Now she'd have to leave Mrs. Larcon to go to another crime scene.

Crap. Just when I was building a rapport. Her thoughts came to a halt. Fashion industry icons murdered.

Her first case in her first two days in homicide just became a serial case by their mere association.

Oh my God, Dara. This is big.

Nick stuck his head in the conference room. "Sam."

She turned toward the door abruptly. "I know. He called me."

"We're staying here. Withers is going. It'll take him at least an hour this time of day. Personnel is on the scene. Just don't tell Mrs. Larcon about it."

"I won't."

Too late. Mrs. Larcon burst into the room in tears. She nearly toppled over Nick, who was in the doorway. "Oh, my God, Detectives. Meghan Mason was shot and killed an hour ago. Pictures are all over Facebook, already. Look!"

With Nick leaning over her shoulder, Sam scrolled down through the posts, showing the barricades set up, on lookers, Meghan's body covered with a white tarp, her two daughters hysterical, the animal caricatures a block away with cops. It was the thrill New Yorkers either craved, or ignored. There was no happy medium. There must have been hundreds of people on the Facebook screens. That precinct would be working overtime, for sure, before they turned over everything to her.

Mrs. Larcon hadn't stopped crying. Her mascara ran down her face, her eyes reddened. She sat at the conference table, hyperventilating with her head in her hand. Sam wondered if she had cried this much over her husband's murder. Probably not. Nick sat down next to her.

"Where's Adam?" Mrs. Larcon asked.

A red flag. Usually under such a stressful situation someone would say, "Where's my son?" rather than something so impersonal. Would Adam know anything about this?

"He's in the other conference room, Mrs. Larcon. Pissed off that I made him miss his appointment. Now I have more to speak with him about, so I'll leave you two ladies alone."

Sam waited until Nick closed the door behind him. Sam leaned in toward the Merry Widow. "Mrs. Larcon, I can see how upset you are. Do you need a moment?"

Mrs. Larcon dabbed her bottom lashes with a tissue. "Detective, what does this mean? Two murders in two days, of people who were in the same industry? I've watched enough TV to know this isn't good. Serial killers? Is that what you call them?"

Sam responded with a weak smile. "Yes, and you can probably help us. What do you know about the business relationship between Meghan and your husband? Think about their commonalities, people they both know."

"They were very good friends. Strictly platonic." Mrs. Larcon relaxed, as if she was more comfortable talking about Meghan than her daughter.

Sam saw her body language change when she had asked her about AriellaRose. Taut, sitting straight up, as if to exert her personal power and, then she had immediately asked to go to the ladies' room.

"Steven told me their specific conversations. She liked to bounce her design ideas off him. Like the outfit we're both wearing. She drove herself crazy, trying to figure out the shape of the studding, which direction they should go. Which would flatter a woman's curves. They never discussed anything of a personal nature. Steven was never the type to air dirty laundry."

"Um, that's strange, Mrs. Larcon. There have been many tweets where he talks about other designers."

"Oh, that?" She poo-pooed it with a callous hand motion. "That's business, my dear. Don't tell me you believe what you read in the media. All that was a publicity stunt. Agreed upon by them all and staged. Even when he ripped apart my rehab. And it was very effective, too. Sales increased by the negative tweets and remained longitudinal with the mundane ones. We have analysts on board who deal with all of this."

"Interesting. Do you know how often Steven and Meghan would see each other, where they'd meet?"

"Steven's office was in Chelsea and Meghan's office uptown on Broadway. He would meet her at a Bistro on Broadway. Maybe he would see her a couple of times a month. People always took photos. They were always in business attire with their attaches by their side. Believe me, if there was any socializing, it would be on social media. Actually, Steven didn't do any socializing. So before you ask. He never had an affair. Totally devoted to me. Our sex life was...how can I say it?...sizzling. Oh, but I will tell you before I forget. Speak with Meghan's ex-husband. She divorced the abuser when the girls were little. It was the first year we launched our cosmetic division. We usually don't divulge information, but she's gone. May she rest in peace. And I would consider him the prime suspect, if I were you."

"Thank you. We will definitely speak with him. But regarding yourself, Mrs. Larcon, this is so different than what you told Detective Valatutti and Doctor Khaos when they came to your home."

"What do you mean?"

"Well, you told them, that after his meetings, Steven went to different clubs and you didn't care enough to question him. That doesn't sound like a warm and fuzzy marriage, if you ask me."

"Oh, I was under the stress of just finding out my husband had been murdered. You've got to understand that. And I always knew that Steven would come home to me, eventually. And when he did, he came home ready to make me a very happy woman. If you get my gist."

Um, what happened to 'we have an open marriage'? Sam put that on the back burner for now. "Yes. I most certainly do. Tell me now about AriellaRose."

A shut down with a smirk. "What do you need to know?"

"Let's start with your pregnancy."

"Ooh, that is going far back. The twins were very much wanted. I was a smoker back then. Stupidly. I haven't touched a cigarette in ten years. AriellaRose blames me for her asthma. So do the doctors, in all honesty. They were lying on a nerve, so I spent the last trimester in bed. Adam was fine. He was the bigger, stronger twin. But they were both premies. Adam was four and a half pounds, AriellaRose, three and a half. Not that underweight." Sam must have shot her a glare of disapproval that Mrs. Larcon caught. "I know what you're thinking, Detective, they only spent a month in the NIC unit," she added, dismissively.

Sam didn't push her, but she didn't like this woman.

Remain objective, Sam. She felt the imaginary twang of Dara in her stomach. "What was their childhood like?"

"Privileged, spoiled rotten by Steven. They got everything they ever wanted. That was the problem. Don't know why they resorted to drugs. I have already told the two gentlemen, and I use that term loosely with that doctor. Ugh, not the type I'd go to bed with." Sam rolled her lips together to hide a smile. "What about you, dear?" Mrs. Larcon asked. "I don't see a marriage band on either of you. Would you romance him?"

Sam laughed. "Romance him?"

"You know. Have sex."

"Uh, I know what you mean, Mrs. Larcon. Inter-precinct relationships are frowned upon. So, uh, no, and we just met yesterday."

"That is not true, dear, if you're discreet."

"Excuse me?"

"I read somewhere that two New York City employees could have consensual relationships where they work, even in their place of employment if it's after hours, with no children around. It was a law passed in 2012. So you're safe."

Sam couldn't contain her giggle. "How did you know that one?"

"I read the paper every day. Okay, so tell me. Is he available? I saw the way my Valerie looked at him. She was consuming his groin with her eyes. That's what she always does. Jumps into bed with any man, if he's rich enough. Doubt if he is, on a civil servant's salary. Adam, I don't have to worry about. He's dating a lovely girl from a lovely family. Calinda is her name. I'm keeping my fingers crossed. I'd love, love, love to have her as a daughter-in-law. Now AriellaRose, I am sure she's still a virgin. Poor thing. But I could see you and that doctor together."

Oh my God! She's worse than my mother. Sam felt her cheeks flush. "Uh, Mrs. Larcon, even though talking about the prospect of Doctor Khaos in bed is more fun at the moment, I need to know more about AriellaRose. She seems shy."

"One more thing about that before we go on. I noticed he definitely has eyes for you, by the way."

"And you know that how?"

"When he stood up and I saw where Valerie's gaze settled, he was looking at you. He may have wanted to intimidate Adam, but believe me, dear, it was your reaction he studied."

Um, this woman is so observant, but she can't understand her children. And was he? Observing me?

Sam chose to ignore that and move on. "Why does AriellaRose appear to be so shy?"

"I don't think she's shy with her friends. She does have some. They met in rehab. With strangers, it's hard to engage her."

"She's twenty-five, right?" A nod. "What does she do for a living?"

"Not much. She did graduate from design school. But Steven

would not hire her until she cleaned up, both with the drugs and weight loss. She never looked the part to be in his company. Adam and Valerie fit the persona, but AriellaRose has been a big disappointment. She's not even as talented as the other two."

"So how does she live? She has an apartment on the upper east side."

"Steven owns the apartment. He lets her live there. Rent free and he pays all of the expenses. One thing, for sure, he was a devoted father. Unconditional love. He always preached that."

∽∾∽

Frank had just gotten off the phone with Nick about Meghan Mason's murder. He didn't know what to think, but he'd rather be with his gangbangers at the gym and investigating Jen's murder rather than entrenched in the fashion world. He had never felt comfortable in the celebrity arena. He had the feeling that would be consuming his time now, unless he could find a way out. He'd keep that to himself for now.

He re-entered AriellaRose's hospital room and found her watching a game show. Interesting choice for such a solemn person. At the same time as the canned laughter, she just smirked, not even a glimmer of a smile. She didn't acknowledge his presence, but stared with tunnel vision at the TV. He stood for a moment as he did when Frankie ignored him, usually when his little guy foresaw an impending lecture. But his wasn't chemically induced. Frank slipped the remote out of her swollen wrist. The IV had been leaking. He pushed the red button to call for a nurse, then shut the TV, still ignored.

He leaned against the bed on his right thigh, and crossed his arms across his chest. *Man, this girl is good at planned ignoring, with a complete disregard for authority.*

Still, he had made it a point never to come across as an authoritarian with a patient. In the gym, that was a different story altogether. He tapped her on the shoulder with his index finger.

"I see you. Go away."

"No can do. Got your toxicology report back. Illicit drugs in your system."

She sneered into his face, "Big whoopee," and turned away in a split second.

"Well, it's even a bigger whoopee than you think."

"No, it's not."

"Yeah, it is. High levels of oxycodone, which we found could exacerbate asthma." She looked at him for the first time. He nodded. "Good. Now that I've got your attention. We also found Vicodin. Why two narcotic analgesics?" He pulled the chair over. "AriellaRose, it's either me you talk to or the police."

"I have my sources."

"Obviously. Who?"

"You actually expect me to rat?"

"Nah. You wouldn't give me a straight answer, anyway. Tell me about your rehab experiences."

She glared at him.

"Your mother mentioned to me you tried it a few times."

"They tried it a few times. I didn't."

"So you didn't put in any effort in when you were there."

She looked away.

"Why not?"

"You are so dense. You know that, Doctor Khaos? I have a sucky life, in case you haven't noticed."

"What makes it sucky?"

"You are such a predictable shrink. Stop repeating what I say in a question, just to show me you're listening."

He laughed.

"I've been shrunk my whole life. Go speak to my mother and listen to her lies. I get it from her."

"Actually, Detective Wright is with her right now. So why don't you set me straight on her lies."

"I don't know what you guys talk about."

"Everything. From your early childhood, friends, relatives. Even back to conception."

"Conception? That would be a good one."

"How so?"

"She would probably go on and on about how they wanted us and what devoted parents they are. It's bullshit. You heard the way she introduced me. And don't tell me you didn't notice. The air stood still. She's always that humiliating. She hated the idea of being pregnant so much, she smoked to kill us. I think we were an accident. She'd tell everyone we were lying on a nerve. That's crap. She's bulimic and so is Valerie. That's how they stay so thin. Every time she eats, she complains that the food is laying on her, so she goes into the bathroom to throw up. She sticks her fingers down her throat. By the time she was thirty-five all her teeth had to come out, 'cause the acid from vomiting eroded them. I'm no dummy, Doctor Khaos. Don't treat me like one."

"I know you're no dummy. So talk to me like an adult. How severe was your asthma as a child?"

"I almost didn't make it to be a child. We were premies. Adam came out okay. I came out not breathing. They had to resuscitate me. I'm sorry they did. I'd be better off dead." A single tear trickled out of the corner of her right eye.

CHAPTER 12

BlackFlower cursed under her breath as she came to a halt in bumper-to-bumper traffic on Richmond Terrace in Staten Island. This area, always heavily trafficked, had multiplied by ten. Delivery trucks had always doubled parked on this two way, four-lane avenue. Now they seemed to be stuck there. Even with her hand out the window, no one had the courtesy to let her slip out of the right lane. Driver's inched up to deliberately close the gap, to which she retorted with the middle finger salute.

What the fuck?

She'd do the same thing. Courtesy was never high up on her list. Okay, she'd have to wait. She tapped on the steering wheel, looked out the window, and grimaced at the run down apartments above the shops.

Ugh, who'd want to live there?

The fumes alone could kill. Funny how her thoughts always went to killing. *Guess because that's one thing I'm good at.*

There had to be an accident. It was after six and she'd miss her appointment for an oil change if she didn't get there soon. Fuck. The one night Philetano's was open late. This shop was the only one that had never screwed up. She'd only entrust her Camaro to them. Philetano's was next to an empty lot and the cars in the right lane usually headed for the service entrance. Now, she couldn't tell where they were going.

She checked her new short Afro in the rear view mirror and smiled ear to ear. Way better than those long cornbraids. This hairstyle filled out her oval face. She felt attractive. She hadn't been this happy in a long time. Her cuts were scabbing and she didn't feel the need to inflict new ones. She had followed Ram's plans to the T. Only one thing bothered her. Tormented her was more like it. She couldn't dwell on it or she'd start cutting herself again.

But she did dwell. She would have to make some cuts tonight to take her mind off it.

She had lost her white band. Where, she didn't know for sure. The symbol of their coven's solidarity. She'd hoped it was pulled off her wrist when she removed the surgical gown and protective sleeves. She had buried her bag in a garbage dump in Queens. That's one thing she had learned researching the perfect murder on the internet. Spread out the evidence as far as you could to make it hard or the cops, or something like that.

There was no way to get a replacement of the band. Ram had made only four. They had been warned not to lose them. Ram had made the consequences clear. Flower would have to figure out how to steal one from Cloud or Moon. No. Then they'd get the clout from Steven Larcon's kill. And it was her kill. Her best to date. She'd rather take the punishment from Ram, than give up the status from that kill.

Cloud had her chance today. And succeeded. Things were looking up and Flower would be very rich, very soon.

Finally, she'd be able to show her dad she succeeded. Maybe, just maybe, he'd now think of her as a daughter, rather than as the druggie who'd made him lose his hundred fifty k a year gig as a corporate lawyer for that pharmaceutical company in Westchester. At least, he didn't get disbarred.

So what the fuck is he still up my ass about?

She shook her head, pitying her parents' pathetic lives. Work, work, and more work. They probably didn't even fuck anymore.

The traffic crawled forward. After stop and go for a good twenty minutes, she saw the police truck, The Lenco Peacekeeper.

What the fuck? SWAT? No, wait a minute, not SWAT. This is New York, not Atlanta, you dimwit. It's ESU. That's right, the emergency service unit.

She couldn't make out what was on the back of their protective gear.

As she edged farther the bold letters *DEA* accosted her gaze. *Holy fucking shit!* And it was right in front of Philetano's car repair shop.

The front gate was down with yellow crime scene tape across

it. Police cars, detectives, all gathered in small groups. She watched a DEA agent hand a business owner a sheet of paper and then climb a ladder to remove a surveillance apparatus from the store across the street from the car repair shop's entrance.

What? The DEA has been watching them? For how long? Damn! Good thing I got what I needed last week. Oh, no! Fuck! Fuck! Fuck!

I'll be on that tape! And so will Ram, Cloud, and Moon.

❧❧❧

In the back office of an Italian eatery near the Todt Hill section of Staten Island, Paulo Philetano sat on the luxury leather couch with his three sons in dark blue, wing chairs opposite him. He hadn't lost his heavy Sicilian accent, despite forty years of living in the United States. Most likely, it was because he'd tried so hard to keep it. He loosened his tie and unbuttoned his Armani suit jacket, but nothing would make him comfortable. "The three of you. You're not doing ya jobs." He rustled an arthritic hand through his full head of white hair. Cracking his knuckles caused him to wince in pain and he blew out a deep breath as he shook his head in disappointment. He rubbed his trimmed salt-and-pepper beard with his fingers, then covered his mouth, feeling as if he were holding back lava readying to burst out in a volcano, right from the center of his heart. He had barely touched his lunch, which had gotten cold. He usually couldn't resist the fresh fragrant savory herbs and the melted cheeses in the homemade lasagna his son prepared. But today, his stomach churned and if he put anything into it, that would mean a trip to the emergency room.

His second eldest son leaned in toward him and put a reassuring hand on his thigh. "Papa, we'll find her. She hasn't answered her phone."

Paulo swiped his son's hand off his leg absentmindedly as he gazed out the sheer curtained window. He leaned in to meet his son. "Carlo, you like this restauranté? Yes?"

"Yes, Papa. You know I do. It's my life."

"Well, if you don't find her soon, you lose it, along with that strip club of yours. Am I making myself clear?" Paulo shot Carlo a stern disciplinary glare, just as he did when his sons were young. They understood that sharp dark-eyed stare. The one that told them they'd better conform or all hell would break loose, usually on their behinds.

Carlo's face reddened.

His father smiled, knowing that he could still intimidate his son, even though the boy was thirty-eight.

Carlo sat up, swallowed hard, and hesitated a moment before he answered. "Yes, Papa, perfectly clear."

Paulo turned his glare on his other two sons. "And you, my hotshot lawyer. How about you finance your practice on your own? And you pay the sixteen-G-a month rent? How would you like that?" His son's eyes opened wide and his mouth nearly followed suit. "Stephano, don't you dare say a word. And you, my high-priced doctor. You're the only one with an excuse. You work all day. But, as God is my witness, Paulie, you better help your fratelli as much as you can. Don't just sit there, frowning at me. I can tell what you're thinking. I know exactly what you're thinking. I'm not losing it. I'm seventy, but still head of this family and no one, but no one, especially you three sorry-ass excuses for sons, will take all that I worked for away."

Paulie changed his seat to the couch to sit next to his father. "Papa, we're not trying to take anything away from you."

"Paulie, close your mouth." He waved a crooked index finger at his eldest. "I will not allow you to dig my grave."

Paulie wrapped a supportive arm around his father's back. "Come on, Papa, calm down. Your blood pressure is high enough. Of course, I'll help Carlo and Stephano. You know we do whatever you ask. Always. Ever since we were little, we've done what you say. We've never once disputed you. Even without the threats. Now, come on. Be reasonable, Papa."

Paulo's soft spot for his eldest showed through. His tone of voice immediately mellowed. "Yes, Paulie. I know. I'm sorry. I'm sorry for my tirade. I'm just so frustrated. All of you out. Find AriellaRose Larcon and bring her to me. With her father's murder on our property and being a close friend with Leonardo, the police will be investigating her too well. I don't need any more collateral damage falling upon us. Leonardo tells her everything. If she knows the weapons supplier, both of them are in danger. She's such a sweet young woman. I just can't imagine what she's going through now. At least we know Leonardo wasn't involved in the murder. He'd been in jail three days before it had happened." He swallowed hard. "Some consolation. So go.

I need to talk with her. Your youngest fratello's life depends on it. And I want to give your mother some positive news. The holidays will soon be upon us."

ৎৡৎ

Sam walked down the corridor to AriellaRose's hospital room. She paused when she heard pained screaming.

"You're hurting me! Stop!"

"AriellaRose, look at me, not your arm. You have to keep your arm still. Come on. I'm here with you." Frank's voice was in his usual comforting tone.

Sam wondered if this man ever showed emotion. They had spent a good part of two days together and he had never raised his voice above a soothing decibel. For such a behemoth, he appeared way too calm.

How does he do that?

Maybe she could learn something from Frank. The only time she was calm had been in her classroom. She had loved being with the little kids. But she had to move on after ten years. She had craved the excitement of law enforcement. She got high on the action, and she needed that high. She needed it to survive her boring, celibate life.

"Okay, we'll be done in a second. There ya go. Done," the blood tech said.

Sam waited outside the door, leaning against the wall and crossing her right foot over her left. Her mind went to the conversation with Mrs. Larcon.

Is Frank interested in me? She laughed silently. It would be about time she had a relationship. But she wasn't sure she was interested in him. *Is he as calm in the bedroom as he appears to be at work?* She couldn't deal with that. She liked her men a little more aggressive in bed. *What am I thinking? He's a colleague. Off limits.*

However, it had been way too long. The last schmuck did a number on her. She was so naive she wouldn't believe her friends when they told her they had seen him with another woman, too close and too friendly. And she was the one who was psychic. Yeah, right. Dara didn't warn her about him. Or maybe she did and Sam didn't listen to the signals. She had no one to blame but herself. For six months, he cheated. And what for? She knew she was awesome in bed. Her ego was exactly where it should be.

No worries, Sam. The right one will come along when the time is right.

The one she felt sad for was AriellaRose. That woman needed someone who'd understand her. Her mother certainly didn't. Sam had had children like AriellaRose in her classroom, withdrawn, saddened by the way their parents treated them. She had become saddened, too. She had become their surrogate mommy. But AriellaRose was an adult and Sam decided she'd do her best to befriend her. On second thought, that wasn't in her job description. *You're a detective now.* She wasn't supposed to become attached to anyone in an investigation.

The tech exited the room and nodded to Sam. Sam waited a second and entered the room. The back of Frank's stark white lab coat stopped her like a brick wall. Her briefcase slipped off her shoulder and fell onto the floor in one smooth motion. "Hi, AriellaRose. How are you feeling?"

Her smiley tone wasn't appreciated. AriellaRose rolled her eyes. Sam took it down a notch. "I just came by to see how you're doing." She turned her attention to Frank. "Hello, Doctor Khaos."

"Hello, Detective."

She nodded in approval at uniform of the moment. "You're looking rather *doctorly,* Doctor Khaos."

He loosened his tie. "Thank you, Detective."

"Oh my God! Why don't you two get outta here and go fuck?"

"Excuse me?" Sam couldn't believe her need was that obvious. *Will he see that, too?*

"Oh, man, AriellaRose," Frank added.

"Knock it off. You both look like you need it, bad."

"Don't worry about us, AriellaRose," Sam said. "I need to talk to you."

"Well, I'm talked out. This motor-mouth shrink won't leave me alone."

Frank nodded to Sam. She got the message. "Okay. I'll let you rest."

"Good. Both of you, out."

"All right. See you later. Keep yourself covered. It's chilly in here." Frank pulled up the sheets for her. He nodded to Sam and they both left the room.

As they walked down the hall, Sam couldn't wait to talk to him. "Motor-mouth shrink? That's an odd term of endearment."

He ignored the small talk. "Why'd you really come over?"

"Loo wants me to go over the file Withers gave to you. I have another one with me."

"Okay. Cool."

❧❧❧

AriellaRose got out of bed and retrieved her smartphone from her canvas tote bag that lay against the wall under the ledge of the window. She heaved. The slightest exertion exacerbated her breathing.

Come on, Arie, you've dealt with this a lot. You can do this.

She guided her life with self-talk. Some positive. Mostly negative.

She sat back down on the bed and bent over. She felt dizzy sending the text. *In hospital. Some shit doc says I have pneumonia. Doubt it. Getting out of here. Meet me at the main entrance on First in 30.* She pitched the phone back in the bag.

She checked the length of the cord attaching the IV to the monitor. Good. Long enough to reach the closet. She had to get out. Her body ached. She needed her meds. Not the ones they were giving her. Good thing, though, she didn't have any stashed with her.

Damn that shrink. He actually had the nerve to want to go through her bag. And damn her for letting him. No. That had been smart. She had shown him she had nothing to hide. But now she needed her Blue. She'd pop at least two when she got home.

She pulled her sweatshirt and sweat pants from the closet. She looked at the IV inserted into her left arm, studying the tape securing it. She prepared herself for the pain as she had nothing in her system now to prevent it. Lifting the end, she pulled it up and around. The tugging on her arm made her cringe. She grimaced and stifled an "Ow!" as she pulled. The plastic stint came out of her arm. Relief. She grabbed tissues from the box on the table and held it over the incision. The bleeding would stop in a few minutes. She'd had IV's before, a few times a year, when she had been admitted for asthma. But this was the first time she'd tried to escape.

She got dressed as fast as she could with her labored breathing. That was actually slow. She had to take a break between pulling on each pant leg. She couldn't bend down to tie her shoelaces. She was too out of breath. She just slipped her feet in. She was sick but she couldn't stay now. The need for her stuff took precedence.

Come on, AriellaRose. You can do this. You once had an attack so bad, but you drove yourself home in a blizzard to get extra prednisone.

Bundled up with the hoodie covering her head, she left the room and nonchalantly held onto the wall railing as she walked to the elevator. Thank God she didn't have to pass the nurses' station.

♥♥♥

Sam scanned the office. Nothing great. A bland doctor's office in a hospital. Sterile. White walls. His diplomas hung on a wall opposite his colonial, dark wood desk. No pictures on the wall. Either he wasn't a showy kind of guy, or he didn't feel that this place was his milieu.

She deduced that it was both. If she was going to help him find his wife's killers, she'd have to know him and, so far, this hunk hadn't let out a clue to his emotionality. Everything she needed to know about him was hidden behind his even temper and soothing, deep voice. She had to make a connection with him, even on a primal level.

"Is this your private office?"

"Yeah. I insisted they get me something where I could write out my reports in private. Hate doing them at the nurse's station. Way too busy for me."

She removed a huge file from her bag and put it on his desk, looking for the slightest reaction. Nothing.

Frank didn't pay attention at first. He didn't seem to be in a hurry. She couldn't believe that it didn't affect him anymore. That surprised her and worried her at the same time. He had probably been through Jen's folders more than a million times and didn't expect anything different from these new ones. Discouraged and pained would describe how he probably felt. It had been over two years. It was considered a cold case now. She agreed with the lieutenant on reopening it. Never give up on a colleague's case, no matter how long. There was no statute of limitations on a murder case, so she'd do what she had to, even wake up the dead.

She imagined what Frank thought about his department's cool attitude.

How can he still be vested in his job?

He must be one strong and dedicated man. She decided she did like him. More like, she appreciated and respected him. She couldn't imagine herself staying with the job after such a painful loss.

He removed his lab coat and hung it on a coat rack in the corner. He didn't stop there and pulled off his tie as Sam organized the paper work on his desk.

"Come on. Sit. This will take a while."

"I have to get out of this first. Feel suffocated."

He unbuckled the belt on his dress slacks and pulled out his shirt. He unbuttoned it as Sam pretended not to watch. She just glanced up out of the corner of her eye. He removed it slowly. The nerve of him to tease her. She felt that was exactly what he was doing. A strip act, just for her. Then he slid his arms out of it.

Oh. My. God! She couldn't help but stare. She didn't know what to look at first—his perfectly defined torso with more like an eight pack rather than six, or his colorful tats that traveled from both wrists up over his shoulders.

Hot. This man was beyond hot. Her pelvis twitched.

Before anything witty could expel from her mouth, without a knock, the door opened. A security guard yelled in. "Doc, the Larcon girl left the building. She just went out the front door."

Shirtless, he ran out of the office. In mid-November. Sam followed him, shocked, as all the women in the lobby stopped dead to stare at him. He didn't seem to care. Okay, there were perks having an office right near the main entrance. He looked out the revolving door and spotted AriellaRose waiting by the curb.

He bolted through the door and grabbed her arm from behind.

She turned around and blinked. "Sorry I interrupted you two."

Passersby stopped and stared at the Hercules. A woman fell down the last step on the Express Bus in front of the hospital. No one went to help her. They just stood still. Sam just blended amongst them.

"Where do you think you're going?" he asked AriellaRose.

Um, a change in his tone. Sam studied him.

"Home."

"No. You are not. Let's go."

He held onto her arm, paying no attention to the people who Sam thought were judging him. Pretty aggressive for a doctor.

Though gasping for air, AriellaRose struggled to pull her arm away, unsuccessfully. "Let go of me!"

"You either walk with me, or I carry you. Now. Your choice."

"You carry me? Yeah, right."

He moved closer and bent his arms to pick her up, glaring down at her. "I could twirl you like a baton. Don't ever test me."

Oh. My. God. Alpha male be born. Take me now. Waves of sensual energy hit her from head to toes. Sam became beyond ready for him. This was not supposed to happen. *Thanks, Dara, for waking up my soul.*

CHAPTER 13

Back in his office, Sam sat opposite Frank as she opened the newest file. She couldn't help but stare at him, now back in his Khaos Rules T and skinny jeans.

He glanced up and caught the stare. "Okay, what?"

She gyrated involuntarily in her seat. "Oh, nothing."

"Say it. Now you're holding your tongue?"

"Nothing. Uh, the flash drives are in the pockets, here."

His intense glare seemed to peer right through her. "That's not what you wanted to say. Spill it."

"Um, you could have stayed shirtless. I wouldn't have minded."

His wickedly sexy smile told her he'd play. "Yeah, okay. And I'd like to see you without that clingy top and bra."

She gasped. *Yup. He certainly would play.*

"But right now, these files—" The phone ringing interrupted them. He closed his eyes and sighed.

Yeah. He didn't want an interruption, either.

He lifted the handset on the phone on his desk on the second ring. "Doctor Khaos…You're kidding?…How does she have the strength?…She won't let you? What do you mean, she won't let you?…Tell her I'm coming right up." He disconnected. "Let's go. Little Miss AriellaRose is being difficult."

☙❧

Frank and Sam raced down the third floor hallway to AriellaRose's room. Staff moved out their way, stood still, and watched. His heavy sneakers thumped in the hall as AriellaRose's raspy screams bellowed.

"Stay away from me! No! I won't let you!"

They heard the clang of the five thousand dollar IV pole with the attached monitor hit something hard.

Frank bolted into the room and saw the mess she'd created. The bed table had been pushed toward the closet. The IV pole and monitor lay diagonally against the windowsill. The sheets had been kicked off the bed and lay wrinkled on the floor. AriellaRose bent forward on the bed, hyperventilated with a panicked, frenzied look in her eyes, shaking her head. Perspiration dripped down from her hairline. Sweat saturated her hospital gown.

He studied her for a moment before he spoke then approached the bed with deep concern. "What is going on in here?"

The nurse picked up the pole, moved the table next to the bed, and started to pick up the sheets.

He put a palm up to her. "Stop, Vera. Tell me what's going on."

The sixty-something, gray-haired nurse was winded. "She won't let us put the IV back in, Doctor Khaos. I'm sorry, we tried."

He paused, put his hands over his mouth before he spoke, and swallowed. "Why, AriellaRose?"

Her breathing had become so labored she couldn't get the words out. "It—hurts."

"We have to get the meds in you. Your breathing is getting worse. You have to let us help you. Which arm?"

"The left," the blood tech responded.

"Put out your left arm now."

AriellaRose looked up at Frank with tears running down her cheeks.

Okay, some emotion. I'll accept that. "I said, now."

She hid her face in her hands, crying. "I need my stuff and you won't give it to me. My stomach hurts."

He sat on her bed. "Okay, calm down. It's okay."

Her legs bounced on the bed as if she was chopping salad. "I don't want the IV. I need to get my stuff."

"You need the IV. Listen to yourself. I heard you wheezing down the hall."

"Don't I have the right to say 'no'?"

"If you were a responsible patient."

"I am responsible."

"I beg to differ. A responsible patient sees her doctor regularly for her meds. A responsible patient doesn't pull out her IV and try to leave without medical clearance. You are anything, but responsible."

"I don't care."

"Okay, then." He retrieved his smartphone from his pocket and put in a pretend call to Nick. "Detective Valatutti, Doctor Khaos here. I need you to get a judge to sign a PINS petition for AriellaRose, assigning her to me." He addressed her in an official tone. "Do you know what a PINS is?"

"No," she replied, whimpering.

"A person in need of supervision. So I'll be able to treat you without your consent. And a judge will want a full report on your drug use. Including your sources."

Sam stared at him. His gaze was steeled on AriellaRose, his face expressionless, lips closed tight. He definitely wanted to intimidate. He glanced at Sam. His assertiveness shook her, too.

"No. I'm not a P…that person. Look at me. I can't keep my legs still, I'm crying. I can't stop the angry voices in my head. I'm freezing. I'm shaking. I'm hot. My stomach is killing me. I feel like I'm going to take a dump in bed. Or throw up."

"That's your withdrawal." Frank continued his call. "Yes, Detective. I need it ASAP."

She gazed up at him with pitiful eyes. "Okay. Okay. I'll let you."

He ended the make-believe call, feeling sympathetic for just a moment. "Vera, get me a glucose reading. Have you eaten?" he asked AriellaRose.

"No."

The nurse returned with the glucose monitor. "Unroll your fist. Vera needs a finger."

AriellaRose hesitated as she put out her hand. Vera gave her a poke on her index finger.

"Ow!"

"Oh, that doesn't hurt."

Vera showed him the number—375.

"Show her."

"So, 375, so what?"

"AriellaRose, diabetes could give you most of the symptoms you're popping those pills for. Did you know that?" She shook her head. He nodded. "Besides, the high amounts of prednisone you've been taking, in addition to what I'm giving you in the IV, could give someone who doesn't have diabetes, diabetes. I'm not an alarmist, but this number is high. I want her on a diabetic diet." Vera nodded and started to leave the room. "And coverage before she eats. Ten units."

"What's that?"

"Insulin. Now let them put the IV in and then you're eating. And while they're doing that, you are going to listen to me."

She extended her arm. "Then give me Suboxone like they did at some of my rehab places."

"No. It's one addiction replacing another. We'll deal with it and you will be comfortable." He needed to engage her in conversation to distract her. "Who were you waiting for at the curb?"

She swallowed her tears. "No one. Just a cab."

"I don't buy it. There were cabs right in front of the door. Why didn't you just hop in one of those?"

She ignored him, just looked away.

"Okay. Be mysterious. That's okay. You can have visitors, you know? Why don't you call up some of your friends?"

"I don't have any friends—any close friends, who'd give a damn, anyway. I'll be fine alone. I've been alone most of my life."

"There ya go. All done," said the blood tech. He gathered his vials, nodded to Frank and left the room.

About fifteen minutes later, AriellaRose sat with a tray on her table. She lifted the metal cover. "Ugh, what's this white stuff?"

Frank was nonchalant in his response. "Boiled fish. With string beans and spinach."

"It looks like wet Styrofoam with green shit."

"Nah. Not Styrofoam. It is wet. More like undrained cod and thinned out butter, and over-steamed veggies."

AriellaRose laughed, coughed, and laughed again.

Good. That's probably the first time she's laughed in years.

"How much of that other stuff do you take?"

She shrugged her shoulders. "The Blue, about two pills every four hours or so. It's not that much."

"Sixty milligrams of oxycodone every four hours. That's quite a bit. And the Vicodin?"

"In between the Blue."

"What does all that do for you?"

"You're a shrink and you don't know about drugs?"

He smiled. "Yes I do, but everyone has their own reasons."

"It calms me down. I can ignore my whiney mother and my judgmental dad. At least he gave me whatever I wanted. I think I'm the only one in my family who's really upset he was murdered. But that stuff lets me hold in my feelings."

"I don't think that's such a good thing. People need to emote to show grief. It's a lot more healthy. How long have you been using?"

"Since I was fifteen."

"What happened when you were fifteen?"

She looked up at him with a solemn expression. Another shut down. No response. She took a forkful of the fish and pushed the tray away. He pushed it back.

"You need to eat with the insulin. You'll see. You will calm down. You won't be so flighty. I know it's hard for you. Hard to trust. Give me a chance to help you."

She began eating slowly. Frank could see she was holding back tears.

"I don't want to talk about it," she said.

☙❧

Nick ended his call as he knocked on the door to Withers's office in the Homicide Investigative Unit at the precinct.

"Come in."

Nick entered and saw piles of folders on his desk.

"Where's the rookie?"

"At the hospital with Frank. She went to see how AriellaRose was doing. Dysfunctional isn't the word to describe that family. Anything come in yet?"

"A little, yeah. The decedent's name moved his case to the top. Call them to come back here. I don't want to have to go through this shit twice. My luck, the case landed in this precinct. So I'll be stuck here more."

"They're on the way. You okay?"

"Yeah. Fine."

"You don't look fine. You don't exactly look your healthiest self."

"Knock it off. My breathing's just a little tight. Doc gave me an inhaler. Said I have emphysema from smoking. Like I didn't know that already. I'll live."

"Okay. Give me a prelim."

Sam and Frank knocked at the door and entered.

Withers gestured at them. "Sit down, both of you and just listen."

They followed the directive without saying a word.

"There were twenty-three cuts made on Larcon's torso, from two paring knives. One was held right-handed, the other left. The cuts ran four inches long, each one, as if the perp measured them. Meticulous cuts, so the knives were brand new. No blood was found on him, other than his. B positive. From the lines of the cuts, they found one company who sells blades with these serrations. Just in case you don't know, rookie, each knife has distinguishing characteristics like bullets. Just like we could recognize the type of gun from the lands and grooves in bullets and their casings, we can find the manufacturer of a knife. Anderson and Son's. They're an online company. A warrant has already been sent to them for their sales over the last six months. No telling how long his murder had been in the works. If we have to go back farther, we will. And a machete chopped him. They're still working on his dick." He looked up at Sam.

She didn't react to his terminology. "What do they have to do on his dick? We know it's his."

"It was feasted upon by the turkey vultures so the lines of demarcation were destroyed. Want to see if he got fucked before he was offed. You were right, rookie, the white band is from the crime scene. Only blood on it was the vic's. No prints. Smudges caused by latex gloves. Good call on that, Wright. I'm impressed."

"Thanks, Withers. That means a lot."

"Don't get too cozy. We don't have a weapon, motive, or any prints yet. This person knew the drill. They did an assessment. Agree with you, rookie. More than one person. Too much for one person to do alone and not be seen. More people cut time in half or thirds. Again, rookie. I'm impressed. I can't believe I said that."

"Twice. You said that twice." Sam kept an impassive expression while Nick covered his mouth and Frank rolled his lips together.

Withers had become annoyed with himself. "From your conversations with the family, no one wanted him permanently dead. Am I right with that?"

"If there's any other kind of dead, I'd sure like to know about it," Sam chided, remaining straight-faced.

Nick and Frank let out boisterous laughs.

"Stop being a fucking smartass, Wright! Nick, what did ya get from the son?"

"He did admit to me his dad gave him a lot of money. He confirmed his meets with his dad at the club. The arguments between his dad and Jaye Manning were over the salary Adam was being paid. His dad felt his kid was worth twice the amount. Manning refused to give in because Adam sometimes wasn't reliable. When I asked him what he meant, he told me that sometimes he'd sleep late after partying and miss a morning shoot. The kid doesn't get it. Doesn't understand what responsibility is. There's a trust for him and AriellaRose. But he can't have control of it till he's twenty-seven. Valerie just got hers and she's spending it. Right now, control went to Mrs. Larcon. He's pissed about that because Mommy isn't as tolerant as Daddy and won't be so free with the dough. He was more *pissed* at Dad about his murder, than grief struck. Oh, get this one. After Sam told me about the conversation with Mrs. Larcon and his lovely girl, Calinda, I asked him how serious he was with her. He shut down. Didn't want to talk about it. Said she's last month's flavor. I asked him why they broke up. He said it was painful and told me to 'drop it.'"

"Yeah, well you ain't going to drop it. Does this Calinda have a last name?"

"I'll call Mrs. Larcon and ask her. I'll find everything about her down to her conception," Sam volunteered.

"Okay. Good. That's good. That's what I wanted to hear. What I have for you, rookie, is a list of everyone Mrs. Larcon gave us. Family, friends, biz associates. Over a hundred people, including what Valerie and Adam shared. And funny thing is. There's no Calinda on this list. What did you get from the daughter?"

Frank sighed. "AriellaRose is one sick puppy. Has pneumonia. Started drugs when she was fifteen. Shut down when I wanted to talk about it. Told me she's probably the only one truly upset about her father's murder."

"Don't believe her."

Frank darted a look at Sam. Withers and Nick followed.

"What are you thinking, Sam?" Frank asked.

"What I'm thinking and what I know are two different things. We need to find her street contacts for drugs."

"What are you thinking, rookie? Don't make me pull it out of you."

"I'm thinking you might have the killer in custody already."

Withers jumped in. "Nope. The second kill of Meghan Mason occurred when the family was here. And she was in the hospital. We're calling it serial."

"I don't care. AriellaRose may have partners. I want a list of all of her friends and a search warrant for her apartment and phone."

"You don't have probable cause," Withers snapped at her with a coughing fit. "You can't stick to the hypothesis you created at the crime scene. How many times do I have to tell you?"

"Listen. This girl doesn't hesitate to say what she means." She glanced at Frank. "I'm saying it."

Withers shot her a glare of disapproval. "Saying what?"

"AriellaRose wanted us out of her room and she told us to get out of there and go fuck. Literally, she wanted us to fuck, not fuck off. Hearing now that she started using drugs at fifteen. What would girls at fifteen want to block out or dull the pain of? Rape. I bet she was raped by a person in a position of trust. An associate of her father's. Or her father. And she was waiting at the curb for someone. Right, Frank?"

His lips curved in agreement.

Sam glared at Withers. "Why wouldn't she want her friends to visit? I'll find the proof. And I'm as sure of that as I'm sure I'll find Frank's wife's killers."

CHAPTER 14

Paulo and Carlo had lunch at their private booth, the one closest to the kitchen in the back of Carlo's restaurant. A *Reserved* sign hung from the ceiling like a chandelier, hovering over them. Paulo gazed out the dark red-and-blue stained glass windows overlooking their booth. He didn't expect to see anything. The thick glass shielded the afternoon sun. The darkness reflected Paulo's mood. He closed his eyes, wanting to escape from the despair that tormented him.

Glancing toward the other patrons enjoying their lunch on the other side of the restaurant, he sighed. He and his sons needed privacy now.

Paulo looked for a distraction so he focused on the pristine white tablecloths. Candlelight from small lanterns on each table projected a romantic feeling. Booths lined one wall and squared tables for four were spaced equidistant around the rest of the space. Stained glass windows ran the length of the wall above the booths, depicting scenes from Venice waterways. Patrons focused on the imported Italian glass throughout their dinner. Paulo nodded in approval that his son took care to provoke elegance in his restaurant.

"I'm finito, Carlo." He stared at the half-eaten antipasti salad and meatball heroes in front of him. "Leave the rest for your frattelli. Stephano will be here in a little while."

"Papa, you need to prepare yourself. Leonardo isn't getting off with just a few years sentence. Judge Malone denied bail. That's a very bad sign."

"Don't tell me how to prepare myself." Paulo glared at his son. "I'll prepare myself when I see it in black and white. Then I'll do the necessary."

"Papa, you did do the necessary. You hired the best criminal defense attorney on Staten Island and I'm glad you listened when we told you and mother not to have Stephano represent him."

"You were right. We would have been too emotionally involved. As it is, the heartbreak is killing us." Paulo swallowed, choking back tears. "After the first time, I thought I'd be used to it. Obviously not. I haven't slept since the night of his arrest. I haven't been able to focus on anything. That's why I need you to oversee the businesses for a while. That damned fool!" He took the napkin off his lap and threw it onto his plate. "And your mother, your poor mother. A mother could never get used to her son being in prison. She's isolating herself from all of her friends. She doesn't want to vent to people who wouldn't care. All she does is bake. I don't need all those extra calories, but how can I tell her 'no'? She's crying herself to sleep every night again. I don't know what to do to console her. He was a bambino the last time."

"Papa. Leonardo was eighteen. Hardly a baby."

"I can't believe he didn't learn from that. He got three years for dealing cocaine. He promised. He swore he would never do anything like that again. The therapy, the rehab, all meant nothing. I threw out thousands on his rehab. And what does he do nine years later…"

Stephano hurried toward the table, clenching a thick folder. His father's heart skipped a beat as he saw the sullen expression Stephano carried on his face. Paulo closed his eyes and took a deep breath. He had to prepare himself now. He knew it was serious, but he didn't know how serious.

"Stephano, eat, then we'll talk."

"No, Papa. We need to talk now. This isn't going away. The grand jury indicted him. That was to be expected. There were weapons this time. And not just hand guns."

"Oh my God!" Paulo grabbed his stomach, feeling as if it would plummet out of his body. His heart thumped in his chest and beads of perspiration formed on his forehead as he inhaled and exhaled rapidly to calm himself, just like his doctor-son had taught him. He wiped his hands over his face, swallowed, and composed himself. "They had to wait six days?"

"Yes, Papa, the grand jury has six days to indict or release. At least his attorney didn't waive his right to that to give the prosecution more time."

"All right. Tell us everything." Paulo waved his finger at Stephano. "Everything. No sugar coat."

Stephano opened the file.

Paulo understood the look of apprehension on his son's face.

"Leonardo sold firearms to three DEA agents on three separate occasions." Stephano paused and looked into his father's eyes. "Not at the repair shop."

"Then where?" Carlo asked.

Stephano flipped through the documents. "Once in a gym parking lot, once in his apartment, and the third time at the mall. Papa, it was in broad daylight where there were children."

Papa closed his eyes, pretending to escape for a moment. "Oh my God. Go on."

"Two .45 caliber Remington firearms, at sixteen hundred bucks each. A .38 caliber Smith and Wesson firearm and a Taurus nine millimeter for fifteen hundred, total. Two Israeli-made Uzi nine-millimeter firearms for twenty-six hundred bucks each. With the Remingtons, he sold five hundred oxycodone and four glassines of cocaine to that agent."

"How could he be so stupid?"

"Papa, they watched him for six months. The agents interacted with him and made smaller buys. They developed his trust. There's much more, Papa."

Carlo placed a reassuring hand on his father's knee. "Are you okay, Papa?"

Paulo took hold of his son's hand and patted it before grabbing on tightly. He held on as he spoke. "Go head Stephano, what else?"

"The top charge is two A-felony counts for possession with intent to sell over an ounce of a narcotic drug. Then arraignment charges. Fifteen B-felony counts." He paused. "That's time seven, Papa, That's one hundred five B-felony counts. The arrest charges were B-felony for criminal possession of drugs with intent. And seven D-felony counts for criminal sale of a firearm with intent, unauthorized person with an assault rifle, and criminal possession of weapons other than handguns." He scanned the court printed charts. "Everything is detailed here, Papa."

Paulo rubbed his forehead and quivered in his seat. "Who was involved in this?"

"Leonardo and two of his mechanics. They were cousins. One has bail at five hundred thousand, one at one hundred fifty thousand. Neither one made it so they're being held at the same detention center as Leonardo. They have legal aid representation."

"I don't care about them."

"Papa, you should. Says here, it was their first arrest. Don't know what they can say about Leonardo to get a better deal. They are more of a threat than any of his friends."

"Who was in charge of this so-called investigation?"

"The DEA Tactical Diversion Squad, the NYPD Intelligence Unit, the NYPD."

"Names, damn it! I want names!"

"All right, Papa. This is what the article says. I'll read it to you verbatim. 'On November 7, 2014 after a six-month investigation, Leonardo Philetano, considered a major illicit drug trafficker in the Richmond Terrace area of Staten Island, was arrested, pulling up the gates to his car repair shop at seven a.m., by DEA Special Agent, Marcus Willtower of the New York Tactical Diversion Squad and NYPD Detective-Investigator Dunnar Vike, along with NYPD officers. The arrest occurred without hindrance. As Philetano was taken into custody, the DEA carried out search warrants for the repair shop, Philetano's home, and the apartments of his two employees, Corrie and Jeff Markson of Sheepshead Bay, Brooklyn. The search warrants resulted in confiscation of four thousand Oxycodone pills, two thousand Suboxone, thirteen glassines of cocaine, and one thousand Adderall, along with assorted drug paraphernalia. Over a six-month investigation, DEA agents filmed cars going in for repairs. Most left sooner than one hour later. The DEA put the investigation together, after calculating the short time of repairs to the number of employees. They used surveillance, physical with undercover agents and electronic, and undisclosed sources. The DEA estimates that over fourteen thousand dollars of illicit drugs per week hit the streets of Staten Island out of Philetano's operation. Philetano is the son of Paulo Philetano who has been on the FBI's most-watched list. But no charges were ever brought against him and no illegalities were ever investigated. High-ranking Mob bosses in his extended family fostered the interest in him. Philetano's brothers are Doctor Paulie Philetano, a highly respected OB/GYN and fertility specialist in Todt Hill, and Stephano Philetano, a high-priced criminal defense attorney. Philetano's brother is not representing him. The DEA would not disclose any information about suppliers. Their investigation is ongoing. These charges are not definitive. The suspects are considered innocent until proven guilty.'" Stephano closed the file. "That's it."

"Okay. We need to speak to all of his friends. They have to know who his supplier is. Especially AriellaRose."

"Papa, there could be many suppliers."

"Speaking of that, tell Leonardo's attorney not to fight for bail. He was using heavily. At least on the inside he'll be detoxed. And I'm sure there are still people out there who don't want him to talk. Those arms dealers scare the shit out of me. I'd rather have an incarcerated son than a dead one."

"Agreed, Papa."

✧✦✧

Sam was in a quandary. She sat on her bed with one leg in her slacks, the other in mid-air, her mind imbedded in the case.

Was it gut instinct or my psychic ability that pinpointed AriellaRose?

She'd always known she was intuitive, as all detectives were. Truly psychic? She'd have to get a handle on it. She was great at putting things together. She knew deep down in her gut, she'd make a great detective. She was great at manifesting things. She attributed her practice of Dianic Wicca to that. She meditated and that was where she'd met Dara. She had just come to her. Sam didn't even know their relationship. Spirit Guide was what she was told at a Reiki Healing circle she went to once a week. So Spirit Guide it was. As good a label as any.

She had no idea how she just blurted things out. Sometimes Dara did that to her. Sam needed to control that. Now she'd have to prove an hypothesis that she hadn't consciously created. *Psychic? Am I truly becoming psychic?*

Dara was the one, rather the entity, who gave her answers. Like when Nick wanted to warn her not to drop the Rose. Dara had told her that in a meditation. Sam was glad she was quick to think of a reason that Frank would buy. She had cut that one close. The guys thought that her showing up in the same outfit as the Larcon women was coincidental. Not so.

Thanks, Dara.

She ruminated on the fact that none of them had asked her about it. Not the men, nor Mrs. Larcon, or Valerie. You'd think those women would want to keep their fashions in their echelon.

She could make a bet that the Larcon women wouldn't wear another Meghan Mason outfit since a lowly cop had worn it. She laughed at their pompousness.

Okay, Sam, you have to shake this off. Focus. Pay attention.

After glancing at the clock on her nightstand, realizing she had to get a move on, she dressed hastily. She needed her morning fix. A cup of joe.

A few minutes later, sipping her hot coffee at the table in the nook in her kitchen, she looked at the cover page on the New York paper. Leonardo Philetano had been indicted on drugs and weapons charges. Three days after the Larcon murder on one of their properties. Exactly six days after his arrest. Um, AriellaRose and Leonardo were the same age. But she lived in Manhattan and he on Staten Island. Still, the drug world was small. He sold the merchandise she consumed. Sam scanned the article. Weapons, high-powered weapons to boot.

Not good, Leonardo. That's ten years minimum in federal lockup.

They hadn't gotten ballistic reports back from Meghan Mason's murder. On first look, there wasn't an exit wound, so they needed to wait for the full autopsy. Sam wondered if there would be a weapon's match from her case to Leonard's. She hated the waiting. But it went with the territory.

The possible drug connection, kept coming back into her mind.

What if, they were friends? What if AriellaRose knew about his weapons connections? In addition to his suppliers, that's what the DEA would be interested in. What if AriellaRose had partners who had gotten the weapon to kill Meghan Mason from one of Leonardo's suppliers? And what are you basing this all on, Sam? Nothing. Absolutely nothing.

It was too damn coincidental. But that sure as hell would be a great conversation she should have with AriellaRose.

Okay, she decided, she needed info about AriellaRose's rehab and people she'd met while there. That would be hard. Doctor-patient privilege. These places didn't share their files. Not even in murder cases. Then she got the one idea that could help her make the connection between Leonardo and AriellaRose. She'd contact NYPD detective Dunnar Vike. If she played nice, maybe he'd share the surveillance video.

She was ready to kick herself. Why AriellaRose? This meek,

poor-self-esteemed, sickly woman didn't look like she had the strength to pull this off. She had dulled herself so much with drugs, she wouldn't be able to think of something so evil. Why Sam picked her, she had no clue. Now she was stuck having to prove a hypothesis that she didn't even think was possible.

Okay, Sam, you're back to square one. Besides, anything derived through psychic intuition will not hold up in court.

She grabbed the paper and stuck it into her tote. Maybe AriellaRose would want something to read.

☧

Sam entered AriellaRose's room to find Frank standing next to her bed, wearing his *doctorly* uniform again. "Good morning, Doctor Khaos. AriellaRose, how are you feeling?"

She sneered at Sam. "Like shit. And he isn't helping."

Sam starred at him, wide eyed. "Shirt and tie again?"

"Yeah. The admin wasn't thrilled with my shirtless escapade in the streets yesterday. But if this little girl hadn't tried to pull a stunt—"

"I won't again. That cop you put at the door keeps popping his head in to tell me he's still there. Don't worry. I promise."

"Doctor Khaos, if you don't mind, I'd like to have some time to speak with AriellaRose."

"Sure. I have other patients to see, then I'm going to the precinct."

"I'll meet you there."

He nodded and left the room.

Sam turned back to AriellaRose. "Seriously, how are you feeling?"

"My breathing is better. I want to get out of here. But he won't let me."

"It takes time. Do you have any friends you want to call? You must be bored."

"I'm watching more TV than I usually do. But no thanks. My friends are busy working."

So she does have friends. Different story now. Glad I asked. "Has Adam or Valerie visited?"

"Adam came this morning."

"Can I bring you anything? Toiletries? Magazines?"

"Why are you being so nice?"

"That's the way I am. And I feel bad about your father."

AriellaRose sucked her teeth before answering. "It's not your job to feel bad. It's your job to find who killed him."

"Yes. It is. But cops are feeling human beings, too."

"Well, don't waste your time feeling bad for me."

"Okay. I won't. So help me find out who killed your father."

"And how do you expect me to do that?"

"By talking about it."

"What do you want to know?"

"Your mom said your father pays all of your expenses and rent."

"Yeah. So what? My shrink—not Tattooman, my other one—says I haven't found myself yet."

"Do you work?"

"Like at a job?" AriellaRose looked away in disgust.

"Yes. Exactly."

"I had a job after college, in a fashion house, but my asthma had gotten so bad, probably from the dust from cutting fabric—" She smirked. "I missed so much work, she had to let me go. She said I didn't carry through on my responsibilities, even when I was there. The bitch."

"What fashion house?"

"Meghan Mason's."

Sam stood stunned but tried not to let it show. "Did you know she was shot and killed the other day?"

AriellaRose blinked and then looked Sam straight in the eyes. "No. Can't be. You're fucking shitting me. When?"

Wow. She really didn't know. "The day you were admitted."

"Holy crap. Damn! I don't watch the news."

"It's been all over social media."

"My phone died. I told Adam this morning to bring me a charger."

"What can you tell me, other than that she's a bitch? Something from when you used to work for her. You know? Something only an insider would know."

"I thought you were working on my dad's murder."

"We're connecting them now, since they're both fashion-industry related. So what about it?"

"Her husband used to beat her up a lot."

"Yes. I know that. Your mom told me about that. We were together when the news came in."

"Yeah. But even after the divorce, the fuck didn't stay away. He came to the warehouse and wrecked it a few times. Set the place on fire once. A real sicko. He got arrested and did jail time. I don't know who he knows, but he got out too quick."

"Anything else?"

"Like what?"

"Your mother said Meghan and your father met a couple of times a month to talk about business."

"Yeah, right. They'd talk about everything but."

"Such as?"

AriellaRose swallowed and let out a shallow breath. "Damn. My mother lives on another planet. More like another galaxy. My dad would talk to Meghan about everything. Even every affair he had. That's why he had the apartment I lived in. I was the excuse for him to have his hideaway."

"Could you give me a list of the women he saw?"

"I was never introduced to any of them."

"Any name come to mind?"

"Only one, Calinda. I heard him speak her name on a call. He was begging her not to stop seeing him."

"Calinda? That's Adam's girlfriend's name. Adam told Detective Valatutti they broke up."

"That's the one. My dad was banging her, hard and often. I never met her. Or even heard her. For some reason, whenever Adam had planned to introduce us, she couldn't make it. She's always working. At what, I don't know."

Um, Adam and Calinda just hit the suspect list.

"Thank you, AriellaRose. That helped a lot."

AriellaRose put her head back on the pillow, looking fatigued.

"I'll let you rest now." Sam pulled the newspaper from her tote. "I took the liberty of bringing you the paper." She put it on the table.

"Thanks. Yeah, I need to rest. I can't talk too much without my breathing acting up."

"Feel better." Sam patted her arm, left the room, and stood by the NYPD guard, pretending to talk to him while she watched AriellaRose lift the paper and stare at the headline. Then she heard what she wanted.

"Oh, no! Leonardo!"

Sam smiled. *This case is coming together from all directions.*

CHAPTER 15

Frank and Nick were focused on the forensic reports that had come in on Meghan Mason as Sam entered the conference room, pulling a dolly piled high with boxes. They looked up, Nick for only a short moment. Frank caught her gaze as it landed on his torso. From the glimmer in her eyes, he convinced himself she had gotten used to seeing him in his T and jeans. He hoped so, because that was what she was getting. He smiled at her in her light blue denim jacket, jersey top that peeked through, and slacks that accentuated every curve.

Those boxes stirred some anxiety in him. He changed his position in the chair. "What's up?"

"Later." She moved the dolly into a corner. "Lots. Mr. Larcon was having an affair with Calinda. 'Banging her hard and often' to give the exact quote."

Frank squirmed in the seat. He didn't need her to be so explicit or dramatic in her delivery. That's what *he* felt like doing. To her.

"And AriellaRose knows Leonardo Philetano."

Nick scratched his chin. "Okay. No wonder Adam and she broke up. We'll bring in the unhappy couple, but what's the connection between AriellaRose and Leonardo?"

"Don't know for sure yet. She was getting fatigued, but I left her today's newspaper. She picked it up when I was outside the room. Her reaction was note-worthy. I think I'll give Carlo a call to see if he knows about their relationship."

Frank shrugged. "Why don't you just ask her?"

"She wasn't forthcoming with any info that pertained to her. Like her mother. And the Mrs. didn't know her husband. Told me he never had an affair. AriellaRose told me he had a slew, in her apartment." Sam paused for a long moment. "Hold on! Didn't that just give us probable cause for a search warrant for AriellaRose's apartment?"

Frank sat back and flipped the pen he held onto the file. "Yeah. It did."

"And if we find illicit drugs or anything else during the search, that's exigent circumstances."

Nick raised a hand. "Hold on, Sam. We don't want evidence bounced. How large is the apartment? How often was he there? Did he have a separate bedroom? If he did, we can't include AriellaRose's room in the search. Even though she might not hide her stash in there. You have to go back and ask her a lot more details."

"Okay. I got that. I'll do it tomorrow. Put in a call to whatever judge will listen. Get someone lined up. What's in here?"

Nick ran his finger over the report. "A .380 hollow point in a Ruger with suppressor terminated Mason."

"That wasn't on the list of weapons the DEA confiscated from Philetano. Crap. That's not our case, so I doubt if we'll be granted an interview with Leonardo. No point in that yet. So what now?"

"It's your lead. So what now?" Nick mimicked her and sat back in the chair, folded his arms across his chest as his lips curled into a smile.

"I have been working on this, Nick. We just haven't met long enough to go through it all. I divided the hundred or so people we have into four teams. Loo gave me staff to work this." Nick looked surprised. She rolled her eyes. "Hey, we can't do all this legwork. It's been two murders and we don't know if any more are in the pipeline. Wallace-Dutton, Smerling-Cohen, Theodure-Ritlin, and Allenry-Holmes. They're taping the interviews so we'll have tons to piece together. They started late last night. On my drive here, I recorded the report of my conversation with AriellaRose." She slipped her recording device out of her bra and handed it to Nick.

Frank admired her unique hiding place, staring at her cleavage. Nick hadn't flinched.

Has he seen this act before?

"Here knock yourself out. While we're waiting for the warrant, I'd like to go through Frank's files, if that's okay with you." She looked at Frank and then the dolly.

Frank shrugged. "Sure thing."

"I'll call for the warrant."

"Wait, Nick. Before you go, what are your thoughts about AriellaRose, Frank?"

"Did some kinesiology testing on her. No muscle strength in her arms or legs. Doesn't take care of herself at all. No way in hell could she drag a body, even if she had help."

"Show me what you did."

"Seriously?"

She nodded. "Yes. I want to get a complete picture of her."

"And I thought you wanted to get your hands on me."

She scowled at him.

Nope. Not the response he wanted. "Okay. Take off your jacket." He moved his chair away from the table, leaned forward with his arms bent at the elbow. He extended his fisted arm to Sam and grinned. "Did this with her, having her dangle her feet off the bed. Grab my fist and try to pull it down."

She removed her jacket and put it on the back of the chair. "Is this a dare?"

Her clingy top worked for him. The woman knew how to turn a man on. It was instant with him. He held his breath for a second, surprised at his own reaction. Yeah. He definitely meant his grin to be a dare. "Hey, you asked me. Show me what you got."

Sam wrapped her hand around his fist, as much as she could wrap around. Their size difference was huge. She pulled, hard. Maybe he moved a few centimeters.

"That's it? Okay, but AriellaRose couldn't budge me."

"I would have expected that." She grabbed on with both hands and tugged. He moved a few more centimeters. "You're a brick wall."

He laughed. "Stand up." He pushed back in the chair and stood up. He couldn't wait to stand. His hard on made him uncomfortable to say the least.

Oh man, this woman had an effect on him. *Maybe Jen did send her down from heaven.* He stood with his feet apart and put his palms out facing her.

"Push against my palms."

"You did this with her?"

"No. Didn't let her out of bed. Tested her leg strength, though. Having her push my hand up and down at her ankles. Couldn't do that either. Her breathing tightened so I didn't push it. But *you* are a different story. Push."

Sam stood opposite him placed her palms against his. "Okay, big shot."

"Wow. You *are* tiny."

"I am not!" Sam pushed into him as hard as she could, using her full body. She twisted to the side to add momentum, as if he were a heavy bag.

He didn't move an inch. "Detective, I need to get you into the gym."

"I work out like crazy in the gym. I do kick boxing. I was the best in my class in the academy. So bring it on, Khaos. I can compete with you, big time, in the gym. Name the time."

Nick laughed through this entire display. He put his hands over his mouth to conceal the permanent grin. It didn't go unnoticed by either of them.

"What, Nick?" Frank dared him to respond.

He knew what his colleague thought. He had discussed Samantha with him. Nick told him to go for it. So did Withers. So did Loo. He didn't have to approach the Loo. Rojas had told him to get it on already the first night when she had entered the conference room. He did make it clear to all three of them that he wouldn't have a real relationship again, with any woman, until Jen's killers were behind bars, or preferably, dead. The heartache of another woman being in jeopardy over him would destroy him. He had to stay well and in one piece for his son.

He certainly knew he wasn't great at hiding his feelings. After meeting Sam, he must have shouted his readiness to the world. Rojas saw the change in him immediately. He transformed from sullen and dead from the neck down, to alive and ready. The only one who didn't know he was attracted to her was Sam. Relationship, no. Sex, yes. *Will Sam do the casual thing?*

"Nothing." Nick retorted.

Yeah, right, nothing. Frank turned his attention to Sam. She probably wondered where his mind went for a minute. "Compete with me? Oh, yeah?"

"Yeah."

"Okay, put your hands on my chest and show me what ya got."

Nick got up, pushed the chair in, and shook his head before he left the room.

She hesitated. Why, Frank couldn't figure out. Then she placed both hands on his pecs. She pushed.

He felt the heat. The vibration. His body steamed up within a few seconds. Heat radiated from his crown to his toes. He laid his palms on her upper back. More heat. She had to have felt it.

"You have great energy," Sam said, looking up at him. "Do you do Reiki?"

She looked at him as if the positive connection he had waited for had been made. He'd take what he could get. "Yeah. Level two."

"Me, too. Never had time to go for master."

"It's nice. Feel it?"

"I'm getting drenched. Yes, I feel it. It's very nice," Sam panted.

He wrapped his arms around her, caressing her frame. "Oh, man. I haven't had a Reiki treatment in a long time. So you are going to give me one."

Sam smiled. She answered without skipping a beat. "You got it."

"Good, we'll do nude Reiki." His grasp around her held tight. She didn't try to release it.

"Nude Reiki? Um, never heard of that," Sam teased.

Oh yeah. She was ready. "Just made it up."

∽∂∽

AriellaRose plugged in her phone and sat on the edge of the bed as she made her call. She trembled, clicking the keys. She had been calming down since Tattooman started her on insulin, but that fell by the way side after reading the article. Hopefully, they didn't know she was friends with Leonardo. That would be all she would need.

"Hey, Arie, where the fuck are you?" Emma demanded.

"You're never going to believe this. I'm in the hospital."

"Still? I drove by like you said, but you weren't there. How the fuck did that happen?"

"When we went to the precinct to talk to them about my dad, there was a shrink there. He saw me wheezing and having a hard time breathing. He was old. Had to be old. He had that old-fashioned doctor bag. I couldn't believe it. He checked me and said I had pneumonia and he admitted me. They said I do. He's giving me a hard way to go."

"How long are you gonna be there?"

"Haven't a clue. And to top it off he put a cop outside my door."

"Why the hell did he do that?"

"I sort of tried to escape, but he caught me."

"Arie, that's not good."

"Tell me about it. I'm dying here. I need you to bring me my stuff."

"Uh, I don't have much left."

"Don't shit me, Emma."

"I'm not. You probably haven't heard. Leonardo got busted. DEA."

"Yeah. They've been watching him six months. Read it in the paper that shit detective brought me."

"Yeah. That's not good. You gotta get out of there."

"What aren't you telling me, girl?"

"I was driving by yesterday to get an oil change and saw a DEA guy climb up on a ladder to remove a surveillance tape. Shit, Arie, you, me, Meredith, and Rachel will all be on that tape. A lot."

✑✑✑

Sam had sorted piles of forensic reports onto the conference table, thinking about their placement carefully. She then tossed the empty cartons into the corner of the room. Frank re-entered the room, carrying bottled water and lunch containers. He stared at ten stacks of varied heights of folders spread across the six-foot table. "Tell me. Where the hell did all this come from?"

"I'm a visual learner. I printed out everything on the flash drive. What did you bring?"

"Water, obvious, and chef's salad. I'm gluten-free."

"Oh. Me, too. Thanks!"

He had to shuffle folders around to find room for the containers. "You slept here last night?" He was being half snide, half teasing.

Sam matched his tone. "Stop moving them. I have them in order. And no, I came in very early. Half is what Withers gave me."

Frank pulled over his chair. "Okay, cool. Didn't need everything. We'll look at it all and decide what we think will be useful. We focus on that."

Sam didn't want to upset him, but she needed to make a point. "Um, how has that worked for you so far? In two years." He slumped back in the chair. A despondent frown replaced the smile. She sighed. "And I have to review all of it to decide what to focus on. I didn't go through anything yet. Each stack has something different. Okay, I numbered them. One and One A. Jen is the single number. New cases, number and letter. One lists the gangs and their precincts. The tallest stack. You guys interviewed over fifteen hundred gang members, validated ones."

He perked up in the seat. "You know what 'validated' means?" he asked, taking a forkful of salad.

"Yes, I do. Confirmed by the police to be a gang member, not a wannabe, or fringe member, in case you want to test me."

He smiled. "How do you know about gangs?"

"Taught in Brooklyn for ten years before joining the department. Had a lot of children whose parents were in gangs. Almost every day, they'd bring in fights that started in the projects and ended up in the classroom for us to clean up. Then I spent four years in juvie. A lot of gang action there."

He nodded, lips compressed.

"You're easy to impress. And also about a thousand crew members and their sets. About five hundred of them go to your gym. Not so many from Brooklyn, though."

"We eliminated them."

"All of them?"

"My gym members. The five hundred with their families and closest gang ties."

"Why?"

"All right. My guys appreciate the opportunity. Love working out in the gym. Learning respect for themselves and others. There are over three hundred gangs in the city, about ten to fifteen in Brooklyn. That's where the case ran cold. Those guys don't make the trek into Harlem. Don't have any beef with me getting involved in their turf. In Manhattan, Queens, Bronx, when I went out with Withers and the Gang Intelligence Unit, they spoke to us. Chased every lead. With me present, they'd talk. With only Withers and the cops, it was wasted. Did get them to come in and take polys. All came up clean. Forensics led to the Bronx. Text message led to the Bronx. Each gang uses their own lingo for weapons, kills, general communication. There are thousands of gang expressions. Went through them all with GIU. "

"The techie stuff is so easy, though, to mislead."

"Not with our lab guys. New York City has the best forensics labs in the country. Our IT can get into everything. Every bullet was put through IBIS for identification and possible match to a gun. It has better odds than AFIS for matching fingerprints to an individual. Everything led to the Bronx."

"What about Staten Island?"

"Same as Brooklyn. Narrow search."

"What do you have?"

"Bullets, their casings. Reports showing their lands and grooves. Some residue did hit Jen. About five feet away. It's a thirty-eight caliber from a Smith and Wesson revolver. No weapon. That's what we've got. Period. Six bullets from the same gun. Shot erratically. Only one bullet hit her, the fatal shot. Went through a bag of groceries into her stomach. The fourth shot. But they didn't have the control to stop."

"You said 'a text led to the Bronx'? You got a text message, personally?"

"Yeah. On my NYPD-issued phone. Not my personal one. Never give out mine. If a kid's in crisis, they can text me. Got one text saying, "Got the biscuit. I'm hungry."

"Excuse me?" She lifted the edge of the cover of her salad container and, not looking at what she was doing, she popped it open and the salad jumped onto her lap. "Oh crap!" She scooped it up with her fingers. "What does that mean?"

"A biscuit is a gun. Hungry, they want to shoot. If they know me, they know my diet, and I wouldn't eat that, so it was interpreted as a personal warning. The next day Jen was shot. No time to do anything. Told Jen not to go out of the house. She had completed two tours in Iraq. Proficient in handling weapons and she carried. I managed to get her a concealed permit, because of me, and her going into suspicious areas. But she couldn't miss work. She was an ER and trauma nurse, and the surgeon needed her for this one. She left the hospital at ten a.m. and went shopping to buy what she needed for my birthday dinner."

Sam sighed and reach out to grasp his left hand. He put his right on top of hers. Just for a moment. Then they released.

"Yeah, princess. She was killed on my birthday. It sucks. I know. She was shot as she was walking to her car. Open area. No cover. The shopping bags were up to her neck. From how she fell, she didn't even have time to take her own weapon out of her holster attached to her bra. My only blessing was that Frankie wasn't with her."

"I'm so sorry, Frank. What did they find?"

"They did find the origin of the text, located the last owner of the phone. No phone, no owner. He had been in Rikers for two days prior to Jen's murder. He said the cops took his phone at his arrest. His wife came to the precinct to get his belongings and they wouldn't give anything to her. That's the law. Then his phone disappeared. They thought she snuck in to the property room and stole it. Have no idea how she pulled that off. The wife then moved out of the city. FBI tracked them to North Carolina. Father and phone owner's wife, dead. Overdosed two weeks apart. It was found not suspicious, nor a cover up. No phone found in thorough searches of their property. Feds spent months on this one lead. That phone has probably floated down to Florida in the Atlantic, by now. What are the other folders?"

"The second group, Jen's crime scene photos and photos of the other gangs are here." She put her palm on the second pair. "A cover page noted that all the scenarios were put into a database. No match." She moved her attention to the third pile. "These two are interviews with Jen's friends and colleagues. The thinnest folders with the least documentation. Are you positive, and I mean a-hundred-percent positive, that this is gang related?" She paused for his response.

"Everyone feels it is. The thirty-eight is the cheapest bullet. What gangs could afford. No one would want Jen dead. If it was a professional hit, they wouldn't have missed five times. Gangbangers do not have gun training. They hold the gun up and shoot. That's why so many innocents get killed when gangs go after each other with guns. They don't know what they're doing."

"No one IDd the car?"

"No plate. Vehicle never found. Probably went straight to a chop shop out of state. Every chop shop in Brooklyn was investigated."

"Could it be anyone that you put away where your testimony got them a stiffer sentence?"

"Went through every arrest they called me in to profile and their families."

"Any prints on the bullets or casings?"

"No. What are these two folders?"

"These are you. The cases you were profiling at the time of the murder. And these go for a couple of years before. Any from Brooklyn?"

"A few."

"Tell me." Her gaze remained peeled on him, taking in his every word. She wanted to solve this case. He was a good guy and he deserved closure.

"Hospitalized two kids—well, not kids, nineteen and twenty three, separate cases for drug-induced psychosis. Both murder cases. One was high on crystal meth, one on another hallucinogen. The nineteen year old stabbed a homeless man to death and the twenty-three year old, a hooker. Their families were happy they got a hospital sentence rather than prison. The vics had no families that could protest. Usually when I get called in, the defense wants hospitalization and they really believe it's what's needed. If the prosecution has enough evidence for incarceration, and the defense knows that, they don't need me. The defense knows better than to try. I don't hospitalize lightly. That's why all my cases have been eliminated."

"Any Brooklyn gang members you threw out of the gym?"

"Now back to gangs?"

"I need to know every possibility. So?"

"Not thrown out. But if they come, they have to do the work. I push hard. Some quit. Always give them the option to come back when they're ready. So the door is never closed."

"Okay. I'm going to go through all of this. And I hope you don't mind if I call you at three a.m. if I have a question."

His eyes hurled daggers. "Don't you dare call me in the middle of the night. I hardly sleep as it is since Jen's murder."

"But I—"

"Okay, sorry. I know you want to help me. It's just that I've been living with disappointment for the past twenty-five months. Call me whenever. Even in the middle of the night."

CHAPTER 16

AriellaRose lay in her hospital bed, head turned toward the window. The chipped and rusted security bars interfered with her avenue view. However, the blaring ambulance sirens, pulling into the emergency room entrance, did make it through her window. It was constant. There was no way for her to block it out. The shrill noises made her tremble. She put her palms up to cover her ears. Not even closing her eyes would carry her to another place. She tried. She focused. Her mind wouldn't move to her fantasy life. She was stuck in the morbid present against her will.

She fingered her hair covering her ears. Yuck! She needed a shampoo and a trim. Rachel better be available as soon as she got out. This woman had skills. The new short doo she did for herself was cool. Even in the perfect shade of blonde. She loved Emma's new short Afro, too. It was shit that Rachel couldn't go to hair-styling school. No one could know she existed, any longer.

AriellaRose admitted to herself that she had felt calmer much of the day. Her involuntary leg gyrations lessened. She was able to lay still without the constant twisting and turning that had plagued her. At least she was able to get some sleep. It had been three days and her discharge was nowhere in sight. She had to get out. The cravings for her stuff hadn't decreased much. She only pretended it did when Doctor Tattooman asked her. She was good at pretending. And lying.

Emma said Meredith would be visiting today. She and Rachel were busy holding down the fort. Saturday was their busiest day. AriellaRose had kept their "business" hidden from her parents for three years already, ever since she was fired from Meghan Mason Fashions. Her parents thought she got along on what her dad gave her. That was a pittance compared to what she was making. The dough she had gotten from her parents had gone to Leonardo for her stuff. She'd take it, without a thank you or appreciation. That's what they expected. That's what she'd deliver.

She'd been living up to expectations her entire life. Her dot com business was flourishing because of it. She had created the fastest growing underground company for affordable clothing for kids in the hood. Yup, "Aries Fashions: For the Warrior Within" had reached the charts. Fastest growing. Wow. That's what the reviews had stated.

Who said I couldn't live up to expectations?

She gave a silent 'thank you' up to Aradia that she was able to save enough for her million-dollar brownstone in Park Slope. No one knew about it, except for her girls, her beholden, and she planned to keep it that way. Nor did they know about her Upper East side apartment. They had always met in the office they had rented for the business, but she gave that up when she moved into Park Slope. She loved to reflect on how far she had come. And by next Tuesday, her life would be complete. She had to get out of here.

She let out a deep breath, or as deep as she could get, grabbing her chest. It still hurt. Damn that shrink. Did he have to be right? She heard the heavy thud of his sneakers come into the room. She barely looked up at him. T-shirt and jeans again.

Fuck. Is he a downer. Just when I was thinking of good things.

"How are you doing?"

"When can I get out of here?"

He smiled. "What's the rush? Got a job to return to?"

She picked up on his sarcasm, looking up at him and trying to keep her face expressionless. "No. You work on weekends?"

"If I have to." He checked her with the stethoscope. "Still tight. You are not going anywhere yet. And from here, I would like you to consider going straight to rehab."

"What you'd like me to consider is shit. Not going. I can control it myself. When I want to."

"We'll talk more when you're not in denial."

"I'm not in denial. I know I use. But I can accomplish things."

He pulled over the club chair closer to the bed, sat, leaned back with his arms in his lap. "I'm all ears."

Damn him. I let out a hint and how in the hell am I going to get around it? He's a shrink and can probably see right through

me. Aradia, please make something happen now to distract him.
"I can accomplish things."

"You said that already. What kinds of things?"

"Well, I'm working on a fashion line that kids my age can afford, not like my parents."

"I would hardly consider you a kid, but tell me more about that."

"Okay, men and women in my age group who are just starting out and don't have that much money."

"Okay, cool. Have a name for the line yet?"

Yes. But you're never finding out. She paused. "No. It's still in the thinking stage. My friends and I want to do it."

Her friend entered the room and stopped at the doorway.

Thank you, Aradia!

"Come in, Merry. Doctor Tattooman is getting on my nerves."

Merry stared, apparently startled at the introduction.

He looked at AriellaRose with a smile. "Doctor Tattooman? Okay. But for future reference, it's Doctor Khaos. And you are?"

"Does it matter?" AriellaRose didn't hide her annoyance. *So this guy likes heavy breasted blondes. Of course, he does. And so did every other asshole in that Vegas strip club Merry had worked in until she did what she had to do and I rescued her.*

"Just being polite."

"Yeah, well, I've been in hospitals before, and doctors don't ask for an introduction of visitors," AriellaRose challenged.

"Okay, fair enough. So you've been in the middle of a murder investigation before?"

AriellaRose and Merry yelled out a "No!"

"I'm Meredith, Meredith Cummings. So, Doctor Khaos, when is my friend being released?" Meredith let the words slip off her tongue seductively as she unbuttoned the top button of her floral print cardigan to reveal some cleavage.

Tattooman must have gotten the message and so did AriellaRose. He laughed and shook his head. She seethed and flushed.

"Okay, Meredith. Just to set the record straight, I am trying to detox your friend. You want her to be healthy, right?"

Meredith gave him a meek nod.

"Good. Very good. So I sincerely hope you did not come over to give her some of her 'stuff' as she calls it."

"Oh my God, Doctor Khaos, no, definitely not. I've been clean over three years, and I'm constantly on her to do it, too.

She's my BFF," Meredith said, putting her hands up to her heart. "And it hurts me so to see her so depressed all the time, but I don't know what to do. I'm nagging her every day, aren't I, Arie?" She looked for a brief moment at her friend. "Yes, I am."

Enough with the overkill, Merry. He can see through the bullshit. AriellaRose winced. "Yes. She's on me all the time."

He put his lips together and stared at them, alternating glares between AriellaRose and Meredith. "Okay. So I am going to have the mean police officer out there step inside and monitor your visit. It's for AriellaRose's protection."

Merry stepped up to him and looked way up. "Doctor Khaos, we need some privacy."

"That so?"

"Yes."

"I can't help you with that. The police officer comes in or you leave."

"He can come in, certainly, but all he's going to hear is girl talk. You see? I just broke up with my boyfriend and I'm all upset, and Arie always knocks some sense into me."

Oh God, what a freaking jerk. Come on, Arie, think fast! "Good. I'm glad you finally listened to me. That guy's a jackass."

"Doctor Khaos. What kind of a doctor are you?"

"He's a shrink!"

"Perfect. Then maybe you can help me, Doctor, and listen to my story?"

"I don't do relationship counseling. Sorry."

"Yeah. He can't control his own…relationships. Speaking about that, how was she?"

"Excuse me?"

"That detective. Samantha."

He gave her a thin lip smirk.

"You didn't yet, did you? Well, what the fuck are you waiting for?" AriellaRose hadn't been this serious in her life. She surprised herself.

"On that note, good bye, ladies." He turned, walked out of the room, and signaled to the cop at the door to enter.

❧❧❧

Yeah, what the fuck am I waiting for?

That comment sang through Frank's brain the entire trip to the precinct. Withers had called a Sunday meeting for the three of them to review some forensic reports that had come in on both murders. Frank was appreciative that at least Loo had assigned Sam to review Jen's case.

He had postponed his training class at the gym until later that afternoon. Dale made the calls to the guys, but Frank was sure they'd be pissed. He rarely had to reschedule on a weekend, but the guys knew they had to be flexible. His contract with NYPD wasn't. No leeway whatsoever. He was on call twenty-four seven, three hundred sixty five days a year. And Jen had been totally cool with it. She knew private practice wasn't for him. Her parents would have wanted that, though. He craved the action, just like in Iraq. He needed to move, not sit behind a desk. As it was, profiling at the precinct at times was too stagnant for him. He did whatever he had to, to convince them to let him go to the crime scenes. Too bad he had missed these two.

He knocked on the door to Withers's office.

"Come in."

Withers sounded annoyed already. Frank opened the door and saw Sam, Nick, and Withers sitting around the conference table. "The gang's all here." Sam smiled as he took the seat next to her, as if they had left that seat open for him. They were ganging up on him, too. "What have we got?" he asked.

"Interviews from pedestrians. Thirty-five to be exact. One, I said one, saw the shooter." All of their eyes lit up. "Don't get too excited. The description doesn't fit the type."

Frank studied Withers. "Descriptions could be of disguises. Who gave it?"

"May not be so reliable. A woman running for the Express Bus. When she saw Meghan fall, she recognized her and didn't get on the bus. She looked right at three women behind her. She smelled what she said was 'something burning,' from the one in the middle. Could be gunpowder. Her description was fairly generic for the area. About five ten, short chin-length blonde hair, hazel eyes. Expensive black leather jacket, with the collar up, navy wide-legged pants, what do you call those things?"

"Palazzo," Sam chimed in.

Withers check the file. "Yeah, rookie, that's right. Also had a big black tote bag. The woman said her makeup was heavy. Don't know what in the hell that means. She mentioned it 'cause she guessed the woman was mid-twenties. And didn't know why someone so young would need that much makeup. The three of them just walked around Meghan and continued away."

"Okay. Stop right there. Mrs. Larcon has a makeup line for women who want to cover up facial scares, even freckles. What was this woman's name?"

"Susan Miller. Call her. 212-555-1979. But she's coming in to give the graphic artist a run."

Sam jotted it down on her pad. "After we get the drawing, I want to call in the thirty-five others. See if I can spark a memory. What else came in?"

"Interviews with her daughters. Sweet kids. Thirteen and fifteen. Dad has been in Italy at a gold and jewelry show for two weeks. He's on his way back. The girls opted to live with their grandparents and they already went to family court. Grandparents don't want Dad anywhere near the girls. Understandable. When we get the visual of the shooter, we'll put it out to the media. Ms. Miller so was so shocked that she couldn't describe the other two. Okay, rookie, now what?"

"Um, I like to hear what Frank has to say. He's the profiler."

He leaned back in his seat. "Thought you'd never ask. Otherwise, I'm wasting my time here." He paused for a moment. "Though it's out of profile for a serial killer, I tend to agree with you, Sam. Definitely women. Changing my mind on that one. Okay, three of them. When you speak with Ms. Miller, ask her if she noticed a white band on any of their wrists, which would link the two murders. These were deeply rooted in anger. The cuts, obviously. I wonder if the killer was a cutter, herself. Probably. Symbolic. She'd be cutting to create physical pain that covers her emotional pain. Getting even with Larcon for something. She'd have open wounds that could transfer DNA. Got to find the clean up evidence. Look for a bandage that could have come off her. Killers who have experience, and I use that term loosely, would hide evidence far away. Look on the East side. The River has always become a big dump. Actually, any body of water. All of them around the city. Between the scenes in the parking lot and park, they had to carry a lot away. Look for those big black garbage bags. Off the pier, too, from the strip club. Cutters usually take Oxycodone to mask their pain."

Sam jolted her head up.

"Yeah, back to Arie."

Withers looked in the file after Frank's last sentence.

Sam laughed. "Arie?"

"AriellaRose. Her friends call her that, but I wouldn't. Oh, and she nicknamed me, Doctor Tattooman."

Nick laughed. "Well if the shoe fits…"

Withers glared. "Cute. Back to profiling, Doc."

Frank swallowed. *Damn, Withers is all business today.* "The Mason murder also anger. The killer dressed up to the level of the neighborhood, so I doubt if they're from that socioeconomic group. Anger about that. One or more of them has a knowledge of forensics, clean up, weapons, bullets. Could get all that info online. Even how to commit the perfect murder. Interesting that they chose a hollow point. They knew that the bullet wouldn't leave the body and hurt any bystanders. That's substantial. Definitely not a gang killing. They wouldn't care. This was calculated and planned. Also, not their first hit. They were very casual about it. Both went smoothly for them. Doubt if the Mob would hire a female for an execution. Male pride thing. That white band is key. Get the IT guys on this. Tell them to do a search on gang attire. Some of the guys come into the gym with special bandanas that they had made, which go straight into their lockers. I'll ask some of the ones who's trust I've gained. They are very secretive about their sources, even about where they get their clothing. It's like a secret society. Wait a minute! That's it. A secret society. Three women who kill and one who controls them. That fourth woman is the key. They're doing the murders for her, carrying through on her agenda, or his. What is the worst hold someone could have on another?"

"Being witness to a murder." Sam's voice escalated in pitch.

"Right. These three have murdered before. Fourth person could be a guy. Technically, as far as a definition, they are a gang. Three or more members."

Sam looked confused. "Thought you said it wasn't a gang hit?"

"Yeah, I did. Referring to traditional inner-city gangs. Gangs don't plan so carefully, nor do they worry about clean up. But they may not know the specifics of gang psychology and want us to think it was gang initiated. Would have been a good detour, but they haven't pulled it off."

Sam looked up at him as if a light bulb went on.

"What?"

"I still have to go through the files, but what if, what if Jen's murder wasn't gang related, either? Even though all the evidence leads to it? What if the killer wants us to think it was a gang and did everything gang-like? It would make sense, since that's the demographic surrounding you."

Withers stretched and let out what looked to be a sigh of exasperation. "One case at a time, rookie."

Frank didn't appreciate Withers's dismissal. "Well, Withers, if you had been more thorough, maybe—"

"No maybe about it, Khaos. We were thorough. Now if this rookie and Loo want another go around, let them knock themselves out. But not on my time. As per Loo, I'm not to be involved unless it's absolutely necessary and you need me to explain things. He's demanding fresh eyes."

Sam sent Withers a disdainful glare. "Don't worry about it, Withers. I'm definitely the fresh eyes."

Frank chuckled at her snide retort while Withers's expression became distant. Frank was content that Sam was on his side. He had needed an advocate all along. *Yeah. Mommy sent her down from heaven for a few reasons.*

He continued, but his thoughts were on Jen. "Okay, previous murders. Obviously cold cases by now. I don't know if I agree with you—" He looked at Sam. "—about AriellaRose. So unmotivated. To do anything. Not in any physical condition to do anything strenuous. Pretends to let whatever her parents say roll off her, but she's a deeply wounded woman. It's those deep wounds that could cause something like this. Angers have to manifest. Her parents pushed her to the side and only hired Adam and Valerie. Angry enough to kill Daddy? When he's supporting her? She had to know all of her part of the trust now goes to her mother's discretion. Why would she want that? Could go either way in my mind, at this point."

"Haven't a clue yet, either," Sam answered, knowing his questions were rhetorical.

Frank shrugged. "Hey, I'm open to anything. When it comes up. When are Adam and Calinda coming in?"

Nick checked the calendar. "Later this afternoon. Around three."

Damn! He'd have to cancel his training class, again. *Hide your anger, Frank.* "Okay. Fine. I'll have Dale cover my class."

"Hold on," Withers said. "Here's something. A blue oxycodone was found on a leaf next to Larcon's body. Could have slipped out of the cutter's possession. Gives credence to what you said, Frank. They will investigate to find the manufacturer and then if there are any matches to any other bust confiscations."

Frank sat pensively with his fingers over his lips. The others waited. "She mentioned a clothing line to me. Need to find out if it exists."

CHAPTER 17

Frank leaned forward, resting his forearms on the desk. "Okay. I want to be a part of both interviews, so this is what's going down." Nick glared at him. "Forget where you are, pal?"

Frank wouldn't accept the offhanded remark. "What do you mean?"

"What's going down?"

Sam laughed. "Oh you don't know by now, Nick?"

Nick looked puzzled. "What?"

"When Khaos is in the house, he rules."

Nick laughed. "That's what he told you?"

"Very clearly."

"Nah. With his gang crew, yeah. But here?" Frank sent him a look that could kill. "Okay, here, when he's called in. How to you want to proceed?"

"Much better. Okay, seriously. Have to get to know this Calinda. Think she'd relate better to you, Sam, and I'd love a crack at Adam if you don't mind, Nick. He could deal with the both of us."

Sam bounced in her seat. "How about making Adam wait? He hates that, so he might let out some things in anger, and you could observe me and Calinda. I don't care how long it takes. Then, I'll watch you two and type in contradictory things to question."

Withers stood. "That works for me. Gotta run. Wife has a dinner planned with the in-laws. She's cooking, which means it's an antacid kind of night. Man, twenty years and she still hasn't learned." He shook his head and left the room, carrying the folders.

"Um, he's upset with the wifey," Sam said, sounding like she enjoyed that.

"Yeah. It's been the past couple of years. Ups and downs, the usual. Cops' relationships fail a lot, the tension."

Frank stared at Nick. "Bullshit. A relationship is what you make of it. Can't blame the career choice. There's tension in every one."

"So you and Jen never fought?" Nick asked.

"Playfully. I like to play. Never seriously. I believe in choosing your battles, and Jen never wanted anything so disagreeable to me, that I'd revolt. We'd play in the cage and I'd let her whip my ass at times. And she knew I was letting her win."

"What's a cage?"

Frank laughed at her. "Oh, man. Like a wrestling ring, but it's eight sided and metal. You know? You have to come to my gym. Have to make the time. I'll show you around and you'll get a sense of the guys there. Maybe think of a lead. Can't hurt, and I'll work you out hard." He hoped he conveyed a dare.

"Done. When?"

"How about tomorrow?"

"Perfect. And I'll whip your ass in the cage, for real," Sam teased.

Oh, man, would I like to get her in a full body submission hold under me. Frank's mind soared to places off the sex meter as Withers opened the door. With him stood Adam and Calinda.

They were less than pleased. She stood, rolling her eyes, in a tight low cut T-shirt with too much cleavage showing. Her breasts shouted augmentation. Tight sleeves hugged her arms to her wrists, and her skinny jeans were tighter than what he'd wear. Certainly not appropriate for a police interview. Her long mid-back-length hair had been straightened.

He noticed some frizz on the roots. Her skin tone and facial features indicated mixed ethnicity with more African American in her than Caucasian. Her oval dark-brown eyes were extenuated by false eyelashes. Frank knew Sam would have fun breaking her down.

Adam stood with his right leg crossed over his left as he leaned against the doorway. His smugness hadn't decreased after his round with Nick. *Okay, wait until he has a round with me.*

"Come on in, Calinda. You're meeting with Detective Wright in this room."

"Who—the—fuck—are—you?" she asked, enunciating each word as her gaze scalded him from head to toe.

Sam said she was a lovely girl as per Mrs. Larcon? That widow is blind.

"I'm Doctor Khaos. Have a seat," he responded, neither impressed nor enticed.

Calinda strolled over, sucking her teeth, then held her lips in a closed mouth smirk. She extended her butt, which lowered her breasts toward the table as she slid into the seat. Settling in, she clasped her hands on the table and batted her eyelashes. "And where will you be?"

Oh, man, old school. "In the next room."

Sam sat at the desk. Frank patted her shoulder, squeezed it, and the three men left the room.

༺❧༻

Sam studied Calinda. "Just so you know, everything in here is recorded. State your name, please."

"I know. My dad's a lawyer. Calinda Alexander." Calinda sat back with her arms outstretched but with hands still clasped on the desk. "He told me what to say and what not to say. And to be honest, I don't feel like talking to you at all."

"Why not?"

"You're too prissy for my tastes."

Sam put her lips together to hold in a grin. "Too prissy? How would you describe that?"

"Just look at you, girl. Too put together, girly girl. A pushover. You know? Not a dangerous chick. Not someone I'd want to hook up with."

"Yeah, I'm not the dangerous type." *Hook up with a woman? Not in this lifetime.*

"Then, girl, you don't know how to have any fun. Bet your life is work and go home. I can see through your conservative outfit. You probably haven't had a good fuck in, like, an eternity."

In the observation room, Frank couldn't hide his laughter. Good thing they couldn't hear him. He focused on the computer screen, watching the comedic conversation.

"Speaking of fucking. I've heard you've been doing that a lot." Sam let the words come out matter-of-factly.

"Yeah. I have been." Calinda's knowing grin accentuated her hardness. She sat up tall and pushed her boobs toward Sam.

"How long had you been seeing Mr. Larcon?"

"Adam and I met three years ago in rehab."

"Well, we're investigating the senior Mr. Larcon's murder. I meant him."

Calinda bolted up, leaned forward, and thrust out her fist. "Who the fuck told you that I was fucking him?"

Sam grabbed her forearm hard, retaliating with a firm glare. Calinda winced and sat down.

Frank wrote on the keyboard. "Take it slow, Sam. Too early to instigate."

Sam backed off a few inches. Frank adjusted the angle and observed Sam peering right into Calinda's eyes, not flinching from her outburst. "Good. Remain seated. Let's back up a bit. You met Adam in rehab. Can you tell me about that? The place. The services."

"Why?

"Well, we're trying to get a composite of what Mr. Larcon's life was like and he paid the bills."

Calinda sucked in her cheeks together and slumped back in the chair. She ogled Sam up and down. "I'll tell you what, girl. Go online and Google drug rehab on Long Island, and they'll tell you what their rehab and services are like."

Sam needed to level the playing field. A little unorthodox, but this bitch needed to be taught a lesson. She let her jacket slide down her arms revealing a very low cut beige silk camisole. *Now let him look. No, let her look. My natural boobs are bigger and firmer than her silicone ones.* She got up and hung her jacket on a coat rack, walking slowly so Calinda would get the drift. After Sam slithered back into her seat, sitting up straight in the chair to protrude the girls, she pretended to lose her place.

"First, It's Detective Wright, not girl. Okay, now Miss. Alexander, where were we?"

Calinda seemed thrown off by Sam's display, mesmerized by her breasts.

Now, if you were Frank looking at me like that, I'd jump into your lap, but you? Ugh. "Okay. Seriously. Did you and Adam break up? That's what he told Detective Valatutti."

"That piece of shit. He doesn't know when to keep his mouth closed. What brought that up?"

"Oh, Mrs. Larcon told us that Adam was seeing a lovely girl named Calinda and she was hoping that you'd become her daughter-in-law one day."

Calinda blinked. Her tone mellowed. "No damn way."

"Yes, Miss Alexander, I kid you not. She brought it up."

"Well, let me tell you something, gir—Detective, that woman doesn't know her ass from her elbow. The thought of her becoming my mother-in-law would be enough to send me into the looney bin. It's no wonder that Adam and Arie have so many problems."

"How so?"

"Man, that woman. Never a nice thing to say about either of them. She comes down on Arie hard. Always about her weight. And she can't help that. It's her meds. And Arie's really pretty cool when you get to know her. Doesn't have a mean bone in her body. I don't know how she does it. Yeah, I do. She meditates a lot, uses crap I don't understand nor care to."

"What kind of crap?"

"Candles, oils, the kinds I don't know."

"Essential oils?"

"Yeah, yeah, that's what she calls them. Some of them are strong, too. Don't get how she can breathe all those in with the asthma."

"I'd wonder about that, also. So tell me, how often do you see Arie?"

"Once in a while. Why?"

Um, Arie told me they'd never met. Confront or let go for now? "Have you been to her apartment?"

Her voice wavered. "Uh, no. We met for lunch a few times."

"Well, she is very sweet and we want to help her. She's in the hospital, you know?"

"Yeah. Adam told me. When is she getting out?"

"I don't know. Is there a reason you're asking?"

Calinda paused and looked away. "Not really." She began shifting in the chair and pressed her right hand on her left forearm. "Are we done soon? I'm not feeling well."

"Actually, we're not. Far from it. Can I get you something? How about a bottle of water?"

Calinda rolled her eyes. She pulled back her hair in her hands and lifted it off her neck. "It's warm in here."

"I can see you need something stronger. What do you take?"

"Nothing. I've been clean."

"Miss. Alexander, I don't mean to stress you out more." *Yeah, the heck I do.* "But we need to solve two murders. And I will be blunt, since you seem to appreciate that. And you have nothing but fond things to say about Arie. But she's the one who told me that you're having an affair with her dad, as well as with Adam."

"Having an affair? Is that what you older bitches call it? We were fucking, just that. He was a great fuck for an old man. Surprised me the first time. And he's into kink. So am I. Told me his old lady wouldn't let him do any of that to her. And he tried. He's been into that BDSM scene for years. Goes to all the clubs in Manhattan. Loves to do it and have it done to him. Whoever killed him must have come from one of those clubs."

"Why do you say that?

"I've been there, not with him. No sex in the clubs allowed, no exchange of body fluids, their first rule. But I'll tell ya, what goes on inside gets carried through on the outside."

"Know the name of a club he frequented?"

"Yeah. He went to Whiplash, on the lower west side."

"Know when it's open?"

"Yeah. Friday and Saturday nights. Midnight to six. Sunday, ten to five."

"Thank you. I'll have to pay the club a visit."

"You? Don't you dare step foot in there. You'll be eaten alive. But that other dude, the one who grabbed onto your shoulder? Now he, he looked like he could handle it."

"Okay, I'll have him go with me." *Oh my God! In a BDSM club with Frank? I just died and went to heaven.* "So how do you feel about Arie telling me you fucked her father?"

"Don't care. He's dead now. So I'll just go after her man. I believe in getting even."

"Who is Arie seeing?"

"Well, she isn't going to be for a while. He got busted."

"Arie's boyfriend got busted?"

"Yeah. By the DEA, Leonardo."

"Oh, so, Leonardo Philetano is Arie's boyfriend? How long have they been going together?"

"About three years. Arie loves his folks and they love her. She has dinner there every Sunday. Man, his mom can cook. And his brother owns the best Italian restaurant on the Island. Arie would bring back doggie bags that would last her a week. She could talk to them about everything. They never put her down, even with her using. And it's shit, he got busted."

"Why?"

"'Cause now I have to look for another mechanic. He was the best in Staten Island." She grabbed onto her left forearm again and winced. A tiny spot of blood oozed through her sleeve.

"What's going on, Miss Alexander? With your arm?"

"Oh, nothing. I burned my arm taking a tray of cookies out of the oven."

Sam remained stoic. "Well, if you did that, and I do that sometime, so I know that can hurt like hell, it would be on the side of your arm not the underside."

"It's a burn."

"Well, let me get you a fresh bandage." Sam spoke into the intercom. "Doctor Khaos, please bring me a bandage from the supply cabinet."

"I don't need a fresh bandage."

Frank entered carrying a first aid kit. "I beg to differ."

"Thank you, Doctor Khaos."

"No problem, Detective. Miss Alexander, roll up your sleeve, please."

"No, I can refuse."

"Well, you see? We police are here to serve and protect. So if someone is in the precinct is in need of medical attention and we fail to give it, we can get sued down the line. Roll it up, now."

She pulled her arm away from his near grasp. "I need to call my father. The attorney. That means all questioning stops."

"You're not under arrest," Sam reassured her.

"Then I'm free to go." Calinda got up from the table and bolted to the door.

Sam's ego needed the last word. "Just so you know, Miss Alexander, what you are doing is speaking volumes. We'll be in touch."

After Calinda slammed the door behind her. Sam and Frank stared at each other, both with widening smiles.

"Well, Miss Alexander is a cutter. She has to be one of Arie's crew," Frank said.

"One of them is lying. Arie said she never met Calinda. Up to going clubbing tonight, Doctor Tattooman?"

Frank grabbed her around the waist, pulled her in close to him, and peered straight down at her breasts. His wickedly sexy smile told her the answer. "Hell, yeah. What are you going to wear?"

Ooh, that tone demanded something sexy. "Oh, I'll go shopping—in my closet."

CHAPTER 18

Sam strode brusquely down the hall on the third floor of the hospital to AriellaRose's room. Her navy blazer was back on with white low-top sneakers to ground her. So many clues bombarded her at once. A lot more than when she worked in juvie. Coming straight from the precinct after a close interlude with Frank didn't help either. The thin layer of her camisole didn't shield much. Her skin tingled as much as if his hands were still on her waist.

She didn't have any time to process the new forensics, either. She would have loved to see the complete file, not just listen to what Withers chose to share. That man sure irked her, and that put it mildly. *Maybe he's being hard on me to push me to the limits so I can prove myself to him and the precinct. Maybe Loo gave him orders to apply pressure. Maybe I should talk to Loo.*

Whatever—she'd have to prove herself to herself, most of all. She had wanted to be a detective for four years. She deserved it. She'd earned it. Now she had to prove it.

She had to push all of that aside and use her training, not her heart. Yeah, sure. AriellaRose appeared to be weak. Okay, physically, Sam would give her that. Something underplayed that. The poor, little abused soul act had run cold. Sam needed to be hard now. No little girl pout. No Miss Nice Girl. No nurturing. She had two murders to solve and, just like Frank transformed to tough guy when the situation necessitated it, she'd have to do the same.

Okay, Sam, take a few deep breaths and do your job.

She entered the room just as AriellaRose disconnected from a phone call.

"Hi, AriellaRose."

AriellaRose rolled her eyes again, lips closed in a smirk, and then she turned her head away toward the window.

That went over well. Take it down a notch, Sam. Follow her body language. Dull. Yeah, like hell, I will. No more catering to Miss Larcon. "AriellaRose, we have some things to talk about."

With her back still turned to Sam, she responded in a whisper. "Like what?"

"Well, for one, you and I have a lot in common."

"Such as."

"I love essential oils and candles and so do you."

AriellaRose struggled to turn around. Her breathing still labored at the slightest exertion. She pulled on her hospital gown to free it up from underneath her. Landing on her left side, arm bent under her head, she let out a shallow breath. "Who told you that?"

"Calinda. We had a very long conversation."

AriellaRose blinked repeatedly. "Calinda? I told you I never met her. I never spoke to her. When Adam wanted to introduce us, she always had to work."

"She told me differently. That you did meet a few times."

AriellaRose struggled to sit up. "I don't know a Calinda."

"You don't know Calinda Alexander?"

"No! Just from what I told you. My dad's conversation and he said her name."

"So you don't know a Calinda, who's mixed ethnicity, has a boob job, mid-back-length hair—which I could tell are extensions—and who's a cutter?"

AriellaRose closed her lips together and her already pale complexion faded to corpse like.

Yup. Cutter did it. "Well?"

"Like I said, I don't know her."

"AriellaRose your words say you don't know her, but your reaction says you do."

"Fuck you, Detective. Okay, I know her. Adam wanted to introduce me so we had lunch a few times. She's cool. What else did she say?"

"Was she ever at your apartment?"

"No." AriellaRose looked straight into Sam's eyes with that response. "Why?"

"Then how does she know about your use of essential oils and candles?"

"It came up in conversation. What difference does that make?"

"Humor me here. I would think that with your asthma, those scents would be irritating to your lungs."

"Yeah, some are."

"Which?"

"Frankincense, Myrrh, Sage. The others I tolerate and I use fragrances, so they're mixed with non-scented cold pressed oils. Which ones do you use?"

Finally, some interaction. "I use lavender and sandalwood a lot. Also bottled mixtures—to manifest things, good luck, prosperity, protection."

AriellaRose curled her lips down. "Prosperity? And you're a cop? Good luck with that one. Why don't you use something to manifest love? Yeah, put a spell on Tattooman."

"I didn't think of that one. You do spells?"

"Some." AriellaRose swallowed after her remark, as if she had second thoughts about letting that comment slip out.

Sam feigned excitement and raised her pitch. "Me, too. I practice Dianic Wicca. Know what that is? White magick? After the Roman Goddess, Diana?"

AriellaRose looked like she was about to pass out. She blinked, as if to regain focus. Her gaze darted to her cell phone that lay on the sheets. Sweat trickled from her scalp, down her cheeks, in a very cool room. And this woman was far from menopause.

Um, hit on something here, Sam mused. "I use the oils on candles to perform rituals and spells. Mostly with Isis and Artemis. Oh, and Lord Ganesh. Who do you invoke?"

"Oh my God. What the hell does all this matter? You're getting on my nerves, Detective."

"I'm responsible for solving two murders. Who do you invoke?"

"Oh, so you think I did a spell to kill my dad and Meghan? That's freaky."

"I never said you were a suspect, AriellaRose." *But you sure as hell confirmed that you* are *one.* "Okay, we can move on. What do you know about the club Whiplash?"

"From spells to a sex club. You're sure organized, aren't you? But at least you stayed the same place in the alphabet. Okay. Okay. My dad liked it. He went a lot. So does Adam. Why?"

"What about you?"

AriellaRose shuddered. "Me never. Hate the pain part. Ugh."

"Well, I'm going there tonight with Tattoo—Doctor Khaos— to follow up a lead Calinda gave us."

AriellaRose paid attention as if relieved the focus was off her. "What lead?"

"Calinda said your dad's killer might have come from there."

"Hope so. That would mean you'd solve his murder quicker, right?"

"Possibly. Anything I should be aware of in preparation to go?"

"Like what?"

"Set up of the place. Rules. Things like that."

"So you've never been in a club like this?"

Sam shook her head. "No." She could lie, too. But unlike AriellaRose, she had been trained.

"Okay. You've got to be dressed for it. Can't wear street clothes. And you can't go in there smelling of cop. Which you do. And no sex. Save that for when you get Tattooman back to your place, or wherever."

"If you've never been there, how do you know?"

AriellaRose rolled her eyes. "Okay, you caught me. I've been there lots of times, but I just watch. I don't like them doing those things to me."

"Okay, good. Then I can be more specific. Who's the owner or the person we should ask to see?"

"Oh yeah. Dominic. Dominic what's his last name? Yeah Trevino. He's totally hands on."

"Hands on? Such as?"

"He teaches first timers how to do everything. Spankings, the bondage. He'll show Tattooman how to do all that to you. And from what you look like, I bet Dominick will take his time with the lessons. He's into long spankings. He'll go for an hour. He's in and out of the rooms to make sure no one gets carried away. Oh, and this is important. You need a fake name. No one uses their real ones. No phones or cameras allowed inside, either."

"Do you know your father's and Adam's aliases?'

"Yeah. I do. But I can't laugh. It hurts."

"Okay. I won't laugh."

"Dad's is Dudley. And Adam is Fido."

"Fido, like the dog?"

"Yeah. Adam is always a sub, but my dad does both. Uh, did both."

"Thanks for the heads up. One more thing."

"What?'

"Calinda says you've been seeing Leonardo for three years and you're close with his family."

"Yeah. Remind me to thank her for telling you my life."

"Well, is he your street pharmacist?"

"He isn't no more, now, is he?"

"What do you know about his suppliers?"

AriellaRose turned away. "I'm getting tired."

"I can see that, but we may need to protect you. How open was your relationship? Your mother didn't seem to know. She thinks you're still a virgin."

"People know. My mother is in denial. But he never did business in front of me, so I really don't know his clients. And every transfer was in private, so no one else saw anyone, either. He never did any parties."

"Thanks, AriellaRose. This has been helpful."

"Can't imagine how. It was all bullshit to me."

Sam nodded and left the room, knowing she had to initiate a warrant for AriellaRose's apartment. First, however, she envisioned herself over Frank's muscular lap with his large, warm hands toying with her naked bottom, patting her first to warm her up, then increasing in firmness as she spread her legs, so he could reward her with his fingers sliding over her clit, intermittently with the spanks.

Oh my God. Her thong just stuck to her crotch.

Sitting in her car in the hospital lot, she put in a call to Nick. She had about five hours before she had to meet Frank to go to the club.

"Hi, Sam."

"Nick, how's the warrant coming? I need to get into AriellaRose's apartment."

"What did you get?"

"She was pissed Calinda told me so much. I have to figure it all out. But she uses oils and candles for spells, and she brought up using a spell to kill her father and Mason."

"Excuse me? How is that possible? You can't believe in all that crap."

Sam sank in the seat. "Uh...I just wanted to see what she'd

use. Maybe we'll find a tool or something. She or Calinda is lying, big time, but she knows her. The cutter comment I made really got to her. Maybe she knows Calinda as someone else, but
she connected. Nick, make that warrant happen."

"Want the good news or bad news first?"

"What do you mean?"

"I got the warrant for the father only. To add AriellaRose to
the warrant, one, would take till tomorrow, and two, it won't fly
based on oils, candles, and spells."

"Okay, I'll take it. Where are you now?"

"Home with my wife. And I plan to stay—"

Sam interrupted him. "Meet me at her apartment. I'm in Manhattan. About twenty minutes from her."

❧❧❧

AriellaRose's apartment was on the upper east side off Second Avenue. Thirty-story residential buildings lined both sides
of the one way street. Her building was a huge, modern complex
with man-made gardens in front, leading to the main lobby. With
the chilly afternoon upon her, Sam decided to wait in the lobby.
After the doorman rang her in, she looked around at the mailboxes on the wall. She found the Larcon apartment but Steven's
name was on the apartment tag.

*Um, they didn't even acknowledge AriellaRose here. This
woman had nothing in her name. Nothing to view herself as an
individual.*

She felt a momentary sadness for AriellaRose. Scanning the
apartments, she came across a familiar name. She couldn't wait
to ask Nick about it. They could get a reliable tip. The breeze
came in through the doors when residents entered. Sam rubbed
her upper arms with her hands crossed over her chest. She felt
like she had waited a half hour when Nick appeared.

"Hi," he said. "Can't seem to get oils and candles out of my
head. That's all so bogus, you know?"

Okay, Guess I have to stay in the closest here. "Take a look at
this first." Sam led him over to the apartment roster. "Here's Larcon."

"So?"

"Look who's right next door."

"Who?"

"Nick! Pay attention." She pointed. "Is this the same Doctor Trenton that Withers wanted to call in instead of Frank?"

He read the tag. "Doctor John and Vicki Trenton. Yes. It is. I knew he lived in the neighborhood but didn't know exactly where."

"I want to call him. Maybe he knows them and could give us some insights."

"No, Sam. Can't step on Frank's toes. No way."

"Not to come in and profile. But to gives some facts that an otherwise civilian wouldn't know."

"He's not here, anyway. He's in Florida."

"I can make a call to Florida."

Nick eyes narrowed and he stared her down. "No. He's on sabbatical. Not supposed to do any police work. Let's go. The superintendent is expecting us outside the apartment." He put his hand on Sam's shoulder to edge her along.

"I'll ask Frank. We're going clubbing tonight."

They got into the elevator and Nick pressed twelve. "Clubbing? To where?"

"I don't want to tell you. You'll yell at me."

"If it's case related, I won't yell at you. Where the hell are you going?"

Sam turned her back to him. "Whiplash."

"Hey, I heard you. Turn the hell around! And why are you going there?"

"Calinda told me Dad and Adam went a lot. We might get a lead there. You heard us discuss it from the other room. Want to come, partner?"

Nick shook his head. "I know what I heard. No. And I don't think you should go there, either. But you're a big girl. Do what you want." The elevator door opened and they walked down the hall to meet the superintendent, who didn't say a word, but took the paper Nick handed him.

He scanned it and opened the apartment door. "Just press this in and the door will lock, Detectives."

Nick nodded in thanks.

The apartment, six rooms that would be considered small for a man of Steven Larcon's status, emanated a coldness, a barrenness that conformed to AriellaRose's personality. The dark forest green upholstery on the couch and love seat situated perpendicular to each other stood centered in the room on almond tiling. A green striped rug was the anchor for an oval coffee table. The walls were painted a golden yellow. But without any art work or family paintings, there was no life. Dark, depressing and, to Sam, full of toxic energy. She stood in the entry hall and stared into space. She needed to do a meditation to protect herself. It was as if she'd walked into a room so full of tension that she'd need three athames to cut through the air. It was heavy and musty, but not from unopened windows. There was central air in here, but you wouldn't know it.

Nick had walked on ahead of her. "Sam, can't tell which bedroom is his—or hers, for that matter. Sam? Where are you?" He came back to the entry way. "Why are you still standing there? Looking into space?"

She jolted. "Sorry, I was, was trying to get a feel for the space."

Nick waved at her dismissively. "Come here. Want to show you something."

Sam shook her head and rotated her shoulders to bring her back to the job. She followed Nick into the first bedroom. "Looks like an indifferent hotel bedroom. Queen bed. Desk on one wall, club chair in corner. In that same forest green. Ugh. Anything in the closets?" Sam opened the folding door. "There's nothing in here." She opened the dresser drawer. "Everything empty. He probably just comes here for sex."

"I already checked out the bedroom next door. Same thing. Nothing. I'll check all the drawers."

"Is there a master?" Sam walked into the living room and stared into the galley kitchen. All beige. Neat. Some appliances on the counter. She opened the fridge. "Nick. Come here quick!"

He sped over to her. "What?"

"Look!"

"What do you mean, look? Sam, there's nothing in there."

"Exactly. So where does AriellaRose live?"

CHAPTER 19

This was the last place Frank wanted to be on a cold Sunday night in November in one of the slimiest parts of Manhattan, parked in a filled outdoor lot at twelve a.m. He palmed the steering wheel of his Explorer as if he needed something to distract him and prayed for a way out. Not only out of tonight. A way out of this case.

How are we going to pull this off? They reeked of cop, just as AriellaRose warned Sam against. He—in his leather jacket, form-fitting black T-shirt, and skinny jeans—could possibly pass. But Sam? He gave her more than a scrutinizing look. She wore a long beige tweed wool coat over a black silk blouse and charcoal gray slacks. Her hair pulled back into a sleek ponytail did nothing for her soft features. At least she had put on heavier makeup than he usually saw her wear.

What is she thinking? Oh, man, this woman was naive. And she expects to walk around a BDSM club looking for leads?

He had no idea what she expected to accomplish. Yeah, she had brought him up to speed and he heard the Calinda interview, but so what? The cutter wasn't exactly a reliable witness. He still couldn't get a handle why that woman's name never appeared on the interview lists.

He blew out a deep breath, faced her. "Ready?"

"Ready as I'll ever be. Let's do this." She opened the car door. As she slipped her leg out, Frank noticed her high heels.

"How are you going to walk in those?"

Sam snickered. "At least you won't be able to tell me I'm short."

A quick belly laugh followed. "Yeah. Well, just think of it as a term of endearment, princess."

"How many times do I have to tell you?"

"Hey. It would make a great alias for you."

"Uh, no. Speaking of that, what's yours?"

"I got used to my nickname, Tattooman."

"No. That's lame. I'll be Barbie, like the doll."

"Uh, don't expect me to be Ken. Okay, I'll go with Drake."

She gave him an inquisitive glance.

"He was my German Shepherd growing up. He died at fifteen when I was away on my second tour. I was heartbroken. I promised Frankie I'd get him a shepherd and we'd name him Drake, but I'm not home enough now for a pup." He shook his head at the nostalgic moment.

"Let's get going. Hope Dominic is there."

They walked the two blocks to Whiplash on the lower west side in silence. The stores in this commercial area were closed, many out of business. There were some vacant plots of land encased with ten-foot high, entwined steel fences. Through the holes, Frank saw garbage that had been pushed through. Some vagrants and hookers meandered on the avenue. The hookers crossed the street when they spotted Frank and Sam. He was right, Sam and he reeked of cop.

Down a flight from street level, the eeriness of the dungeon enveloped them. The gray popcorn finish on the walls added to the cavernous feel. The yellow tapered candles in gothic-styled wrought iron holders gave off a citronella scent. He knew that one as a bug repellant. Ugh, bile rose in his throat. He coughed, then swallowed. His mood soured as he grimaced. The flames reflected yellow-circle shadows around the candles. He guessed there were over thirty of them spread between both sides of the stairwell. His hand searched for a light switch. None. Sam couldn't help but let her palms swipe the walls as she walked.

Oh, man! She's like a little kid.

They reached the bottom of the stairwell and were greeted by a hostess dressed in dominatrix garb, a leather strapless bra-like top connected to a G-string by a black mesh material. Garters held up mid-thigh black mesh stockings.

Not figure-flattering. 'Nuff thought.

Her long straight black hair looked too severe for her porcelain skin and her red lipstick totally missed the mark. Frank tried to contain his bitter attitude by surrendering a weak smile. The hostess gave him a clipboard stating the rules. Sam looked over his arm and read them with him. He sprawled his name, Drake, on his signature line and then Sam did the same, signing Barbie.

The hostess pointed. "The lockers are through there. Put everything in. But shut off your phones, now."

"Is Dominic here? We need to speak with him first." Sam tried not to sound so official.

She didn't pull it off. Frank shook his head.

The hostess reviewed their sheets. "Just so you know, Drake and Barbie, cops are considered rattlesnakes in here. No one will rat and, if you think you found a snake, they'll slither away. But they sure as hell will bite first, then rattle out your presence. Know what I mean, honey? The phones?"

Frank ignored the warning. He and Sam shut their phones. "Where is he?"

"Before you take another step, it's fifty for the both of you. We don't give discounts to our friends in Blue. No credit cards, no receipts."

Frank sucked in his cheeks. He knew that he couldn't declare this adventure on his monthly stipend account. He jiggled his wallet out of his jean's pocket, retrieved a Grant, and handed it to her.

"His office is first door to the left. But he might be watching or teaching a scene."

"Page him." Frank meant, now.

"We're not allowed to interrupt a scene. Our patrons pay good money for the experience."

"We'll go to his office and wait. I'm sure our presence right outside his door will be fascinating for your patrons' experiences." Sam's impatience couldn't be mistaken.

"Very well. He'll meet you there when he's done. Go there and I'll have someone find him. We have fifteen rooms here. It may take a while." She depressed a pager as Frank and Sam walked to his office.

They didn't see too much. Just a few scantily dressed aging and overweight patrons sitting on stools around a bar that served nonalcoholic beverages and smoothies. Frank eyed the menu hanging on the wall behind the bar.

"Carrot juice, carrot, apple, pear, beet with kale and yogurt. Yeah, I could go for one of those." Frank turned toward the bar.

"Later. There he is." Sam tilted her head in Dominic's direction.

Dominic unlocked the door to his office. He was mid-sixties, a little paunchy, wearing jeans, a vest without a shirt underneath. Sam and Frank made it in right behind him. Dominic turned abruptly and slammed the door.

"Before anything else, IDs."

This guy was sure the boss. His tone was clear enough. Frank looked down at the man half his size. About five eight, he looked worn out from the job. Dominic sat at his desk, moved his right ankle across his thigh, and stuck a menthol toothpick into the corner of his mouth. Frank and Sam slid their IDs across the desk. With one hand, Dominic first flipped opened Sam's, took a good look, sneered, and sent it flying across the desk back to her. He did the same with Frank's but studied it more.

He gave Frank a condescending glare. "You want a second job?"

"As what?"

"A dom. You got the look. I'll test you out tonight. One of my guys went on to greener pastures."

"No thanks."

"What do you want?"

We're investigating two murders, Mr. Trevino. And—"

"I'm not talking to you, Detective. You look like a school marm. Don't belong here."

She gasped.

"Hush. I'm talkin' to him. Who got whacked?"

"Steven Larcon and Meghan Mason."

"Yeah. Yeah. Read it in the paper. Why did ya come here?"

Frank returned the hard glare. "A lead, from someone we interviewed."

Dominic sat stone cold. "Don't know them."

"Know a Dudley and Fido?" Sam chimed in.

Dominic perked up in his seat. He swallowed. "Who'd you speak to?"

"Talking to me?" Sam asked.

"Yeah. Answer me."

"Actually, I'm not sure. Doubt if she gave me her real name."

Dominic licked his lips. "So what do you want here?"

"Not sure about that, either. Want to look around, listen, and observe scenes. We are allowed to watch, aren't we?"

"Yeah, sure. Can't interrupt, but you can watch through the observation window. But not the way you two are dressed. For some reason, the smell of cop inhibits the…the experience."

"I'm dressed for it underneath." Sam's voice softened.

Frank looked away and studied the stained, worn faux wood paneled walls. Cruddy wouldn't describe how this place appeared to him. He could just imagine how this baby-boomer club owner spent his time in here.

"Oh yeah? Show me." Dominic doubled checked the forms they had signed. "Uh, Barbie. Hey, I got a better name for you. Princess. You look like a sub all the way. Yeah, princess. Show me."

Frank smirked and sat back in his seat, arms filling the arm rests. "Yeah, princess. Go ahead."

Sam stood up, facing Dominic and let her coat slither down her arms. She pulled the coat around her and placed it on the back of her chair. She unbuttoned her slacks, then unzipped. She slowly unbuttoned her blouse, still facing Dominic, her back toward Frank. All Frank could see were Dominic's reactions. His eyes widened more at every button Sam undid. So did his. After the fifth button, Dominic sat up in the chair and as Sam slid the blouse down her arms, Frank could have sworn Dominic drooled. He removed the toothpick from his mouth and tossed it to the carpet. She removed the blouse to reveal a strapless black lace bustier that came to a V down her spine outlining a perfect muscular, but feminine back. Dominic gazed at her breasts with his mouth gaping. Frank could only imagine how much cleavage she displayed.

"Just so you know, they're all mine."

"Oh, yeah. I could tell, princess. I could tell." Dominic's mouth catapulted to involuntary sucking motions.

So did Frank's. All he knew was that he wanted to see them, too, and more.

"The bottoms."

Frank squirmed in the chair, not happy that Sam was so quick to oblige to Dominic's demand. He became hard, and that wouldn't help him investigating tonight.

She slipped off her heels and put them upright on the desk. Every seductive move was deliberate. Frank's body temperature rose beyond warm. He rubbed his sweaty palms on his thighs and watched Dominic do the same thing.

Then she slipped her thumbs into each side of her slacks and, with her index fingers and thumbs, inched them down. Frank saw the high cut on each leg with black mesh covering her firm upper thighs. Then she bent over with her butt extending into Frank's lap and edged her slacks down, exposing her perfectly rounded— naked—bottom with a thong separating her butt cheeks.

Dominic looked like he died and went to heaven. His face flushed. Frank thought the man would pass out.

A second after she was fully exposed and her slacks lay at her ankles, Frank bolted up from his seat. "Oh, no, you're not!"

ം෩ം෩

AriellaRose finally had some relief. Three days of IV steroids and antibiotics eased her breathing and began to heal her infection. The clock on the wall read one a.m. The cop outside had left at midnight. Thank God. He had been a real pain in the ass. He popped in at least every thirty minutes to check on her. All he'd say is "I'm still here, sweetie." Ugh, sweetie. She was far from being a sweetie. The only ones she was sweet toward were Leonard's parents. Otherwise, she considered herself death warmed over.

Her mind went to Calinda. Who the fuck was she? They never did meet, but she'd had to tell that detective something. The only one she knew matching that description was Emma. Emma Sanders. *No way in hell could Emma pull that off. Screwing Adam and my dad? No. Impossible. Not with the tight rein I have on my beholden.* AriellaRose wasn't sure Sanders was Emma's real name either. When they met in rehab, they only met with their first names. In the years that they had played together, they had only used their Wiccan names, except at times like today, when Merry was here. She couldn't possibly introduce her to Tattooman as BlackMoon. Now, could she?

There has to be a million women who fit Calinda's description. Okay, Arie, no time for that reminiscing bullshit.

She grabbed her phone lying next to her on the sheets and sent a text. *B @ my place @ 3.* She had to get out of here. Maybe a walk would help her think. Her pulmonary doc said she could get out of bed.

She tore the sheets off her, brought her legs over the side of the bed. Damn, her ankles were swollen. Probably from all the fluids and just lying in bed. Her feet touched the floor and she used her palms to push herself up. She grabbed onto the windowsill for balance and slipped her feet, one at a time, into the slippers Adam had brought her.

She disconnected the IV pole from the wall socket, wrapped the long cord around the hooks underneath the monitor, and slid the pole around the bed. She was okay. Her breathing held up. She could do this. She tied the green hospital gown, making a sloppy bow around her waist. Twisting around to make sure her rear was covered, she crept to the door. Then she remembered her cell phone and plucked it from her tote. Her wallet, too. Luckily, for her, there were pockets in the gown.

She peeked outside. No staff lingered in the hallway. The lights shone as if it were daytime. Looking both ways, she inched out of her room. She knew that the exit signs were the opposite way to the nurse's station. She'd walk to the exit first, unsure of what she'd do when she got there. Wheeling the IV pole, she strolled down the hall to the end where the window overlooked the rear of the hospital. It was pitch black outside. Around the corner she spotted a sign on a door. Supply closet.

Maybe I can find a weapon in there I can use to escape.

AriellaRose tugged on the door handle. Not only did it not open, a piercing alarm went off.

Oh crap.

She froze.

Two security guards in blue uniforms came out of nowhere. They saw her standing there.

"What are you trying to do, miss?" the mid-sixties one asked.

"Uh, my gown is sweaty, and there were no nurses around. I went for a walk, which my doctor said I could, and I passed this closet. Sorry. Didn't know the alarm would go off."

The younger burly guard extended his hand to support her arm. "Obviously. Let's go, back to your room, hon."

AriellaRose pulled away, scowling at him. Before she could think about it, as if something took over and controlled her mind, she grabbed the IV pole with her free hand and, as if in slow motion, the pole came down, and the monitor smacked onto the guard's head. He fell back with blood gushing from his skull. She started yelling as loud as she could but her screams pierced the hollow halls as raspy chokes. "Get—away from—me—you fucks!"

Staff came running. She was overtaken by fear. She remained motionless like the guard on the floor. Doctors surrounded him.

The older security guard struggled to hold AriellaRose. A psychiatric nurse grabbed her in a hold from behind. He wrapped his
arms around her and held hers close to her body. She couldn't
move if she had wanted to. She turned her head around. Fuck. He
was bigger than Tattooman. He lifted her off the ground, carrying
her away. She kicked a few times, her slippers tossed to the wind,
but lost strength. Her body went limp.

"Call Doctor Khaos," the nurse yelled to anyone who'd listen.

AriellaRose groaned. *Fuck. I've certainly caused enough of
my own chaos here tonight.*

CHAPTER 20

With Dominic eyeing her approvingly, and Frank, the opposite, Sam removed the butt cover for her outfit from her small clutch evening bag. She held it up teasingly between two fingers as she stood up tall. She knew her boobs excited Frank, and now the rest of her would. She twisted around taunting him with a full view. Frank snatched it from her and moved her toward the desk.

Sam placed her palms on the desk, bent over, and extended her rear up high. She looked up at Frank with her little girl pout.

Dominic grinned, standing with his hands on his hips. "She wants you to spank her."

"I know what she wants, but she's not getting it."

"Are you two a couple?"

"No." Frank was curt.

"Did you ever play a scene?"

"No."

"Did you ever fuck?"

"No."

"We just met a few days ago," Sam said.

Dominic didn't get it. "What difference does that make?"

Frank dismissed him. "Working a case."

Dominic lost patience. "You two aren't exactly teenagers. What the fuck are you waiting for? For your prostate to act up and start givin' ya problems?"

Sam giggled and Frank ignored the questions. He placed the patch over her bare bottom, pressing the Velcro together that held it on. He scowled at her as he took his time.

She wanted him to go slowly. His hands felt so good caressing, cupping her bottom. His fingers lingered at the base of her spine sending a thrill through her. *Is he truly pissed at my unex-pected display or jealous that my act wasn't only for him?*

"What about you, Drake?" Dominic barked.

Without a second request, Frank yanked off his T-shirt and pulled off his jeans. He stood there, hands on hips, in tight, black, skimpy swim trunks and mid-calf cowboy boots.

Dominic's mouth went slack. He grabbed a cowboy hat from a hook on the wall and tossed it to Frank. "Like I said, you'd make a cool dom."

"Maybe, in my next life, man."

Dominic gave Sam the once over and then turned to Frank. "You got a weapon in those fancy boots?"

Frank slipped his hand into his right boot and retrieved a Ruger. "Loaded, safety's on."

Dominic opened a wall safe. "Put it in here. What about you, princess?"

Yup. They couldn't evade that direct question. Sam retrieved her revolver from her coat pocket and put it into the safe. Dominic closed the safe and swirled the combination lock.

"Good. Okay, what kind of scene do you want to start with? Doctor-patient?"

Sam eyed Frank. "No. Too close to him."

"Teacher-student?"

Frank tilted his head at Sam. "Too close to her."

"What did Dudley and Fido play?" Sam asked.

"Parent-child. I know your next question. No. Not with each other. We knew they were father and son. It wouldn't be al-lowed."

Um, so Dominic slipped. He did know them. I've got to get him to talk. "That sounds good."

"Okay, follow me." Dominic left the room, they followed, and then he locked his office.

As they proceeded down a narrow hallway where different rooms lined both sides, Sam noticed how quiet it was. Very creepy. "Where is everyone?"

"Divided into the different rooms. We have very good sound-proofing. Can't have yells and screams interrupting our patrons. All right, in here. This is the observation room. Make yourselves comfortable on the bench. A father and son scene is starting. It'll take about half hour and then you two will be next. I'm assuming Drake, you're the Dom and she's the sub. Correct?"

"I don't necessarily want to play."

"Come on, Drake. I want to." She shot him her little girl pout again.

Dominic left them at the door, shaking his head.

Frank glared at her. "Knock it off, princess. I said, no."

She lowered her eyes for a moment, then looked around the room. The same popcorn finish covered the walls surrounding the one-way mirror. The room was long and narrow with just the six-foot-long, worn wooden backless bench, in the middle. One air vent in the ceiling couldn't eliminate the musty odor. They were definitely in a dungeon. Sam ran her hand over the bench before she sat. Last thing she'd want was a splinter. They made themselves as comfortable as they could be.

"You know, going through the experience ourselves may give us a better understanding of the dynamics of all of this, and aren't you all about profiling?"

"Don't have to commit murder to understand the mind of a killer. I said, no. End of story. Deal with it."

Crap. He'd sure make a great Dom. Before she could retort, the black screen on the window lifted. The parent-child room housed a twin bed in the middle, a spanking bench next to it, some children's toys on a desk against the wall with the entrance. There was an exit door on the far right. The same popcorn finish adorned the wall. The floors were gray concrete, just like throughout the dungeon. Nothing child-like about that. However, they were easy to clean up. The thought gave her uncomfortable chills. No turn on there.

A man wearing a mask over his eyes entered the room with another man wearing a knit, full face stocking. The older man looked like he was going to a Halloween party and the younger one looked as if he was going to rob a bank. They were both dressed in black.

The older man, obviously the dom, began the scene. "How many times do I have to tell you the same thing?" He pushed the sub toward the spanking bench. The younger man almost fell over but saved his fall, grabbing onto the padded bracket, where his stomach would soon lean.

Sam had never seen a spanking bench this close up. She had never been over one. She preferred an OTK—over the knee—spanking when both she and her partner were nude and she could feel his length swelling, hardening against her body. But tonight her chance of getting Frank to pull her over his knee seemed to be nil. She exhaled a breath of exasperation.

Frank sat hunched forward, looking bored with his knees apart and his hands clasped between them.

Maybe this wasn't such a great idea.

"I'm sorry," wept the younger man. "I can't help it, sir."

"Why can't you help it?"

"I need it. I need my Blue." the younger man whined.

Sam and Frank both perked up. Blue? Oxycodone?

"So what are we going to do about it now?" the dom bellowed.

"I need you to teach me how to behave, sir. I'm such a bad boy, sir."

Sam gasped. "Oh my God, Frank. That sounds like Adam!"

Frank sat up and paid attention. "I believe you're right."

"I am sick and tired of paying for your rehab. For your drug dealers that threaten your mother and me. Maybe once and for all, a good whipping will snap you out of it. Fido, pull down your pants and assume the position."

"Oh my God, sir, another one?"

"Yes, you bad boy, another one. And this one will be harder than the last one. You will be screaming and begging me to stop. But I won't. Not even yelling Red will make me stop. Not until you tell me everything that I need to know. Assume the position, you bad boy."

Who is that man and what does he need to know? Sam squirmed in the seat. She wrapped her right arm under Frank's left and swallowed. This might become too intense for her.

The dom walked to the wall where flogging implements hung on a rack. Whips of varying lengths, paddles of varying thickness, about ten in all. He chose a thin wooden paddle about three inches wide with a handle that extended straight out, one that looked like a spatula used to pick up one slice of pizza. Sam had one in her kitchen drawer. The dom walked back to Fido, now bent over the cushioned bench with his pants pulled down to his knees and his black briefs still covering his butt that faced the observation window. His hands touched the floor, his feet positioned opposite his hands.

"We're starting with this one." The dom stood in front of Fido's face, smacking the paddle against his hand. "Now, how many do you deserve, you bad boy?"

"One."

"One. Seriously? How many of those damn pills do you pop each day?"

"Six or seven."

"Then we start with that." He walked over to the side, raised the paddle about nine inches from Fido's butt and swung. "You will count after each one." The paddle made a crisp smacking sound as it connected.

"One." Fido said as his crying commenced.

Another smack.

"Two. That hurt, sir."

"It's supposed to."

Smack.

"Three. I'm sorry, sir. I have to stop now, sir."

"Why?" A harder smack with a twelve inch swing.

"Ow. Oh, fuck! That hurts." Fido barely got the words out. "My—supplier—got—arrested."

"You forgot to count. We start over. But this time…" He pulled Fido's briefs down past his butt. "And now it will be harder and faster." The dom walked to the wall, replaced the paddle, and grabbed a short flogger. The handle was made of leather, about eight inches, from what Sam estimated, with a wrist strap so it wouldn't slip out of the dom's hand. There were about five tails that would make contact. Sam closed her eyes and squirmed in the seat from just imagining the damage this one could do to the recipient's flesh. Heat swelled in her. Not from excitement, but from envisioning the pain. Fido's red butt assaulted Sam's gaze. She put her head into Frank's arm. "I think I had enough."

"You think?"

"We'll get him to come in."

Sam started to slip off the bench. Frank grabbed her arm. "Hey!"

"What?"

"We're not leaving."

"Uh—"

"You wanted to come here to get a lead, and you're not leaving." His voice was firm. "You're a detective. You can't leave a scene, and I mean, any scene, if you're uncomfortable. Doesn't work that way. Deal with it."

His stern glare went right through her. Chills replaced the warmth. "You're right, Frank. Absolutely right."

The dom waved the flogger in front of Fido's face. "You're going to feel the pain. Tell me you're ready."

"I'm ready, sir."

The dom flailed the flogger through the air and landed on Fido's rear. He screamed out. Lash after lash, from a farther distance, Fido's wails got louder and his butt reddened, welted—bled.

Fido sobbed almost unintelligible words. "I'm—sorry—my—father—got killed—I'm—sorry.

"Do you know who killed your father?"

"No—no—I—don't."

The thrashes multiplied in intensity. The sounds echoed against the walls. "Fido, tell the truth. Tell the truth for the first time in your life," the dom shouted.

Sam jumped in her seat with each thrash. She clutched Frank's hand and squeezed. Her hands became clammy. This was way out of her comfort zone. He stared back at her straight-faced. Tears welled in her eyes. Her scalp prickled. Her stomach quivered.

Am I cut out for this? Am I cut out to be a detective? She took some deep breaths and exhaled slowly to calm her rampant heartbeats.

"I—know—who—killed—him," Fido cried.

Sam and Frank shot each other looks of amazement. A black screen shut down over the window to signal the end of the scene. Sam and Frank bolted off the bench and out of the observation room into the hallway. Frank tugged at the doorknob to the room that scene had taken place in. To no avail. Locked tight.

℮℈℮℈

AriellaRose lay in bed. Sedated. Breathing shallow. Wrist and ankle restraints in place.

℮℈℮℈

After Dominic told them that Fido left the club via a back entrance immediately after the conclusion of the scene, Frank convinced him to let him use a phone. He called in a BOLO to Nick, who'd get units out searching for him.

Sam wanted to stay at the club to find the dom.

Frank held the plastic container with his smoothie between his hands, sitting at the bar with Sam. His mind was rambling, more about Sam's ability to handle homicide, than the case. He looked ahead, not at her. "We have a lot to talk about, princess."

Patrons in the club passed by, women in various stages of nudity, deliberately swiped Frank's arm with their bodies. It was a continuous trail. He just smiled and hiked his eyebrows in response. He wasn't impressed with any of them.

"I know. But later. First, I want to find his dom. I have a lot of questions for him. And if Dominick knew we were looking for them, why would he take us directly to them? Coincidence?"

"I beat you to it. He said he didn't have time to check the sign-in sheets. We interrupted him from doing his job." Frank assessed her. Okay, respiration normalized. He ran his index finger down her arm. She smiled.

Okay body temp back to normal. Good, she recoups fast. That's a plus. "What do you want to ask—" He took a gulp of juice. "—the dom?"

"Their history. How much he knows about the real Fido. How and why they created that particular scene."

"Well, I could answer all that. Looked like they've been partners a while. Scenes are discussed beforehand and agreed upon. Sometimes scenes are more than just for pleasure, pain. They could be used as a catharsis. To release traumas, buried emotions, even grief. Remember Adam told us he wasn't going to grieve?"

"Yes."

"This is his way of letting it all out. And if he really knew who offed his Dad, all the more reason he'd be uncooperative with us."

Sam looked around, finished her carrot juice, and slipped off the bench. Standing tall now, Frank absorbed her entire body. Oh, man! He wanted her. Her lace top barely covered her nipples and her breasts held up just fine. She leaned in toward him. He faced her and she wrapped her arms around his neck. He didn't know what possessed him to do it but his hands slid down her back and landed, caressing her bottom. He squeezed.

"Ooh," she purred.

"Later." He pulled her close in between his knees and kissed her face gently, letting his lips peck her cheek down to her neck. He lingered there, sucking, kissing her. His warm breath bounced off her neck. She shuddered. He felt the sensations travel through her as she quivered against his bare chest. Her warm body went limp on his as she nestled her head on his shoulder.

He whispered in her ear. "Did you just come?"

She looked up into his eyes. "Yes."

"You owe me, princess."

As she giggled, she recognized the dom a few feet away from them, leaning against a wall. "There he is. I'm going." She released herself from Frank's warm arms and stood still for a moment to, Frank assumed, regain her composure.

Sam walked over to the dom who seemed to have been eyeing her and Frank. Frank pretended to pay attention to his smoothie, but he sure as hell would watch that guy. Too bad he couldn't hear from that distance. The techno music in this section of the club drowned out all conversations.

ᥱᚴᥱᚴ

Sam approached the masked dom leaning against the wall as if he was the pillar holding it up. He wasn't a huge man, about five ten, not athletic, but his aura protruded not only dominance, but arrogance, and danger. Sam felt his toxicity, but she needed to do this. This was a man she'd usually run from. She greeted him with a fake, warm smile, hoping he couldn't read her. "Hi."

"What's the matter, sweetheart? Tired of your boyfriend?"

"He's not my boyfriend. We just completed a scene."

That's sort of the truth. "I'll be honest with you, sir. I observed yours."

"You don't say? What's your name?"

"Princess." She delivered it with her pout. "What's yours, other than, sir?"

"Ty. And you want me to repeat it with you?" He uncrossed his legs and slipped his hands into his pockets.

Another obnoxious gesture. "Well, maybe. " She shrugged. "But not really."

He laughed at her. "Why not?"

"I mean, I'd want to talk about it first. Isn't that what you need to do? Talk about it, first?"

He shook his head. "You're new at this, I'm assuming."

"Yes."

"And you chose my scene to observe. Why?"

"I like the daddy-daughter scenes and Dominic brought me in to observe. It happened to be yours."

"Okay, that's cool. Why do you like daddy-daughter scenes? Fantasize them? Like being punished by your…Daddy?" He grinned from ear to ear, accentuating his dimples.

Sam's cheek's flushed. "Yes."

"Tell me."

"Uh, now?"

"Yes. Now. So when I play Daddy, and I sure would like to play Daddy with you, princess, I could recreate your fantasies to a T." He looked down at her and then over her head. He froze. "But I don't play with cops, bitch." He escaped down the hall with long strides.

Sam turned abruptly to come face to face with the hostess who shook a baby rattle in her face. Sam swiped her hand away as she stormed back to Frank. "Guess we've outworn our welcome."

As soon as they hit street, Frank checked his messages. "Damn! Six messages from the hospital. Hold on." He listened, as they came in succession. "Looks like our playtime is on hold. AriellaRose became violent."

CHAPTER 21

The morning shift at the hospital hadn't commenced yet. Half hour to go. Housekeeping was in process on every level. Pairs of nurses stood outside patients' rooms, one giving the other updates. Nurses wheeled medicine carts to patients in a progression. A floor polisher swirled out of the way as Frank and Sam hurried down the hall to AriellaRose's room. It was Monday morning, already.

Feelings of fatigue and frustration ran through his mind and body. He didn't know which was more prominent. He knew what he looked like when that happened. Shit. He looked and felt like shit. He was probably pale and needed a shave. He hated that scruffy feeling when he hadn't aspired to it on purpose. At least that protein shake would tide him over. They had come straight from the club. So not only didn't they have time to clean up and change, their playtime was put on hold. That's what angered him the most. Actually it was a combination of anger and lust at the same time. He hadn't expected that from Sam. Her willingness to expose herself like that. He had taken her for a tight-ass. Boy, was he wrong. His profiling skills sure let him down. All he knew was that he needed her in his bed. Immediately. Tonight. Walking around in the condition he had been in the last few days wasn't healthy, on any level.

Sam looked rearing and ready to go, unless her makeup concealed her fatigue. To him, she was the energizer bunny. He couldn't understand that. Neither of them had gotten any sleep in over forty-eight hours.

As they reached AriellaRose's room, Frank heard moans, then clanging on the security bars on the sides of the bed.

He signaled to Sam to wait outside. She shot him a glare

which he returned. The last text message had said that AriellaRose only would talk to him, and she was yelling for him. He wanted to honor that. He approached the bed.

AriellaRose had been turning her head from side to side but when he came near, she faced him.

"What happened?" he asked in a low-key manner. He knew the entire story, but he needed to hear her side.

"I don't know." AriellaRose gasped. She tugged at the wrist restraints that drew his attention.

"Why did they restrain you?"

"I don't know," she cried.

He pulled over the club chair next to the bed and sat, pulling his jacket out of the way. "Okay. Tell me what happened before the restraints."

"I don't think I remember." She had a look of pleading in her eyes.

"All right." He swallowed and paused. "I was told you hit someone over the head with the monitor on the IV pole."

She stared into space in non-recognition. It took a few moments for her to refocus on him.

He made sure she paid attention before he spoke. "You were walking and tried to get into the supply closet. You told them, for a clean gown."

"Now I remember, yes. But I don't remember hitting anyone."

"Well, just to let you know, the security guard needed twelve staples on his scalp and he has a concussion. He's going to press charges for assault."

"But I didn't do anything. I wouldn't hit anyone."

"There were several witnesses, AriellaRose. Think. Very carefully now."

"Doctor Khaos, you've got to believe me. I'd never hit anyone. I'm not a violent person."

His cheeks expanded as he blew out a breath. "Before you grabbed the pole with your right hand, before you swung, a witness said you paused for a few moments. Remember that?"

AriellaRose closed her eyes. It was as if she tried to visualize the event. She blinked rapidly. To him, that meant she remembered.

"No. I don't." She looked away. "Maybe it slipped from my hand. It was heavy on top and the pole was wobbly."

"AriellaRose. That isn't working. I've been with you enough

to tell when you're not telling the truth. This is one of those times." He leaned back in the chair and clasped his hands in his lap. It took all his strength not to close his eyes and doze off.

She erupted. "That's too fucking bad, Tattooman! Get the fuck out of here!"

Whoa! He shot up in the chair. Not good coming out of a relaxed composure. The dark side of AriellaRose smacked him in the face. "AriellaRose, why the change in tone?" He kept his own low-key.

"There's no fucking change in tone! This is the real me. Get the fuck out of here. Before I knock you over the head with this pole!" She snarled, showing teeth. Her gaze shouted violence, mixed with lunacy. Her round eyes converted to icy glaciers. She started to pull her wrists from the bars. She couldn't free them. Then she tried her legs. Also held tightly. "Get these the fuck off me, Tattooman!"

"Not now, I won't. You're proving to be a danger to yourself and others. So, AriellaRose, you give me no choice but to admit you for a seventy-two hour psych eval. Starting now."

"Nooooo! You can't do this to me! Go fuck yourself!"

He didn't respond. Slipping his fingers into his jeans pockets, he left the room, bypassed Sam, and headed to the nurse's station. He heard AriellaRose screaming obscenities down the hall, as did bewildered staff who froze in their stance.

∽∾∽

Frank parked in Sam's Brooklyn driveway behind her Murano. He was exhausted. But he needed to go over the events of the past twelve hours. He checked his watch. Nine a.m. "Man, it's been a long time since I pulled an all-nighter. Okay. So the warrant yielded nothing."

"It yielded plenty. AriellaRose has another place. Doctor Trenton lives next door. Nick did find erotic paraphernalia in the dresser drawer in one of the bedrooms. No sign or scent of essential oils or candles, though."

"We'll call Trenton later. He's a good guy. Okay, what else? Ah, when we were in transit, Nick left a message. The knives place…"

"Anderson and Son's," Sam reminded him.

"Yeah. Out of business. That sucks. Website taken down, too.

Nick's investigating when all this happened. Calinda. Still ruminating on that one. From AriellaRose's outburst tonight, there's a side that she might let out often, or not. The anger and change in personality show itself during stress. I'll be doing a full workup on her and testing the stress level. How about going for Italian tonight? Maybe Carlo could enlighten us on the dark side. Adam is still on the run, or in hiding. Maybe he went to someone for aftercare."

Sam cocked her head. "You know about that?"

"Yeah, I do. After what he got last night, he'd need someone to make nice. Okay. And that guy. The dom. What was his name?"

"Ty."

"Yeah. I'd sure like to hear about your conversation with him." He couldn't help but let out a grin.

Sam plucked her recording device from her cleavage, handed it to him, and smiled. "There you go. And I'd love Italian tonight."

"Oh, man. You *are* something else. You know that?" He shut the engine and began to exit the car. "Come on. I need a shower bad." He grabbed a duffle bag from the back seat.

In the house, Frank took less than a second to check it out before he bolted up the steps.

"First bedroom to your right." Sam took off her stilettos and followed him.

Once inside the bedroom he pulled her close to him. His hands cascaded down her back to her bottom and rested there. *Oh, man. This tush feels good. Even with two layers of clothing over it.* He gazed at her breasts, peeking through her blouse, and couldn't wait to ravage them. Boobs and butts, his two favorite parts of a woman's anatomy, though an exceptional brain and heart had to top them off. This woman met his criteria and more. Jen's parents would love her. And encourage him.

"Uh, I need a shower, too. Worse than you. The smell alone from that place stuck in my nose."

"All right. Go. And get rid of that makeup. Way too much."

"I needed it for the occasion."

"Yeah, well, but not for the occasion that's happening soon."

He made sure she read that clearly. As she turned, he swatted her bottom. She smiled, her mouth forming an O.

Sam retreated to her bathroom. Frank heard the shower starting. He heard the hamper cover shutting. Then he heard splashing of water in the sink. He could guess what she was doing. He yanked off his clothing with urgency, nearly ripping his T-shirt that had glued to his sweaty torso. He'd give her a few minutes and then join her in the shower. Scrutinizing the bedroom, he decided he liked the king-size bed. Even her color scheme in the teals and blues met with his approval.

Oh, yeah, we'll have fun playing in here.

He sat down on a cushioned chest at the foot of the bed and pushed his palm up and down on the fabric. Oh, yeah. This would be real comfy for what he had in mind. He massaged the palm of his right hand with the fingers on his left. Then he balled his right hand and released a few times, just as if he were exercising for a marathon. Excitement ran through him envisioning the next hour or two, or three. For some reason, he had just become invigorated.

He listened to find out what Sam was up to. The shower door snapped shut. Okay, another minute and he'd surprise her.

Nude, he entered the bathroom, opened the shower door, leaned against it on his hip, and grinned.

℥℥℥

Her eyes devoured him from the top of his head to his furrowed brows and the eleven lines between them. So damn sexy. Her gaze canvased around his dark oval eyes, down his rugged, hair-shadowed cheeks to the cleft in his chin, to his chiseled torso, settling on his well-endowed manhood.

She hiked her brows, widened her eyes, but didn't take her focus from below his navel.

"Well. Coming in? It's big enough for two."

"Excuse me?"

She caught on, still staring at his now-hard length hitting way above his navel. "Oh my God, Frank. I—uh—meant the shower. It's big enough for two. Not your—"

"Yeah. Yeah." He didn't hesitate joining her and grabbed her in a bear hug.

Her arms clutched around his waist. "You'll just smell from lavender."

"Yeah. I'm getting to like that smell." The four spouts expelled a pulsating stream of water onto them at varying heights.

"For such an old house, you did great with the renovations. This will be lots of…uh…fun."

He snatched the bottle of lavender-scented shampoo out of her hand, flipped the cap open, and deposited a liberal amount on top of her head. His fingers ran through her locks, creating mounds of suds. He took his time, massaging her scalp.

Oh God. He was better than her hair stylist. His electric touch sent tingles around her scalp, ears, and down her neck. She relaxed with deepened breathing. He leaned her head back under the tallest spout to rinse her hair. He ran his hands through it and she shuddered from his energy. She closed her eyes and moaned.

She wiped her eyes with her finger tips, squeezed scented bath gel onto a mesh sponge, and soaped his torso. She looked into his eyes, smiling. He bent down and lowered his lips onto hers in a soft sensual kiss. She kept her face raised. She wanted more. He didn't oblige, just returned a teasing grin.

She relaxed her fingers. The sponge slipped from her hands and fell onto a mound of bubbles on the tile floor. He teased. He must have known what she wanted, but he was denying her.

Um, bad boy. Okay, she'd play. She could play the bad girl.

She retrieved the sponge and brought it up to his stomach. She lowered it a bit. Just a bit, then slid it around to caress his back, then lowered it to his butt cheeks, and swirled the sponge around. He grinned, pulled her close.

He snatched another sponge from a shelf, poured gel on it, spun her around with her back leaning on his lathered chest. She loved that he took charge. She put her lips together and closed her eyes.

He scrunched the sponge between his hands to increase the suds as Sam made herself comfortable against his eight-pack. He caressed her with the sponge, starting at her neck, and crept downward. He was torturing her with his gentle touch. With his right hand, he moved the sponge over her right breast, as the fingers on his left followed the soapy path, making circular motions on her chest. The warmth of his hands on her caused her to moan in surrender and lean her entire body weight against him. His fingers lingered on her pebbled pink skin that surrounded her hardened nipple, driving waves of excitement through her. He teased her in his slow pace, making her wait. With his left arm, he held her up on her rubbery legs. The grin hadn't left his face.

Control. He definitely controlled her pleasure.

He leaned forward and let the sponge travel millimeter by millimeter down her midriff, but stopped at her thatch. Sam moaned, edging her pelvis up, giving him permission to go lower. She was going to have him soon. The anticipation thrilled her and terrified her at the same time.

His hardened length settled on the crack of her butt cheeks with it reaching the small of her back. It felt so good there she almost didn't want to move. She needed him, his touch, in her most sacred place. She turned slightly and spread her legs for him, raising her leg as he brought the sponge down to her sex. When it reached her clit, he kissed her neck and she closed her eyes in deep desire and trust.

Again he made circular motions—this time on her mound— with the sponge. She gasped, low guttural moans. The heat rose from her core. He continued to peck at her neck. Then he dropped the sponge and inserted two fingers into her, probing, massaging the most sensitive part of her.

She let out louder moans. "Oh my God. Ooh. Ahhhhhh."

He found her G-spot and lingered. He moved his fingers over the spot, one at a time, tapping, as if his fingers walked within her. Her entrance swelled. Tingling sensations ran through her, driving her close to the apex. The feeling within her mimicked wanting to pee. She knew she couldn't.

As if on cue, he removed his fingers, halting her climax.

Damn him!

"I want you under me, princess. Now." His voice commanded the only words he uttered.

Yes, he was her dom. A gentle one. But a dom, nonetheless. He flipped her limp body over and held her tight as he rinsed both of them off without another word. He shut the shower, opened the door, and wrapped her in a towel. Then he grabbed one from the rack. As Sam finished drying herself, Frank did the same on himself.

They exited the steamy bathroom, looking into each other's eyes. The coolness of the hall hastened their retreat into her bedroom. Her sex throbbed. Ached.

He plopped her down on her back on the bed with towels wrapped around them. He pulled his off and dropped it to the floor. Sam gazed up into the eyes of the overpowering specimen who was about to consume her. He drove her insane with lust. She wouldn't be able to take much more of the heat that had mounted in her core, sending tremors through her body. In a few moments she'd have to beg him. Beg him like the bad girl he wanted her to be.

With seduction on his face, leaning over her, he tugged on Sam's towel. He gently lifted her body to slide it out from under her. Kneeling on the bed, he lowered his body onto hers. He caressed her face, moved his hands down her neck to her breasts. Cupping her right breast, he lowered his face to kiss the mound he held in his hand. She let out low gasps. His lips moved to her mouth, her arms went around his neck, welcoming him.

Just as their lips were about to meet, both their phones rang at once. His had an alarm ringtone. Hers, the bark of a dog.

"What the—" Their voices trampled each other's.

Nick had called Sam. Loo had called Frank.

CHAPTER 22

The drive from south Brooklyn to north Manhattan took two hours in rush-hour, Monday traffic, a week and a half before Thanksgiving. Bad timing. Holiday shopping had been underway in New York weeks ago. Crap, bumper-to-bumper on the Belt Parkway, Gowanus, into the Hugh L. Carey Tunnel and West Side Highway, traveling north. He'd go to his gym the same way in an hour, during off times.

Knock of the pity party, Frank. Murders aren't convenient at any time.

They had guzzled down whey protein drinks, tuna and egg salad Sam had in her fridge, got dressed, all in less than thirty minutes. He would have loved to ignore the phone. He couldn't. Neither could Sam. He was pissed.

Patrol officers guided him into a cordoned off area to park outside the church's rear parking lot. Sam looked out the window and nudged him with her elbow to face the direction of Nick and Withers, standing inside the lot, near tarp covered bodies.

Frank got out of the driver's seat, slammed the car door, put his elbows on the roof of the SUV, and scanned the site. Damn! Every emergency service team in New York City was here—fire trucks, ambulances, Crime Scene unloading their van, detectives from the Central Park Precinct, and about ten uniformed officers. Then he noticed Lieutenant Rojas speaking with the Bureau Chief of Homicide, Burt Hazelton.

That meant trouble for him, Sam, Nick, and even that bum, Withers. It had been three days since the last murder.

And what have we accomplished? Squat! That's what.

They'd all feel the heat. The forensic reports hadn't come in yet. No one would give a damn. They had a couple of leads. AriellaRose was now contained in a psych ward. Adam had gone into hiding. Calinda—who the heck *was* she? Something had to give. Sam had already gone through the gate over to Withers. She flashed her badge, dismissing an officer who tried to detain her.

Yeah. She was pissed, too.

Frank pulled his shades from the nape of his T-shirt, put them on, and joined them after flashing his ID at the same officer.

Sam stared at the tarps. "When?"

She nodded to Nick, who signaled hello from where he now stood. Then he resumed conversing with this precinct's detectives.

Withers gave her a hard stare. "Around ten-fifteen. They were coming out of an AA meeting. They left a few minutes early. As soon as they came down the steps to the parking lot, they caught it in a drive-by. The bodies are still in the exact position they fell. No witnesses. Anyone who was going to be here already was." He paused and studied her. "So what do you make of it, rookie?"

Frank was taken aback by Withers's affront. He put it on Sam awfully fast. But she didn't flinch or miss a beat.

"What did the first responders report?"

"Never mind them for now. Crime Scene just got here. Scene same as it was found. This precinct knows it's ours."

"Not appropriate, Withers. The first responders have—"

"Zip it, Khaos. Who invited you to this shindig?"

"Whoa, Withers. Watch it." Frank removed his shades and stared Withers down to the size of an ant.

"Wow, temperamental this morning, hey, Doc? The two of you look like crap. Didn't get much sleep last night, did you?"

Frank got the message, but backed off, giving a snide retort. "No, we did not." Let Withers mind wander where he wanted. His brain was usually in the gutter, anyway.

Sam ignored them and looked around. Frank saw her photographic mind at work. She seemed to be absorbing every detail. She rubbed her lips together before she spoke, as if she wanted to choose her words carefully before she let them out.

That was a first.

"They took a big chance here. Way too public. What were they thinking? Different from the park kill. Similar to the Mason kill. Church right on a main avenue. They knew they'd be exiting at the rear. Their car in here?"

Withers nodded.

Sam walked to the entrance gate. "Too narrow for cars coming and leaving at the same time."

That, Frank could see.

She walked the direction that the getaway car needed to go. "They came in, drove around this row, and must have waited by the steps, facing the exit. Each row flows in one direction. They don't enter and leave through the same gate. The gate we walked in is the entry gate, and the one opposite is the exit. Um, they knew about timing. No one else would be exiting while they did this. Obviously prepared. May I see the bodies?" Sam yanked latex gloves from her pockets, slipped them on while she gave her full attention to Withers.

"Yeah. Sure, rookie. Go ahead. They haven't been processed yet. The tarps are held up on spikes so they don't make contact. Make sure they don't slip."

Sam nodded and approached the bodies. She crouched down and lifted the first tarp, closest to her. Frank followed her, stood behind her with his hands in his jeans pockets. He kept his distance, but he needed to convey that she had an ally.

She scanned the body from head to toe, bending down farther to get a full view. "Hey, Withers! Want to come over and listen? Or do you prefer my tape?"

Without a response, Withers knelt next to her.

"Valerie Larcon. Three bullet wounds in torso. One in left shoulder. Looks like from a thirty eight. Some residue on her coat. I'll let the lab guys estimate the distance." She stood up and walked around to the second tarp. She lifted the edge closet to the head of the victim. "Mrs. Larcon. Oh shit. Two to the face. Looks like from closer range. Powder residue. Those black spots aren't makeup." She stood up and let out a short breath. "Know why they left early?"

"Yeah. As long as you asked. A member said, the Mrs. got an emergency call. He couldn't hear what, but the Mrs. turned pale, got up fast, and ran out of the room. Valerie followed her. That's it."

"The driver's side was over here. Car facing the exit. That's a definite. Hypothetically, I think there were two shooters. One shooter in the back seat. I think that's Valerie's killer. Both probably used suppressors." She walked the distance from the body to the first row of cars. "About fifteen feet here. Shot's within that. Then I think for the Mrs. Larcon kill, the killer may have been here." She walked a few feet away to the row of cars again. "This would be where the hood of the car would be, so after the kill, the perp could run around the front and jump into the passenger seat. Only two shots, close up, to do it quick, while Valerie's shooter could get two more rounds off."

Sam's gaze seemed to scrutinize the ground. Withers stood with his usual sour expression. He must love lemons. The more Frank saw him, the more it reinforced that he couldn't stand the man. Frank shifted on his legs farther back from the area where Mrs. Larson had been taken down.

Sam shouted, "Don't move, Frank!"

He froze. "What?"

She bent down and picked up a blackish-blueish round piece of gook that lay by his toe.

Withers yelled at her. "What the fuck, rookie? That's old bubble gum!"

Sam put the glob up to her nose. Frank furrowed his brows. She sighed. "Okay. How do I say this so you don't have Doctor Khaos commit me on the spot?"

"Just say it, rookie!"

"First, this is where Mrs. Larcon's shooter stood. Second, this isn't bubble gum. This is candle drippings. It's called an amulet. See the pentagram, the five pointed star engraved on it?"

Withers didn't know what to make of it and shook his head. Frank stood straight-faced. On purpose.

"Amulets are used for good luck doing something. Lighter colored ones for good things, dark ones for evil." She lifted the amulet to her nose. Each sniff yield a different scent. "Jasmine—Basil—Pennyroyal. Oops. That one could cause a miscarriage. I bet these women work with black magick. Spells. Like AriellaRose slipped out."

"And you know that, how?" Frank's tone was out of curiosity not condemnation. He was careful about that.

"I work with oils and candles, too. In meditation. Nick already knows."

She threw that out, Frank guessed, to minimize the effect.

"There's a lot more to it than what you're saying, but okay, so what?" Frank needed to know but he'd wait.

"How soon can we get a fingerprint ID?"

Withers held out his hand. "Gimme." She placed the amulet into Withers's gloved hand. He peered at it suspiciously. "Give me a while. We'll see if we can get a print." He left to find a crime scene investigator.

"When were you planning to tell me?"

"Tell you what?"

"About your interest in Wicca."

Sam stared at him with her mouth agape.

Twenty-five minutes later, Withers returned with a smile on his face. The first smile Frank had ever seen. "Ordinarily, they don't do this at the scene, but we got lucky, rookie. The guys they sent owed me a favor. Our buddy AFIS made an ID. Great job! Emma Sanders. Busted three years ago. Stealing from her dad's employer, a pharma in Westchester. Got probation cause Daddy's a big time corporate lawyer, but he did lose his job. What she stole was proven to be for her own use. Don't know how they pulled that off. She moved away to Atlanta and came back six months ago. And guess who she is?" Withers flipped the phone toward them to see the pic.

"Calinda Alexander!" Frank and Sam said in unison.

Sam grimaced. "No wonder her name wasn't on any list. Before our guys went out to interview, they validated IDs. Anyone they couldn't verify was ignored. Need to confirm that, though. Get a BOLO out for her and Adam. Psych ward or not, can I borrow the amulet and white band?" she asked.

"The band's at the precinct, and the am…what the hell did you call it?"

"Amulet," Frank filled in.

Sam frowned and shot him an inquisitive stare.

"Yeah. It's being packed up now. Come back to the precinct and let's see what we could put together."

"Good. I need a computer," Sam said as if she had a lot of ideas.

❧

At the precinct, Sam shuffled files around on the desk in the War Room. Frank made himself comfortable on the couch behind her. Nick and Withers meandered in a few minutes later. Sam glanced at the wall clock, two p.m., and narrowed her eyes at them, showing her annoyance at their tardiness. They pulled out chairs and plopped down. They understood her non-verbal reprimand. Good. This was her case and it was about time they realized who was really in charge. In her mind, it certainly was not Withers.

"Okay, guys. We have a lot to do this afternoon, so I hope you didn't plan any family time. This is our first meet to put it all together. Nick, what did Central Park tell you?"

"A lot. Valerie and Mrs. Larcon had been going to this church for just a few months. There's about twenty AA meetings in the area. They've hit all of them. It seems that when the sessions become too hot for them, when members ask too many questions and push them, they split. So the killers are people who know them personally. Dingo caught me up on your assessment at the scene. I agree. So good job on that."

Sam gave him a cynical smile. "Sorry, no Brownie points. What else?"

"Oh, man, Sam! Who didn't get what she wanted last night?" Nick laughed, glaring at Frank, who also perked up at her remark, responding with a guttural laugh.

Sam turned around and glared at him. "What, Frank?"

"Hey, I didn't get what I wanted, either!"

"Frank," Sam scolded. "What we got or didn't get is nobody's business and has nothing to do with it. What pisses me off is that four murders happened right under our noses. I believe the person who knows the most about it is already in custody and we can't find the other two key witnesses. Nick, what else?"

"Interviews came in from the teams. Very thorough. Unbelievably, all the reports are positive. People were very cooperative. No one wanted the vics killed. All leads went to the kids and their dealers. A couple of reliable sources led to Leonardo Philetano as their only supplier. Like Calinda said, AriellaRose and him are a couple. Adam is still MIA. Possibly the driver in the last two kills. We know Calinda is still around."

Frank leaned forward, still on the couch. "From what we saw at the club last night, Adam has a lot of hostility and guilt toward his parents. Wouldn't be surprised if he orchestrated the kills and his puppets executed the plans. He and AriellaRose, as twins, have a lot of the same personality traits. I'm confident he does know who did the kills."

Sam nodded. "Okay, so Adam tops our suspect list now. What did the graphic artist come up with? That witness ever come in?"

Withers referred to the file. "Yeah. Gave an accurate account. Found her quickly. Rachel Hawthorne. Late twenties, five tenish.

Which fits, if we compare her height to the height of the bullet entry wound. She was taller than Mason, so she'd be able to keep her trigger hand lowered and not seen by passersby. She's wanted in Atlanta for murdering her grandmother last year. Here's the pic." He turned the file around so they could see.

"Atlanta? That's what info on Calinda said. Find out if AriellaRose or Adam ever went to rehab in Atlanta," Sam said.

Frank raised a hand. "Hold on. One of her friends that I met, Meredith Cummings, had a southern accent. So I believe, gang, we just found our three killers. Address on Hawthorne?"

"Funny thing is, she's listed as homeless. In Staten Island. But she didn't look homeless from what she was described as wearing." Withers closed the file. "No way is she fucking homeless."

"Okay, so both Adam and AriellaRose are financially set enough to support these women. Now, we have Doctor Trenton. He lived next door to AriellaRose. Suppose we make that call now," Sam said.

"All right. I know him well." Nick took his smartphone out of his pocket, checked his contact list, and dialed from the phone on the desk keeping it on speaker.

A young boy answered. "Hello."

Nick looked surprised. "Is Doctor Trenton there?"

"Yes. Who is this?"

Nick laughed silently. "Who's this?"

"Ricky, his son. Hold on. Dad!"

Nick looked at the team, putting his palms out in bewilderment. Guess he didn't know him as well as he thought, Sam ruminated.

"Doctor Trenton, here."

"Hey John. It's Nick Valatutti. How are you?"

"Hey Nick. Doing well. Going out of my gourd with boredom, but I'm busy."

"That's what you get for staying down south. You know what they say about Florida?"

"Yeah, the one foot in the grave, but I'm far from that."

"Isn't that the same little guy you rescued three years ago?"

"Sure is. Came back to us last February, and we'll be finalizing the adoption next month. Amazing how things can be manifested."

Sam perked up at Doctor Trenton's choice of words.

"How's he doing?" Nick asked.

"It's been a fun ride. We're homeschooling till he catches up. He's a great kid."

"So what are you doing to pass your days?"

"Finishing my book, teaching criminology at the community college."

"Bor—ing."

"What are you asking me, Nick? I get the feeling your call isn't just social."

Withers butted in. "Still with the feelings crap?"

"Well, if it isn't Dingo Withers. Spoke with your brother last week. He's still wrapping things up on the Gemini case. Finding more bodies, so the families can have closure."

"Good, okay. Listen, I got a rookie here who needs to talk to you. Detective Samantha Wright."

"Sure." Trenton's smooth tone came through clearly.

"Hi, Doctor Trenton. We're investigating four high-profile murders. The first vic is your neighbor in Manhattan. Steven Larcon. What can you tell me about him?"

"Wow! I hadn't heard. Who else?"

"His wife, daughter Valerie, and designer Meghan Mason."

"Hey, John, how about coming up and taking this over? Get rid of your boredom. And I never did get the chance to whip your ass in my gym."

She shot Frank a how-dare-you glare. "Uh, Frank, we're not talking about the gym now. Doctor Trenton?"

"Okay, Khaos, how long have you two been going together?"

"We're not going together. We just met last Wednesday," Sam said, flatly.

"What does that matter?" Trenton asked. "I met Vicki the same night I came here to see my parents, and by the next night I knew she was going to be my wife."

"Oh? That was kind of quick. Can we discuss that later, please?" Sam didn't like her own pleading tone.

"Yeah, Doc. When I said rookie, I meant it. All business. She doesn't even have a week under her belt in the rank. And get this. She's the lead on this case."

Trenton laughed. "Wow, I like that. How'd you pull that one off, Detective?"

"I'm good at manifesting, too. Did you know Mr. Larcon, personally?"

"Yes, I did."

"What can you tell me?"

"What do you want to know?"

So he's testing me, too.

"All right. I'll be specific. Did you see women coming and going, other than AriellaRose?"

"All the time. Very loud. Very rough sex."

"Any names?"

"No. When people are involved in the scene he was, introductions were never made."

"Any men?"

Without missing a beat, Trenton responded. "Yes."

"Who specifically? You answered quickly. I get the impression you know."

"Very good, Detective. Using your instincts. I like that."

"You like it that much, John, how about coming up?" Frank asked.

"No can do, Khaos. I know it's out of your specialty, but how do you say it? Deal with it? Besides, Vicki is due this week. Twins. Not leaving Florida."

"Oh, how sweet. Congrats! Now who?"

"Another designer. Jaye Manning. He designs my suits. He'd stop by my apartment before…their…appointment."

"Okay, this is a stretch. But, by any chance, would you know his alias?"

"You know about that? Yes, I do. I'd hear the screaming through the walls. Ty. Why did you ask?"

"Went to Whiplash last night with the guy who wants to whip your ass in the gym and observed a scene with Ty and Fido—uh, Adam."

"Yeah. The three of them were partners. And, yes, it wouldn't be allowed in clubs, but Steven and Adam were partners, too. Not for sex. Just for the discipline component—" A big dog's loud barking in the background interrupted the conversation. "Okay. I have to run and walk him. A shepherd. Duke. Got him as leverage for Ricky. I'll tell you, it worked. He's an amazing dog. Look, call me if you need me. And, Detective Wright, I'm impressed." He disconnected before any of them could say "Goodbye."

"Crap! I didn't get to ask him about AriellaRose."

Frank shrugged. "Hey. We got plenty. Call in Jaye Manning. Not going to that club again."

"Okay. What did our tech guys get?"

Withers looked at the blank section in the file. "No reports yet. But neither AriellaRose or Adam had any social media accounts, which is more than bizarre for their age group. That tells us a lot, actually. They didn't want any attention. They wanted private."

Sam scowled. "Not good enough."

"Hey," Frank protested. "It's only been five days. Complete forensics takes two weeks."

Frank's rational approach wouldn't make a dent. Sam glared at him and pulled the laptop close to her. "Enough bullshit. I'm going to find where AriellaRose really lives and whatever else." She Googled AriellaRose Larcon and stared at the screen. Images came up with AriellaRose and her family. The first page articles showed a happy family at events and charities—the most recent in 2012. "Okay. Find out what happened in 2012 or 2013 that ceased attendance at these functions." She continued the search. Articles about Larcon Fashions took up most of the first five pages. On the sixth page, there was a link entitled, *AriellaRose Larcon, seen in Park Slope*. Sam clicked on that. The article was dated six months ago. She scanned it. It was written by a fan of her dad's line. The pic showed AriellaRose carrying grocery bags, walking down a side street to Garfield Place. "Got it! Got it! She lives in Park Slope, Brooklyn. Now to find an address."

Frank grinned. "Very good."

Nick gave her a high five. "All right, Sam, excellent. You two, go home and get some sleep. We'll work on this."

"No. I want to confront her with the amulet and white band. And someone has to tell her about her mother and sister. And there's a lot more I need to find out."

"Now I know how exhausted you are, Sam. Believe me she already knows. And you'll do that tomorrow. Get out of here. Now. The both of you!"

Nick's demand was appreciated.

CHAPTER 23

Tuesday morning, ten a.m. sharp, Nick escorted Jaye Manning into a conference room. Looking at him, Nick became self-conscious. He examined Manning's attire, trying not to be conspicuous. For a man around sixty with an abdomen that had spread, he still had style. Black silk shirt with several buttons undone, exposing his gray haired chest. Indigo skinny jeans, but more ornate than Frank wore. Manning's had a black on black embroidered geometric pattern up the sides on the legs. Yet it was still masculine. Nick didn't know what made him focus on this man's attire. He'd never paid attention before, not much anyway, unless it was describing a witness or in official case business. But, then again, this qualified. Here he was in his Khaki slacks and brown blazer, the usual cop gear. Bland, but in style. "Have a seat, Mr. Manning. We'll be with you shortly. Waiting on members of my team to arrive."

"No problem. I want to help."

"Thanks," Nick said as he closed the door behind him.

Nick observed Manning on the computer monitor. He seemed sincere in wanting to help, relaxed, leaning back in the chair away from the table, his left leg crossed over his right thigh. He ran his fingers through his hair which Nick could tell, had once been blond.

Okay, maybe he's a tad nervous.

Nick sat back in his chair. This lifestyle bothered him. Not that he was a prude, far from it. He and his wife still had awesome sex, even after twenty-three years. What he couldn't wrap his brain around was the pleasure-pain part. Yeah, he knew about all the feel good chemicals that were released from the brain, when it was done right, but he could swear he released those same chemicals in his wife after sex. Oh man, sometimes judgments got in the way. Even with the best investigators. He just hoped he could control himself and not knock this Manning character out.

Sam and Frank joined him. All cleaned up and rested. Sam wore black denim jeans with studs scattered throughout the legs, from ankle to upper thigh and her jacket matched in pattern. Frank wore his usual—a black T-shirt and chambray colored jeans.

Nick nodded in approval. "Nice outfit." He paused. "Hold on. I never say that about a woman's outfit. Only sometimes to my wife. This case is having a real bad effect on me."

"Aw. And I thought you meant me," Frank chided.

Sam laughed. "Well, you should. Women like to hear it." She took off her jacket and hung it over the back of her chair. "Did he say anything yet?"

"No. Waiting for you." Nick couldn't help but stare at her white sequined pullover top either. *Come on, Valatutti, snap out of it.*

"Okay, Let's do this." Sam opened the door.

"I'm staying here and observing," Frank said.

"Sam, I'm letting you conduct the interview. I need to distance myself for a bit," Nick said.

She looked at him suspiciously.

"Not. It's not a test. Don't want my disapproval of the lifestyle to come through. And, more importantly, too many people throw the process off."

"Fair enough, Nick."

Nick nodded and he and Sam left the room.

They entered the conference room. Jaye Manning sat up tall when he saw Sam. He wet his lips and put them together. He rubbed the back of his neck before he brought his hands down and curled them on his stomach.

Good. He's embarrassed.

Nick unbuttoned his jacket.

"Hello, Mr. Manning. I'm Detective Samantha Wright, and you've met Detective Valatutti. Thank you for coming in." She and Nick sat next to each other at the table opposite Manning.

"Sure, Detective Wright. It's a shame what happened. I lost a very good friend and business partner."

She clasped her hands in front of her on the desk. "We know.

How long were you and Mr. Larcon business partners?"

"We were in design school together so we go back over thirty-four years or so." He sighed at the memory. "But we partnered up ten years ago."

"How did that come to be?"

"Actually, a client of both of ours suggested it. She bought a teal gown from Steven and then brought it to me to see if I could make a matching shirt for her husband to wear under his tux for their son's wedding. It was like an epiphany. Why hadn't we thought of that? But glad we did. Brought us in a bundle over the years."

Nick wasn't sure where she was going, but he needed to trust her. He'd interject if he needed to. Right now, he sat listening attentively. From Manning's reaction when they entered the room and he saw Sam, he knew Jaye had recognized her, yet they were both pretending otherwise. Nick mentally prepared himself for a long meeting.

"Oh, that is a long time. What did you like best about working with him?"

"His mind. The man was a creative genius. He could visualize a gown, for example, tell me what he saw, and a few minutes later it was on paper. He always had the gift. Even in school, he blew everyone else away. Sure, every designer can do that, if they're good, but Steven's visions were uncannily detailed."

"I'm sure you heard about Meghan Mason's murder."

"Yes, another tragedy of a true gift."

"Um, did you know, probably not, hopefully not, because we've kept it out of the media, that Mrs. Larcon and Valerie were also murdered yesterday?"

"Oh my God! No, I didn't know. Oh my God." His voice ended in a whisper. "Why? Why is all this happening?"

"We don't know, Mr. Manning. All we have are Adam and AriellaRose, who are quite high on the suspect list. We need to solve this case to keep them both safe. We have no idea if either of them are safe. What can you tell me about them? Please, we need you to be completely honest."

Nick stifled a smile. *Okay. She sent a clear message. Let's see how this aging yuppie responds.*

Manning sat back. "All right, enough games. You know me from the club. I'm guessing you know Fido is Adam. Do I need an attorney?"

"We have no plans of considering you a suspect. I'll be frank. You asked Adam about who killed his father. He said he knew. Did he tell you?"

"No. He didn't. And that's the God's honest truth. I swear." He took a hankie out of his jeans pocket and wiped his brows. "He ran out of the exit and I haven't heard from him. I tried to reach him as I always do after a scene, but he hasn't answered my calls or texts."

"Okay, so tell me how that particular scene played out. How did it develop? Who wrote the script, so to speak? How did you know which way to go?"

He let out a deep sigh. "No script for this one. I was so angry, I wanted to know for purely selfish reasons. I had lost my business partner and my partying partner. Him knowing who killed Steven came as a shock to me, as well. Okay, okay. How do I say this without you thinking I'm a total creep?" He paused for a long minute. "Okay. Obviously, I've known the twins from before they were born." He paused another long minute. "I want complete immunity in this."

"Mr. Manning, obviously, what you want to tell us is grave in nature. You'll feel better if you get it off your chest," Sam assured him.

"I want to consult my attorney. But I swear to you I had no knowledge of the murders, nor had any part in them. I swear on my children's lives."

ⲉⲟⲉⲟ

With that, Frank stormed in. That was the message to Sam and Nick that he was taking over. "Hi, Ty, remember me?" His tone was caustic. Manning paled. His eyes rolled back. He looked like he had gotten dizzy. "Doctor Frank Khaos. Forensic Psychiatrist." He made himself comfortable on a chair next to Sam and blew out a nasal breath. "I'm not good at coercion, so just tell us what's on your mind."

"I—uh—care—a—lot—about—the—twins," Manning stammered.

"Then help me save them. I have AriellaRose in a psychiatric ward now. She attacked a guard and he needed twelve staples on his head. Yeah, sure. You have every right to consult an attorney, and our conversation will stop. But that's the easy way out and

AriellaRose could wind up behind bars for life."

Manning blinked a few times, as if to regain confidence. Before he spoke he exhaled a long breath. "She has a temper, yes. But I'd never known her to attack."

Frank leaned forward in the chair. "Think carefully, Mr. Manning. How often do you see them?"

"Often. Okay, this is how we usually devise a scene." He looked down.

"Mr. Manning. Look at me." Frank tapped on the table to get his attention. "We're beyond that now. I could tell Detective Wright how to devise a scene. How often do you see the twins?"

"A couple of times a week."

"Why so often?"

"Well, Adam works for me. He's in the office, working in the studio. Our paths cross a couple of times a week."

"And AriellaRose?"

"She comes to my office to complain about her parents. I'm not as judgmental as her mother. I helped her out."

"With what?"

After a contemplative pause Manning let it out. "With her clothing line."

"Yes. She told me she was thinking about creating a line for young adults that they could afford."

"Thinking about? She swore me to secrecy. She'd kill me. Oh, no. That was a poor choice of words. And the people she didn't want me to tell are gone. She's had the line for three years. She's making a shit load of money because she listened to my advice. Her father, as much as he knew about business, wouldn't share his knowledge with his kids. Steven wanted control as if he begrudged his children their own success. That peeved me to no end."

Frank tilted his head in an understanding nod. "Name of the business?"

"Aries Fashions." He laughed. "She named it after her astrological sign. And her nickname is Arie. Completely online. She sends orders all over the country. We haven't spoken about it since its inception—well, only marketing ideas, but she made enough to buy her brownstone in Park Slope."

"What kind of clothing does she design?"

"Some hip hop accessories. Belts, bandanas, caps, fancy shoelaces. Stuff I don't understand, nor care to."

"Have an exact address?"

"Of the business?"

"And her house."

"Not offhand. But she has a warehouse in downtown Brooklyn, Never been there. The brownstone is on Garfield Place or something. She wanted complete anonymity and independence. It was as if no one knowing about her made her important. I never understood her thinking but I respected it. That's something she never had. Respect. Never appreciated anything anyone has done for her."

Frank shook his head. "Mr. Manning. Things aren't adding up. What you've told us so far is nothing that would make you out to be a creep. Helping the kids of a close friend is commendable, especially when they're having a hard time dealing with their own parents."

Manning slumped in the chair.

"Mr. Manning?"

"All right." He sighed. "I am the twins' biological father."

Silence overtook the room. Just for a moment.

"Do they know?" Frank asked.

Manning cleared his throat, swallowed. "They found out ten years ago. At fifteen. Kathryn, Mrs. Larcon, had a mental breakdown. She was committed and was having a nightmare in the hospital. The twins were in her room. She woke up screaming for them to get their father. Adam called Steven in from the lounge. When he came into the room, she started screaming again, 'No not him! Jaye! Jaye is your father.' Well, they thought it was her medications and her illness playing tricks. But Steven knew better. He never saw it coming, however, he saw the truth immediately. The twins were blond like me. Valerie was darker like him and Kathryn. He freaked out, the screaming was horrendous. He had to be sedated. The twins escaped into drugs after that. Their relationships were made rocky, permanently. And before you ask, no Steven never wanted a divorce. He felt there'd never be another woman who'd allow him his…uh…extracurricular activities without complaint.

"And Kathryn and I were no longer seeing each other. Ours was nothing but a short fling and we became careless. So she conceived. She and Steven were still having sex so it was believable and Steven never thought twice. And what you heard in the scene was true. It was I who paid all of their rehab expenses. Steven refused to pay for anything for them after that. And, yes, even the apartment. It's in Steven's name, but I pay the three thousand a month mortgage."

Frank hesitated in an effort not to sound judgmental and moistened his lips before he spoke. "And you still remained partners in business and otherwise?"

"Yes. Money and our fun trumped all. Even family." Manning paused. "So I guess that does make me a creep."

♥≫♥≫

Sam entered the section where AriellaRose's room was in the psychiatric ward. The stark whiteness of the walls, and how they blended with the staff's white uniforms, jolted her. The boundary between human and concrete seemed to have faded. She had to consent to a mini search that meant she had to walk through a scanner. Even though she handed in her weapon to be put into a lock box, the metal studs on her pants and jacket triggered the alarm. The hefty security guard looked at her as if she should have known better. She had, and thought about it after she had gotten to the precinct, less than a mile from the hospital. Frank had placed her on the approved visitors list, so the guard let it slide and admitted her into the wing. Frank also told her that everything in the room was recorded, visually and audibly, so she left her recorder in the car.

She walked into AriellaRose's room. It was a little smaller than her private one at the hospital with the same colored walls. Light green. There were some oceanfront lithographs on the walls. Not too bad.

AriellaRose faced the door when she heard Sam enter. "What do you want?" She crossed her arms across her chest, laying them on top of the white sheets. She didn't bother to sit up.

"Well, at least you're not restrained."

"Yeah. Where the fuck am I going to go?"

"Nowhere. So as long as you know that, we'll talk for a while. Have some things to discuss with you."

"You can sit over there. I'm not talking."

"We just met with Jaye Manning. Sorry you had to find out the way you did. I never went through anything like that, but I can imagine how it made you feel."

"Yeah, well. He's more of a dad to me than Steven was."

"That's a plus."

"I guess."

"I need to show you something." Sam retrieved the white band in a manila envelope with the clear plastic window from her tote. "Recognize this by any chance?"

AriellaRose stared. "No. Not at all." Her face reddened, redder than a beet—a sweet roasted beet, as two minutes of silence passed.

"Know where we found it?"

"Where?"

"Near where your dad's body was dragged and left."

"I'm not feeling well. You need to leave."

"Not just yet. There's something more." Sam plucked the second manila envelope that held the amulet from her bag. She turned the clear plastic side to face AriellaRose. "Let's try again. What about this one? We found it on the ground—close to where your mother fell in the parking lot of the church, coming out of her AA meeting with your sister who also fell."

AriellaRose began to cough, then choke. She brought up phlegm that stuck in her throat. Her complexion whitened. Sam ran to the door and screamed for the nurses. AriellaRose's eyes widened, then almost rolled back in her head as she gasped to catch her breath. Her hands clutched her throat. She couldn't dislodge the phlegm. Her gagging made her retch.

It seemed like more than thirty seconds, to Sam, before nurses ran in and shoved her out of the way. One nurse had to fight the panicking AriellaRose to hold her still. The nurse pushed her shoulders flat. AriellaRose punched her away and bobbed her body as much as she could to fight her. A second nurse grabbed her arms, one at a time, and forced wrists restraints on her that attached to the steel security bars on the side of the bed. When both wrists were secured, the second nurse held her face still, pinching her cheeks to open her mouth in order to insert a tube down into her throat to aspirate her. AriellaRose gagged, kicking her legs in protest.

After a minute, the nurse removed the tube filled with mucous. It looked to Sam, like a turkey baster filled with fat. AriellaRose began to catch her breath. The nurse removed the restraints. More mucus spilled out of her mouth into a tray that a nurse handed her. AriellaRose sat up, bent forward, and rocked like an autistic child. Then she pulled up the bed sheet and used it to wipe dribble from her chin. She heaved heavily at first, then her breathing became shallow after a couple of minutes.

Her gaze rocketed evil, that looked like a death wish, straight at Sam. Sam felt the negative surge of energy, but thanks to the pendant around her neck and healing stones in her pockets, the negative energy went right back to the sender. Sam smiled as the jolt of returning energy smacked AriellaRose in the face. She saw AriellaRose's body sway about a millimeter upon impact. Sam's energy was strong and it would behoove AriellaRose to get the message. From the look in her fear-ridden eyes, she had.

"Feeling better?"

"Get the fuck out of here!"

"AriellaRose, please listen to me. Someone, or a few people are killing your family. You and Adam could be next. We want to protect you. I know you work with spells and amulets. Do you know to whom these belong?"

"No, I don't. Get out."

"We know who the amulet belongs to."

"Then why are you asking me?"

"We need you to tell me where I can find them."

"Who? Who the fuck are you talking about?"

"The amulet belongs to an Emma Sanders. AKA Calinda Alexander."

AriellaRose looked stunned.

"You see? We have a contraption that attaches to a computer that reads a fingerprint. Then there's a program called AFIS that identifies the person based on a match. Emma was in the system because she stole drugs from her father's employer, a pharmaceutical company in Westchester. He lost his job. And the judge told her if she did it again, which she has, escalating to murder, there'd be jail time. Did you know that?" Sam paused. "Yeah, sure you did. Is that the hold you had over her?"

AriellaRose kicked her blanket off her. She must have had a surge of adrenalin because she grabbed a plastic knife she had had on her sheet and launched forward to attack Sam with the knife. She almost made it off the bed, but Sam grabbed her arm and pushed her back down. Sam held her down until the psychiatric nurse rushed in and took over. He held her shoulders down and leaned over her, until she calmed down.

While holding AriellaRose securely, he turned his head toward Sam. "You okay, Detective?"

Sam looked up at the man who was bigger and a lot younger than Khaos. She read his name plate. "Yes. Thank you, Jake."

He gave AriellaRose a hard stare. "Are you putting her under arrest?"

"Actually, I'm not. She's been through hell. Between her meds and what's been happening, I'm going to let it slide. Just a woman-to-woman courtesy. Is she allowed visitors?"

AriellaRose looked stunned, stayed quiet and attentive.

"Only if they're on the approved list."

"Um, is she allowed phone calls?"

"Not in this ward. No way."

"Jake, is it possible to bend on this? I mean, AriellaRose has just gone through some major trauma losing her family. She needs the comfort of friends. Who else does she have to turn to? Please? Can you cut her some slack?"

He sighed, as if in deep contemplation. "All right. I'll return her phone. I have it at the nurses' station. AriellaRose, I'll give you your phone to make two calls, max. Then I take it back. Clear?"

AriellaRose looked confused but nodded.

"Come on, Detective. She has to rest now."

"Feel better," Sam said as she left the room with Jake.

When they got to the nurses' station, Sam felt both relieved and uncomfortable. "Thanks, Jake, for going along with this. We know she arranged for these murders. I hate the deceiving part. But she's in custody, so to speak, and we need to find her partners."

"No problem. With the warrant Doctor Khaos just brought over, her phone is already tapped, location services turned on. And we have that other thing, for just in case. So good luck, Detective."

"Thanks." Sam left, head down, knowing she was doing a wrong to make a right.

CHAPTER 24

For whatever reason, AriellaRose understood not to cause a problem with Jake. He would not be as soft or consoling as Tattooman. She had already experienced his hard hands around her. He didn't hesitate to demonstrate his strength. Fuck him, her ribs still hurt from his grasp. Those eyes alone, in that piercing dark brown, conveyed there was a very hard man who lurked behind them. From the screams she'd heard from the patients next door and down the hall, he must deal with men three or four times her size, and with multiplied craziness. He probably considered her a druggie with mood swings. Big deal. She'd be a piece of cake for him to handle. She still had no idea why she was committed. She'd had an angry outburst. So what? Hadn't Tattooman ever seen one of those? She looked toward the door when she heard it open.

Jake entered the room and handed AriellaRose her phone without saying a word.

She looked up at him in his pure white uniform and gave him a hesitant stare. "Thank you."

"Okay. You have two calls," Jake told her. "A few minutes each. Nothing more. You have no idea how lucky you are. Detective Wright really likes you and she wants to get you out of this mess. And to keep you alive. She's probably your only advocate right now. Understand that?"

"Yes, I know. I am thankful for that. She's the only one who wants to help me. Don't worry. I understand. Can I call later? My friends are working and their bosses don't want personal calls. I know how worried they must be about me."

"Sure. Okay, then. I'll take the phone back and you buzz me when you're ready." She placed the phone in his open hand. "Try to get some rest." He started to leave the room and turned back when AriellaRose pushed the sheets off her and got off the bed. "Where you going?"

"Bathroom. I feel like I'm getting my period. Got my pads in here." She lifted her bag. "It's the only thing you let me keep, except for my panties." *I'm not waiting till my friends get off from work, you dirt bag. The bitch detective is way too close and I've got to take care of business.*

"Okay. Go." Jake left the room with quick strides.

In the hall, he sent a text to Sam. *No go. I still have the phone.*

Crap. Got the bug in place, though, right? Sam responded.

Yes. In the paper roll, Jake answered. *Was in place when you were here. Dr. Khaos had someone in housekeeping do it, so we'll have to wait and see. I'll keep you posted.*

AriellaRose disconnected the IV pole, wrapped the cord on the hooks below the monitor and slid the pole to the front of the bed. With her bag in the pit of her arm, she dragged the pole close to the bathroom door. The cord was long enough for her to enter the bathroom and leave the pole outside. It was about a foot taller than the door frame. She closed the door as tight as she could without squashing the IV tube.

Thank the universe there were no recording devices in here. At least that's what they had told her. She'd inspected the bathroom before and hadn't seen any. The tiles were a pristine white on the walls and in the shower stall. The curtain had a striped black and white pattern. She searched again for anything that looked out of the ordinary around and under the sink, in back of the toilet. She bent down and let her fingers roam around the pipes. Nothing.

She took out a large plastic bag of sanitary napkins from her tote bag, pulled back the tab at the top of the bag, and removed twenty heavy flow napkins that were individually wrapped. Next, she pulled out a small smartphone that lay on top and in the middle of about fifteen more pads.

"Thank God, all these psychiatric nurses are men. They wouldn't have thought to go near this. And another thank you, Aradia, for no scanner. Ah heck, they knew I couldn't have anything on me. I'm almost naked under this crap gown. Sorry, Hecate, can't forget you. Thank you for making me aware to always carry this hidden phone. Actually, what would I do without my Goddesses of the Dark? I'm really blessed."

First she sent a text. *Get my message 2 L. What I told U yesterday. Last contact.*

She stared at the number before she made the call. She was pissed. Her beholden fucked up. They would pay. Definitely Flower, Emma, Calinda. Who cared what she called herself now? AriellaRose's mind wandered to the consequences she'd be dealing out, visualizing Moon and Cloud binding Flower to the restraining poles. Both wrists and ankles. Flower being stripped naked. Her clothing cut off with shears. Cold, sharpened shears that would poke and scrape against her bare skin, preparing her for the worst that was to come. Her wails, asking for forgiveness, knowing it would be to no avail. The thin, sharpened blades, two at a time slicing through her delicate brown skin. The blood oozing. She'd remind them to make sure they didn't overlap on healing cuts. She wanted fresh ones to remind Flower of her disobedience.

How many cuts should I delegate as the punishment?

That she'd have to think about after she spoke to them. After all, she was a fair leader. Her punishments were always warranted. Chills went through her. She held onto the sink with both hands and closed her eyes until the terrifying waves of energy ceased. It was almost as scary as an orgasm. She was so pissed. But which one lost the band? Now they had an ID with the amulet. And that bitch talked way too much. *The fuck-ups stop now.*

Oh Aradia.

She couldn't think straight. Her thoughts jumbled in her brain. *Who would do what to whom?*

She had to plan. Had to be the one who gave the orders. She had been the one they depended on to make sure everything went as planned. She was their leader. The Warrior. It sucked she couldn't do this from her ritual room. She tapped the call key.

Cloud answered the phone on the second ring. "Ram, where are you?"

"In a psych ward. They got an ID on Flower. She lost her fucking amulet but which one of you bitches lost your wristband? It was in the park, the three of you were there."

From the pause on the other end of the line, AriellaRose sensed Cloud knew.

"I have mine. I swear. And so does Moon. I saw it when she pulled the trigger on Valerie."

"Where are you now?"

"At the warehouse, packing orders."

"The three of you?"

"Yes," Cloud whimpered.

"Send me a group pic in a text of your wrists showing the bands. Now."

Less than a minute later the pic came through. Cloud had her band as did Moon. Flower's brown wrist was bare.

"I don't have time to stay on the phone to listen, but do the necessary, now, in the back room. For the amulet and band. Make sure the floor is covered and get rid of the tarps. And no Blue to mask the pain. I'm doing without it and so can she. Different ones. On virgin skin. I expect her to bleed—a lot."

AriellaRose disconnected the call. She placed the phone back into the bag, replaced the napkins, re-sealed the top, then sat on the toilet. Fuck. She'd surprised herself. She did get her period. Soaked through her gown and panties, too. Damn, she felt wet. *Thought that was the thrill.* She depressed the emergency nurse's alarm in the bathroom.

Jake came in ASAP. "AriellaRose, what's going on? What's taking you so long?"

"I did get my period. My stomach is killing me and I soiled my gown."

"No problem. I'll get you another one." He pulled one out of the closet. "May I open the door?"

"Yes."

He opened the door, stuck a hand in with the gown, and she took it. "Okay, leave the soiled one on the floor," he said. "Have extra underwear?"

"Yes, in my bag."

She planned to tell them she had changed her mind about making calls. Leave it to that bitch Detective. She had probably gotten a warrant to wiretap her calls. But they'd never find this number. Yeah. She was one step ahead of them. She planned to stay that way.

☙☙☙

Sam, Nick, Frank, Withers, and a two man team of crime scene investigators, stood staring at AriellaRose's impressive brownstone in Park Slope, attached on both sides with brownstones in similar gothic designs. The tree-lined street was definitely the higher end of the neighborhood. Sam unrolled the blueprints they had gotten from the realtor. Five floors, one room on each floor with a finished basement. First floor, living room and half bathroom; second floor, kitchen; third floor, master bedroom and full bathroom; fourth floor, guest bedroom and bath; fifth floor, another bedroom. No bath. Black wrought iron security bars with antique scrolling spread about two inches apart on each, encased all of the windows. A small balcony extended from the master bedroom floor. The building's beige tone projected a calm feeling. One that was probably the opposite of the happenings inside.

Sam took charge. "Okay. Need to find the location of the warehouse. I can just imagine what they're doing to Emma and it isn't pretty. And I want to read that text. Good thing she didn't find the device inside the toilet paper roller. Let's do this."

"No," Nick said. "We need to wait for ESU to clear the building. She's savvy enough to do what she's done, no telling what she could do to her place to wire it."

"You're so right," Sam replied.

Withers snorted. "Don't become overzealous. That'll make you careless."

She stared at him. "Yes, I got it. Thank you for the second reminder. So where the hell are they?"

"Rookie, listen to me. I know you're far from hardened, but this Calinda, she's a murderer, multiple times, no sympathy from the rest of us."

"She's still a human being. Any news on the text?"

Nick frowned. "Yeah. Her back was to the camera. Her body concealed it. Damn! Okay first things first. But we'll get a warrant for the phone."

The ESU van pulled up. Men in full gear—helmets, body shields, Kevlar vests—exited quickly. They dressed as if they were entering a war zone. Three men nodded to the awaiting team and plodded up the ten steps. Sam followed them. With a hand-held electronic device, one of the men focused the laser around the door. He listen to the device and heard nothing to halt the inspection of the premises. He put out his hand to Sam for the key and then motioned for her and the team to back away. Sam stood, defiant. Frank bolted up the steps, lifted her up in one arm, sprinted down, and carried her across the street. He put her back on her feet, firmly. She scowled at him while everyone else laughed. The ESU cop waited until they followed his directions and shook his head at Frank's display.

Sam pulled out binoculars from her bag. She intended to view first hand, no matter what. She focused the lens. The ESU cop held a device to an alarm box on the wall above the doorbell. He must have decoded it, because a minute later, he depressed the right keys. Sam shifted her view. She saw the red light on the keypad turn to green. But her wait wasn't over, yet.

He put the key in the lock. It was a double bolted security lock. The realtor told them that. The cop stepped back. Checked again with his monitoring device, turned the key. He opened the door about an inch. No wires. He entered the first floor, with his two team mates following.

Sam shifted on both legs. After about five minutes, which seemed like an eternity, Nick got the "all clear" signal in his ear-wig.

"We're on."

Sam raced ahead of them and bolted up the steps. They entered the first floor and scanned the room. Nothing that unusual. Leather couch, love seat, ottoman, all in a bright apple red. Glass coffee table with finger print marks. Crime Scene noticed them before her and were on it.

The walls were off white. The floor was a natural sand colored wood. Overall, good taste. With gloves on, Sam walked over to the knickknacks on the end tables. Every accessory was in red. Small plates, bowls in a red milk glass, bud vases. But very nice. Primary colored abstract oil paintings hung on the walls.

To Sam they were eerie, irregular patterns, colors looked splashed on the canvas with red, being the dominant color, vomited on top.

They ascended a black, wrought-iron spiral staircase in the middle of the room to the second floor, the kitchen. Sam stopped dead. This was striking. Red veining within the white marble on the counters, white cabinets in a galley construction. Appliances on the counters, all with red bases. The usual, blenders, mixmaster, toaster, confection oven, coffee maker. Lighting fixtures on silver bases hung from the ceiling, with the bulb ornamentation covers all in red. A round kitchen table in a painted red wood was surrounded by six red upholstered swiveled arm chairs.

No clutter. No mail left carelessly on the counter or table. No dishes in the sink.

Frank seemed to be taking it all in. "Doesn't look like a home of a depraved murderer."

"You're telling me. I want to know her decorator. Upstairs to her master." They hiked up another spiral staircase, larger than the first. "You know? With all this stairs climbing, you'd think she'd be in better shape." She pulled her grasp from the landing. "Fingerprints, guys. Maybe they all went upstairs."

The master bedroom must have reversed Frank's initial impression. He stared, standing in one position, his gaze circling around the room, in sync with Sam's. Everything in red—headboard, bed frame, bed linens, comforter, red wood dresser, night tables, red based and shaded lamps, red around the mirror over her dresser, and red walls.

Frank stared at the wall behind the dresser. "This just hit me guys, in this room, all blood red—at all stages of blood hitting oxygen. Some dark purple veins designs hand painted throughout the walls. Looks like the shade of blood drawn through a syringe. Then these darker splotches on the walls, like oozing blood that had dried. These other reds look as if they were letting blood out of cuts." He moved to a corner near a window. "Hey, over here. See the splatter? Resembles blood spraying from bullet wounds."

"Glad we had the good doctor with us," Withers mumbled.

"Holy crap! This is too much. What the heck does all this red mean?" Nick exclaimed.

"Okay," Sam began. "Um, red is the color of Aries. They can be violent, but there are violent traits in each sign. The Warrior. And blood. What do you think, Frank?"

"Oh, man. The first thing that hits is anger. No matter *what* the sign. This woman is turbulent. Anger rules all of her actions. Overwhelming. I get the feeling she has murdered before. Not orchestrated it, but she herself. It's that strong. Maybe she had another partner, a fourth that she had disposed of. Or fifth. Or sixth. Nothing would surprise me. All I know, is I'm glad she's where she is. I'm putting a call in to Jake to secure her room, completely. Nick, make sure you get that warrant for the cell phone she used." Frank moved off to the side to put in the call to Jake.

"Nothing would surprise me, either," Sam went on. "Hear me out, please. What if—what if, each line, each marking, each splatter—" She pointed to the splatter. "That it's all symbolic of a cut or kill she made. She told them to cut Emma. Maybe they're trophies? Have Crime Scene count them. Just a thought."

Wither nodded in the affirmative.

Nick and Withers followed Sam up the next spiral staircase. Crime scene investigators were already working the two lower floors and putting out markers. When Sam, Nick, Frank, and Withers got onto the landing, they stood in awe of an open closet. The entire floor held clothing racks.

Sam counted ten. Casual clothes, dressy, sports clothes, evening wear, some racks had size labels on top. "Hold on. All these sizes are too small for AriellaRose to wear. And the lengths appear to be too long for her height." She pulled out the rack on rollers that mimicked the clothes worn at the Mason kill. Suits, jackets, blouses, pants, different shades of browns, grays and blues. Each piece was labeled with laundry tags with markings. Sam couldn't decipher them on first glance. She picked up the sleeve on a black leather jacket that matched the witness statement.

A manila tag on the cuff read *Thurs. 3 p.m., C.* "What does this mean?"

Frank took the tag between his gloved fingers. "Three p.m. Thursday was the time of the Mason kill. C, not for Calinda. This woman is taller. About the five-tenish in height, the witness described. What the heck? How many aliases do these women have? Tell Crime Scene to bag all of this."

"Believe me, they will." Sam started reading tags. "Wait a minute. Three p.m. on Thursday for Mason, four to five a.m. for Steven Larcon, 10 a.m. for Valerie and the Mrs." She thought hard for a moment before she let it out. "Okay, guys. Another reason he'd commit me, but hear me out, please."

"Go ahead, rookie."

She sneered at Withers. "These murders happened in what we call 'the moon in Mars conjunct hour.' It's the hour in which planned murders will be successful. She's using black magick to persuade these women to kill for her. No, it's not actually working. They're suggestible. But—and it's a big but—the hold she actually has on them is that she knows about their past murders. They'd better do as she says or she'd turn them in. Obviously she set it all up, prior to her hospitalization. They knew whom to murder and what to wear. They must have access to the house even when she isn't here. They'd have to come in to pick up an outfit. Um, on the racks, tell Crime Scene to note any spaces between them. Maybe there was a outfit there, that was just removed for another kill. And find the spare key they use for entry.'"

"Okay, I follow but what do you mean by 'what we call'? Nick asked.

Um, so Nick listens. "I practice Dianic Wicca, white magick. This guy—" She tilted her head at Frank. "—would think it's meditation, the mind body connection, which it is. If I saw her ritual room, I could tell you everything. Possibly even ID the other two women. But I'd love to read all the tags, too. The times would be when the kills occurred. There's an hour for each one. How much time do we have?"

"As much as you need," Nick encouraged.

Sam scanned the racks one at a time. "Okay, can't do it all now and do it justice. Get everything bagged and labeled. Tell Crime Scene I need tags photographed, size on outfits, actually the outfits, photographed. I could possibly find previous murders. Um, ritual room, basement."

"How do you know it's in the basement?" Nick asked.

"Mine is." Without hesitation, she skipped down two flights of stairs to the living room. Go downstairs yet?"

"Not yet, Detective. Waiting for directives. This isn't a crime scene."

"Maybe. Maybe not." Sam's gaze scrutinized the hand railing leading to the basement. This one was the original red-brown mahogany. She saw smudges on the hand rail. She yelled. "Fingerprints, here!"

An investigator perked up and laughed at her attitude, but he came running with the portable fingerprint ID unit. She backed up into the living room to give him space. He photographed about ten sets of prints. "Give me a while. Don't go downstairs yet." He connected the unit to the laptop and connected to the AFIS database.

Damn, the basement was the room she most wanted to inspect.

A Black Magick coven?

She had never been in one. The anticipation made her hands clammy. She slipped both her hands into her pockets, pulled out of her right a clear quartz rough stone, and grasped it to her heart to cleanse her aura. She replaced it in her pocket. Out of her left, she pulled a black tourmaline tumbled stone, and a rutilated quartz, also tumbled. They would definitely protect her from absorbing any negativity from the room. She couldn't afford to get sick.

She was so preoccupied in meditation that until she finished and looked up, she hadn't noticed Frank watching her every move.

Yup. I'll be next to be put into the psych ward.

CHAPTER 25

Leonardo Philetano wore the short-sleeved buttoned-down orange shirt and elastic waistband polyester pants of a maximum security prisoner as three hefty guards dragged him into the solitary visitation area. If it weren't for the guards' hold on him, he wouldn't have kept his balance. He had only been here a week, but they sure had done a number on him. The drugs they had given him to calm his anger didn't mix well with the detox meds. Confusion overtook his brain. He didn't care what they did to him. He'd be spending the rest of his life in here, anyway.

Fuck his father, the big shot Paulo Philetano. Fuck his brothers. His attorney had told him about the Steven Larcon case and that some bitch detective put his girl in the hospital. Well, fuck that Samantha Wright, too.

He gazed through the bars to the other side of the visitors' lounge, where minimum security inmates were allowed some contact with their visitors. Thirty inmates, at least, sat at red, green, or gray tables, matching their uniforms, with seating for each visitor. Three max. Couples had a three second hug, held hands. Daddy's held their little children on their laps while the Mommy and Grandma wept. It was Tuesday afternoon in Manhattan and his visitor had just arrived with only ten minutes left.

Two correction officers supported Leonardo under his arms, guiding him to a stool by the bars, while the third stood in the at-ease position by the door. They sat him down and backed off. His body swayed back and forth, out of control. He stared vacantly into the eyes of his visitor. All he could manage were blinks, at thirty second intervals in slow motion, and nods. He couldn't get any words out.

A gong, like a church bell, echoed through the halls. His visitor got up and left.

Leonardo only hoped his visitor had understood his message.

❧❧❧

Sam paced around the living room. Crime Scene had brought up bridge chairs from their van for her team to sit on. The men sat. She couldn't. This excited her. This reminded her why she wanted to become a detective. The action. The analyzing. The uncertainty. Teaching had become too predictable. Boring. She loved the children, and all, but her life wasn't complete. Now her fulfillment was getting closer. At least she felt she had a reason to get up and go to work every day. Every day would be an adventure. She tapped her foot on the wooden floor and checked her watch every few seconds.

Come on, Sam. It's only three seconds later than the last time you looked. Let these guys do their job. She had to scold herself to give herself a dose of reality. After thirty minutes, she got some news.

"We have IDs, Detectives!" The investigator shouted from the top of the stairs leading to AriellaRose's living room.

Sam, Frank, Nick, and Withers surrounded him.

"Okay, AriellaRose Larcon, Emma Sanders, who we had, and these two new ones. Meredith Cummings and Rachel Hawthorn."

"Cummings is the one I met in AriellaRose's hospital room," Frank said.

"She's wanted for killing her john in a Vegas strip club last year. And this Hawthorn is wanted for killing her grandmother. All gems."

Sam nodded. "That's the hold AriellaRose has on them for sure. I'm going downstairs."

"Be careful, Detective. It sure as hell is eerie down there."

Sam grinned from ear to ear. "Not for me."

Her gloved hand lightly touched the poles on the left side of the stairwell that ran from the top to base of the steps. Again, red-brown mahogany. She paused after each step, one foot in front of the other, as she gazed at the rose toned tiled floor. She noticed specks of dried wax on the tiles. She stood at the base of the steps, taking it all in. The space was massive. Easily thirty-five feet by twelve. Unbelievable. This was the same design and wood she had in her own basement. Only hers was smaller, by maybe about ten feet. The time this house and hers were built must have been the same. The late 1920s, early '30s. She was mesmerized by it. Her eyes scanned robotically as she analyzed everything.

Oh my God. This is awesome!

She turned left from the stairwell and approached a stand-alone bar. This was AriellaRose's ritual altar.

Oh my God!

Again, the same as hers. The engravings in this wood were more ornate than in hers, more Mediterranean. Hers was more colonial in style.

Wait till Frank sees mine. Uh, oh.

Frank, Nick, and Withers stood in the center of the space, not getting it. Sam had one word to describe their faces. Bewildered. She signaled for them to come over. "Listen as I explain all this. And with an open mind, please."

She heard a crunching sound as Frank moved over. She looked down. "Okay, Frank, you just stepped into a ritual circle, actually desecrated it."

He examined the floor and smiled. Nick and Withers didn't share the same enthusiasm.

"It's salt crystals, to keep away any energy or entity that would prevent their ritual from going smoothly. Look here on the mantle. The same amulets. She must have just made these. Don't know if she gives them a fresh one for each kill or for each ritual. The ritual she did for these kills had to include all of them. Here's why." Sam stared at the candles. "Oh, no. There are five, seven-knobbed candles around the main one. One more murder to go."

"Rookie, be a little more specific for us non-believers. Okay?"

"Okay, these candles are called seven-knobbed. You burn one knob, one for each day of the week. There's four more knobs to go. Obviously she snuffs the candles before she leaves the house. That's why there's so much candle left. There's the center one. I think the five surrounding it are for people. Black for evil. Red for Aries. To have the energy and strength to carry it through. It's color symbolism. They have candles in every color, depending upon what you want to accomplish. So I'd interpret it as five murders in seven days. Today makes seven days. So today or tomorrow will be another kill. There could be some leeway. We have to find out who."

"Adam?" Nick asked.

"Don't know," she said. "Would she kill her twin?"

Frank jumped in. "Usually, no. But, hey, look at the Gemini case. Barbara Montgomery did it," he explained. "But, on the other hand, they had been separated at birth. One had a great life, she, the killer, a life of anguish. These two were raised together."

"Hold on. Hold on." Sam paused for a moment. "Got an idea. Aries. The Aries myth. A Golden Ram was begged by Nephele to save her children. The evil stepmother wanted them killed. As the Ram was crossing the strait, one of the kids, Helle, fell off his back. The son, Phrixus, though safe, was ungrateful and killed the Ram as a sacrifice to Jupiter. The theme is ungratefulness and that's a negative Aries trait. Now, who has helped the twins but been totally unappreciated?"

"Jaye Manning," they all said simultaneously.

"I'm putting in a call to get him into PC." Nick went upstairs to get better reception on his phone.

"It fits. Meghan Mason tried to help her out, too, and gave her employment. And I'm sure Valerie, and even her mother at times, weren't all bad. Ooh. Ooh. The evil stepmother. Mrs. Manning. Tell Nick to get her into protective custody, too."

Frank sent a text to Nick. Sam stared at him. "What? I want to hear what you have to say, too."

Withers snickered. "What else, rookie? Though I'm probably not going to be able to call you that for long."

"I like that. Look at all these oils here. They're labeled with purposes. This one says, Death Commanding Oil." Sam opened the bottle. She sniffed. "Yes. Jasmine, basil, and pennyroyal. What she used on the amulets. These are the oils of Hecate, the Goddess of the Dark. Well the jasmine and basil are. This is Hecate's statue. Isn't she beautiful? Look at the engravings to show the pleats in her gown. She's holding torches. Wow." She lifted up the ten-inch-tall statue.

In a child-like trance, she was oblivious to the stares of the men. "She's made from resin. I have several, but not this one. And here's Aradia, the queen of all witches. Wow, look at these oils. Listen To Me, Beg Me, Do As I Say, all commanding. None asking for peace, prosperity, or love."

"She actually thinks these work? You actually think these work?" Withers asked.

"Yup. They do in combination with a ritual and with someone trained in the right way to perform it. AriellaRose probably went to a coven to learn. There must be one in this area. And she may have met other women who she used and disposed of. Something to investigate if need be. And she wanted me to do a spell on Tattooman, here."

Frank's eyes opened wide.

"Yup. A sex and love spell."

He returned a wickedly sexy grin that Sam knew even Withers would understand. "Won't have to."

"I know that and I didn't." Sam winked at him before she looked toward the benches. "Oooh. Three pillows. Each one of her beholden—yeah, that's what she'd call them, because they are beholden to her since she knows their secrets. There'll be finger prints." She walked over to them. "Um, all paisley, multicolored. She didn't use their signs. That's because she's the only one who matters." She picked one up. *BlackCloud* was sewn on the upper right hand corner. "BlackCloud, that's her Wiccan name." She picked up the second pillow. The label read *BlackFlower*. The third pillow was labeled *BlackMoon*. She paused for a moment. "Okay, I bet BlackRam is AriellaRose's Wiccan name.

Frank hiked his eyebrows. "And you know that AriellaRose's name is BlackRam, how?"

"Just a hunch. Black cause the rest have it and she's Aries dominant. The symbol of the Ram. Her fashion lines is Aries Fashions, too, remember? There's got to be a laptop here somewhere. Now we have to match these to their IDs. Bet there'll be DNA transfer from their backs. Get these processed ASAP. Oooh, I know. I bet the C on the outfit is the initial of the Wiccan name. Which ones was that? Who's about five feet ten?"

Withers found the ID. "Okay, the shooter of Mason, the one five ten, Rachel Hawthorne is this here, Black Cloud. So how does that help us?"

"Don't know yet. Give me a chance to process this. Now where the hell would she keep her laptop? Probably hidden if it has all her client info."

Sam stayed in one place and just pivoted around to check out each area. Her eyes scanned the tiles beneath the bench, the open wall units that hugged the side opposite the steps. At closer look, the shelves held design books, probably ones she had kept from school. The bookshelf next to it held metaphysical and Wiccan books. Sam recognized many of the same titles she had.

Damn! We really do have things in common.

Sam thought for a moment about where she could have wound up if her mind and actions had gone to evil. She shook it off, not wanting to address the negative realm, and walked behind the bar. "This could have been a wet bar had it been hooked up."

She checked the compartments which turned up empty. She looked around and opened the cabinets on the wall behind the bar. No files, just Wiccan supplies.

She listed the items. "Crystals, jars of dried herbs, different sized and colored candles, chalices, incense and holders, oils, parchment paper, Hathor's Mirror, meditation DVD's, several crystal pendulums, different Tarot decks, different sized knives. The usual Wiccan tools."

Looking around, she slowed her breathing and found another door to the right of the bar. Her excitement level was high and she needed to be careful. She had to exert a little pressure to push the door open. It squeaked from the top bolts.

She wandered into the laundry room—dryer and washing machine that drained into a slop sink. The sink was rusty around the rims of the hot and cold faucets and the drain, filthy, and full of lint. There was a big crack in the porcelain that looked deep enough for water to seep through to the floor. The hose that hung into the sink had a stocking over the mouth. She guessed it was to prevent lint from clogging the drain. The sink was dry but with that crack it couldn't be functional.

What is the point of the stocking then?

Didn't look like this room had been used in a long time. There was soot on top of the washing machine and dryer. The oil heater took up most of the space. She nodded. That's where the soot came from. To the right of the oil burner, in the corner, was a dirty white metal cabinet that stood about six feet tall. She wouldn't run her fingers over it, but the smudges looked like oil soot, as well. She exhaled a deep breath and grabbed onto the handle of the cabinet, which pulled apart at her touch, leaving her with only a dangling piece to grasp. She tugged the cabinet open.

Bloodied towels fell from the crowded top shelf. She jumped back to the wall behind her in an automatic startle reflex. "Guys, in here, quick!"

Nick, Frank, and Withers shoved into the cramped space. They grimaced at the sight. Sam had counted them, moving her eyes to each one, as the towels laid in a pile overlapping, cross contaminating. Some landed across her toes as they ricocheted after their fall. *Damn! Another pair of my sneakers just became evidence.*

Formerly white hand towels, someone had folded them neatly around an implement of some kind.

"Twenty here. My guess is that knives are in each one. Maybe murder weapons? From more than just ours. And it stinks. Decomposing flesh. The odors from the oil tank masked the human odors, preventing them from seeping through to the rest of the basement."

Nick's disgust mimicked her own. "This case has just multiplied."

"Yeah. Maybe by years," Frank grumbled.

CHAPTER 26

Flower lay naked on a white tarp on the black concrete floor of the warehouse in a commercial district in downtown Brooklyn. Her body temp dropped, clammy from anxiety, and because the stinking landlord kept the heat down low. The colder November air seeped through the bottom of the gate. The draft blew directly on her. There was nothing that blocked the wind. She was in the middle of the space that Arie had wanted kept open. No clutter. She whimpered when her louder moans fell on deaf ears.

The other two women didn't care and the traffic noise, coming in from the commercial area, drowned her out. The cars, beeping, trucks pulling into driveways continued through midnight for some of the shops. And they weren't planning any deliveries here, today.

Cloud, who held the knife loosely in her hand, and Moon both sat back on their knees on either side of her.

"Come on get it over with already," Flower snapped. "Just tell me how many more."

Moon and Cloud exchanged hesitant looks. Moon's eyes looked vacant, but Cloud definitely had something on her mind.

"What?" Flower protested.

"There'll be no more. We gotta think. Ram is locked up in a psych ward. They're going to find us soon. We'll get life without parole. More than her. We did the kills. Just let me take a pic of the cut we made. She'll want to add it to her bedroom wall. I'll send a text. Get me the towels."

Moon stumbled up, walked across the ten thousand square foot space to a cabinet that spread the length of an entire wall, removed a stack of new white hand towels, and returned, all in robotic movements. She handed them to Cloud and sat down, leaning back on her knees, without uttering a sound.

"I can tell you're using again, Moon. You look like a space cadet," Flower said.

Moon didn't look at Flower when she responded. "I am, so? We'll be locked up soon. And I wouldn't mind having that shrink as my doctor. You should have seen him. Even unbuttoning my sweater to expose my—boobs—didn't—interest—him. But—I—could—dream." Her speech slowed and slurred.

"Are you telling me that you started using again, just to have him as your doctor?" Flower asked.

Moon closed her eyes and rolled over onto the floor in a fetal position. They paid her no attention.

Cloud unfolded a towel, dabbed the one twelve-inch surface cut she made on Flower that ran from under her right breast diagonally to her left hip. It had barely bled. No worse than a paper cut. She placed the blood spotted towel over her thigh. Then she dabbed another spot on the cut. She placed that towel over Flower's stomach, not covering the cut she had made.

"Good. She'll think we made a lot." Cloud took a pic on her smartphone. She checked it and showed Flower. "Perfect. Okay, and, there, clicked 'send.' Let's bandage this and get going."

She stared at Moon lying on the floor. Cloud put her finger under Moon's nose and felt her breath. "She's still with us."

Cloud opened a towel, placed it on an untouched part of the tarp, near an outer corner, placed the paring knife in the center. She folded the right side over the knife, then the left side. Next the top over and the bottom of the towel, up. She had a neat bundle. "Okay, we'll go to the brownstone and put this into the cabinet. Arie will be happy we're continuing her quest."

"Yeah, Moon's all right for now. Remember we got another kill, tonight." Flower insisted.

"You're actually planning on doing him? Snap out of it. Maybe if Ram wasn't locked up. We'd have to, or she'd turn us in. Remember, these kills weren't our first show. I could get the death penalty if my kill of my grandmother in Atlanta gets found out. You. You only did her dad and mom. You're safe in New York. Get dressed. We have to get rid of the tarp."

"What are we going to do with her?"

"Ya know what? Let her sleep. She'll catch up with us later."

Flower put on the white long sleeved, low cut T-shirt and

black skinny jeans she had worn to the precinct for her interview. Okay, she'd have to make Calinda disappear soon. At her apartment, she'd shred every paper with that name and close her accounts. She'd tell the banks she was moving. Absentmindedly, she grabbed one end of the tarp while Cloud grabbed the other. They came together in the middle as if they were folding a flat queen size bed sheet. They picked up the corners and came together again. One more time and they had it. Cloud folded the tarp over her sleeved forearm.

"Where we're going to stash this, I don't know," Cloud said.

"All right, let me just make sure we have everything. No we don't. We don't have our outfits for the last kill. When we stop off at the brownstone, I'll run upstairs and get them."

"You still want to do this?"

"Yeah. I want the clout," Flower demanded.

⁊⊱⁊⊱

Emma and Rachel stared out the front window of the Camaro as they looked down the block. They couldn't drive down. It had been cordoned off by that yellow crime scene tape that they've seen quite often lately. From their doing.

"Looks like that puts a damper on our plans." Emma pounded the steering wheel with her fist. "Fuck! What did Arie say to tip them off? She promised we'd get away with it! I didn't give anything away with that bitch detective."

"Yeah. You sure did. Don't bullshit. You said you told her all about that sex club, Arie and Leonardo are an item. And you really thought you could hide that you were fucking her dad and get away with it? They probably found out there is no Calinda Alexander. And you lost your band and amulet? Come on. The cops aren't stupid. They probably have all our IDs by now. Yeah. I'm sure they do. I even said that before." Rachel sat for a moment. "Holy shit. Holy shit. Holy shit. What kind of assholes are we?"

"What are you talking about, now?"

"We sent Arie a text of the cut we made on you. She's in a psych ward." She smacked her forehead with her palm. "We sent the text to the cops! They gotta have her phone."

"So now what the fuck are we supposed to do?"

"For one, I can't add this cut to her collection. That'll be a downer. And it was a good one. I feel bad it won't make it onto the wall of blood. It would have been preserved forever." Rachel sighed. "But we can't do that last kill, either. Don't have the clothes."

"You're really a moron. Know that, Rach? Doesn't matter what we wear on this gig. We get too put together, he'll know something's up. I have what we're using already at my apartment. What's there to prepare? I say we do it tonight. Tomorrow at the latest. So what if it's a day out of plan? I've got to get myself back on Arie's good side. She's wanted him out of her life for ten years now."

"Where do you want to go now?"

"Back to my place. This cut burns like hell. Need to take something."

"Emma! Go back to your place? Are you fucking kidding me? I'm not going back to mine. Hell, no."

"Do what you want. I'll drop you at your car."

❦

Jesus Parvos had gotten the message all right. And several messages from Leonardo's weapon suppliers. Put down anyone he sold weapons to. No trail was to lead back to them. No one left to rat them out.

Okay. Fair enough.

The one on top of the list was a bitch named Emma Sanders. She bought guns and ammo from him and distributed them. The suppliers said to also do her friends. And after the confirmation he got from Leonardo last night in his visit to the jail, another one was dumped in his lap.

Leonardo didn't have to speak. His eye blinks and nods confirmed what he had to do. Jesus had read the papers. He knew the detectives on the Larcon case. He'd been a part of Leonardo's crew long enough to know who he'd want whacked. He had never made a hit for him, but anyone late on payments, Leonardo could count on him to deliver a strong message. Jesus still thought about the guy in the wheelchair.

The one that he had turned into a quadriplegic.

Too bad, Leonardo never wanted Adam taught a lesson. If any one deserved it, it was him. Guess he didn't want the brother of his girl permanently damaged. Mrs. Larcon had quivered whenever he or a member of his crew showed up at their door for payments. Leonardo had never agreed to a drug installment plan for anyone, except for Adam. Guess he really dug AriellaRose.

But Jesus knew who AriellaRose ran with. They were all there when the last deal was made. That wasn't the first time, either. He had met them all when they hung out on the beach at the Jersey shore. Oh, man, their partying at Seaside Heights, back in the day. All behind him now. And this Emma Sanders and the other two cunts wound up on two hit lists. AriellaRose's and the weapons dealers. These kills would really put him up there.

Yeah. He'd finally be able to make his mark. They'd finally be able to count on him to carry through. He put his jobs in order. One. Make that detective, Samantha Wright, disappear. Two. Do the same to Emma Sanders, Rachel Hawthorne, and Meredith Cummings. Three. No, that's four. Five. Bust AriellaRose out of that hospital. He'd need to call his crew in for that one. No telling how many cops were around her now. He hadn't seen her mentioned in the paper. Guess the cops wanted to keep her under wraps. They still hadn't gotten any of the suspects. No one was specifically mentioned in the paper.

Sitting on his worn couch, he looked around his studio apartment. Oh, man, would he like a bigger place. He could afford it. Leonardo and the other street pharmacists he worked for treated him well. He did his job and nothing trailed back to them. That was the way he planned for it to stay. But he had to stay low key. Nothing expensive. He had furnished the place with second and third hand stuff from a consignment store and Salvation Army. He pled poverty and was even receiving food stamps. He made his appearance so outrageous with tats on his neck, and nose, face, and ear piercings, he put it on the state of New York that he couldn't get a job.

What a joke. He grossed more a year than a cop and a teacher put together. All cash. And no taxes. Too bad he had to keep it all in his apartment.

He perked up. Got a major thought. *Whack a cop? Not such a great idea. But she was a new detective. Probably not as skilled as the others. Ah. She'd be easy. Okay. Be smart about this, Jesus. Move the pig down a few notches.*

He'd take care of Emma Sanders first then he'd find the other two. He knew where they lived.

ം૦ം

Sam, Nick, and Frank were anxious. Taking a working dinner break, they sat around the conference table in the War Room in the precinct. Sam and Frank had their usual chef salad, and Nick indulged in a veal parm hero. Withers joined them, carrying stacks of folders.

"Yours is over there, Dingo. Sausage and peppers hero. Just be careful not to drip on the paperwork," Sam warned, receiving a unappreciative glare in return.

"Yeah? Well, I'm starved. So I'm eating first. Smelled the sauce all the way down the hall." Withers placed the files on a shelf behind them and sat down at the table in front of his foot-long hero. He spoke as he unwrapped it. "Okay, Crime Scene is back at the lab. They found the computer in the master bedroom in a dresser drawer. Our AriellaRose must be a techie. She had an app on her smartphone that remotely wiped her hard drive clean. Our guys are smarter. They recovered everything in the slack space. Accessed it. The passcode was easy to crack. Went along with the Aries theme, rook—uh—Wright. Think it's time. You did good. The passcode was Golden Ram 1989. The year she was born. They found a lot. Every order she sent. You were right, Khaos. She probably wanted to make us think the kills were gang related, especially for the first one. She created gang-related attire to the hood. Sent all over the country. Very little in the city. All money was wired to a place in Philly. We could let the dough stay there for a while. Legit business. She paid taxes. Listed employees. Same three women for this year. Now it gets creepy from here."

"Why?" Nick asked.

"She's had the biz three years. There were different women listed as employees for the first and second. We don't know if they are aliases for these three or she eliminated others as need be. But their addresses were different from year to year, so she either had them moved with a new identity or we're going to be looking for nine women, not three." Withers added. And then he took a big bite of his hero. Sauce plopped out onto his tie.

Sam snickered. "Okay. There were enough outfits up there for nine women or more. We could figure out the times and wouldn't there be some DNA transfer on those outfits even if they've been dry cleaned? And we can compare the DNA on those knives and towels. Let's start at the addresses for these three. That should be easy. Nick will get the warrants. He's attached to the hip with

Judge Martinson by now, and I'll direct the teams out to their apartments. We'll synchronize the arrests, so they won't be able to warn each other. How's that for a plan?"

Nick nodded. "Okay, I get it. I'll call the judge after we make it solid. Don't you think we should arrest AriellaRose for conspiracy to commit murder by now?"

Frank swallowed his mouthful of food. "She's locked up tight. All of her personal belongings taken. No pockets in her gown, now. Still on IV, needing meds. A cop is outside her room. Door's locked, so she can't open it from the inside. She's handcuffed to the security railing with her left hand, her non-dominant one. She was having temper tantrums, so I ordered a Tylenol based relaxant. Just to keep her comfortable and calm. I'll go to the hospital with you two if you want to make the arrest tonight. We have more than enough to warrant it. As for Mr. and Mrs. Manning, they both refused protective custody. Couldn't believe that. Even after I told them there was going to be one more hit on someone. Told me, they'll go to their summer house in the Hamptons. They haven't heard from Adam, either. But I agree, we better make the arrest tonight. I think the Manning's wanted to stay around if AriellaRose needed an attorney. Actually, I wouldn't put it past Mr. Manning to already have one on standby for her. Then she won't be able to talk to us at all. What addresses are we going to, with the three beauties? Actually, I'd really like to go to Emma's, Calinda's, whoever it's listed under." He paused to take a breath, pulled the file, and copied the address onto his pad. "Okay, here is Emma Sanders's address. In Staten Island. Off Victory Boulevard."

Withers put down his hero. "Rachel Hawthorne is a Brooklyn gal. Wasn't she the one listed as homeless? Guess she isn't. Coney Island. Down Ocean Parkway, off Surf Avenue. And Meredith Cummings, that southern twit you met at the hospital, Brooklyn, too. Where Flatbush intersects with Nostrand Avenue. Oh, yeah. That's the Junction near the college."

Nick left the table. He sat on the couch, talking on the phone. He seemed to have gotten the person he wanted. Sam watched as he nodded.

"Thank you, Judge Martinson. We'll stop by your office and pick them up…Okay. By the reception desk. We could be there in thirty."

Sam sat back confidently. "I'm all game to pay Emma a visit,

tonight in fact. Maybe we could stop that fifth kill. I'll put in a
call to the teams. Tell them to meet us at the judge's office. I
think, gentleman, tonight we'll solve this case."

CHAPTER 27

The avenue was desolate, and dark. Businesses all locked tight. Delivery trucks parked in driveways. Jesus tugged at the padlock on the closed warehouse door.

Oh, man, is that a big sucker.

He'd need bolt cutters to break that one. The door was a heavy stainless steel. *What the fuck does AriellaRose store in here? Has to be more than fabrics. Are they worth that much to protect like this? What the fuck. Everything in Brooklyn needs to be protected.*

He walked down the entire block length of the front, turned the corner, and went to the back entrance. Through a tiny window, he saw a woman lying on the floor in a fetal position. She had long red hair. That was all he could make out. Certainly wasn't his target tonight. He checked his smartphone. Yeah, she was on his list. Meredith Cummings.

What the fuck? Screw it.

He was no do-gooder. He'd let her lie there. Maybe she'd OD before he had to pull the trigger. He sprinted around the corner, got into his sedan—next stop, Staten Island.

He bet no one would miss Emma, especially if she could leave a so-called friend like this. They'd be happy when they found her dead. Yeah. He was doing the citizens of New York City a favor, murdering one of their scum. One less for them to worry about and he had a feeling, just a feeling, that this was the broad who did Steven Larcon in. Adam didn't give him the details of who did what. He just knew his sister was doing no good. When people started showing up dead, he knew it was her. Finally, she'd admitted it to him, when she ordered the three girls taken out, the other day. What was Adam supposed to do? He wouldn't think of turning her in. Jesus chuckled at what Adam had told him. That AriellaRose was half his soul. If AriellaRose was smart, Adam would be next on her hit list.

Emma was banging Mr. Larcon *and* Adam. What a cunt she was to break up a happy marriage. Yeah, right. The thought of a happy marriage, especially for him made him nearly vomit on his steering wheel. Maybe he'd bang her before he did it.

The ride south on the Staten Island Expressway seemed to take forever, even after rush hour. Finally, he made it to the Victory Boulevard exit. He got off, bore to the left, and, at the corner, made a left turn. About a mile up, he made another left, and her apartment was on the upper floor of a private house. Parking was scarce.

He saw her Camaro in her driveway. He had to drive around three blocks to find a spot. Okay, good. He'd casually walk back to his car after he did it. No sweat. This would be a piece of cake. He pulled his Taurus with a suppressor out of his glove compartment and tucked it under his sweatshirt in his back belt. His jacket would conceal it, no problem. He checked his hair in the rear view mirror, removed his nose and lip rings and eyebrow studs, and put them into his glove compartment. One thing witnesses remembered were face piercings. He'd stand out. No good. Then he pulled his hood over his head to cover his forehead tats and his long ponytail. He pulled the strings around his neck tight. That would work. It was cold enough.

He got out of his car, zipped up his jacket, and did some pretend warm ups, stretches, as if he was going for a jog. People might wonder, but heck, everyone was used to guys jogging around polluted Staten Island. He took off slowly for a block, then jogged faster, and the last block, Emma's block, he slowed. A few people came out of the house next door to hers, but ignored him. He blended in with the rest of the residents—the same age, mid-thirties, looked like a blue collar worker. No big deal. When he saw them pull out in their car, he sprinted up the steps and rang Emma's bell.

A groggy voice answered. "Who's there?"

Sleeping already? Man, it's only nine. "I'm a friend of Arie's."

"Who?" The voice came from a distance.

"Emma, I can't scream it and wake up the neighborhood."

He heard her plodding down the steps, coming to the door.

And sniffles. Then the lock turning. She opened the door. "Who the fuck are you?"

"I'm Adam and Arie's friend, Jesus. Remember we met in the shop last week and in the Heights last summer? I brought you some stuff, girl." He pushed his way past her, ran up the steps into the apartment.

She followed, holding on to the banister. It took her a while to make it up thirteen steps. At the landing, he pulled out a baggie full of Blue and handed it to her.

She stumbled into her apartment after him. "Oh thank, God, Jesus, I'm all out." She took the baggie and stashed it in her robe. "What do I owe you?"

"There are ninety in there. Twenty-seven hundred."

"No problem. Have—a seat. I'll—bring it—out." She wobbled to the bedroom, eyes half closed, as he sat on her couch and looked around.

He stared at his reflection in the mirror on the wall opposite the couch. Damn. He looked pretty acceptable without his piercings. Had a decent build, too. He could have gotten a job in construction. His six-foot-two-hundred-pound frame could handle it. That was, if he wanted a day job. Nah, being self-employed was much better. He definitely had that entrepreneurial spirit. And boxing gave him some legit dough when he could arrange a match.

Emma came out of the bedroom with the cash and handed it to him.

"Why don't you sit down, girl, while I count it?"

"I'm really wiped. I drank a bottle of cough syrup, I was so stressed. Why don't you just shut the door behind you? I'm going to bed."

"I said, sit." He pulled on her arm and, being so wobbly, she fell on top of him. He was stunned for a moment, trying to figure out how to position her. He flipped her around while she lay limp across his lap, got up with Emma in his arms, and laid her face down on the couch. He stretched out her body.

She squirmed and twisted her head to face him but had no strength. "What—are—you—doing?"

After he put the cash in his left jacket pocket, he retrieved a plastic zip tie from his jeans pocket and bound her arms behind her back. Without thinking about it, he yanked his Taurus 9 mm from his belt. The suppressor added two inches. He put the nuzzle at the base of Emma's brain and pulled the trigger, watching his handiwork. Her head bobbed from the force, her chest stopped moving the instant the bullet entered.

"Okay, Mob hit number one. Done," he said, pretending he were marking a list. No emotion. No sentiment.

He searched her pocket. No Blue. He darted into her bedroom and pulled open every drawer. He didn't want to waste time looking, so he re-entered the living room, looked out the window, and, with it clear, opened the door and went down the steps, closing the door behind him.

He grimaced as he hoofed it down the block. Man, was the barrel of the Taurus hot as it pressed against his lower back.

❧❧❧

Sam, Nick, and Frank parked lengthwise in back of Emma's car in her driveway.

Sam grabbed her bag from the car floor. "Okay, let's see if we can get at least one out of three."

For the first time, Nick showed compassion toward her. "Sam, we'll get them, relax. You have to not be so tense. You won't think straight after a while."

She pushed the door to his SUV open. *Wow. Better accept that when I can.* "Thanks, Nick. I'm glad Loo let us keep a watch on the other two. They may have skipped. They know AriellaRose is in a psych ward and their game will soon be over. They're getting careless. I can't believe they sent the text of the cut they did on Emma."

She stood looking around at the congested block. All attached homes. All looked alike. That little wrought-iron-framed porch, just big enough for one person to stand on, up six steps, where anyone else had to stand in a descending line. The neighborhood was lit up by street lights. Leaves blew from the sparse amount of trees.

Then it hit her. She was cold standing there in just a bulky ribbed knit sweater over her blouse and slacks. Better move. She hopped up the steps and rang Emma's bell. No answer.

Crap. Why did I expect anything different?

She rang the landlord's bell.

"Who's there at ten o'clock at night?" The woman's voice shook with fear.

Sam double-checked the warrant in her hand. "It's the police, Mrs. Smith."

She heard footsteps approaching the door. Mrs. Smith opened it wearing a red fleece robe with her hair in curlers.

Oh God, Sam had had her fill of red. "Mrs. Smith. Sorry to bother you so late. I'm Detective Samantha Wright. This is Detective Nick Valatutti and this is Doctor Frank Khaos. We have a warrant to search Emma Sanders's apartment." She handed the dazed woman the warrant.

"What did she do?"

"It's part of an investigation. We may have to speak with you later," Nick told her.

"All right. Wait in the hall while I get the key." A minute later she returned. "Hope everything is okay. She's a good tenant. Not the best. But good."

"What do you mean?" Frank asked.

"Her father pays her rent on time. No wild and crazy parties, but too many men coming and going. I'd be surprised if she didn't have one of those sex diseases. Here you go." She handed Sam the key to the upstairs apartment. "Just slip the key back into the slot on my door when you're done."

They walked up the thinly padded, worn carpeting to Emma's apartment. They didn't have to use the key. The door was ajar. Sam pushed the door open. Emma, with her hands tied behind her and a bullet wound in the base of her skull as she lay face down on her couch in a robe, was not the sight they expected. Sam threw her arms up into the air. Nick checked for a pulse in Emma's neck. None. He grabbed his phone, put in a call to 911, then Withers, who'd call Crime Scene, again.

Frank shook his head. "Is this what AriellaRose meant for the other two to do her?"

"I'm looking around." Sam pulled gloves from her pocket. She went over to the body, looked around, and bent low to the ground. "Bullet casing, edge of couch. Looks like nine millimeter. Only one. I'm leaving it here."

She walked into the attached bedroom. A few dresser drawers were open. Sam ignored them. She headed into the bathroom. Pretty sloppy. Hair tools all over the sink. Assorted brushes. Face creams, anti-acne medications. Toothpaste tube uncapped. Makeup and toothpaste stains in the sink. She pivoted around and noticed an empty bottle of an antihistamine cough syrup in the trash. She hastened to the body and sniffed at Emma's face. "Okay. She drank a bottle of cough syrup, probably to drown the pain from the cut they gave her. Bottle's in the trash."

"Did they make her drink it, so she'd be an easy kill?" Nick asked.

"Maybe, maybe not." Frank walked into the bedroom. "Unkempt, bed not made. Looks like she was in bed when whoever killed her came over." He approached an open drawer. Just underwear. The second drawer, tank tops, shorts. He didn't look under them. "I'd sure like to tear this place apart."

"Me, too. Can't yet." Sam joined him in the bedroom. Something had come over her. She perked up, shook her head, and, with a frown as if she didn't believe it herself, walked over to a covered wicker basket next to the left side of Emma's bed. With the tip of her index finger she raised the lid. She stopped for a moment, appearing dumbstruck. "Frank! Nick! Look!"

They raced and leaned over her. Inside the box was a Ruger handgun, suppressor, box of .380 hollow point bullets, rubber band wrapped hundred dollar bills and a bag of Blue.

Sam frowned. "Why would she drink a bottle of cough syrup if she had this much oxycodone?" She blinked. "I know why! The person who killed her brought her the drugs." She pivoted to the dresser. "After he or she killed her, they went looking for the pills to take them back. They couldn't find them in the drawers and didn't look around this side of the bed. We need prints on this bag."

After an hour of waiting, a team of two men in Tyvek protective gear entered the apartment. At least they weren't dressed for combat. The lead investigator approached her with a smile. "Officer Wright. What have you got here?"

"It's Detective now, Perry. Manhattan Mid-Town South. This case has taken us across boroughs."

His smile indicated more interest than just for the case. "Congratulations! What's going on?"

Sam understood it, too, and glanced in Frank's direction. So had he.

"The vic, Emma Sanders, is wanted in two murders so far. The Steven Larcon family kills. What I need here are whatever fingerprints you find and, of course, the bullet identification. Found a Ruger in the bedroom. Need to know if it was the same weapon that killed Meghan Mason. They used a hollow point.

Need to find the weapons that killed Valerie and Mrs. Larcon. Bullets were thirty-eights. Collect all knives. And there's a baggie of Blue. Fingerprints there, too." She turned to Nick and Frank. "Let's leave these guys to work. First, I want to ask Mrs. Smith if she saw this guy here tonight."

Downstairs, Sam rang the bell.

Mrs. Smith opened the door, as if she had been standing, waiting for them. "I guess it isn't good news. All I want to know is, will I have to find another tenant?"

"Unfortunately, yes."

"Damn it. She's my third tenant this year."

"I just wanted to ask you if you saw any man come here tonight."

"Yeah, a guy. I looked out the window when I heard the bell ring.

"What time was that?"

"You missed him by a half hour. He only stayed a few minutes then jogged down the block."

"Did you get a look at him?"

"No. The porch light is out."

Sam grimaced. "Thank you, Mrs. Smith The investigators will let you know when they're done. We may have to speak with you again." She turned and ran to the car. The temperature had dropped. She jogged in place until he opened the door. "Come on, Nick, open the door and put the heat on."

Once comfortable in the back seat, with Frank next to her, she put her hands in her pocket, leaned back, and closed her eyes. Nick busied himself inputting data into the computer that took up the passenger seat while he waited for the heater to warm things up.

Frank snapped his fingers in front of her face. "Oh, no, you don't, Sam. Not fogging out on me now. You have some things to clear up."

She grabbed his fingers. "I'm up. What?"

"Okay. First. What made you go to the other side of the bed to the basket?"

"I don't know. Intuition, maybe."

"Uh, uh. What kind of intuition?"

"Female, cop. I can't put my finger on it. Does it matter?"

"Well, you didn't look confident. Quite doubtful, in fact. Want to tell me about it?"

"Nothing to tell. Just made a good call."

"You're in denial," Frank intonated.

"Of what?"

"All right, We'll get to that."

Nick pulled out. "We should be there in about forty-five minutes. Never too late to make an arrest." His comment went unanswered.

"And just how well do you know this Perry?"

"Now you're prying."

The trip to the hospital took less than forty-five. They were outside AriellaRose's room by midnight. Frank unbolted the door with the key the security guard handed him.

He assessed AriellaRose with his shrink hat in full gear. *Does she belong behind bars in an upstate prison for life? With no chance of parole? Or should I incarcerate her in a hospital for the criminally insane?*

This decision would weigh on him and he wouldn't make it lightly.

AriellaRose turned toward the door when she saw the three of them enter. Her left wrist was still handcuffed to the side railing of the bed. "What the fuck do you three want?"

Sam got the honor. "AriellaRose, you are under arrest for orchestrating four murders. That's for starters."

"Well, for starters, are you out of your fucking mind? I've been here a week. So how could I have done anything?"

"We were at your brownstone. Found out a lot." Sam read her Miranda rights as AriellaRose looked distant. "Do you understand your rights and responsibilities?"

With her right hand, AriellaRose grabbed an envelope from under her blanket. "Here, read this and shove it up your ass." She turned toward the window.

Sam opened the unsealed envelope and withdrew a formal sheet of paper. She took it over to the door. "Frank was right, Jaye Manning hired an attorney for her."

"Okay. we can't talk to her anymore. Let's go," Nick said.

"I just want to tell her about—"

Nick pulled her away. "No. You can't jeopardize this case."

Frank rubbed his chin. "I can speak to her. Call her attorney, Stan Hartman. I mean now," he insisted.

Nick was more forceful than his usual manner. "Frank, who's side are you on? Prosecution or defense? If it's ours, he won' let you talk to her until he has all the documentation. Listen, we're all tired, out of sorts, and pissed off. I'll put in a call to him to let him know we made the arrest, but I, for one, need some sleep. We'll pick this up tomorrow."

CHAPTER 28

Sam drove down her block at two a.m., cognizant of her surroundings as she always was. Her neighbors cars were parked in their own driveways. She didn't notice any strange vehicles. A single woman living alone in Brooklyn, no matter how safe the neighborhood presumed to be, had to be careful. She paid attention even before the academy. Now, more so, knowing about all of the hidden crimes that civilians never learned about. She pulled into her driveway, letting the car lights stay on as she peered down the path to her garage. She shut the engine, got out of the car quickly, and walked up the steps to her front door, then punched the code to her security alarm, missing a digit. The red button didn't turn green. She realized she was a bit jumpy and in desperate need of some sleep tonight. She tried again. It worked.

She entered the foyer and depressed the keys on the inside box. Worked the first time. She blew out a calming breath. Safe and secure in her own home, she checked the drawer on a wall table to the left of the entry. Glock .40 caliber in place. She sprinted up the steps and into her bedroom and checked both night tables on either side of the bed. A Taurus and Smith and Wesson, both loaded, and in place.

After a relaxing shower, she slipped into bed and pulled the floral print comforter up to her neck. Her mind was reeling. To the case, then to Frank, and back to the case again. She needed to find the fifth vic before it was too late. She needed to accomplish something positive. Her first case as a detective and it was going down the tubes, fast.

The murderers kept doing what they did best and no one stopped them.

Who hit Emma Sanders? Is it Adam or Jaye Manning who is the fifth? Where did the other two women go? Crap.

She needed to sleep. She rolled onto her side into the fetal position that always comforted her under stress, but it took her longer than usual to doze off…

ⵀⵀⵀ

She was trapped in a cave. In the middle of the dessert. She didn't know where. All she saw was blood dripping from the holes in the walls around her. Blood red. Drip, drip, drip. The puddles of blood spread all around her feet. She couldn't move. Her wrists were tied above her head with metal cuffs bolted into the walls of the cave, her feet chained to the floor with metal ankle restraints. Her neck was held still by a tight spiked cuff, also chained to a spike in the wall. Rusty old spikes and chains. That was all she felt against her body. She was cold and clammy. She couldn't move her head. He had stripped her naked. Her T-shirt and jogging pants lay crumpled in a puddle of blood. Where was her underwear? Why was she thinking of that? Her body had not been harmed. She hardly noticed.

He approached her, laughing. He mumbled words she couldn't understand. She couldn't identify him. His face was covered with a red knit ski mask. She scrutinized him, but she could hardly see.

The blood drops from the wall hit her head and rolled into her eyes. She blinked several times to clear her vision. Then she made him out. He wasn't a huge man, nor small. His body was hairless without any tats. He was naked, too. Then she let her gaze travel down and saw it.

He was missing his genitals. Steven Larcon.

He was trying to tell her something. She couldn't understand. No. It was more like she wouldn't let herself understand. She felt as if she had earmuffs on.

From the distance—almost as if in wisps of air, a whirl of air, in gold and silvers—she saw Dara come through to her. She wore her usual sleeveless white flowing gown, with pleats throughout it and a low V neck. Her blonde curls were pulled up, away from her face, held with a barrette at the back of her head. The rest of her waist-length blonde hair cascaded down her back. Dara, her spirit guide, whom she hadn't learned to trust completely. Her spirit guide whom she had been trying to ignore. Her intuition, that she had been trying to deny.

Dara came up behind Mr. Larcon. He pivoted toward her. Dara spoke to him. He responded. Damn! Why couldn't she hear their conversation? Mr. Larcon stepped out of the way. Dara waved her hand and the wrist, feet, and neck restraints dissolved. Sam fell forward into a puddle of blood. She landed in the same position in which runners begin their races, fingers on the ground, knees bent, backside out. She bent her neck up toward Dara and Mr. Larcon. He pointed behind him. What was he pointing to? What was behind him? His past.

He was telling Sam to look into his past.

Sam jolted awake in a cold sweat, rattled from the dream.

Oh my God. Analyze it quick, Sam before you forget.

Dara had sent a clear message. Sam should start trusting her and her own intuition. Steven Larcon had told her to look into his past.

So maybe Adam or Jaye Manning isn't the fifth target.

જ⁄જ⁄જ

Sam, Frank, Nick, and Withers entered the War Room, each carrying folders up to their eyeballs in one arm and large coffees in their free hands. It was exactly one week and five murders since she had entered the rank. She didn't consider that to be a good beginning at all. Folders placed on the table, they all sat in silence.

Sam broke it. "Let's get started. This will be a long meeting." She pulled a ponytail scrunchie from her pocket and tied her hair back. "What forensics have come in so far?"

Withers swallowed before he spoke. "They IDd our guy, whose prints were on the baggie. Jesus Parvos." He turned the file open in the center of the table so they could all see.

"Eww! Tats on his face. Piercings. He shouldn't be too hard to find."

"Hold on, Wright. Not so easy. He's wanted by the FBI and DEA. Parvos's prints were on several of the weapons in the bust of the Philetano car repair shop. Either he's the supplier or the middleman, but whoever he is, his rap sheet indicated he is armed and extremely dangerous. Already spent a nickel in federal lock-up for trafficking weapons. High-powered ones, too. He's a boxer with some heavy hitter matches under his belt. Light heavyweight class. Strong and violent. Was in the box several times for a few months each, when he was upstate. Then he was moved to a different facility, each time. All for fights. He busted up some guards pretty bad. And they were armed. Okay, next, the Ruger we found in Miss Sanders's apartment was the gun used in the Mason killing. Not for Valerie and Mrs. Larcon's. No prints other than Sanders's. That was sloppy. Surprised she kept the murder weapon there, unless she planned to use it for the fifth kill, which I'm not agreeing will happen, based on a candle count."

Sam leaned back in her chair and frowned.

Withers gave her a hesitant stare before he continued. "She did drink the bottle of cough syrup you found. That was good. No other drugs found in her system, so she didn't have time to take one of those Blue. The count was ninety. Enough for her to share and sell. Crime Scene found four semi-automatic handguns and enough ammo for several kills. Serial numbers were filed down but they were able to retrieve them. Researching the sources now. No revolvers. Two revolvers were used for the Larcon women. AriellaRose's attorney has denied you any visits, Frank, until he goes through all of the documentations and evidence. That was to be expected. He'll be meeting with AriellaRose at the hospital today, and don't you dare step foot into that building today. Take a day off, go to your gym. Got it?"

Frank nodded. "Okay. Anything on the bloodied towels we found in AriellaRose's basement?"

Withers flipped through a file. "No. No DNA yet. That could take a couple of weeks. The knives, though, matched about a hundred other packaged ones from the extinct Anderson and Sons found at the brownstone in a locked cabinet behind the bar. We might get lucky if any of the paring knives found in the cabinet match Steven Larcon's cuts. That would mean the rest are trophies, too. Pray for that. It would solidify the case for murder against her. That AriellaRose knew about them. No doubt."

Frank let out a nasal breath. He seemed to be deep in thought.

"What, Frank?"

"Need to figure out what we want to happen. No one has to be told that this is the work of a deeply disturbed woman. She's ill physically, as well as mentally. Do we want her incarcerated in a prison for life or is her attorney going to plead insanity? Killers who take trophies, in her case, bloodied knives from kills or cuts, usually have the trauma it represents in their past. That was done to them on some level. Doesn't have to be physical cuts. AriellaRose isn't a cutter. Cuts must be a mental symbolism. Someone who cut away at her self-esteem. Someone who cut away a part of her life. Definitely someone in her past triggered this and she was holding onto to it until she was able to carry through, maybe financially, until she could afford to pay the others to help her."

Sam grasped onto what Frank had just said. "Speaking of her past. Mr. Manning told us she escaped into drugs at fifteen. We thought she may have been raped at fifteen, since she told you, Frank, she started using then. I'd like to look farther into the family's past, to when the twins were fifteen. Okay. Which folder has the interviews with family? I believe the Allenry-Holmes team was on that. Oh, and, Frank, I got that angry persona out of her when I stressed her. Crazed wouldn't describe it."

"Good to know. Thanks."

After shuffling the folders and examining the cover sheets, Nick handed it to her. "Went through this, Sam. Nothing negative found."

"Not looking for that. Looking for any person who was in their lives ten years ago or thereabouts and was close to AriellaRose. Age fifteen. That's important. Give me a minute, please." She ran her fingers down the page, line by line, turning page after page. "Um, this may be something. Mr. Larcon had two brothers. Mitchell, who's older, told the detectives, and I quote, 'He's close with them as far as parties, birthday and Christmas cards, and presents. But they don't get together and socialize. Not because of time. But because he didn't like 'Steven's ambition and lifestyle.' But Mitchell said that their younger brother, Timothy, hasn't spoken to them in over nine years. And when Mitchell asked about the distancing, Timothy never told him why. He gave them the last known address, but it wasn't good. No Timothy to be found. I think we need to add this Timothy to the list. Based on what Frank said, this could be a buried trauma. What do you think, guys?"

Before they could respond, Lieutenant Rojas opened the door. A well-dressed, suited man, with a long braided ponytail, entered with him. Rojas left and closed the door behind him. Frank smiled from ear to ear and jumped up from his chair. He and the suited man gave each other bear hugs.

"How are you doing, bro?" Frank asked.

"Man oh man, Khaos, didn't expect to find you here. Thought you'd be in an ER somewhere, patching up people."

"Used to. Forensics and psychiatry grabbed me by the balls and haven't let go. Great to see you, bro." Frank turned toward the group, who sat stunned. "Marcus Willtower. We go back to Special Forces in Iraq."

"Yeah, this guy, here, patched me up a few times."

"More than a few. What are you doing here, bro? I saw in the paper you're DEA now. Come on. Pull over a chair. These are Detectives Nick Valatutti, Dingo Withers, and Samantha Wright."

Marcus nodded. "DEA, New York City, Tactical Diversion Squad."

"Yes. I saw it in the paper you made the Leonardo Philetano bust," Sam said.

"Yes. That's why I'm here. We've got a problem, Detectives. I need you to watch this surveillance video."

He removed a flash drive from his pocket and put it into the laptop on the desk. Sam depressed a remote and a screen came down a wall. The video played on the screen. Inside, the Phileta-no repair shop, with cars on lifts lining the back wall, the scene depicted an SUV with an open trunk in the center of the floor. Leonardo placed weapons into it. One semi-automatic and two automatic handguns with boxes of ammo. Around from the side, Jesus Parvos appeared with a semi-automatic rifle across his chest. He looked edgy, eyes darting around. He was big, ominous-looking, with beady eyes, straight posture, and his finger was steady on the trigger. Emma Sanders jumped out of the driver's seat.

Rachel Hawthorne appeared from the front passenger seat. Meredith Cummings and AriellaRose got out of the rear seat. Emma handed Leonardo a roll of Ben Franklin's in exchange for a bag of Blue. Then Leonardo handed a baggie of assorted pills to AriellaRose. She handed him a wad of bills. Their backs blocked the view.

But he sealed the deal with a hug and long kiss to her. AriellaRose backed away, smiling. The four women jumped back into the SUV and exited the garage.

Willtower sat back despondently. "We've been watching them over six months. This incident took place four days before we made the arrest. The night before the arrest, DEA agents were undercover as customers at the repair shop. From the reports we read, your murder spree started three days after we took Philetano down. Do any of these weapons match?"

Sam didn't hesitate to lash out. "And you're sitting there, telling me you just let this happen?"

"We didn't see it happen. It was on the tapes we watched. These women were on several tapes. This, by far, was the most merchandise transferred. Had we seen it, the bust would have been made right then. We had so much evidence to sift through, we just got to this one last night."

"The DEA can spend over sixty grand a month on surveillance and you had nothing in place to watch this in real time? Do you realize how much drugs hit the streets of the five boroughs because the almighty DEA didn't move faster? You guys wait too damn long! All to nail one person? Five murders, four of innocent people, could have been prevented!" Sam's voice escalated to a bellow.

Willtower blew and jumped up into Sam's face. "You yelling at a federal agent, Detective?"

Sam bolted from her seat and stood tall. "You're damn straight, I am! I'm in charge of this investigation and you'll address me with respect. I don't give a crap how far back you go with your bro!"

"Whoa, Sam. Marcus sit down. We're all stressed. This case has pushed all our buttons." Frank tapped Sam's arm. "Come on, Sam, sit down."

She sat down and stared through Willtower, stone cold. She made the black man turn red. She'd become real good at that lately. "So what are you here to tell us?"

"We have jurisdiction over this case since we've been on it six months. Is there a possible weapons match?"

"Don't think so," Sam said. "And bullshit. Where's Dunnar Vike in this? He's NYPD."

"His division is investigating and turning over everything to the Staten Island District Attorney's office. Intra-agency cooperation, which I see we're not going to get from you. But I'm sure Lieutenant Rojas will have the final word."

"Too late. We arrested AriellaRose Larcon on murder charges last night. She's lawyered up. We're turning everything over to the Manhattan District Attorney's office. And we have an ID on

Parvos. Teams are out looking for him and the other two women," Sam retorted.

"Two women? What happened to the third?"

"Parvos executed Emma Sanders last night. The one in the driver's seat. That's how we got the ID. Prints on a baggie of Oxycodone he had brought her," Sam said, one-upping him.

"Where's the Larcon woman?"

"In a psych ward. In Manhattan," Frank said matter-of-factly.

"How long have you been in rank, Detective?" Willtower asked.

"A little over a week. Why?"

"A week? Okay, that explains it."

"Explains what?" Sam made sure her inflection spewed defiance.

"Your outburst to a federal agent. You didn't know any better. Okay, I'm prepared to make you a deal."

"A deal? With the DEA? Fat chance," Nick said.

"No, seriously. We don't want the hassle with the guy, but the feds do. So it'll be up to you to fight them. I'd like to watch you mouth off to a fed, Detective Wright, and you'll see where it gets you. In cuffs."

"What's the deal?" Withers asked.

"You find, apprehend, or eliminate Jesus Parvos, and you can have the women, including AriellaRose Larcon. We want them on drug trafficking. Murder tops us. So our charges will be added consecutively."

"Deal," Sam said without missing a beat. "I have a feeling there's going to be another murder, but we don't know who the vic will be."

"Okay, then we're done." Willtower got up and left the room without acknowledging them.

Frank looked at Sam. "You did good. Proud of you."

Nick and Dingo nodded in agreement.

Sam pulled the laptop over and Googled Timothy Larcon. "Oh, great. One million, three hundred forty seven thousand. How could he just disappear? I'm giving Jaye Manning a call." She checked the file, made the call from the phone on the desk.

"Hello."

"Mr. Manning, it's Detective Wright. I have some questions to ask you."

"I know you arrested AriellaRose. Her lawyer is seeing her

today. And he advised me against speaking with you."

"Mr. Manning, Doctor Khaos here. We believe there's going to be another murder. We want to prevent that at all costs."

"Oh God. Well, it isn't me or Adam. He's safe here with us."

"Okay, good. Very good. Could you put him on the phone, too? We have it on speaker."

Adam's arrogance hadn't changed. "What do you want?"

"Adam, know where your Uncle Timothy is?"

"Why?"

"We were looking through the files and learned from interviews with your Uncle Mitchell that he had broken off ties with your family almost ten years ago. Mitchell didn't know why. Do you know?"

"Yeah. I know why."

"Tell them," Mr. Manning urged. "They'll find out soon."

"He raped AriellaRose. He forced roofies with liquor down her throat. She didn't know what hit her."

We were right.

Frank and Sam exchanged looks.

"What happened?" Frank asked.

"I found him doing it and pulled him off her. He had already jerked off. I told my dad, uh, Steve, but he didn't want to report it to the police. Said it would look bad for the family business. My mom and he pretended it never happened."

"When did it happen?" Sam asked, thinking about the ten year statute of limitations on statutory rape.

"We were almost sixteen, two months before our birthdays."

"Know where he lives?"

"Somewhere in Queens. I saw him at a tennis club a few weeks ago. Before all this happened. The big one up there. I ignored him and he pretended not to see me."

"Okay, thanks." Frank disconnected the call. "So much for the Aries myth.

"Well, it led us in the direction of who to call. So, okay. Timothy Larcon is our fifth vic," Sam said as the rest of them looked worried.

ᘒᘓᘒ

Nick exited the Belt Parkway at Cross Bay Boulevard into Howard Beach, Queens. Frank and Sam followed in his SUV, and patrol officers from the local precinct tailed. The tennis club wasn't far from the exit. A couple of blocks and they'd be there. The club had confirmed Timothy Larcon was there, right on schedule. Sam was excited she'd be making her second arrest. They had two more months till the statute of limitations ran out, and Nick had deferred the honor to her. Nick pulled into the parking lot, pulled a ticket from the dispenser and drove into a spot. Frank followed, but the local cops in their cruiser parked outside.

They walked into the main lobby, where the sounds of balls smacking onto rackets ricocheted through the building. They headed down the halls with glass-enclosed courts that were occupied with two or four players. The players dressed in the white and blue uniform of the club—men, shorts, and women, short pleated skirts that hit their upper thighs. The remnants of an ammonia based detergent accosted Sam's nose as she passed the men's room. She ignored it as soon as she spotted Timothy playing in a foursome. Yay! She could embarrass him in front of more people.

Sam opened the door mid-game, lifted, and flashed her badge that hung around her neck. "Police! Hold the serve!"

A cranky woman yelled at her. "What the heck, lady?"

"It's Detective Wright, and I suggest you close your mouth, ma'am. I need to speak to Mr. Larcon."

"Well, I'm his wife," the woman retorted.

"Oh, sorry to hear that," Sam muttered to herself. "Mr. Larcon, please come over to the side."

"Sure. Detective. Hey, I know what happened to my brother and his family," he said as he strutted over. He and Sam walked to the bleachers. "We were never close, so—"

Sam cut him off. "Mr. Larcon, I don't know if you know this."

He frowned.

Sam made sure she spoke loud enough so his tennis partners would hear. *Unprofessional, but so what?* "When this crime was committed, in New York City, there was a ten-year statute of limitations on the rape of a minor, as in a niece, which is incest. So, Mr. Larcon—"

Sam didn't get a chance to finish. Timothy bolted to the door, opened it, ran, and was met with a clothes-line-to-his-Adam's-Apple by Frank's rigid forearm. Timothy tumbled backward. His sneakered feet swung out from under him, landing him on the ground, flat on his back. Nick jumped him and flipped him over. Timothy tried to fight as his feet pummeled the wood floor. Nick brought his hands behind his back and cuffed him. He and Frank lifted him up under his arms. Timothy stood trembling.

Sam approached and continued. "Mr. Timothy Larcon, you are under arrest for the drugging and rape of your niece, AriellaRose Larcon, nine years and ten months ago, when she was fifteen and ten months old. Officers, read him his rights and book him."

Two patrol officers read him his Miranda rights and took him outside to their patrol car. Sam, Frank, and Nick left the building as they heard his wife's hysterics inside the court area.

"Wait till he finds out we just saved his life." Frank stretched out his shoulders and twisted his neck from side to side. "Oh, man, do I need a workout."

"Why don't you go, then? We have units out for Hawthorne and Cummings," Nick said.

"Thanks. Hey, Sam, want to go?"

"I don't have my gym gear. It's in my car."

"I have uniforms at the gym. They'll fit."

"Yes. I'd love to. Thanks, Nick."

"I'm going home, too. Don't thank me."

Sam's lips transformed into a sexy smirk. "Finally, I'll have the chance to whip your ass in the cage," she told Frank.

CHAPTER 29

Frank used the electronic key fob to open the ten-foot gate to the parking lot of his gym in central Harlem. The doors swung open and he parked closest to the entrance door. The gate closed behind them. Security lights went on, forming a two foot radius around his Explorer. His was the only car in the forty-space parking lot.

"Where is everyone?"

He grinned and hiked his eyebrows. "Just you and me, princess. Gym closes at six on Wednesday. No one here until six a.m. tomorrow."

She bit her lower lip and gyrated in the seat. "We're spending the night?"

Very good. She's enticed. "Maybe. Maybe not. Depends upon your behavior." He jumped out of the driver's seat and depressed another key. The steel gate to the gym rolled up. He turned around and looked at Sam, giggling in the passenger seat. "Hey, you coming?"

She jumped down from the seat and ran in with him, just as the gate descended behind them. The lights went on by quadrants. She stood still, her eyes following the lights, her mouth agape. "This is awesome!"

"Yeah, it is. Come on."

She followed him to shelving divided into cubbies on the left side of the main room.

He pulled a Khaos Rules T-shirt from one cubby, short shorts from another. "Wearing sneakers and socks?"

She pulled up her pants leg. "Yup."

"Okay, good. Here. A small should work. What size bra do you wear?"

"You have bras, too?"

"Yes. Women can't wear those strapless things in here."

"Thirty-four D."

He handed her a nude-colored sports bra from a closed drawer.

"That's fine. Thanks."

"Locker room's through there. Everything goes in. Weapon, too."

"Got it."

A few minutes later, Frank, already in his T-shirt and shorts, was in the workout quadrant in the gym, in the rear left of the space. He called to Sam. "Over here!"

She jogged over to him, passing the cage, her head turned toward it. She reached Frank, though her focus wasn't on him. The ceiling lights glaring on the metal rings made her squint. "I want to go in there!"

He laughed at her enthusiasm and at the way her face scrunched from the glare. "We will. I can guarantee we will." He turned her around, pulled her close, held her around her waist, and pecked her nose with his lips. "First you have to prove to me you've earned it."

She looked up into his eyes with her arms clasped on his hard biceps. "And how may I do that?"

"Show me how you work out. Not looking for an injury or accident. Not on my watch."

For the next hour, Frank put Sam through the ringer. Calisthenics with high reps and intensity, dumb bells, pull-up bar, boxing with the small and heavy bags, step exercises, twelve-pound kettlebell swings, a hundred reps.

After the kettlebell count Sam bent over, hands on her knees. Panting, flushed, the shorts and T-shirt saran-wrapping her body with sweat, her hair at the hairline damp, with tendrils of hair loosened from her ponytail, she looked up at Frank, who had completed each exercise with her. He probably could have gone another round, but something more fun was on his mind.

She sighed. "I'm done."

He handed her a second bottle of water. "Drink. Then stretch out. Then you'll be done." He was damn serious.

She guzzled the bottle of water, stretched low and long with her legs spread out. Sitting on the floor, with her legs in a wide V, stretching her arms to grab and hold her toes, with her breathing normalized, she managed to get out the words. "In your humble opinion, King Khaos, am I ready for the cage?"

"Oh, yeah." He extended his hand, which she grasped, and he pulled her up. in one smooth motion." How much do you weigh?"

"One twenty-five on a good day. Maybe one twenty-seven on a bad."

"Okay, you're five six, one twenty-five, lightweight."

"And you are?"

"Super heavyweight. Still think you could whip my ass?"

"Do I have to follow the rules?"

"In here, absolutely!" He was shocked she'd think otherwise.

"So that means no strikes to vital organs, no head kicks, no joint tugging, no sticking my fingers into your nose, eyes, or ears…uh…no jumping on you, think they call that stomps, no punching your nose, no elbows to your head, and no groin pulls. Right?"

"And you learned that, how?"

"In the academy we were taught to do exactly those."

He laughed. "Oh, man, okay, so if a perp ever got a hold of you—"

"They wouldn't stand a chance. And that would be before I pulled my weapon." She jogged to the cage, ran up the steps, and bounced up and down on the tarp.

Good, she's feeling the resiliency of the tarp.

She spread her legs, bent at the knees, hands fisted in front of her and prepared to attack or be attacked. "Come on, King Khaos," she shouted from the middle of the ring.

He jumped up the steps, laughing. *She actually thinks we're going to spar?*

That wasn't what he had in mind. Not at all. But she'd soon find out. He positioned himself for the first confrontation. Palms out in front of him, fingers curled, he waved his fingers in a "come on" gesture and leaned over, knees bent. "Let's go. Show me what ya got."

"You asked for it!" She lunged forward and, with her full body, landed smack on his torso, her hands pushing on his chest.

He skidded back three steps then regained his balance. With his right arm, he pulled her into mid-air, facing the matt, away from his body. His left arm went under her and, with both arms on her underside, held her straight across him like a dad would hold a child teaching her how to swim in a pool. Sam kicked her legs, laughing. *Guess she feels like a little kid, too.* He curled her up and down along his forearm and up to his biceps a few times, as if she was his human barbell. She laughed the entire time. "Now what, princess?" he said as he held her across his arms, his grin permanently sealed.

She bent her elbows and, using his straight left forearm as a rack, riveted herself off him into a standing position. Without hesitation, she slid her leg in between his and tried throw him off balance to push him down onto the tarp. Her plan backfired. He braced her legs and flipped her with his arms under her rear end so that she landed on her butt. The sound of her thud, echoing through the gym, startled her. "What the—"

"Microphones under the tarp. Makes landings seem harder than they are."

She bolted up, ran to the outer perimeter, and back again, to attack him from the longest distance. He moved out of the way, stuck out his left leg, and tripped her so she landed flat on her stomach.

"That's not fair!"

"Sure it is. Hey, if I let you run with that momentum, you'd crash into the cage. We've seen enough blood this week. Don't you think?"

She rolled over onto her back and threw her arms over her head so they rested on the mat.

He dropped to his knees, rested his palms on this thighs. "Bad move, princess."

"Why?" Her sparkling eyes told him she knew why.

He laid down directly on top of her, with his arms covering hers and his legs concealing the rest of her. He looked her in the eyes. Their T-shirts were saturated with sweat, their shorts clung to them, and perspiration leaked out of every pore.

"Oh my God, Frank! We stink."

He nestled his head on her neck. "Don't care. I like the way you stink."

She laughed and crinkled her nose. "Oooh."

"Okay, so how are you going to get out of this? A full body restraint."

"I never heard of this submission hold."

He kissed her cheek. "Made it up. So what are you going to do about it?"

"What if I don't want to do anything?"

"Have to do something."

They were nose to nose, lips to lips. Sam tilted her head up and kissed him. A soft, gentle kiss. He didn't reciprocate. She kissed him, again. He just smiled. She kissed him again, longer, harder, closing her eyes.

"You're killing me. You know that?"

"So what are you going to do about it—King Khaos?"

Without another word, their lips met, their hands tightened, interlaced above her head on the mat, and he didn't want to come up for air. He kissed her more than he had kissed a woman in a long time. Over two years and one month. They moaned. The kisses deepened. His mouth moved to ravage her neck and he whispered in her ear that he wanted her, as he pecked his lips against her soft skin.

He could melt into her skin. "When was the last time you had a cock inside of you?" he whispered into her ear.

She paused for a moment and her breath hitched. "With a man attached?"

Her response was more clinical than sexy, though her eyes teased him. His eyes widened. Here he was trying to talk dirty to turn her on and he didn't expect a comedic response. His mind went to Steven Larcon. "Sam! Oh, man. Yeah, with a man attached."

He couldn't stop laughing. Not the feeling he wanted, right now. He put his face down on the mat, next to her neck. They lay cheek to cheek.

"It's been a long while," she responded with a tone that made him think there was another option.

"Okay, then without a man attached?" He had no idea why he had asked that. Yeah he did. He'd always be up for a game.

"A couple of days." She shrugged her shoulders.

"What?"

She tossed him a hesitant look and bit her lower lip. "I happen to have a pretty effective dildo. And he vibrates."

"You gave your dildo a gender?"

"Hell, yeah. He couldn't be a she, now could he?"

He kissed her cheek. "Does he have a name, too?"

"Yeah, but I'm not telling you." Her voice was coy.

"I can just imagine."

Or hope.

He rolled over onto his back, shaking with deep laughter. "Okay, that's it. Now you're in for it."

He stood up, put out his hand. She grabbed it and he pulled her up and into his arms. He grabbed her on her butt, shimmied her up his body, and, with her legs wrapped around him at his waist and her head nestled in the crook of his neck, carried her down the steps, and into the locker area.

ᥩᥴᥩ

Frank walked into the ladies bathroom when Sam was finger-combing her hair. She had a white towel wrapped around her that opened in the front in a V, revealing her thatch. She stared at his hard length protruding from under his own towel and closed her eyes for a moment.

Oh yeah, he planned to do plenty to her with his manhood.

"Have any trees in here to swing on, Tattooman?"

Without saying a word, he scooped her up in his arms, threw her over his right shoulder, and carried her out of the bathroom. "Isn't this what they used to do in those days?" He completed his question with a pop to her behind, keeping his left hand on her butt.

"Ooh, think so. Where are you taking me?"

"You'll see, princess. Be patient." As he carried her, he patted her butt cheeks, softly, as one would do to an infant to calm them down. Lightly. To warm her up.

"Oooh, that feels good. Don't stop." They entered the main section of the gym. "It's cold in here."

He opened the door to his office. "You won't be cold for much longer."

"Your office? We're going to play in your office? Your desk is crammed with paper work."

"Would you stop?" He gently smacked her bottom, again. "You're one bad girl, you know that?" He punched keys on a pad on the wall opposite his desk and slipped her down off him so that she could see as the wall slid open. "Come on in to my secret place."

As they entered the room, dimmed lights went on. Electric candles illuminated one by one in wrought iron holders placed intermittently on the walls. Sam seemed to be entranced as her gaze scanned the room.

She didn't notice that he had slipped both their towels off and let them fall to the carpet.

"Oh my God, Frank, this is beautiful." She touched the wall and let her fingers roam on the three dimensional waves. She walked the length of the room with her fingers dancing on the blue-green water. "These murals, hand painted?" He nodded. She did, too. "The water, the sand. Looks so real. Down to the pebbles on the beach." She peered at them closer. "This is magnificent." She turned to take in the rest of the room. "On all the walls. It's like we're really there. Like we're on a beach, within a cave. Frank, is this real place?"

"Beach on the Greek Isles. Jen and I went there on our honeymoon. This was replicated from a photo we took." He turned on the audio—ocean water, waves crashing into rocks. Melodic sounds, so relaxing. So sensual. He wanted this night to be special for him and Sam.

"It's amazing." She turned to the center of the room. "Ooh. A round bed."

"I love round. Like this tush." He lightly pinched her bottom.

She laughed and stuck out her bottom for him to do it again. He patted her, moving her toward the bed.

"Frank, this is gorgeous. It looks like the bed is within a cave, with the shades of brown as the backdrop." She sat down on the bed and her hands slid over the sea blue comforter. "Silk?"

He smiled, slipped his hand under her, and pulled the comforter out of the way. He tapped her shoulder and she fell back onto the pillow.

Her arms spread wide on the bed. "Yikes, it's cold."

"Prepare to be warmed up, real soon."

"No wonder you insisted we shower first. Didn't want gym sweat on your silk sheets."

"There'll be plenty of sweat on them, soon."

Her smile welcomed him. She opened her arms to draw him in. He went down on top of her and they kissed, gently at first, then increased to wet, succulent passion. Her mouth opened and his tongue entered, dueling with hers. His belly tingled. His length quivered. He kept kissing her until he almost came. He slid his lips to her face, neck, down to her breasts, uttering soft grunts, while she, gasps and moans.

He shifted his body onto his side, cupped her left breast, and brought his mouth down to suckle her. She moaned in contentment. He'd read her right. His tongue whirled around her boob. "Warming up yet?"

"Oh God. Yes." She let out gasps of contentment, purrs, her right arm resting on his left shoulder.

They turned onto their sides facing each other. Their legs interlocked. The warmth of her taut, silken legs flush against him excited him. He loved the touch of her skin against every part of him. His hand caressed her hip, then brought it around her, and settled it on her bottom. He ran his hand over each smooth, firm cheek, squeezed, and patted her. No more than love pats. He wasn't planning to go harder than love pats. He had certainly gotten warm. She had to have also. He kissed her neck and his fingers lingered in the small of her back. She moaned and squirmed. He had found another one of her sensitive spots. Tonight, he planned to explore every inch of her. He would know what his princess wanted and desired. Her breathing deepened, as did his. She was relaxed and open for him.

He leaned her back on the bed, extended his left arm, and pulled open the drawer to the night table. He tossed three packets of condoms onto the table, inhaling deeply to absorb the warmth of her breasts on his chest. Oh, man, did he relish every part of her.

Her eyes opened wide.

"Hey, I told you. No one will be here till six a.m. Oh, man, do you feel good under me."

"And you feel so good on top of me." Her arms slipped underneath his and she wrapped her arms around him, as much as she could. Her hands couldn't meet. The warmth of her hands sent intense heat through his back, up and down his torso.

He put his head down next to hers. He was so relaxed he could have fallen asleep. But that wouldn't fly. He needed to switch things up a bit. He rolled over and pulled her on top of him.

She went willingly.

Okay, she likes being in control, too. He'd go along with her, for a while.

She straddled him and positioned her sex over his hard length. She arched her back, her palms on the bed, sliding up and down, and moaned, her decibel increasing as her wet folds caressed him. She slid high, making sure she teased his tip, massaging her clit in circular motions against it. She screamed out in ecstasy He felt her swell. He leaned back and moaned with hitched breath. Intense energy began to hit him. Not yet. Too soon.

He lifted her off him and plopped her down on the bed. "Not so fast, princess."

"Frank, you're killing me. You know that?" she panted.

"I don't rush. And you need to calm down and relax." He kissed her as he placed his left hand over her heart. "Everything you do, you rush. Want it. You try to get it. You need to relax during sex."

"I am relaxed. Don't go clinical on me."

"I don't think so. Just go with me, okay?"

"Are you always going to be so gentle and slow?" she whined, caressing his cheek with her palm.

He laughed. "Until we get to know each other sexually. Yeah. And I never did like wham-bam-thank-you-mam-roll-over-and-snore."

She burst out laughing. "Oh, my God! Okay, King Khaos I'll go with you. As long as you put it like that."

"No more talking." He shut her up with his lips on hers.

∾∾∾

Sam hungered for him. Her body was scorched, her sex awakened from his mere touch. From her mere thinking about him. She felt her center, wet, almost dripping out of her, as she tingled all over her body. Pressure was building. Now she had him and wanted him inside of her. She didn't know how much longer she could wait.

Take control of me, Tattooman.

Her longing eyes must have conveyed the message.

He grabbed her, pulling her up close to him. His hands cascaded down her back as he kissed her neck. She arched her back, protruding her breasts into his chest. He followed the lead and sucked on her pink nipples, alerting them. His tongue swirled the pink flesh around them, making her skin pebble. She quivered. As rippling sensations ran through her, she purred. He pushed her back onto the bed then lowered his lips from her breasts down to her navel.

He pecked her, right above her thatch and toyed with her curly hair between his fingers.

She jolted at the twinge, let out a low gasp, and spread her legs for him. His lips pecked her clit. Then, with his the tip of his tongue, he tickled her. He teased.

Damn him!

She took control, touching his warm head, pushing him down. His tongue, flattened, encircled her mound. She wanted more. The carnal pressure wanted to burst. She screamed out, loud, long, moans. "Consume me," she begged.

He knew exactly what she wanted. He repositioned her on the bed, so she laid across it, parallel to the headboard. Her upper body fell back off the bed and her arms dangled above her head, opening her body to the energy. He held onto her hips as he submerged his head between her thighs, kissing her inner, upper thigh, right outside her womanhood. She widened her legs more and held them high as he moved to suckle her swollen mound and let his tongue slide down to enter her canal. His teeth and tongue took turns on her folds, bringing her to ecstasy. His teeth pinched, his tongue soothed. Her juices flowed.

"Oh God, Frank," she screamed out in complete abandon.

It didn't take long for the waves of climax to ride through her. Her body writhed, from her toes up to her head. She quivered on the bed, drenched. Damn! She had wanted it to take longer. For him to have to spend more time.

Her breathing hadn't even calmed down before he slid her full body onto the bed. He wasn't done with her. Her body was riddled with excitement. He was taking control and she loved it.

He kissed her and her own scent filled her nostrils. He paused to put on a condom. Again, he held her at her hips. Her legs spread high and wide for him. He guided his shaft into her wetness. She still hadn't stopped quivering from the waves that had penetrated her just a minute or so ago and her sex was still sensitive. He thrust in, gently at first, then with more intensity as the as the pressure mounted. She moved her hips in sync with his rhythm, up and down. He slowed. She wanted it faster, harder. She emitted a loud moan. "Ahhhhh."

He was panting. He teased, but gave in. She felt the thrilling tingling on her mound as his shaft rubbed the walls of her entrance. She was feeling his heat. He had to have felt hers. Their temperatures soared, their bodies wet and shimmering from sweat.

Faster. He thrust faster. His thrusts pulsated on her clit as the top of his groin met with her pelvis. He grunted louder as he came closer to his own apex. Her climax shot through her, a combination of nub and canal frenzy. The strongest kind for her. She panted, breathless, as he came after her. He moaned, collapsing on top of her.

Oh my God. He certainly knew how to please a woman. He certainly knew how to please her.

She knew right at that moment she must have more of him. She needed him in her life.

He pulled out and remained glued to her. His sweat blended with hers, becoming one.

They had become one, in spirit and lust.

She wrapped her arms around his neck. "That was so wonderful, Frank."

"Yeah, it was. Wasn't it?"

They kissed with passion and appreciation for each other. His kisses told her he felt the same way about her. She hadn't been this content or pleasured from any other man in her life.

He kissed her nose then shifted onto his side with his left arm over her stomach.

She looked up, noticing the mirrored ceiling for the first time. She blinked the sweat out of her eyes. "What made you construct this room?"

He exhaled, falling onto his back, his breathing still hard. "After Jen's death, I knew I couldn't remain celibate. And I vowed, I'd never bring another woman into our bed until after her murderer was found, and unless it was the woman I planned to marry. So I created my secret place. No one knows about it except me and you."

"So you've been celibate for two years?"

"Hell, no. The women I've hooked up with had their own place. Short-lived relationships. Very short lived. Like no more than twice."

"Never met a woman you wanted a longer relationship with?"

"Another vow. I will not have a relationship with any woman, a permanent relationship, until Jen's killers are found. I wouldn't be able to put another woman in danger and live with myself."

"Well, then. Let's find Jen's killers."

"Glad you said that, princess. I want you and Frankie to meet."

CHAPTER 30

J esus packed with urgency. One duffle bag. That's all he'd allow himself. He pulled two black hooded sweat shirts and two pairs of black sweat pants from a small chipped mini-chest in the corner, adding some underwear, socks. His wardrobe was set. Then his laptop and cords.

Better grab those forged credit cards.

They were truly a work of art. Even duplicated the signature bar and security code on the back. After he took care of business, he'd be skipping the country. For a brief moment he considered that he was glad he didn't have any baggage. At thirty-five, no kids. No nagging old lady. No ifs about that. He had plenty of room left in the duffle, mainly for his weapons, ammo, and cash. Lots of cash. A hundred grand in small denomination bills.

He hadn't seen Emma Sander's murder in the paper. Guess they were keeping it under the radar, not wanting to alert the other two. He'd be spending a lot of time in Brooklyn the next few days. After he offed Rachel and Meredith, that detective would get hers. He'd have to do those two quick but he'd take his time with Samantha Wright. He knew Leonardo would want her done slow, deep, and painful. Jesus would become her worst nightmare. The worst she'd had in her life. Killing a cop would be major clout. He'd be wanted by the biggest and the best. He envisioned his future unrolling before him. Oh, yeah. He'd be in great shape in a few days. Anyone who had ever doubted him would now be by his side.

He left his apartment, scanning the block before he got in his car. *Good bye, Staten Island. Hello, Brooklyn.*

He came to the corner of Rachel's block off Surf Avenue and halted. He noticed an unmarked police car parked outside the building. Black, tinted windows. He couldn't see if there were passengers in there but his nose smelled cop. He wasn't one for taking chances. No way. Hell, no. There could be a million reasons the cops parked outside a thirty story building. He wasn't going to find out the hard way. He drove past and pulled into a burger place parking lot three blocks away.

He had made it a point to get chick's numbers. Just in case he needed to get laid. Rachel was as good as any. And she was tall. He liked tall. He called her.

She answered on the third ring. "Hi, Jesus."

That was cool. She had him in her phone book. "Hey, girl. How are ya?"

She didn't pause. "I'm doing great! How are you?"

Was she dumb or what? Nah. She just wasn't telling him the truth. She didn't know a hit was put on her. And didn't know Adam had given him the low down. That's for sure. "Where are ya?"

She sighed. "We got some cop trouble. Uh. The usual. Can't go back to my apartment."

"So where are ya? Want to get together for a bite to eat? Maybe I could help you out?"

"That would be cool. I could use some way to go. Where?"

"Are you in Brooklyn?"

"Yeah."

"Wanna meet me?"

"Where?" She sounded nervous.

"How about far from you? Near Marine Park. Parking lot inside the park. Be there in thirty."

"Okay. Later." She hung up.

Jesus sat thinking about the conversation. She was certainly jittery. He was thinking how he'd do it. Ah, he'd figure it out as he went.

It was as if he'd gotten hit over the head with a brick. All of a sudden, it came to him. He couldn't do Rachel or Meredith. Police would be after them, following them, leading them to him. And she knew that.

What the fuck was he thinking? He had gotten away with one murder but there was no way he get away from the cops if he did this. He already spent five years of his life behind bars. And he wasn't planning on going back.

Did the cops say they'd give her a deal if she'd lead them to me? What the fuck? That's it. That bitch is setting me up. Rachel knew Arie was in the hospital.

He bet she knew everything.

"Hold on, Jesus," he said aloud. "You don't know that. Adam hasn't told the cops anything. Just nail them. The suppliers just said nail them. I got paid twice for the same three women. How hard can it be to hit these two? I did Emma like a snap. I expect the same with the other two."

It was eleven a.m. Wednesday morning, cold. Snow was predicted. No one would be in the park at this hour. People would be at work. She'd pull into a spot. Even if there were cars there, no one would be in them. If he spotted a tail, he'd pull out like he had just come from a jog. His black tinted windows would conceal him.

Okay, Jesus. You can do this.

The drive to the park took fifteen minutes. He made sure he wasn't tailed. He did his usual thing. Made every right turn for four blocks, then every left, for four. Even if it took him a mile out of the way. One thing great about Brooklyn that was different from other boroughs was that he could drive around in a square and, on the fourth turn, wind up where he started. He nodded. He liked that. If a car followed his exact turns, he'd know he had a tail.

He didn't. He relaxed. The cops probably hadn't IDd him yet. The studio apartment he lived in wasn't listed under his name. For all purposes, Jesus Parvos's apartment was in Yonkers. Let the cops knock themselves out looking for him. They'd never find his Staten Island digs. He had been good at hiding for the past four years once his probation had ended.

Inside the park, he pulled into a spot close to the exit. The trees were barren, leaves on the ground blew into the lot. No one was jogging on the track. No teams played on the fields. Kids were still in school. He sat bored for a few minutes, tapping the steering wheel. Then he spotted her driving in her broken down Chevy. Oh, man. That ride must have at least a hundred K miles on it. He felt his Taurus in his back belt. Silencer in place. She pulled in next to him. He surveyed the area in and out of the lot. No cop cars. No unmarked ones. She rolled down the passenger window. He rolled down the driver's side. The cold wind sent a chill through him. The chill wasn't from nervousness. Fuck. Maybe it was.

Rachel rolled her lips together. "Where do you want to go? I'm starving."

As he moved his hand around his back to remove the gun, he shrugged. "Don't know. What you in the mood for?" The gun lay on his lap.

"There's Chinese not far from here."

He turned his body toward her. Just enough for her to think he was paying attention. "Okay, babe." With that, he raised his hand and shot through the open window, hitting her in the neck. Blood splattered as she fell forward. "Okay, hit number two. Done." He pulled out and left the lot without thinking about it or looking back.

搇搇搇

Sam, Nick, and Withers, convened in the back lot of AriellaRose's warehouse in downtown Brooklyn. Sam peeked in the window first, hunching her shoulders in frustration. Her solemn expression prompted Nick to look through the narrow window, using his hand across his forehead to block the glare. Then Withers took his turn and shook his head. Meredith Cummings lay on the concrete flooring in a fetal position.

The wait for ESU took longer than Sam had patience for. When they finally arrived, the lock was easily cut with monster-sized bolt cutters. ESU ran in, canvased the area, as EMS technicians checked out Meredith. She was ice cold. Dead and iced cold. The EMS tech didn't find any means of a violent death.

Sam approached him. "Could it be an overdose?"

"Probably. But I doubt if she was alone. They probably left her. Crime Scene will get everything."

"Thanks." Nick approached Sam just as her phone rang. He stood next to her while she answered and put the phone on speaker. "Hello, Lieutenant," she said.

"Sam, there's been another murder this morning."

"Where?" Nick interjected.

"Jesus Parvos struck again. Rachel Hawthorne was shot in the neck in Marine Park. There was a phone conversation between them. They were both in Brooklyn, and we still can't get a definitive residence on Parvos. I want you both there, ASAP," Lieutenant Rojas said before he disconnected.

After hearing the last part of the conversation, Withers swiped his hand over his head. "Where the hell is Frank?" he demanded, accosting Sam.

"Frankie's class is having a Thanksgiving party. It was his job to bring in sweet potato pie for thirty kids."

Withers laughed. "Been there."

"Well, his mother-in-law cooked but he wanted to go. He feels he's neglected him this past week. Dingo, we've got to get in to see AriellaRose."

"Not until her attorney clears it."

"How do we make that happen?" Sam demanded.

"We'll get Frank to deal with that."

"We have to get out of here," Nick said.

ೲೲ

In a corner booth, away from other diners, Jesus sat in a crowded deli on the avenue, digging into a couple of dogs, loaded with mustard, sauerkraut, relish, with a kasha knish on the side. He had already downed the bowls of coleslaw, cucumber salad, and herbed chickpeas they had put on the table, along with a bottle of water. For some reason, his jobs made him famished. Up until now, his jobs had only been as a guard, an enforcer, to make sure a deal hadn't gone sour. They never did. His mere presence convinced buyers and sellers not to fuck with his employers when he was around. He was never shy about throwing a punch, or two, or three. He smiled at the mental images that came to mind. Broken noses, cracked jaws, his own bloodied knuckles. He made a fist and turned his hand to check them out. Hell, yeah. But bullets were so much cleaner.

Now that he could be a hit man for hire, his appetite soared. He'd better watch it. He had to remain in the same weight class for his upcoming boxing match in Vegas in six weeks. He patted his six-pack. Rock solid. He also needed to take care of this detective so he could devote his time to training. He went to grab a piece of knish and it wasn't there. Fuck. Then it registered. His mind had been elsewhere. Not good in his line of work.

He thought about how he'd find her. He decided to take a look in the park. Maybe the cops found Rachel by now. It had been an hour but New York City cops were pretty fast. He had no information about the detective bitch, so he'd need to get the down and dirty by himself. He checked the bill the waitress put on the table. Even though there was a cash register to pay at, he threw thirty bucks on the table and sauntered out of the restaurant.

He parked outside the park on the street, but the one nearest the lot. As he expected, police were there as well as investigators. He pulled binoculars from the middle compartment. After adjusting the lens, he saw her. The same blonde ponytailed detective he had seen in the paper. Samantha Wright. He zoomed in. Fuck, she was sure hot. He'd have fun with her. For sure, he planned to fuck this one. Before he killed her. The thought made him hard. He surprised himself. Fuck. He needed to get laid.

From the newspaper, he knew the precinct she worked in. He couldn't go there. The police had Rachel's phone. They'd ID him from the conversation. By now, they'd finished their cleanup of Emma's apartment. He had been careful not to touch anything. He revisited it in his mind. He didn't touch furniture.

Fuck! The plastic ties! My prints will be on those for sure. And the baggie of Blue. Okay. Two big mistakes. They definitely have me. What are my choices? Skip the country now? Fuck. And not do the hit of a lifetime? Hell, no!

He had never been one to listen to his internal dialogue and he wasn't about to start now. He'd follow her. Not his smartest move. But he sure wanted to fuck her.

He sat for thirty minutes before they dispersed. Samantha Wright got into her own vehicle. The other two cops, in suits, he presumed they were detectives, entered another, parked in front of hers. Good he'd get her plate. Through the binoculars, he zoomed in. He got a clear view and jotted the plate number down on the back of his hand.

After they drove off, he pulled up the duffle that lay on the floor of the passenger seat. He retrieved his laptop, and one of the bogus credit cards, sticking the card between his teeth. A good a place as any. He booted up the laptop and Googled match license plate to car owner. A bunch of web sites popped up. The cheapest one was five bucks. Okay.

He looked at the card. Henrietta Cohen wouldn't notice the five bucks he put on it. He filled in the info, paid with the card, and then more questions arose, like why do you want to know? One option was, *I want to purchase the vehicle.* Perfect. He checked that and, instantly, Samantha Wright's home address in the Madison section of Brooklyn popped up.

"Thank you, Henrietta Cohen," he mumbled under his breath.

೧౨ೲ

Jesus waited until ten p.m. to pay his visit to Sam. Knowing this was an expensive family neighborhood, he figured anyone with kids would be home with their little ones tucked in bed. In the meantime, he visited one of his hacker friends, "Jerry," who provided him, with no questions asked, a house alarm decoder. Also a master key for a high security lock for the front door. "Jerry" kept his anonymity, as did his clients. Cash only. No receipts. Nothing that the purchaser could declare as a business expense on their taxes. Jesus laughed out loud. In contrast to Emma's block on Staten Island that didn't have a parking spot to spare, Sam's block of detached, one-family houses had plenty. The driveways could hold two cars lengthwise. Her car was parked toward the front porch. Didn't look to him like she had company. The spot in front of her house was vacant. He didn't want to park there to give her any hint of a vehicle that she might not have been expecting. He parked three houses down.

"Jerry" had told him there might be a slight chance of her alarm having a warning sound if someone entered the house, if she was inside. That made sense. Another downer was that her alarm could be connect to the local precinct. The nearest precinct was three miles away. That should be more than enough time for him to mess her up bad. Fuck. Doubt if he would have the time to fuck her. But it was a chance he'd take.

He exited his car, zipped his jacket and brought his hand around his back to feel his gun in his back belt. Then he walked the three houses to get to hers. He hopped up the four steps. He held the decoder under the metal piece that protruded from the bottom of the square box. He depressed the "Read" button. About fifteen seconds later, the red button on Sam's box turned green. He retrieved the key for the lock, inserted it, and he was in. He pushed down the lever on the doorknob, pushed the door open, and wound up in a small foyer. He closed the door behind him, walked a few steps into her living room, and smiled.

He heard the voice coming from the security alarm microphone. "Detective Wright, are you okay? Press the green button if you're all right."

Jesus stepped to the side, so as not to be seen in a camera if there was one set up, extended his hand around to the box, and depressed the green button with his index finger.

"Thank you, Detective Wright."

He smiled. He heard the shower running. That meant she couldn't have heard him enter, or heard the alarm company. Walking on tiptoes, he made sure his steps up the carpeted staircase wouldn't be heard. Good thing the stairs didn't squeak. He reach the four-foot-square platform at the top of the staircase and stood a foot back from the bathroom door, grinning. The shower shut off. After a few minutes the bathroom door opened.

Detective Wright stood before him.

Naked.

CHAPTER 31

Sam stared at him for a split second. His shit eating-grin delayed any action as he focused on her breasts and took his terrifying gaze down her torso and legs. During that second, she tapped a button on the doorframe, pretending to hold onto it. She hoped he didn't notice her index finger movement. She didn't know what he was going to do, so she went at him with both hands on his chest and pushed him backward.

He threw his arms around her, hugging her, and, in a squat, shoved his butt down against the edge of the staircase in an attempt to avoid falling down the flight of stairs. With her weight on his upper body, he couldn't prevent it, and they slid down the thirteen steps. Sam rode him as if she had lain down on a surf board. They bobbed on the trip down.

Okay, I can tell his weapon is in his belt, around by his back.

He kept his head raised during the slide and landed on the carpet on his shoulder blades. His long legs lay on the steps, tilting up like a plank. She tried to wiggle free, but he had her arms pinned under her and, as he held her tightly, her butt and legs were straight up on his. He wrapped his legs around her calves to immobilize her.

"You fucking bitch. I'm going to fire your ass up!" With full hand swings, he connected with her butt, alternating cheeks, with eight hearty smacks.

"Ow! You're hurting me! Stop! Ow!" She buried her head into his chest to distract him.

While he raised his hand to pummel her butt again, she wiggled her left arm out from under him, made a fist, and punched him in the nose as hard as she could. She heard it crack. His head bounced back onto the carpet, but he rebounded fast. He screamed out in temporary pain. Before she could jab her fingers into his eyes, he grabbed her arm. They wrestled and he won. He tucked her arm down by her side and held onto her tightly.

On his back, he shimmied—with her on top of him—toward the center of the living room, until his body lay flat. "What the fuck did you do that for, bitch? I had my nose broken so many times, I don't feel it no more!"

His hold on her was tight. Her arms were pinned at her sides. She had no shoes to protect her feet. If she kicked him, she could break a foot. Crap. This man was strong and in shape. She had to think, in spite of her burning ass.

He rolled over and tucked Sam under him.

She squirmed, her ass stinging from friction on the carpet, and she gasped. "I know who you are, Jesus."

"Well, when I get through with you, you'll remember me for life, bitch. Your very short life."

"What are you going to do?"

"After I give you the fuck of your lifetime, I'm gonna take care of you. Got orders. You'll go to hell happy. Look at me, bitch."

She looked away, her mind on an escape plan.

He grabbed her face with his right hand and pulled her face around to his as his shoulder pressed against hers. "I said look at me!"

Sam looked him in the eyes. She had done wonderful things to men with her eyes. *Will it work on a sicko like him?*

She had to try. She softened her facial expressions and tried to relax. He felt it because he loosened his grip on her cheeks. She looked left eye to left eye with him, the way to make a connection with anyone.

He fell for it and softened.

"Oh, man, those blue eyes. You could melt a guy with those eyes. Know that? How about I punch you in the face good? Won't be so pretty then, uh, bitch?"

She moved her face away, but even as she faced sideways, he ran two fingers on her nose from between her eyes down to the tip. "Ever get a broken nose, bitch?" She shook her head. "Yeah. I could tell. Yeah. I'll do that. Won't be so pretty then, either. But I'll wait on that. Got a lot of things to do to you, first."

He shifted his legs on her thigh. Sam felt his length swell against her leg. She forced a smile. Then she swallowed. He was exerting his full body weight against her. Even though he was slighter in build than Frank, he felt much heavier. His anger made him stronger.

"Yeah. I'm in the mood to get laid."

She couldn't fight him. He had a weapon and she was nowhere near one of hers. Couldn't Karate chop a bullet. She had to be smart. "I'd think twice about fucking me, though."

"Why you say that?"

She swallowed. "Just got diagnosed with genital herpes. It sucks." She remained straight-faced. "Still contagious. Actually, at the most contagious stage. Doc says I got a real bad case, too. I'm so itchy and burning down there. Even condoms won't protect."

"No shit?" His eyes widened, his complexion flushing. "You're just fucking with me."

"I kid you not. Wanna take a chance?"

His erection petered. Sam felt that, too.

"Oh, man, you're something else. Ya know that?" he asked.

"What?"

He ran his fingers through her damp hair. "What's such a hot chick like you doing as a cop? You should be in a magazine, girl. Or what are you doing to catch that shit?"

She forced a smiled. "Well, we both know each other, then."

"Seems so."

"Why did you break into my house? You have to know we're looking for you." Her tone was compassionate, not denigrating. Hard to do under the circumstances, but her training prevailed.

"What are you looking for me, for?"

"Jesus, come on. I'm trying to solve some high-profile murder cases, and you went ahead and offed two of our main suspects." She wanted to make it sound like he took away her thrill by getting to them first.

He gave her a quizzical look. "What?"

"You really don't know?'"

"Enlighten me, bitch." He pushed away and sat up next to her, keeping his arms secure on her midriff. He couldn't take his gaze from her breasts. "Don't you dare move. I could break you in half."

She exhaled deep breaths, relieved that he was off her. She was safe, for the moment. Now she'd make a move when the time was right. She remained still, hands lying at her sides, gaze kept on him. "My name is Samantha, not bitch. Emma Sanders and Rachel Hawthorne are—were—wanted in the murders of Steven, Valerie, and Kathryn Larcon, and designer Meghan Mason. Where did the hits on them come from?"

He did a double take, darted up, and thudded around the living room, running his hands through his long hair, stomping his foot so hard that the lamps on her end tables shook.

Sam sat up, legs extended in front of her, with arms behind her. He stood, gaze down at the carpet, one hand snug inside his jean's pocket and the other fisted, tapping his mouth. With caution, she stood up. "Jesus, tell me what's the matter. Come on, sit down. Let me at least get myself decent, okay?"

He nodded. She slipped to her coat closet to the right of where he stood, opened the door slowly so as not to startle him, and pulled out a long, pink duster. She held it out, showing him there were no hidden pockets. He watched her every move and he was close enough and strong enough to do serious damage to her. Her throbbing backside and her heated body, remnants from his body weight upon her, were reminders. She pulled the duster around her shoulders, slipped one arm in at a time, then tied the belt. She walked over to her loveseat that hugged the wall in front of the staircase and sat on the left side, next to an end table that had a drawer, that was lodged into the corner. Rubbing her lips together, working through the sting on her butt, she rested her arm on the armrest. "Jesus, come on, sit down."

He sat on a teal club chair that matched the couch, opposite her. "They knocked off how many people?"

"Four so far. Who ordered the hits?"

He bent over, with his hands clasped between his legs, and remained silent.

"Jesus, up until now you were a bodyguard. Why escalate to murder?" Her tone remained compassionate and respectful.

He kept his gaze on the carpet. "Money. Loyalty. I was making a shitload of dough as an enforcer, probably more than you make as a cop. Then they wanted them whacked. Got paid eighty grand, twenty for each. And then I got paid twice…" He let his voice trail off.

"Who's 'they'?"

"The weapons guys."

"Eighty grand? That's for four? Who are the other two?"

"I got one more to do, Meredith Cummings."

"Too late on that one. She did it to herself. ODed. Okay, so there was one more."

"No."

"Jesus, eighty divided by twenty equals four. So who else did they want you to eliminate? Me?" She shifted onto her left hip.

"No. Not you, by them. Oh man! I was gonna bust her out of that damn hospital for Leonardo. I can't fucking do that and then whack her."

"AriellaRose?"

He nodded.

"So all this is about Leonardo?"

He sat back slumped in the chair. "Yeah." He swallowed so hard his Adam's Apple protruded. "His weapons suppliers wanted anyone who distributed for Leonardo disposed of, so no trail could lead back to them."

"They must know he'd be facing hard time and try to deal. And you were about to say something else. You were paid twice?"

"This just keeps getting worse. Doesn't it?"

"Well, yes. Murder is never pretty. And it's always complicated."

"Either way, I'm fucked. You know that, right?"

"Listen. And seriously listen. We could help you. The feds would love to know who the weapons dealers are."

"I'm not ratting on them. No way. I'd be a dead man, no matter where I'd go, and I have enough dough to go anywhere in the world. Even off the planet."

"I believe you. But I'm also hearing in your voice that you're not thrilled about looking over your shoulder the rest of your life, either."

He let out deep breaths, licking his lips. "AriellaRose has a twin you know." He rubbed his forehead with his fingers.

"Yes, Adam."

"He wanted the three of them hit. But he didn't tell me why and I didn't ask."

"He told you nothing?"

"No."

"Not even that he was doing this at his sister's request?" Sam knew she was putting words into his mouth, and that was "no-no" but he spoke openly enough to make it stick.

"No."

"Um. You know? I like to read a lot of crime novels. A lot where hits are made. The guy called in usually asks a bunch of questions so he/she knows what they're getting themselves into. And so he can name his price."

He sat pensively for a moment. "Yeah, I got some information about AriellaRose. I know what you're getting at. If I talk, what are the chances of me getting into witness protection?"

"That's not my area of expertise. But I'd be happy to ask. I'm assuming you have a weapon?"

"Yeah."

"Why don't you slide it over on the carpet toward me, please?"

He sat for a moment as if contemplating his options. Sam didn't like how his facial expression turned from hesitant to decisive. His eyes went from a calm haze to the intense beady stare she saw in the mug shot.

No, Jesus, don't make the wrong decision. Not now when I am so close to reaching you.

With that, Jesus pulled his Taurus from behind his back belt, but his hand went up, as if to shoot, rather than down, as if to slide the weapon toward her. He fired straight at her, as Sam ducked, rolled onto her left side, and down onto the carpet between a coffee table and her full size couch. She pulled her weapon from the drawer in the end table and, aiming over the barricade, her coffee table, fired her Glock .40 caliber, twice, hitting Jesus in the chest both times.

He slumped back into the chair, and his weapon fell to the floor next to his feet. Sam got up and slid the Taurus to the center of her living room with her bare foot. She checked his neck, no pulse.

She collapsed on her love seat, with her head in her hands. As she leaned back to get a hold of herself, she felt the hot spot. His bullet had pierced the back pillow of the love seat. An anxiety attack overcame her.

Oh my God. I've killed someone.

She trembled. Sweated. Her heart palpitated. She was alone in her house—with a dead man. And she had caused his death. She ran upstairs, grabbed her cell phone, and put in a call to 911, then Nick.

⁓⊷⁓

Her house had become a crime scene. Jesus lay back on her brand new chair, droplets of blood spreading through his hoodie. She knew it was a good kill and she had the video, but that meant they see her in the flesh, and getting spanked. Embarrassing, hell yes.

But she had to hand in the tape. Her career depended upon the truth.

In her bedroom, she checked her butt in the mirror. Red handprints, fingerprints, but no welts. Still hurt. She took out a jar of Arnica cream from her night table drawer and rubbed some on her bottom. She winced but it took the sting away. She got dressed in a T-shirt and jeans while waiting for them.

Nick had called Frank and he arrived first. The shock of her first trigger pull hit. She collapsed in Frank's arms, shaking. He sat down on the couch with her, hugging her.

"Oh my God, Frank—I was so close. So close to talking him in to turning himself in—it was going smoothly once we started talking—I didn't want to have to do it. But he didn't think twice about killing me. He fired, but missed," she cried. "Look, he hit the loveseat."

"All right, Sam. It'll be all right." He caressed her and ran his hands from the top of her head to her back, patting her. "Sssh. It's okay. You're all right."

This precinct's patrol officers came in and stopped, looking at Jesus. Sam looked up at them, sniffling.

"You okay, Detective?"

"Yes."

The officer put in a call to EMS and Crime Scene. He took the preliminary report as the first responder and spent forty-five minutes interviewing her. Nick and Withers appeared through the doorway when he was done.

"You okay, Sam?" Nick asked. He sounded official, no warm and fuzzy feelings from her partner.

"Shook up. Whatever happened to 'some detectives don't pull their weapon in twenty-five years on the job?' Obviously, I broke that myth. Here." She put her hand in her pocket and retrieved a flash drive. "I recorded it. But I must warn you it's X-rated. It better not wind up on YouTube."

"Hey! Why didn't you give that to me, Detective?" the patrol officer yelled.

"It's personal, and I wanted to give it to my team, sorry. I knew they'd be here and it's our case. It's going straight to evidence."

"Hold on. Recorded?" Frank asked.

"Yeah. When I entered juvie, I put recorder devices around." She sniffled. "They're disguised in the doorframe. A friend of mine suggested it. This was the first time I ever used it. Has everything. Conversations and the trigger pulls." She rubbed her arms, chills were still going through her.

Nick looked at the coffee table. "Is that your weapon?" Sam nodded. He put it into a manila bag with a see through plastic, labeled with the date, time of use, his ID, and signature. He sealed the bag with tape.

After she gave the report again, and Withers drilled her for a another good half hour, Crime Scene investigators arrived. This would be a quick one since they had the recording.

Frank hugged her. "Glad you didn't try to be a maverick and fight him. That was smart."

"I did. You'll see."

He felt her, shaking. "Okay. Don't want you staying here tonight."

"I agree. Where can you go?" Nick asked.

"She'll come to my house. I have a couple of guest rooms."

She wiped her eyes as she gazed up at Nick. "What happens next?"

"You should know procedure. Loo and Internal Affairs will look at everything, your report, tapes, crime scene evidence. You may have to work in the office a few days but I'm sure, from the looks of it, you'll be cleared. You will have to be debriefed, though. Be prepared to talk a lot about it. A shooting takes its toll. Don't kid yourself. Everyone is vulnerable. So word of advice, partner, don't pretend to be strong. It'll catch up with you and bite you in the ass."

"That was a poor choice of words." But she nodded. Nick was a hundred percent right. "Can I pack a few things?"

An investigator answered her question. "Did he go upstairs at all?"

Sam nodded, again. "He came up the steps. I pushed him and we both fell down the flight. But he didn't go into any of the rooms."

"Sore anywhere?" Frank asked.

Sam dug her head into his chest so Nick and Withers couldn't hear. "Yeah. I'll never ask you for a spanking, ever again."

❧❧❧

Sam and Frank heard laughter coming from Loo's office at eight a.m. the next morning as they walked down the hall. It was loud laughter. Sam recognized the voices of Loo, Dingo, and Nick. But there were a couple more voices she didn't recognize.

"Who the hell is in there?" Frank asked.

"I recognize your pal, Marcus."

"Seriously?" Frank knocked on the door.

"Come in." Loo choked out.

As Sam and Frank entered, Loo feigned a coughing fit, to stop laughing in front of her. The two men she didn't know stared at her, both with their mouths agape.

Loo introduced her to Internal Affairs investigators, Milt Granger, a mid-fifties gray-haired guy who looked at her with a sympathetic gaze. The other, Casey Ferman, younger, hipper dressed, shot her a mischievous look. She nodded to Marcus Willtower, who just grinned. She wanted to kick him in the teeth.

"Have a seat, Detective." Loo began.

Sam and Frank sat at the conference table with the men.

"First, Detective Wright, relax. You're in the clear," Granger told her. "We viewed the tape. It's all good. They found Parvos's car three houses down from yours. In a duffle bag, he had a laptop which is now with our IT guys and over a hundred grand in cash, which can be traced. Here's what's going to happen. Technically, Jesus Parvos is yours since you took care of him. But, and it's a big but, we need you to hand that case over to Agent Willtower, who is working with the FBI to get Leonardo Phileatano put away for life. In order to do that, we need concrete proof he did indeed order a hit on you and it was not just in Parvos's imagination, what he thought Philetano wanted him to do. That's a loophole that his attorney will drive an armored truck through. Whatever evidence you collected on the three women when you—one, spoke to AriellaRose and that Emma Sanders, aka Calinda Alexander; two, retrieved from AriellaRose Larcon's home; three, any interviews from the case, yeah, the Jaye Manning and Mrs. Larcon interviews too, are to be copied and handed over to Agent Willtower, as well. Notice I said copied, not transferred. You are keeping the AriellaRose case and her brother, Adam, who is a suspect in arranging the hits. The rest are dead, so don't worry about federal charges usurping yours. Those will be added on, after. Response, Detective Wright?"

She exhaled a deep breath. "Okay. Thank you for telling me I'm cleared, first. Yes. That's all fine with me. So then the FBI and DEA will be investigating the arms dealers?"

"Correct. Hopefully, there'll be correspondence on Parvos's laptop. Now, if anything with AriellaRose or Adam leads in the direction of those dealers, you're expected to let us know. Clear?" Willtower said.

"I will. But are you expecting me to interrogate with that in mind?"

Willtower smiled.

"Yeah, sure you are. Okay. I'll see what I can do. When can I get in to see her?"

"Her lawyer said to call to make an appointment, but Detective Wright, you'll be in the office a few days to debrief," Loo said.

"I'm fine."

Frank shook his head. "Sam, you're not fine. You were jittery all night. When I checked in on you, you were moaning in your sleep."

"Frank! Thanks a lot!"

"Hey! I wear my shrink hat in the office."

"You were together over night?" Loo's question was official.

"We live near each other and they didn't want me to be alone. I was in a guest bedroom."

Loo put his glasses on the desk. "Then Frank, you can't debrief her."

"Okay. You know what? Let Doctor Trenton do it. He could Skype it."

"I'll call him and set up appointments. Jittery is no good, Detective," the lieutenant said. "Just think of it as a time to prefect your paperwork and get everything over to the DA."

"Okay, Lieutenant. It'll also be a good time for me to go over all the files in Frank's wife's murder case."

All of them nodded in approval.

Except for Dingo Withers.

CHAPTER 32

Frank's light gray shirt, solid dark gray tie, and charcoal gray pants created the foundation for his long white lab coat. The dreaded stethoscope hung around his neck. He strode down the hall to AriellaRose's hospital room in the psychiatric ward. He heard her screams for Tattooman and frowned, listening to the torment in her voice, though it was strained and distant.

Waiting outside her room, her attorney, whom Frank thought was Stan Hartman, looked like he was out of his element. The short, stout, seventy-plus-year-old man sweated in the cool corridor. He looked tired, hunched over, and this case was just beginning. His black-rimmed glassed kept slipping down his nose. His complexion seemed to be scaly, possibly psoriasis, definitely stress related. He better be able to handle this case. Frank planned to increase his stress in about five minutes.

"Hello, Mr. Hartman. Doctor Khaos."

Hartman swallowed in relief. "First, I'm not Stan. He's my son and winding down a multi-million dollar case now. Final arguments in court. I own the law firm, but retired years ago. My health forced it earlier than I had planned. Just here, trying to help him out. I'm Murray. So thank you for coming, Doctor Khaos. I can't get a straight story from her, and for six hours non-stop, she's been screaming for you. Apparently, by the nickname she gave you."

"What information do you have?" Frank was intent on listening. His tone softened. Not what he had intended.

"Everything the detectives and investigators gave the DA. I don't understand that magick angle at all. I might push that and use it for an insanity defense. I need you to assess her."

"Forget about using that for her defense. Too many people do use candles and oils, successfully, positively, and they're emotionally stable. I know a couple, personally."

Hartman removed his glasses and wiped the lenses with a hanky. "I want to be in on your interview with her. She needs to be questioned in the presence of her attorney. It's her right."

"Agreed. But I'm not a cop. I'm her psychiatrist. Let me ask you this. From all of the information you have, do you believe in her innocence?"

"I don't have to believe she's innocent. I have to give her the best defense possible."

"And I have to give her the best medical treatment possible."

"But I have questions for her and she's not answering me. She doesn't seem to understand what I'm asking."

"We'll deal with that. But not today. She has to feel comfortable if I am going to get her to talk. She closed down with you. For six hours, you said? You wait in the visitors lounge. Everything will be taped. It'll go to the DA and you'll get an exact copy."

"I need to have a conference with her. Doctor, please."

"You will, but not with me present. I'll arrange for someone from the DA's office to come. Wait in the lounge. I'll let you know when I'm done." Frank put his hands in his pocket and stared the attorney down, remaining silent.

Head down, Mr. Hartman plodded down the hall. Frank saw his pants hem dragging on the ground, at least an inch too long for him. The cuffs on his suit jacket came down to his first knuckle on his hand. Frank had sympathy for the man. Yeah. He was definitely in over his head.

Frank exhaled a deep breath, unlocked the door, and entered AriellaRose's room. He stood at the door, observing her. Her hair stuck to her scalp, sweat ridden, her eyes slightly pink on the rims, probably from holding in tears, and her complexion pale. Her gaze up at the ceiling didn't change, even though the door made a sharp clang when he closed it behind him.

"AriellaRose." He stood with his hands in his pockets and kept his face stern, like he did when he needed to reprimand Frankie, lips straight across and closed.

She kept her gaze on the ceiling. "What the fuck took you so long?"

"Your attorney knows I'm speaking with you and he'll get a

copy of our conversation." She didn't respond but Frank knew she heard him. She swallowed. Planned ignoring was one of her favorite behaviors. "We had a lot of things going on," he said.

"Such as?"

"Okay. Here's the list. Your three friends, Emma, Rachel, and Meredith are dead."

She smiled. He moved out of the way to make sure the camera caught the grin.

"Want to know how that happened or do you already know?"

She didn't look at him. "I don't know."

"Okay. Meredith ODed at your warehouse."

Her fists, that lay on top of the sheets, tightened. Again, in camera view.

"Emma and Rachel were shot by Jesus Parvos."

"Who?

"This guy." Frank pulled his smartphone out of his pocket. He pulled up the video his DEA agent bro gave him. He positioned the phone in front of her eyes. "Here. Watch."

"Oh, that dirt bag. I only saw him that one time. Don't know his name."

"Really?"

"Yes."

"Okay, we'll find out. We have his laptop and yours."

"Mine?"

"We found your Park Slope brownstone. Yeah. We know you wiped the hard drive clean. Our guys retrieved it."

"Big whoopee for them."

"I need you to answer some questions."

"Why?"

"For your defense."

"I didn't do anything." She whined.

"AriellaRose, we have enough evidence against you to put you in prison for life without any chance of parole. That's a lot of years." Her eyes narrowed, fearful. He pulled a chair over, next to the bed. "Listen to me. I need you to talk to me so you get a fair trial. No matter what that would entail." He reached out and clasped her hand. She was ice cold.

She yanked her hand away and pouted like a defiant child. "No."

'Okay. You've been screaming for me to come for over six hours. Why?"

"Eight hours."

"Why?"

"I wanted to find out what you've been doing. How's Detective Samantha?" Her tone was childlike but insinuating.

"Well. This guy Jesus Parvos, who murdered your friends, also broke into her house and tried to kill her."

She looked at him for the first time. "Did he?"

"No. He hurt her. She'll be okay. She killed him."

"No shit?"

'Nope. Now it's your turn to answer some of my questions. Fair?" She nodded. "Good. Very good. In your basement, we found bloodied towels wrapped around knives. Turns out they're the same type of knives that made the cuts all over Steven's body. They'll get DNA soon, but are any of those knives a match to his cuts?"

"What do you mean?" She sounded younger.

"The knives that cut Steven, were they in that pile of towels?"

"Maybe. Maybe not," she said, trying to be sly.

That's not going to work. "Okay. So there were many towels in that cabinet. We also found out that for every year you've had the business, you had different employees. Why such a quick turnover?"

She laughed as deeply as she could. Phlegm spit out of her mouth and dripped down her chin. Evil spewed from her cold, hardened eyes. "You'll never find them." Her face went blank and her vacant gaze turned toward the ceiling.

Oh man, this case is far from over.

"I also want to tell you we arrested your Uncle Timothy yesterday."

Her eyes widened. "You're shitting me?"

"Nope. Is that why you did all this? To get revenge on all the people who let this happen without helping you?" She wasn't in any way mentally astute to express it. Not now, anyway.

She nodded and then broke down crying.

"Then why Meghan Mason?"

She sniffled. "I couldn't fit into her clothes. No matter how I tried. She deserved it. That skinny whore."

"All right, AriellaRose. It's over. No more people have to die. Did Adam arrange the murders of your three friends?"

"Maybe. Maybe not. He knew that guy. But how would I know what he did?"

"Did Adam know what you were doing?"

"Maybe. Maybe not."

"How much did Adam pay him?"

"Ask him. Is Adam in trouble?" Her voice regressed in years.

"I would say so."

She smiled again. Ear to ear. Again in camera view. "Good. That'll teach him to get everything."

"What did he get?"

"Everything. He always got everything. Lollipops. Ice cream. I got nothing cause Mommy said I was fat." Her voice had regressed to the high pitch of a three-year-old.

Frank realized what he needed to do. He patted her hand, got up and left the room, his lips rolled together, shaking his head.

ଔଓଔ

Nick and Sam sorted files on the Larcon case. Her bottom still burned and she shifted in the chair. Nick got up, pulled a pillow from the couch and handed it to her. She took it, laughing.

"Sit on it," he said.

She laughed.

"Seriously, he hit you hard. Harder than I'd ever spank my kids."

"You spank?"

"Very gently, but my son likes to make me feel bad so he carries a pillow around."

"How old is he?"

"Five."

Frank came in and, unlike Nick, he wasn't humored by her sitting on the pillow. He patted her on the back of her head. "How are you doing?"

"Okay. Finalizing all this to go to the DA. Forensic reports will go directly to them. There's enough here to indict AriellaRose for murder. What happened at the hospital?"

He sat and clarified. "I didn't ask about the case. I asked about you."

She picked wisps of hair off her face and put them behind her ears. "It was scary. Not something I'd want to do every day. Or ever again. What happened at the hospital?"

"Changing the topic?"

"Frank. Stop. I can't talk about it right now. I have to process it myself. Let me breathe. Okay?"

"No. You need to talk about it. Nick told you that, too, very clearly. You're going to have to dig deep. Into real emotions. Not witty sarcasms that pop out of your mouth without thinking. The real you, Sam. You have to let out the real you."

She looked down at a file, not seeing anything. Doubt riveted through her.

Am I cut out to be a detective?

Nick's cell rang. He answered on the second ring. "Valatutti...Good...No problems?...Excellent...Thanks." He disconnected. "It was the precinct in the Hamptons. They had picked up Adam and charged him with conspiracy to commit murder and hiring a hit man. He's being booked now. Okay. Got to take care of this. See you guys later." He patted Sam on the shoulder and nodded to Frank.

"Before you go. AriellaRose told me, actually admitted a lot. May have been more murders she had initiated. Don't know if it'll hold up in court. She had regressed to a three-year-old child. I left orders for the psychologist to administer a battery of tests."

"All right, good. I believe we have enough without it, though."

"Not so fast. I have to determine if she's mentally able to stand trial. The grand jury will indict her, but I don't know for sure that I want her in a prison environment. It's my call."

"As long as she's locked up somewhere." Nick shrugged, nodded, and left the room.

Frank leaned back in the chair and faced her. "Back to you, Sam."

"Crime Scene called me. They removed my club chair and loveseat from the house, and there was no blood splatter on my carpet, so I can go home tonight."

"Don't know if I want you to be alone."

"Frank. If I'm not home, my parents will be worried sick."

"How will they know?"

"They live three blocks from me. They drive by and see if my car's there. I was praying that when Jesus was there, my dad wouldn't just pop in. The shock would have killed him."

"I can imagine so. You mean to tell me they just pop in without notice?" He laughed. "That's intrusive."

"I'm an only child and they're not thrilled with my choice of career."

"What did they want you to do?"

"They would have loved for me to be a doctor like them. My dad's a neurosurgeon and my mom's a pediatrician. They accepted teaching but wanted me to work toward becoming a principal. When I went for my master's in criminal justice, I didn't tell them in what. They thought it was in administration."

He frowned. "You're how old and you're still lying to your parents?"

"I told them mid-way through," she responded, as if that made it okay.

"What have you done to make them not trust you?"

She rolled her lips together. "I'm not sure I like your shrink hat."

"Come on. Spill it."

"I was very overprotected. But then I went away to college, and I sort of became a wild child."

"And that hasn't changed. Okay, wild child, how about Italian tonight? I want to ask Carlo some questions. And I want you to meet Frankie. He'll come with us. He's been nagging me to meet you."

"Yes, I was bummed you didn't wake him this morning. And I have questions for Carlo and anyone else in the Philetano family who's there, as well."

❧❧❧

After Sam had gone home and packed clothes for a few days, at Frank's insistence, she pulled into his driveway next to his Explorer. She'd leave her overnight bag in the car, not planning to bring it into the house until after Frankie went to bed. She double-checked her appearance in the visor. Minimal makeup to please Frank. Hair flowing straight down. Wearing a T-shirt and chambray jeans to match his casualness. Okay, she was ready to go. Meeting his little guy would be a big step.

She exited her car and stood looking up at his house—much more modern than hers, and larger. She hadn't had a full view last night. She was still shaking when he brought her here at two a.m. She had wobbled her way up the steps on unsteady legs to his porch that framed the first floor.

She took a deep breath, looked at the steep steps, and slowly walked up, holding the wrought iron banister. Crap, her butt still flamed. She certainly wouldn't want to schlep up these steps carrying groceries.

She rang the doorbell and waited.

She heard the little voice. "Coming." His footsteps sounded like he skidded across the hardwood floor. He opened the door and stared at her, wide eyed. "No! Go home!"

He slammed the door in her face before she could respond. That threw her. Her heart fluttered and her stomach felt queasy. Not good, if she planned a relationship with Dad.

She heard footsteps running up a staircase then Frank. "Frankie!"

His stern intonation made her take a step back.

Frank opened up the front door. "Come on in. Don't know what that's about. But I'm sure as hell going to find out. Have a seat." He pointed to a free standing couch in the center of the huge living room. "Frankie," he bellowed up the staircase.

From the top of the staircase Frankie yelled, "No. She looks just like Mommy. Tell her to go home. I hate her!"

Frank and Sam exchanged double takes. He sprinted up the staircase, leaving Sam, stunned, on the couch. This had started wrong, that was for sure. She got up and tiptoed to the base of the stairs to listen, glad Frank hadn't closed Frankie's bedroom door.

"What are you talking about? You've been nagging me to get a girlfriend and you wanted to meet Sam."

"Dad, don't you see it? She's Mommy. She came back from the dead. Like on that vampire game."

"Come here." Frank's voice softened. "No one comes back from the dead."

"She looks just like Mommy."

"Just her blonde hair and blue eyes."

"That's enough."

"Come on. You're coming downstairs, and you're going to be nice. Understand me?" There was a pause. "Okay. Good. We're going out for dinner, but if you don't want Italian, I'll drop you at Grandma and Grandpa's."

"No, I'll go. I want Italian."

Sam snuck back and sat on the couch.

"Okay, let's go. Get your butt down the stairs and say hello to Samantha."

Frankie slowly walked down the steps, making all sorts of facial expressions, contorting his cheeks. He walked over to her.
"Hi, Samantha," he said, pouting. It was obviously something he
was doing under duress.

"Hi, Frankie. I wanted to meet you so bad," she said, lowering
her sentence structure to match his age.

He stood there, looking her up and down, and smirked.

Oh my God, he's a miniature Frank. That's for sure.

⌘

They were seated in Carlo Philetano's restaurant after a ten
minute wait. Sam was famished. Frankie had warmed up in the
car and had at least spoken to her. He told her all about school
and how his teacher was boring, sometimes.

From their table, Sam noticed three suited men, who resem-
bled Carlo, sitting at a table in the rear left of the restaurant. She
nudged Frank. "Know them at all?"

Frank looked over and smiled. "Yeah, I do."

Frankie perked up, sprinted off his chair, and yelled, "Doctor
P!"

Paulie Philetano turned around as he opened his arms and
Frankie lunged into them. "Oh, man! Are you getting big!" He
ruffled Frankie's hair.

Frank met him with Sam at his side. They shook hands.

"He looks great, Frank."

"Thanks."

"And isn't this the little lady detective that met my son, Carlo?"

She smiled warmly at the patriarch. "Yes, I am, Mr. Philetano."

"How's the case coming? I read about all those horrible murders in the newspaper. How is AriellaRose? My wife and I are so
worried about that little angel. I hope you have her protected. I've
been trying to reach her, to reach out if she needs anything, anything at all, but her phone is not picking up. Not even to leave a
message."

Frank grimaced. "Yes, she's protected. I have her in the hospital. Brought her in for an episode of asthma. Found out it was
pneumonia."

"Oh thank God." Mr. Philetano put his hand over his heart. "We love her like a daughter."

Sam couldn't believe his sincerity, and it appeared he meant it, but it was time to burst his bubble. "Thank you for your concern, Mr. Philetano, the case is almost wrapped up. I'm sorry that Leonardo had to get messed up in it. Along with his current charges, this isn't good."

The elder Philetano squinted and flicked his gaze between Sam and his sons. "What do you mean?"

Stephano spoke up. "Uh, Detective Wright. Don't say a word, please. I hadn't told Papa yet. I planned to at our dinner. But I can assure you, Leonardo would never order a hit. Especially on a cop. Especially a woman. That was fabricated on that bum's part. There will be absolutely no evidence to support it."

"What? What hit? I demand you tell me now, Stephano!"

"Why don't you three go and enjoy your dinner while I fill Papa in on everything?"

Sam pursed her lips and nodded. "You're right. This is a sensitive time."

She turned and walked away. The senior Philetano was about her own father's age. Any bad news needed to be delivered softly, not like she had done—with a bat, over his head. She regretted what she had said, the way she had said it. Then again, they lived in a rough circle. He should have been used to it. Crap. The thought hit her again. *Do I deserve to be a detective?*

CHAPTER 33

Monday morning, in a small conference room with the computer set up on the table in front of her, Sam waited nervously for her video conference with Doctor Trenton. Loo hadn't prepared her much. He only said this was mandatory protocol when a detective had pulled the trigger. She had no idea of what Doctor Trenton knew about the case or if he had seen the video.

Should I be totally open and honest with him?

She would have been so much more comfortable had Frank been allowed to debrief her. But she understood why he couldn't. She was never one to get nervous meeting people or conversing. She never divulged much personal information, never got much into her feelings.

Yes, she had them. She knew what made her happy, sad, angry. She knew Frank had made her feel more like a woman than any other man she'd been with.

But to tell someone how she felt…well, that didn't come easy. Especially about her secret she had held in for a few years. Maybe that's why she wasn't married, or even looking for a permanent relationship, until recently—like the last week. It had finally hit her. She couldn't blame her parents anymore. She was isolating herself, period. And that was all there was to it.

When Frank had asked her how she was doing, he'd meant how was she feeling. Her response was to avoid, change the subject. Frank saw right through her and he didn't like it. One thing she liked about working with cops was that they shied away from talking about their personal lives. No one realized that she was doing that on purpose.

How much longer will I be able to deny my feelings and that I crave love, without it hitting me over my head that I could be alone for the rest of my life?

She got up and checked her appearance in the mirror on the wall. She'd chosen a white silk blouse with a silk sash that she tied into a floppy bow at her neckline. No cleavage showing now. Not in an interview that could be used to determine her fitness for the job. Charcoal gray, wide-bottomed linen pants finished her corporate casual look. In the conference call, he wouldn't be able to see them, anyway. She smoothed out her hair with her fingers, tucked stray locks behind her ears, and rolled her lips to smooth out her pale pink lipstick, even though the color was already perfect.

She returned to the chair when the video call came through. She accepted it. Doctor Trenton greeted her with a warm smile. His longish jet black hair that covered his shirt collar showed some graying at his temples. His dark blue eyes were bright and attentive.

He dressed corporate casual in a light blue button-down short-sleeved shirt, but way more dressy than Frank. She couldn't see his slacks but she did notice, right away, that his arms were sans tattoos. And he was built. Smaller than Frank, but built, nonetheless. In a split second, Sam could tell that he was vested in their conversation.

However, she doubted she was.

"Hello, Detective Wright. Nice to meet the face behind the phone call." His warmth and sincerity came through in his mellow tone.

"Likewise, Doctor Trenton." She heard her voice shake. He must have, too. "How's your wife?"

"Vicki's doing great. Very impatient. We both are. She's due in five days."

"You must call us when she delivers."

"Will do. Tell me what's going on?"

"Do you know anything about the case?"

"That's not our focus. Tell me a little about it, what necessitated our interaction."

She nodded. "Well, Wednesday will be just two weeks that I'm a detective. And I pulled the trigger for the first time two days ago. I was in juvie for four years and never un-holstered my weapon."

"Where were you?"

Thank God, he didn't see the tape.

"In my house. A hit was made on me and the guy busted into my home."

He studied her a moment. "What made you decide to pull the trigger?"

"He was pulling his weapon. I had hoped I would be able to talk him down. But when he pulled his weapon, he aimed at me. I had a weapon hidden in the end table next to my couch. It was close. He fired and missed because I rolled down and out of the way. I go over and over it in my mind why he didn't fire again. I can only think that he wanted me to shoot. Suicide by cop. That would be the better alternative to what he'd get from the arms dealers, who commissioned the hits."

"That very well may be. So what's your status now?"

"IA cleared me. I had it taped. I installed a system when I was in juvie. I figured out a way to activate it. They saw it was a good kill."

"Did I hear you say you had a weapon in your end table? And you had it recorded?"

"Yes. My house is an arsenal."

He smiled. "Okay, I now know why they assigned you to me."

"Why?"

"I'll tell you some things about me. I can really say, I know what you're going through. Maybe you heard about it, the Gemini case? Last February, a woman was dumped in my lap for a seventy-two hour observation. Turns out, through my examination, I discovered that she was a predatory murderer. She escaped from custody, creating a nightmare in New York." He paused, looking sullen. "She murdered my entire NYPD team. My friends." He swallowed. "She made it down to Florida. Broke into our house, where my wife was staying on a visit to her family. My wife, Vicki, pulled the trigger, and she isn't a cop. We had a surveillance camera on, too."

"Really?"

"Yes. Another story for another time. Getting back. The trauma of having to kill someone lasts a long time. So, with that being said, what are your feelings right now?"

Sam swallowed. "Oh my God. That is similar. It's eerie."

"Well?"

"It's hard for me to talk about my feelings, especially fear."

He gave her another warm smile, his facial features softened. "Why is that?"

She moistened her lips. " I don't know. It's easier not to address that one."

"How did that come about?"

She took a deep breath. "You ask the hard questions. Don't you?"

"Always. You know? Having a handle on your feelings, especially fear, determines how you optimize your skills as a detective. How badly do you want this career?" He stared at with an intensity that said he was damn serious.

"Very much! I worked so hard to get here, Doctor Trenton, I don't plan on leaving." She sat back, shocked by her own imperative tone.

"Okay. Good. What feeling did you just let out to me?"

"Anger. I know my feelings. I know what makes me angry, sad, happy. And releasing anger isn't one of my issues."

"How did you feel after you pulled the trigger?"

"Scared. That came out first. I was trembling. Then anger."

"Okay. Good. Very good. Tell me about the anger first."

"I was pissed at him for making me do it. I was pissed at myself for not being able to talk him down."

"It's the last statement I'm concerned about. How many people had this guy killed?"

"Two before he came to my house."

"How would you describe him?"

"Big, arrogant, angry, sexual. He wanted to have sex."

"How did he approach that?"

"The sex?"

Trenton nodded.

"He was vulgar. Said he was going to fuck me, before he killed me. One thing I can do well under stress is have a fast come back. I told him I had an STD. It made him hesitate. I felt his erection collapse."

Trenton laughed. "Oh, yeah. That would make a man deflate. How did you feel his erection?"

"He had me pinned under him, on my carpet. I just keep trying to go through my mind as to what I could have done differently."

"Okay. And you're beating yourself up about it, right?"

"Yes."

"It's only been a couple of days. However, do you know what going to happen if you keep doing that?"

"I'll start doubting myself, and then I'll be no good to anyone, especially my partner."

"Exactly. How do you feel when you doubt yourself?"

"Scared shitless. Out of balance. Out of control. I don't like being out of control. I'm sort of a control freak. Like I'm losing, and I don't like to lose. And that pisses me off. I don't like myself for it."

"It sounds like you're not giving yourself permission to do something that goes against your predetermined plan."

"That's exactly it. And I know being effective in this job requires flexibility, to change at a moment's notice to plan B."

"Yes. That will come with experience. You've only been in this position a little more than a week. So what happens to you physically when you're fearful?

"Oh God, my tells are easy, I perspire, get clammy, stomach gets queasy. I tremble. So how do I stop doing that?"

"What do you do to get over anger?

"I meditate, deep breathing. I lay my palms over my heart. The warmth of my hands calms me down. Or I work it through in the gym, on the punching bag."

"Do the same thing when you experience fear. It takes time. Stop beating yourself up. Start trusting your intuition. That'll eliminate some doubt. Are you in tune with that part of yourself?"

"I'm trying to be."

Her voice must have come across as evasive because he narrowed his eyes.

"Okay. What do you feel in your body when your intuition is giving you a signal?"

"What do you mean?"

He smiled. "Detective, I see right through you. Why are you still in hiding?"

She knew what he meant, but didn't think she could be open, yet. "What do you mean? How can you see right through me?"

"Actually, around you, too. I see auras."

"Excuse me?"

"Hey, I'm your ally here, so I'll let you off the hook. For me, my intuition comes through my crown chakra down my right side. Actually, it's my spirit guide, Max."

Sam's eyes widened as her world suddenly opened up. She relaxed. Happy tears almost flowed. "Doctor Trenton, I've never been able to talk about that to anyone before, except for my Reiki circle, and none of them are cops. I didn't think I'd be accepted here. Just the opposite. I thought I'd be shunned."

"Tell me."

"I just started becoming in tune with my guide, Dara, a couple of years ago. I started working with crystals, healing stones, and chakras about then. In the beginning, thoughts would just spit out of my mouth, spoken in third person. People around me would stare, thinking I was talking to myself. Then in this case, Dara started blurting out, again. She identified the killer, AriellaRose Larcon, in a very early meeting. I had no idea why that popped out of my mouth and I was stuck proving a hypothesis I didn't consciously create. Then a couple of days ago, I had a creepy dream, where I couldn't hear what was being said, but Dara was speaking to one of the victims. He gave me a signal to look behind him. We were looking for the reason for the killings and for the next victim. He pointed behind him. I woke up and tried to interpret the dream. All I got was to look behind him, into his past. The next day, we were going through case files, and Frank—uh, Doctor Khaos—talked about deep rooted trauma from AriellaRose's past. I grabbed onto that, and it was a relief, so I didn't have to tell them about my dream. I looked in past records and found the fifth victim. We arrested him on rape charges but actually saved his life. I don't know how I would have approached it if Doctor Khaos hadn't discussed past trauma, first."

"You said you couldn't hear in the dream. What prevented that?"

"I had earmuffs on. When Dara released my hands and feet from the restraints, I didn't pull them off. What does that mean?"

"What do you think?"

She paused for a long minute. "Damn! I'm preventing myself from hearing. Closing myself off. Not listening to my inner thoughts."

"That's right. I'd recommend embracing your intuition. You saved a man's life."

"I listened to Dara when she had given me messages in private. Well, sometimes, not even then. But it's when she appears in public that startles me, embarrasses me."

"What are you afraid of?"

"That's a biggie. Not being accepted. Tossed out of the department. When we were at AriellaRose's house—in her basement, she had a ritual room—and I explained her black magick ceremonies to the guys, I thought the next stop for me would be Manhattan Psych."

"But that didn't happen, did it?"

"No."

"Okay. So what do you need to do?"

"Be more open to receiving."

"Yes. Believe me. It can be a challenge. Max, has given me many clues in cases. Especially when I look at files. Yes, you have to prove them scientifically and with evidence, using your training, but don't ignore them."

"How do I make the men here understand?"

"I suggest, starting with Frank. He'll help you out."

"Frank knows about this?"

He smiled. "Talk with Frank." He checked his watch. "Our time is up for today, Detective Wright. We'll talk again in a few days."

"Thank you."

"You're welcome." He disconnected.

Sam sat stunned. Then relieved. "All right, Sam. Time to come out of hiding. Time to start trusting your intuition," she muttered to herself. "And then it's time to confront Frank."

She approached her desk, piled high with folders from Frank's wife's murder case. Loo had told her she'd be here for a few days, so she planned to make use of her time. As soon as she sat down at her desk, her cell rang. "Hello, Detective Wright." She frowned when she heard the voice on the other end of the line.

"Detective, Marcus Willtower here. Just wanted to let you know that Jesus Parvos's computer led us to the arms dealers. The feds are forming a sting now."

"Oh, thank God. Thank you for telling me."

"Sure."

"One thing, though. I spoke to Mr. Philetano last night, actually three Mr. Philetano's. The father, the son who's a doctor, and the son who's a lawyer said that Leonardo would never order a hit on a woman, much less a cop. Any evidence on the computer about that?"

"No. Not yet."

Sam paused for a moment. "Did you check his visitor log at the detention center?"

"Not yet."

"Do that. For a few reasons. Find out if Adam or Parvos visited him."

"Why do you think that?"

"Just a hunch."

"All right. Just as good a reason as any. Will do. See you around, Detective."

"Thanks. Bye." She ended the call and sat for a moment. *Okay, Dara, here's to a new beginning for you and me. I promise, I'll listen to you from now on.*

She pulled out the stacks of folders. She had already gone through them. But her head had been on the Larcon case. Now that things were winding down, she could focus.

She opened the gang related files first. They were the most copious. She needed to shuffle them around and clear her desk. She placed all of the other files on the floor. The pile reached the seat of her chair. She was thankful that most of the reports had been typed. Years ago, handwritten ones were acceptable. But that made it so hard. Cops' handwriting was as hard to read as doctors', maybe worse, because they were in a rush. She smiled, grateful that this had been before her time.

She tackled the Manhattan gang files first. That was Frank's main turf. There was the list of every gang in every precinct. There was an X next to each gang as they were eliminated. There were fingerprints for each gang member in here She turned to the evidence sheets and focused on the chain of evidence, taking out evidence from the boxes, returning them, comparing who had signed them on the withdrawal and on the return, who added new seals when the previous ones ripped. These seemed to be in order.

She opened the crime scene photos folder. She focused on Jen, the position she fell in—backward, arms away from her body, bullet wound in her stomach, groceries scattered around her. Sam stared at her face—eyes open from the angle they shot the photo. Yeah. She could understand why Frankie had gotten scared when he saw her. She and Jen could pass for sisters. Definitely same eye shade and hair color. Sam's nose was straighter. Jen's turned up at the tip.

Okay, Sam, think.

The fourth shot was the fatal one. She was about six feet from her car. Frank had told her Jen had completed two tours in Iraq.

Jen, you heard three shots. Why didn't you drop for cover? Why didn't you pull your weapon? It was right on you, under your shirt. Something doesn't make sense. I promise, Jen, I'll will investigate this until I find out who did this. Frank deserves closure. So does Frankie. And you. I know you must be tormented, Jen, in your grave, knowing the police didn't find out who did this. The folder of your contacts was the thinnest. No one ever threatened you, no one would want you dead.

At that moment, Sam felt queasy. *Could that have been Dara? I didn't listen when Dara gave me a mental clue, so she'd have to affect me physically. Is that what's happening?*

She decided to go with what Doctor Trenton had said, though it was implausible with what all the documentation had shown. Go with her gut.

Jen, by any chance do you know who did this? Sam had no idea why she asked this question. She had to learn not to be fearful or doubtful of her intuition. This case would test her limits. Even if she had to go against the entire department within the five boroughs.

She sat still for a moment and replayed it to herself. If she recognized someone, her guard would be down. Correct. The shock of knowing who shot at her could delay her reactions. Correct.

Did Jen know who shot her? Dara help me now. Lead me in the right direction. Sam stared at the pile of folders on the floor. Starting at the top, she slipped the folders off, onto the floor, and created another pile. She didn't find the one she wanted until the end. Her luck, she'd need the bottom two. She put the folder of the interviews of Jen's contacts on her desk and opened them, not knowing what to expect. She'd look at Jen's work history.

Okay, she was a surgical nurse in emergency services. Brooklyn South Hospital. That's near me. Bachelor's and master's in Nursing. Also supervising nurse in her ER. Okay, specific duties? Here they are. Mentor nursing interns, write their progress reports, place pharmaceutical orders, oversee invoices and supplies, liaison between nursing staff and the hospital administration. Um, nothing crazy, like report doctors who screwed up. Wonder if she had to do anything like that.

She went through the folder and read every report. Her colleagues applauded her. Wondering if anyone just said they did, just for the police, she looked at the signatures of the investigators from Brooklyn South. She didn't recognize any of their names. Her former precinct was in Brooklyn North.

The lead homicide detective was Dingo Withers. She knew that. The text message from the Bronx came back into her mind. "Got the biscuit. I'm hungry.'

Had anyone at Jen's employment known what her husband did for a living? Was that text message and Jen's employment related?

CHAPTER 34

Sam picked up all the folders from the floor, made a neat pile on her desk, and stuck Jen's employment folder into her tote. She grabbed the handset of the phone on her desk and depressed a key. "Hey, Nick."

"Hi, Sam."

"Where are you?"

"In Loo's office, finalizing some reports."

"Okay, I'm coming in." She straightened her white silk blouse, pulled on the ends of the huge bow at her neck. On second thought, she opened the bow and let the sashes cascade down her chest. They laid smoothly, minimizing her bosom. These men had seen enough of the girls to last an eternity and her embarrassment still hadn't waned.

She walked down the hall, around the corner, and knocked on the door. She gave herself the much-needed courage with a few deep breaths.

"Come in." As she opened the door, Lieutenant Rojas' expression turned stoic, smoothing out any of his facial lines. He must have read the intent on her face. He leaned back in his chair. "What can I do for you, Detective?"

She sat in an armchair next to Nick's. "I'm going through the folders Detective Withers gave me and I need to ask you some clarifying questions."

"Such as?"

"All of the investigation has been done so thoroughly. Every folder. Except one. Jennifer Khaos's employment folder. Minimal information. Why is that?"

"It's a habit we have. We don't spend time in any place where we don't see a purpose. Next?"

"I'd like to reopen that area, Lieutenant."

"Have you conferred with Detective Withers on that? I told him to work by your side, going over every facet."

Sam exchanged looks with Nick. "I just started dissecting all of this, Lieutenant. I'll call him. Thank you. One more question, please. May I please stop by the hospital that Mrs. Khaos worked at? It's actually very close to where I and Doctor Khaos live. I'd like to go, today."

"Have you read the reports from Homicide?"

"Yes. I have the detective's names. I'd really like to give it fresh eyes. I do have the names of people they interviewed, as well."

He pushed his lips into a frown. "What are you thinking?"

"Nothing concrete, yet."

Doctor Trenton's words popped into her mind. '*Trust your intuition.*'

"I looked at the crime scene photos," she continued. "The fourth bullet was the fatal shot. She was a trained marksman. Why didn't she drop the groceries and open fire? Only one reason comes to mind, Lieutenant. That is, Jennifer Khaos was immobilized by shock because she knew her killer." Confident, Sam sat looking straight into the lieutenant's eyes.

"And you will prove this how?"

"I need to re-interview everyone at the hospital, to start."

The lieutenant nodded. "All right. Now that everyone in the Larcon case is in custody or at the morgue, I'll let you out of my sight. But only with your partner, here. So, Nick, go ahead and humor her. Talk to everyone you can get your hands on, even if they aren't in the records, already."

"Ready to go to Brooklyn, Nick?"

"'I'll drive, then bring you back for your car."

"Thank you, Lieutenant." Sam exuded confidence as she closed the door behind her. In the car she didn't waste time opening up to Nick. "Didn't Loo tell us something different from what Withers did at last Sunday's meeting?"

He pulled out of the parking lot. "Exactly the opposite."

"And yesterday, when I said that I'd now have time to work on this case, everyone nodded in approval, except for him. What's up with that?"

"I noticed that, too."

"Tell me about him. So when I do ask him questions, I'll

know how to approach him. I mean, I don't care about stroking his ego, and I don't care if I make him out to be a jerk, but what's his history?"

"We were together in the academy, so we go way back. He's had his share of tragedy in his life."

Sam had a sympathetic thought, for a moment. "Like what?"

"His first wife died from ovarian cancer when they were rather young. Mid-twenties. Left two young girls. One and three."

"Oh, that is sad."

"He met his current wife, Lisa, about five years after Lynne passed. She had two young boys. The family blended really well. Four years ago, when his oldest daughter, Melinda, was twenty-six, she was diagnosed with ovarian cancer. She worked as a hairstylist and had very poor insurance that she had to pay for herself. She had aged out of his insurance. On a cop's salary, he couldn't afford very thorough coverage, even though Lisa had helped pay for it. They lost their house. In a small apartment now. But it's just the two of them. The kids are on their own."

"What happened to his daughter?"

"She's okay, thank God, but they're in debt up to the moon from her medical expenses. So he grabs whatever overtime he can. And believe me, Sam, he did work day and night on Jen's case. He didn't go home to sleep for days at a time. He slept at the Brooklyn precinct, so he could be close. No one could fault him on how he conducted the investigation. He knew exactly what it felt like to lose a young wife and be left with, not one, but two, small children. He could identify with Frank all the way."

"Oh God. I had no idea. I'm glad you told me. And he doesn't seem to carry the weight of it on him. I thought his gruffness and irritability was just impatience. No people skills or he was just mean-spirited."

"No he doesn't engage in self-pity, and he won't tolerate a pity party from anyone he works with."

Sam exhaled a deep breath. "Wow."

"I thought he just didn't approve of you wanting to reopen the case because he felt it was stepping on his toes. Now, anything else?"

"Not about Dingo, no. That was more than enough. But Frank doesn't seem to give a shit about that. He faults him."

"Yeah. He and Jen were inseparable. That started in Iraq. He shut down. Hasn't opened himself up, until he met you."

Sam smiled.

"Who are we seeing now?"

Sam pulled the folder out of her tote. "Okay, Jen worked in the ER. I want to speak with Melody Johnson who shared the same shift as her for two years. The reports said they were good friends. If she's not there, we'll grab anyone who worked there at the same time. I didn't call ahead. I like surprising people."

⁊⊃⁊⊃

Sam and Nick entered the ER, through the sliding doors, and approached the guard at the sign in desk in the lobby. Clean, with just a few upholstered arm chairs in a small waiting room off to the side, this was a community hospital that had a reputation for having a friendly and competent staff. People were coming and going, visitors, and staff as they were close to the shift change. Sam flashed her badge, as did Nick. After explaining what she wanted, the guard pointed her in the direction of the nurses' administration office. They walked down the hallway, on scuffed tiles. Reaching the door, she saw a sign that read, *Doctor Penelope Casting*. Sam knocked on the door.

"Come in, Detectives," the gentle voice responded.

Sam opened the door and she and Nick entered. In the car, Nick had told Sam that she should conduct the interrogation.

Doctor Casting's warm brown eyes were mellow and sincere. "Have a seat, please. My guard called to let me know you were coming. What can I do for you?"

Sam looked around at the corporately furnished office. Huge wood colonial-style desk, matching wall units. This woman must have been in charge of something important. "Doctor Casting, we're continuing our investigation of the Jennifer Khaos murder, two years and one month ago. Were you here at that time?"

She smoothed out her hair that came to a bun at the nape of her neck. "No. I wasn't. I came on board right after that, actually. Moved here from Albany."

Sam read her body language. Nervous, to say the least. Her hair had already been in place. "Do you know what happened to the doctor that had your position previously?"

"No. I wasn't told. I wanted a position in hospital administration, did my research, and submitted an application."

"What's your background, if I may ask?"

"Of course, you can. I have a Ph.D. in Nursing and an MBA The mix is quite helpful in admin. Didn't the police do any investigation here earlier?"

"Minimally, since they felt the origin of the shooting came from another area. But I want to start anew. We need a list of Mrs. Khaos's colleagues and time to interview them. And she had admin duties here as well, is that correct?"

"Yes, very much so. She was the supervising nurse in the ER."

"We need to speak to the person who took over her position."

"That would be Melody Johnson. They were very close friends, from what I was told, but I don't know if they got together socially out of work, as well."

"From the police reports, Mrs. Khaos also put through orders for the department. Is that right?"

"Yes."

"What would she order?"

"Everything from paper clips, to bedding, cleaning supplies, pharmaceuticals, anything that was needed in order to keep our cabinets in the ER fully stocked."

Nick put his lips together. Sam thought he had something to ask but didn't want to step on her toes. "Go ahead, Detective Valatutti."

He jumped in. "Doctor Casting, for those orders, did Mrs. Khaos have her own computer?"

"Yes. For her own reports. The other nurses use the one at the nurses' station."

"So no one else used hers?"

"No. What are you getting at?"

"Do you still have that computer here?" Nick definitely seemed to have something in mind.

"Yes. Mrs. Johnson has it. She needed to continue the work and have the previous records."

Sam looked in her files. "There's no record of the police requesting the computer or doing any search. We need that now."

"Detective. That's not possible. There's highly sensitive information on it."

Sam hiked her eyebrows. "Highly sensitive?"

"Personal. Nurses evaluations, financial data."

Nick took out his smartphone.

Doctor Casting sat up straight in her chair, her eyes widened.

"Who are you calling, Detective?"

"A judge for a warrant. Technology is too important to forget to check. That raises a big red flag to me regarding this investigation. Is Mrs. Johnson here now?"

"No. Her shift ended for the day."

"Does she take the computer home with her?"

"No. It's not allowed to leave the building," Doctor Casting informed them.

"I'm going to get what we need for this investigation, so why don't you turn that computer over to us now?" Nick's flat tone reeked of suspicion.

"I can't do that. The police didn't request it before, as you said, and I will not tolerate this intrusion."

Nick walked to the far corner of the room to make the call.

"Intrusion?" Sam asked. "That gives me the impression you and the hospital have something to hide. What kind of situation did you find yourself involved in, Doctor Casting?"

The doctor hesitated. "No situation. I didn't know the woman."

"Oh, so just because you didn't know her, you don't care that one of your most respected nurses was murdered? Guess your Ph.D. made you a cold human being."

"Detective! How dare you?"

"Well then, prove to me you're not."

Doctor Casting quivered. "I don't have the authority to just hand the computer over to you."

"Call someone in your legal department."

"It's after five. They're closed for today." She looked relieved, as if she'd found a way out.

Fat chance.

"Doctor Casting, if we do find a clue or substantial information to conclude that Mrs. Khaos's murder did indeed stem from the hospital, and you do not help us, you will be arrested for impeding a murder investigation. That's prison time and I'm sure the correctional facilities in upstate New York could use someone with your medical knowledge in their infirmary."

"But I wasn't *here*, Detective." The Doctor's tone pleaded for mercy.

"All the more reason for you to be willing to help us—unless you have been warned."

"Warned? W—warned about what?" she stammered.

"What were you told about the doctor who had this position before you?"

"Everyone here welcomed me. I get along with my staff, and they all do a great job."

"That's not what I asked. So, if they're all warm and fuzzy, they must have let things slip about their previous admin. So?"

"A sudden departure. The day after Mrs. Khaos's murder. That's it. No one was every told why. This is a moderately sized hospital with a lot of turnover in staff. People come and go. No one questions it."

Nick returned to the two women. "I caught Judge Martinson. A courier is bringing a warrant for the computer within the hour."

Sam grinned. "Wonderful! Now, Doctor Casting, speaking of fast departures, did any other personnel leave from this department, the ER, right after the murder?"

"I wouldn't know offhand."

"How about doing a search on your computer, right there?"

"Does your warrant include personnel?"

Nick tossed her a snide smile. "The warrant includes complete hospital business records and personnel. I overheard what you told Detective Wright and included that. We'll add patient records if our investigation deems it necessary. So while we're waiting, Detective Wright and I would like to interview some nurses who were here when Mrs. Khaos was."

The doctor logged in, typed in codes that Sam and Nick didn't see, pulled up a list of nurses, printed it, and handed it to Sam. She promptly logged out.

"There's only eight names here. Where are the names of people who left?"

"These are current employees, nurses who worked in the ER the same time as Mrs. Khaos. To access personnel who left, I'd need the warrant."

"This is a mid-sized hospital, only eight?"

"There's been attrition. Retirements, relocations, not everyone loves Brooklyn. A few transferred to Manhattan or out of state. That's the best I can do until I receive the warrant."

"Okay, of the eight, who's in the building now?"

"Let me see the sheet." Sam handed it to her. Dr. Casting studied it a moment. "The only ones here now are Virginia Carter and Stephanie Maxe."

"Call them please and then give us a private area where we can talk."

◖◗◖◗

Sam and Nick split up the two women. Sam and the mid-thirties woman, Virginia Carter, sat is a small lounge attached to the nurses' kitchen area. Carter wore a light blue uniform with a lollipop design throughout.

"Mrs. Carter, what can you tell me about Jennifer?"

"We loved her but she was tough. She was my training nurse right when I got out of school. She was fabulous at developing rapport with the patients. I was an intern at the time and under her supervision. But heaven help us if we made a mistake. She said her toughness came from the military. No doubt in my mind."

"When would she become tough?"

"In our reviews. She didn't hold back. If we made a mistake during rounds, she'd tell us, even within the group. But not in front of patients, though. She wouldn't hesitate to write a negative report. The only person who'd see them was the person it was written about. We had to sign them and it went into our files."

"Um, were there any nurses she gave a negative review to that lost their job because of it?"

"A few."

"Hold on a sec, please. I saw something like that in my file." Sam pulled up a list. "Tell me if these were the same people. Mark Stratton."

"Yes."

"Louise Mullray."

"Yes."

"Delores Winter."

"Yes."

"Okay, thank you. These people have been interviewed at length. All cleared. Anyone else leave right after the murder?"

"Not that I know of, and I don't know all hospital personnel."

Sam nodded. "Mrs. Carter, were you interviewed?"

"Just for a few minutes. I was in a patient's room at the time of the murder and I think the police eliminated all of us as suspects on the spot."

"What makes you say that?"

"I got the feeling they didn't believe it stemmed from here from the beginning. They looked around minimally, didn't ask too many questions. I felt they were just here to fill up a file. Like they knew where it came from and it wasn't here. They brushed us off, sort of."

"How long did they spend here?"

"Not long at all. Maybe two hours, tops."

"Um, brushed you off? Was there something you or the other nurses wanted to say, that you didn't have a chance to?"

"Yes and no. The past couple of days prior to her murder, Jennifer had been more edgy. She seemed to have less energy and stayed in her office area more than usual. We thought it was her pregnancy."

"Pregnancy? I didn't see that in the photos."

"She was only two months along. The beginning nausea and all. They were hoping it was a little girl."

Oh my God! Why didn't Frank tell me?

෬෩෬

On the car ride back to the precinct, with Jennifer Khaos's computer on the back seat, Nick told Sam about his interview with Stephanie Maxe. "The same lax attitude of the police came through to her as well. Maxe, too, noticed Jen was nervous, keeping to herself the previous day or two, not speaking to her friend Melody Johnson. Maxe thought Jen and Melody had a spat, but when she had asked Melody, there was no such thing.

"She did say, when something bothered Jen, she kept it to herself and refrained from talking about it. Her colleagues knew not to pressure her. I was surprised to hear about the pregnancy, as well. The staff felt something may have been wrong with this one because Jen had miscarried once a few months earlier. Frank didn't tell anyone about this one. He had been so excited the last time and then she miscarried. He and Jen must have made the decision not to tell anyone until she was farther along."

Sam grimaced. *Well, that explains why Frank didn't tell me.*

CHAPTER 35

First stop, the New York City crime lab to see her friend, Tom Taeo. Sam had met him when she worked in juvie. Tom had helped her crack a case involving an adoption ring, which turned out to be a major case under her belt. If this guy ever wanted to cross over, he'd make a hell of a hacker. He had the skills to take down corporate America, if he was so inclined. In his jeans and T-shirt, he looked like an average graduate student with his long straight black hair and wire-rimmed glasses. Well, looks were certainly deceiving. This guy had a double doctorate, one in computer science and the other in digital forensics.

He put the computer on a table in the lab and inserted USB cords, connecting the laptop to other computers that Sam couldn't begin to comprehend, nor care to, as he gave her his undivided attention. "What are you looking for, Sam?"

"Okay. I'm just going to run off at my mouth. At this moment, I have no idea why I'm asking for this stuff, but just bear with me."

"Go ahead."

She paused to think for a moment and closed her eyes in concentration. Doctor Trenton's voice came into her mind again. *'Trust your intuition.'*

Sam rattled her list off. "I'm looking for reasons why Jen could have been so edgy and withdrawn from her colleagues a couple days prior to her murder. Why the nursing administrator suddenly left the day after. Need to know everything about her. Name was Alicia Freed. Next, any personnel who left the hospital's employment, after or soon after the murder, no matter their department. Any invoices or bills she sent, invoices she ap-

proved, who made out the checks to the vendors, and look for a
match for orders and products actually received. Who put the
products on the shelves. I doubt if she played stock girl. Personnel reports of anyone she gave a negative review, with their contact info. And if anyone has a police record. And if anyone is
related to a cop. Just out of curiosity." She took time for a breath.
"Actually, all that came from our interviews today, except the last
one."

"And you want this, when?"

"ASAP."

"How about tomorrow morning, first thing?"

Before she could answer, her cell rang. It was Withers. "Hi. I
was going to call you."

"Yeah, well, making people unhappy and intimidating hospital administrators won't serve you well, Wright."

"Uh—"

"Yeah. Doctor Casting called the local precinct who was doing the initial investigation until we rudely removed it from their
jurisdiction when I was assigned. The captain called me. He was
not happy. This hospital has taken very good care of our guys."

"I had to get through to her and she wasn't getting it."

"Then I suggest you hone your interviewing skills. Now why
did you want to call me?"

"To tell you we were going to investigate the hospital. That's
it. Thank you." She disconnected her call and addressed Tom.
"Tomorrow will be fine. Thank you."

"Okay, Sam. I'll personally bring it all to the precinct."

ন্তর্জ

Sam pulled into her driveway, smiling. She saw Frank's SUV
parked in the spot in front of her house. When she shut off the
engine, he exited his car at the same time she exited hers. "Hi.
What are you doing here?"

He pulled her into his arms and kissed her. His warmth on the
chilly November night made her anxiety dissipate. He was what
she needed.

She wrapped her arms around his neck, welcomed the kiss,
then thought twice and released from his grasp. "Frank, the
neighbors."

"It's eleven o'clock. Everyone's asleep. You wanted to go back to your house, and I don't want you to be alone, yet. So, I'll stay here."

"I don't have a guest room. My second bedroom is a den, and the third, an office." She ran up the steps, punched in the keys, opened two bolted locks and opened the door.

He grabbed a duffle from his car. "I had no intention of staying in a guest room, by the way." He was behind her, entering her living room, and patted her behind. "How's the tush?"

She laughed, running up the steps to the bedroom and plopped down, sitting on her bed. "Fine. Get that look off your face. We have so much to talk about. I went to the hospital. Have so many questions for you."

Frank pulled off his jacket, tossed it onto the chest at the food of her bed, yanked off his T-shirt in one smooth movement, and stood over her.

Sam stared at him in a combination of frustration, anger, and confusion with her arousal mounting. "How can you not focus on this?"

He sat on the bed next to her. "All right. You're right. What did you find out?"

She caught him up on the interviews with the administrator, two nurses, what she requested from Tom, and the tongue lashing she got from Withers.

He dropped onto his back. "Sam, I so appreciate what you're doing, but nothing has led from the hospital. It doesn't make sense."

She leaned over him and rested on his chest. "What doesn't make sense to me is that all the gang interviews yielded nothing. I have to ask you. The nurses said Jen had been withdrawn a couple of days before. Do you know why? What did she tell you about work, anything?"

"Wow. No. Jen and I had made a pact. We discussed nothing about work. We spoke about our common interests, what we wanted to do, had lots of sex, which is what I want, now," he said, sitting up and pulling her down onto the bed.

"Not so fast. She never asked you about any cases? Asked for any medical advice?"

"No. And I never told her about any police cases. Our jobs were very stressful. We didn't want to bring that stress home with us. We lived enough of that at work. Home was *our* time, since we didn't have that much of it. I'm on call twenty-four-seven, so the *we* time was sacred. That's the way it is with most cops and doctors. Privacy, confidentiality. All that."

"Did you notice she was closed down? Come on, Frank. Think with your shrink hat on. I can't believe you wouldn't notice something."

"She hadn't told anyone, but it came up in the autopsy. Jen was two months pregnant. We hadn't told because she miscarried a few months prior. The day before the murder, we didn't even see each other much. She had the night shift. We spoke briefly. I was in deep with a murder case and in court as the medical analyst. Come on. Tom will get what you need by tomorrow morning, and we'll take it from there. There's nothing you can do tonight."

Sam unbuttoned her blouse, slipped her arms out, let her slacks drop as she lifted her foot out to entice him. He got rid of his jeans and briefs. They were under the covers, nude, and in each other's arms in less than a minute.

"I'm sorry, Frank."

He lay on his back. "About?"

She rested her head on his pecs. "Everything. The murder, not having another child."

"Yeah, princess, me, too. I was raised an only child. Didn't want Frankie to be one."

Sam could see this saddened him. "How come your parents didn't want any more children?"

He smiled. "I was adopted at ten. They were older, early fifties."

"Where were you until then? I really know nothing about you."

"No. You don't, do you?" He laughed. "When you hear what I've been through, you'll probably run."

She ran her hand down his arms and rested it on his forearm. "No I won't. You didn't commit me. Tell me."

He rotated onto his right side, facing her, his left hand caressing her hip. "I was born to teen parents, who gave me up for adoption. Right thing to do at the time. I was in a foster home until I was four. I thought they were my real mom and dad. Then one day social services picked me up at the nursery school and I never saw them again. Nothing was explained to me." He paused, pensive a moment. "I went to another foster home. I was very difficult. Thought my parents abandoned me. Didn't trust. Didn't listen. They disciplined me but it wasn't harsh. Nothing they did could make me behave or show any love. Then the cycle began. Bad behavior, horrible in school, being sent back to a group home, back and forth, foster care, and group home. At nine, it appeared I'd be there until I aged out. Then my adoptive parents came into the picture. Theresa and Peter. They had wanted to adopt. Their attorney sent them to the home. They looked at the computer, saw a picture of me, and Theresa pointed and said 'He's the one. We want him.' I think the headmaster must have dropped on his knees and said a prayer to God." Frank shook his head and laughed. "I was such an impossible kid. Had absolutely no respect for authority, never did homework or classwork, but I had high marks on tests. Wouldn't sit. Just walked around the room. They thought I learned through osmosis. I was suspended at least once a month. Then I'd come back, take a test for something I missed, and still get a hundred. Oh man, I was bad. The teachers would give the class more tests because that was the only time I'd sit still. The kids hated me for it. Theresa and Peter took me home and I couldn't understand why. I was so mean to them. Had my own room, every toy imaginable, and I just laughed at them. Then one day I came home and Theresa asked me to show her my social studies test. I was like, 'What test?' Then she stared at my book bag. Just stared like she was concentrating and said, 'You got a ninety-seven on your test. What happened to a hundred?'"

"Oooh."

"Yeah, I thought she had called the school. She swore she didn't. I asked her how she knew. She said, 'I see things.' and I'm like, 'Yeah, right.'"

"Don't tell me she was psychic?"

"Yeah, she was, totally. Like you, but you're denying it."

"So you recognized it? I spoke with Doctor Trenton about it today.'"

He let out a sly mile. "Good."

"You told him. Didn't you?"

"I mentioned he should go in that direction."

"You sneak!" She whacked his arm. "Okay, then what happened? What turned you around?"

"Honestly, patience and love. Theresa was able to see everything I did. Even when I wasn't home."

"How did she do that?"

"Oh, man! She and I must have had some kind of connection. She said we did, from a past life. If I stayed out too late, she'd go into the den, sit in her favorite chair, and meditate. She'd see me, where I was. Then she'd send out a cord, an imaginary one to attach to me. And with her hands, she dragged the cord into her heart until she saw me in front of her. I was usually home within twenty minutes after that. Very weird. But it worked every time."

"Holy crap. That is amazing."

"Definitely. Eventually, Peter asked me why I was behaving like this and I told him that every time I became attached, my foster parents abandoned me and got rid of me. I told him what happened when I was four. He and Theresa researched what had happened. Turned out, I wasn't abandoned. My foster parents, along with a foster sister, were killed in a car accident earlier in the day. By a drunk driver also high on drugs. I became hysterical. I couldn't get why no one had told me. It's the reason I don't drink, and probably why I have never done the drug scene. Then my pediatrician told them to take me to a child psychiatrist, which they did. He told them I needed a physical outlet and that got me into Tae Kwan Do. Major turning point."

"Oh, Frank. I'm sorry you had to go through all that. But it's our soul's journey, you know? And you turned out more than okay."

"Yeah. I certainly know about that. Enough talking, princess." With his arms around her, he scooped her up on top of him.

Her body felt so warm, so natural on top of him. He wrapped his arms around her torso with their lips locked. Her hand was at the base of his neck, drawing him in closer. They had no intention of coming up for air. His hand cascaded down her back to her bottom. He laid his warm hands on her butt cheeks and squeezed gently, causing her to moan and then purr. She rested her head on his pecs, as he tickled her bottom, making circular motions with his index fingers. She gasped and buried her head in his chest, as tingling roared through her, like a river running wild during a storm.

The text sound came from her department-issued phone, still in her tote, that she had placed on her dresser. She glanced toward her tote for a second. They ignored the first beep and continued kissing. Then the sound came again.

She pivoted off him. "Let me just see who it is. It'll keep

coming till I get it." She retrieved the phone, looked at the text, stopped dead. "Frank."

He threw the blanket off him with a frown on his face, begrudgingly got out of bed, went over to her, and stared at the text.

Got the biscuit & UR next if U don't stay away.

Dumbstruck, Sam called Tom to see if he could track the text. He needed the phone to connect. He was at the crime lab in Manhattan. Crap. Then she called Nick. Okay, they were onto something. They'd all meet at the precinct ASAP. She and Frank got dressed in fifteen minutes.

Almost out the door Sam remembered. "Hold on. I have the evidence files with the phone info downstairs in my office. I haven't gone through it yet." She bolted through her dining room, through the kitchen, and down the steps leading to her basement.

Frank followed. When he reached the base of the stairs he looked around, appearing stunned. Sam smiled at his response.

She sorted folders lined up on the red-brown mahogany bench that hugged two walls and, grabbing the right ones, she talked with her back toward him. "Yeah, just like AriellaRose's, but that's a conversation for another day."

Holding the folders, they ran up the steps, into the kitchen, through the living room. Sam was ready to open the front door.

The doorbell rang. She jumped back.

Frank looked through the peephole.

"Open the door, Doctor Khaos," the ESU cop said.

He opened the door and, fully dressed in their combat gear including the laser shields, four men entered the living room.

Sam stood, mouth agape. "How did you get here so fast? In twenty minutes?"

"So you'd rather wait forty?" The sergeant sneered at her. "The precinct we're housed in is three minutes away. Be thankful. Have you packed for a few days, Detective?"

"What? Uh, no."

"Do so. Check to see if it's clear," he told one of his men.

"No one else is here."

The sergeant didn't listen to her. One of his men went upstairs, looked around. "Clear."

"Go. You have three minutes."

She raced up the stairs, packed an overnight bag, and made it back on time.

An officer brought in gear for Sam and Frank. He handed Frank his. "Come on, Detective, let's get this on you."

"Why?"

"No time for questions," the sergeant said. "Wait till we get into the truck. Weapon?" She removed it from her waist holster and handed it to him. He slipped the Kevlar vest around her. Put on her helmet with the plastic face shield down over her face, tied a laser shield around her and one around her back. The sergeant then signaled to his team. They led Sam and Frank out and down the steps, sandwiched between them. After a quick search of the driveway, the sergeant asked, "Have any weapons in your vehicles?"

"No," Sam and Frank responded in unison.

They were led around the back to the truck. An officer opened the doors, a plank descended. Sam walked up as fast as she could with forty pounds of protective gear on. Frank followed. She was edgy, not being able to ask questions. Being silent was not one of her strong points. She was a green personality, as they called it. Someone who needed to know and compare every detail. This wasn't sitting well with her at all. But she did know that when ESU was on the scene, their power usurped hers, especially with someone of a higher rank running the show.

Three officers entered, two in the front seats, the plank was brought back up, shields removed from her, Frank, and the team. She was seated on a bench, seat belted in—all in silence. They drove off.

"Now you can ask your questions, Detective," the sergeant said.

"What is going on?"

"The both of you are now in protective custody."

CHAPTER 36

The ESU team walked into the Chelsea precinct, surrounding Sam and Frank, one man on each side of them, one in front and back, not even allowing them to carry their bags. Sam thought the VIP treatment wasn't called for and, at this moment, she resented it. She clenched her fists to restrain from yelling at the next person she'd lay eyes on. When she got her hands on the guy who destroyed Frank's life, he'd pay. Sam and Frank were marched into Loo's office, with the night shift, about ten uniformed men and woman, staring at them.

Sam and Frank entered the lieutenant's office and the ESU closed the door behind them. Loo, Nick, and Tom had waited for them, Loo by the window, upset.

The lieutenant's expression remained sour. "Sit down."

Sam and Frank sat without saying a word. This man was sure intimidating when he intended to be.

Tom stuck out his hand to Sam. She plucked the phone out of her tote and put it on his palm. He gave her a property form to fill out and, while she did that, he checked the text, showed Loo and Nick, and then took the document from Sam and left the room.

"You okay, Detective?" Loo asked.

"Yes, Lieutenant. I'm fine. I don't see the need for all of this security."

"You don't?"

She opened her mouth to respond.

Loo cut her off before she said a word. "That was a rhetorical question. When that text came in two years ago, there was a murder the next day. I intend to prevent that. Whether it's for you or Frank, I take it to be more than a warning."

"Nick was on the case with me. He didn't get the text."

"Obviously, the person knows you're the instigator in this."
He addressed Nick. "Where the hell is Withers? He should be
finished up by now."

"What happened?" Sam asked.

"His daughter, Melina had severe cramping the past few days.
It got bad tonight and he rushed her into the ER. They're hoping
the cancer didn't resurface," Nick said.

"I'm so sorry to hear that." Sam paused for a moment to respect the news, but Sam being Sam didn't dwell on that. "What's
happening now? I have folders I want to look at from two years
ago about the phone. If it's the same one that sent the text tonight, that FBI investigation was a waste of months. And what's
with Frank and I being in protective custody?"

"For a few days, until we find this perpetrator. You can work
as much as you want on files. You have a choice. You can stay at
the precinct or in one of our safe houses. Frank, where's your
son?"

"At my in-laws. I'll call them in the morning."

"Is their house secure?"

"Yes. They were military. It's very secure."

The lieutenant nodded.

"I vote to stay here. I need access to all the files. Speaking of
which, I want to look through this." She removed a forensic file
from her tote, jumped up from the chair, and pivoted around to
the conference table.

"Hold on, Detective, you weren't dismissed."

Startled, she returned to her seat. "Oh, if I'm in protective
custody how will I go out and interview the people that come
up?"

"We'll bring them in here. You need to listen to what I have
to say." The lieutenant's tone was curt. "You're all over the
place. It's making me nervous."

"Sorry, Lieutenant."

"I agree that you're on the right track. Possibly very close.
But I'm not happy with your approach. You need to take it down
a notch."

"So Withers ratted me out?"

The lieutenant smirked.

"Well, this is what I say to that. I don't think he did the good
job that everyone thinks he did. His handwriting sucks and he
didn't bother to type some of it. Thank God, most of it was com-

puter generated, but for some pages, it's hard to decipher his handwriting."

"That so? Frank, where do you want to be?"

"I have my own safe house. I'll go there if Sam comes with me."

"Absolutely not, and I'm not going to even ask you where or what it is. You'll stay here, then. We have a couple of cots set up. Why don't you get some sleep."

"Not me. Too hyper to sleep. My mind is on a spinning wheel."

The lieutenant was more than serious as he addressed Frank. "You need to calm her down. Just don't pump her full of pharmaceuticals. Okay, Detective, go to your files."

"Can I go to my desk?"

"No. Nowhere that open. You'll stay in here."

"Lieutenant, I feel like a third grader who was sent to the principal's office to do her work."

"So were you?"

"More than I cared to admit, yes."

"Then you should be used to it."

Nick broke into the nonsensical conversation as he sat down at the conference table. "Come on, Sam, show us what you think."

Frank and Sam followed.

The lieutenant joined them. "I want to hear what you have to say, as well."

Sam opened the file and turned to the transfer of evidence page first. "Hold on. The phone was never in the possession of anyone in Jen's investigation. It was like a phantom that no one could locate. Or was it? But the report says, the phone was still active. Guess they paid for the month. They tracked it to a convicted felon in prison. Was he interviewed?"

Frank recapped. "Yes. Denied knowing about it. Said the cops took his phone when he was arrested. Didn't know what happened after that. We went through this, already."

"Hold on, I accessed that guy's file. Wilbur Hemming, right?"

The lieutenant stared at her, wide-eyed.

"I take initiative, Lieutenant. I had to go back in time. Where is the transfer from his possession to the police? They have to mark it. Who arrested him?" She turned some pages. "Here it is.

Mark Collins out of Manhattan North. Two years, and almost two month ago. Where is he now?"

"Who?"

"Collins."

"Collins retired to Florida."

"Where is Hemming?"

The lieutenant shrugged. "I guess, somewhere upstate. The Department of Prisons has his file now. Where are you going with this, Sam?"

She looked farther down the form. "Okay Let's start at the beginning. When he was arrested, all of his belongings were given to the property clerk at the 053 in the Bronx. A wallet, a watch marked y/m, and a necklace marked y/m. A phone. But a couple hours later, at the shift change when the paperwork was caught up, no phone."

Frank nodded. "When we interviewed him, he didn't give a damn about the phone. He was screaming about his Rolex and nineteen gram 14K gold necklace. That's some yellow metal."

"Ooh. I would have liked to see that."

"He couldn't get it back. They would only give it to him, personally, and he was locked up."

"Okay. So it says here, after ninety days, they auctioned off his watch and gold chain." She scanned the next page. "Hold on. His wife did come to get his belongings when he was arrested. They absolutely would not give them to her. That's right, Frank. No one had seen her, but they think she might have snatched the phone off a table. Am I reading this right? How come no one saw her? And she snatched the phone, not the expensive stuff? This doesn't make any sense. Let me look back. What was this creep arrested for?" She flipped to the first page. "Ooh. Murder. Three ladies of the night. So our bum here, was a pimp. No wonder they thought his wife had taken it. To keep his contacts out of our hands. But wait." She glanced up at Frank. "Then he would have cared about the phone." She opened another file. "Now in Jen's file, it says, the feds still investigated that phone. His wife and father moved to North Carolina as soon as he was indicted. By the time the agents caught up with them, they were both deceased, two weeks apart, a few months after moving there. That's weird. The reports said overdose and it wasn't suspicious." Sam sat back, frustrated. "How can that be?"

"Why don't you two go get some rest." Loo said.

"Okay, Loo, I'm wiped," Frank said, equally as frustrated as Sam.

❦❦

The lieutenant brought in breakfast for Sam and Frank. Platters of scrambled eggs, sausage, fresh fruit, but no bread or potatoes. Guess Loo knew Frank's culinary preferences. Nick joined them as they were finishing. He held the door open for Tom, who was behind him with files up to his forehead.

Tom grinned. "Good morning, Detectives, Doctor Khaos. Sam, you're either going to love me or hate me." He put the folders on the conference table and then handed Sam forms to sign that she had received the documentation.

"The phone text is a match from the one two years ago. I'm working on getting a ping signal. Your interviews and what you requested yielded a lot. I haven't read it all. Jennifer kept accurate records. You'll know the relevance. The cover sheets are self-explanatory. Call me if you need anything."

"Thank you so much, Tom," Sam said as she handed him the signed papers.

Tom nodded, did a quick military turn, and left the room.

She looked at the amount of documentation and gulped. Acid regurgitated in her throat. She must have been a hell of a lot more nervous and overwhelmed than she'd admitted to herself. She stared at them, scanned the cover sheets, and picked up the folder about Alicia Freed, the nursing administrator before Penelope Casting.

"Frank, did you know her, Alicia?"

"Briefly. We met at the holiday parties. In all the years Jen worked at the hospital, I was only able to get to two. Definitely not the past three years. Jen and my work schedules conflicted. If Doctor Freed walked in here now, I probably wouldn't recognize her. Except for the fact she was matronly looking."

"Okay, let's focus on why Doctor Freed suddenly left." Sam exhaled deeply. "This will take a long time to go through. I definitely can't assess this all at first glance."

"Let's divide this up. Give me Doctor Freed. Not having a relationship with her, I could be objective." Frank slipped the folder in front of him. "You take the files that Jen created."

"Fair enough." Nick pulled a few folders in front of him.

"Okay, here's her quarterly evaluation reports. I think we should focus on the negative ones and Jen's comments as well as her follow up conferences with them."

"Okay, good." She placed two other files in front of her. "These are orders she placed, the invoices from the vendors, and the products she received. Did she write the checks herself?"

Frank smiled. "No, Sam. There's a checks and balances system. The checks are written to the vendors through the accounting department. I believe there has to be two signatures on the checks. I know that's true for pharmaceuticals, at least. Sam, do you think you could sit still and remain quiet for an hour so we could get at preliminary read?"

"What do you think I am, twelve?"

"Closer to eight."

"Frank, just read."

Nick laughed.

For the next hour and a half their noses were buried in the files. They took notes on yellow legal pads, not being able to write on the documents themselves.

Loo opened the door and stood there, looking grim.

"What's up Loo?" Nick must have read his expression as did Sam.

"Dingo called. The cancer did return. In her stomach, stage three. He's taking a week off so the family can discuss treatment options with Melinda's oncologist."

Sam put her pen down and sat with the same grim expression. "Oh, no. So sorry."

"Send some of those positive things you do, Detective. Melinda's going to need it."

"I will, Lieutenant. I will."

Loo quietly closed the door behind him.

The trio sat solemnly for a few minutes. Sam broke the silence. "Anyone have anything to discuss? I may have."

Frank started. "Okay, let's start talking these things through. Alicia Freed. She's an MD and was in this position for twenty-five years, so she had to know her stuff and be cognizant of what was going on. Every meeting she had with personnel is documented with the date and time and a summary. She met with Jen, which was not unusual, at least once a month for the eight years Jen was employed there. Okay, so far, so good. For the last month, Jen met with her twice. The second meeting was September thirtieth. Three days before Jen was killed. The cover sheet lists that meeting with Jen, but, there's absolutely no documentation as to what that second meeting was about. Nothing. I looked through the entire file, thought the pages weren't in order. So, with my shrink hat on, I assume that Jen saw things occurring that she needed addressed, but this good doctor felt it should be swept under the rug."

Sam nodded. "Excellent find. Let's call in Doctor Freed."

Nick put a halt to her enthusiasm. "Not yet. Go through the rest of this. Let's find out why Jen went to her. Then we can be specific. So when we ask her questions, we'll already know the answers, and any lying will be obvious. There's nothing that would raise a red flag in these nurses' evals. Jen seemed to defuse any anger. No one ever threatened her. At least, Jen didn't document that anyone had."

Sam held up a file. "Okay, I think I found something but I'm not sure how to interpret it and it could correspond with what Frank has. Which one of you guys is a mathematical genius?"

Frank pulled Sam's folder in between them. "Show me."

"Yes, of course you are. The one hundred percent test taker," Sam snipped. "Okay, Tom went back for three years, since Jen took over the supervising nurse position."

"No, Sam, Jen was the supervising nurse eight years."

"Oops. Then Tom only gave us the last three. That should be enough." Sam made two stacks. "This stack is the product list Jen ordered. This stack is the merchandise Jen received. She sent orders once a month. So three years, thirty-six sets of orders. I can do some math. I went through them, starting from three years ago to present. In the first thirty, Jen had checked off each product and cost and signed the bottom of each form. All is good. Everything matches. Then the last six months, things got weird."

Frank raised a hand. "Hold on. Jen put the orders through but she didn't do all this checks and balancing of the order sheets. She received and checked off the inventory. Why would she be looking at all this? Would take away too much time from her patients."

"I don't know, but these next six months are all mixed up. Here's Jens' orders, same form. Here's the invoices sent to the vendors, quantity more, cost more but the same item and item code. This form was not included with any order earlier than these six months. Then the receipts which Jen got, which matched her originals."

"If Jen found something wrong, she'd never wait six months. Wait a second." Frank pulled some of the sheets out of the folder. "There's a date on top when the files were accessed. Here it is. September thirtieth." He slumped down in the seat.

"Crap," Sam muttered.

"And the first undocumented meeting with Doctor Freed. We're onto something. Let me look at the numbers." Frank pulled his smartphone out of his pocket and tapped the calculator app. "Remember, this is only for the ER. There are an innumerable amounts of departments that all send their invoices to accounting. At my hospitals, there are a few people cleared to write checks."

"Do it," Sam said.

Frank looked at the invoices. "These numbers are huge. April tenth. The invoice sent to the vendors totaled five hundred thousand but Jen's order was for three hundred fifty thousand. That matched the product she received. Hundred fifty thousand dollar difference." He pulled the vendor's invoice closer. "Hold on, this isn't an official form. Look. The font on the form isn't an exact match to the hospital stationery. The hospital uses Times Roman. This is Arial. A forgery. Apparently the person who collated these, didn't write the check. Probably a clerk, who didn't eyeball them. Maybe these forms weren't supposed to be included. Who knows?" He checked the rest of the invoices. Same thing. "Okay, May tenth. Seventy-five thousand. June tenth, fifty thousand. July tenth, fifty-three thousand. August tenth, twenty-seven thousand. September tenth, back up to sixty-two thousand. The grand total is…drum roll, please…four hundred, seventeen thousand dollars over the actual cost of supplies. Embezzlement. Jen was killed because she uncovered embezzlement. Someone must have tipped her off and she requested the files. But that doesn't matter. Who wrote the checks?"

Nick pulled over the employment files.

Sam took a deep breath. "I only asked Tom to print out the employees, along with their history, who left right after Jen's murder." Saying the last two words gave her shivers.

Nick opened the three-inch-thick file. The listings were alphabetical by department. He ran his index finger over each department title.

Frank pursed his lips. "Check accounting first."

Nick found the listing and stopped dead. His face whitened.

"Nick, you okay? What it is?" Frank sounded alarmed.

Nick slumped back in his chair and swallowed. He covered his mouth with the fingers of his right hand and grabbed onto his stomach with his left hand, as if he was going to vomit.

Sam's cell rang. "Wright."

"Got the location of the text."

"Where, Tom?"

"At the foundation of the Verrazano Bridge. Then the ping disappeared. Phone probably tossed into the water."

"Okay, thanks, Tom." She disconnected and stared at Nick.

Frank grabbed his shoulder. "Nick, what's going on? Now, pal."

Nick closed his eyes, put his lips together. "You have to take it easy, Frank."

"Just say it."

"The employee who wrote the checks was the one who left, the day after the murder. No explanation. Just didn't show up for work."

Sam's eyes darted back and forth between Frank and Nick. This didn't bode well.

"Who, for crying out loud?" Frank bellowed.

Nick swelled his cheeks and blew out a breath. "Mallory McDonald."

Frank reddened, slamming his fist on the desk. "That's Dingo Withers's wife."

CHAPTER 37

Later that day, Doctor Alicia Freed sat paralyzed with fear in the conference room. The woman's gray and white streaked hair, parted down the middle, curled under her chin. Her complexion, riddled with deep crevices, paled, with just a small dot of blush on the apples of her cheeks. Her eyes looked vacant with her lids collapsing close together, her short eyelashes making them to appear slit-like. At sixty-five, she had weathered many personal traumas that further investigation had revealed, and that Frank intended to grill her on. Sam didn't know about this yet, but he had his own sources in the court system. This was not the first time she had sat in an interrogation room. She wrung her wrinkled hands together on her lap, as they lay on her long, checkered, denim skirt.

The police unit who had brought her in had found her in the midst of packing. She told them she had planned a trip to visit her daughter overseas.

Frank leaned with his back against the wall, his knee bent, with the sole of his right sneaker scuffing it. When her attorney, Maximilian Dempsey, entered with Nick and Sam, Frank sent Dempsey looks that could propel him to hell. Frank's fists clenched and he banged the wall with his hands behind him in a rhythmic pound.

Dempsey shifted in his chair at the intruding thuds and smirked. "Who's he?"

The usually compassionate shrink had flown off the galaxy into Netherland, as Frank walked around the table to face them. "I'm Doctor Frank Khaos. Your client, Doctor Freed, worked with my late wife, Jennifer Khaos, at the hospital. And my late wife went to your client to complain about discrepancies she noticed from the accounting department. Obviously my late wife was ignored. And your client mysteriously retired the day after my pregnant wife—was—murdered," he growled, pounding his fists on the desk.

Frank's phrasing jolted Dempsey who swiped some stray gray hairs off his forehead and unbuttoned his jacket. A missing button on his shirt revealed a spread midsection. "There was no documentation as to that. I read the file."

Sam clasped her hands on the desk. "What was missing tells us a lot. Other meetings were documented in full. Where were you traveling to, Doctor Freed?" she asked, her tone deliberately curt.

"Switzerland."

"How nice. Why did you only get a one way ticket?" Sam already knew.

Shaking, she cleared her throat, her eyes scanning the room. "My daughter—wanted me—to stay a long time," she stammered. So I didn't—know when I'd return."

"Doctor Freed, we need permission to access to your bank accounts," Sam said with a flat tone.

The petrified woman stared back and forth between her attorney, Nick, Sam, and Frank, then focused on Sam to answer. "W—why?"

"You're behavior is showing us it's warranted. You seem so nervous. Why is that?" Sam planned to make her nervous until she collapsed.

Frank nodded. He knew how Sam operated by now. For sure, she was his ally.

Doctor Freed grabbed her attorney's arm and shuddered. "Max."

Nick pulled his smartphone from his pocket. "We can get a warrant for it within an hour. I've become attached at the hip with Judge Martinson."

"If my client cooperates and answers your questions, what will she get?"

"Participating in embezzlement is a felony. Concealing that you know about embezzlement and, as a hospital administrator, not reporting it and making a police report is also a felony, but knowing about a murder that is about to be committed is considered conspiracy to commit murder, and that's a very long prison sentence. And given Doctor Freed's age, adding them up would mean the rest of her life behind bars without chance of parole," Nick retorted matter-of-factly.

"Murder? Oh my God, I knew nothing about murder. I didn't know they were going to murder anyone. I swear to you. On my grandchildren's lives, I swear to you!"

"Swearing won't help you. Why did you retire the day after the murder, Doctor Freed?" Frank pushed, his voiced raised.

Doctor Freed broke down, hysterical. "I didn't retire right away. I just never went back to work. I used my sick days."

"Why did you do that?" Frank persisted.

"I realized Jennifer's murder must have had something to do with those invoices. I had approached the accounting supervisor right after Jennifer came to me. She said she knew nothing about it, but I know she did. From just the way she looked at me. Then Lisa approached me three days later, the day of the murder. Oh—my—God!" she sobbed.

"Lisa?" Sam asked.

"Yes," Dr. Freed took a deep breath. "Lisa McDonald. On the hospital paper work, it's Mallory, but she goes by her middle name, Lisa, and her maiden name. She suggested I retire. No one would suspect because of my age." Doctor Freed couldn't catch her breath. Sobs overtook her. "She said they wouldn't put me in jail for not saying anything because of my age and failing health either, but she said she'd 'sweeten the pot.' Yes, she used those exact words. She gave me sixty thousand dollars to put through my retirement papers and keep quiet." She bobbed her head up and down. "But I didn't get any money from when they were doing it.'

Frank roared and stood up, leaning over the table. "And you chose the easy way out! To do that and not report it so my son and I would have over two years of anguish. He was five years old when his mother was taken from him, Doctor. Had you made a police report as soon as Jen told you, you could have prevented her murder. What a sorry excuse for someone who took the oath!" Frank spun away and slammed his fist into the wall behind him. The plaster board split and fragmented, just like his life felt at this moment.

"But I wasn't the only one," she cried in a whisper.

Frank turned around abruptly. "What was that? You weren't the only one for what?"

She hung her head and wrung her hands in her lap. "There

were five people in the accounting department who knew about it. And got money. Why should I be the only one being blamed?"

"Who? I want names now," Sam said flatly.

"They still work there. Lisa left after she came to see me. The supervisor, a Mrs. Langston, then three others, still work there. I don't know their names."

Sam got up, leaned over the table, and got into her face. "You better think of the names, now!"

Doctor Freed scooted away, shoving her chair back. "Oh my God, you're upsetting me. Okay, Two men. Paul, he was Irish. Spoke with a Brogue. Teddy, he was Haitian. And Karen. I don't know what she is, but she rode a motorcycle to work."

Sam licked her lips and nodded with a sarcastic slant. "If you weren't involved, how do you know who was?"

"It was a Thursday. Lisa came over to my house on Thursday after work with the money. The day after. She came with them. They all frightened me. I didn't know what to do. So I never went back to work, at all. I used my sick days until my papers went through."

Frank returned to the table and sat. "Doctor Freed, what did you use the money for?"

She sniffled. "Personal reasons."

"You need to tell us. My partners need to know everything."

She stared down at her skirt. "My son's bail."

"What was he arrested for?" Sam asked.

"Embezzlement. He worked for a large discount store chain."

"And you didn't learn from his arrest that it was not okay to do that?" Nick sounded flabbergasted.

"He had gotten away with it for years, the other ones more than six months and me, a measly one time."

This doctor was not all there. Frank knew her attorney would grab onto her mental instability. He should if he was worth a penny. Frank was leaning toward a diagnosis of early dementia. "Where is he now?"

"In Switzerland."

"The sixty thousand you made, did it go entirely for his bail?"

"Yes." She sniffled again. "The bail was six hundred thousand. I paid, sixty in cash. I was so relieved I didn't have to dig into my own money."

"Look, Detectives. These people obviously did their due diligence, researched, and knew that her son had just been arrested.

They saw how vulnerable she was. Is. She's still vulnerable."

The attorney's explanation didn't make a dent.

"Do you realize that money obtained in the commission of a crime is not allowed to be used as bail money?" Nick asked.

She shook her head.

"Then I suggest, Doctor Freed, that you contact you son to come back."

"But—but—but he'll go to prison."

Sam and Nick sat, as dumbfounded as Frank at this woman's lack of ability to make connections.

The lieutenant entered the room and put his hand on Frank's shoulder. "As will you, Doctor Freed. Doctor Khaos come outside for a while. Doctor Freed, did Mrs. McDonald tell you who pulled the trigger?"

Through her sobbing, she shook her head. "No. I swear."

"Did you call anyone to tell them you were being brought in?"

Again, she shook her head.

"Did you tell any of the other people involved you were leaving the country?"

"No, I haven't spoken to anyone since right after the—Mrs. Khaos—I'm so sorry."

"Then how did you know to leave the country, now?" Lieutenant Rojas persisted.

Doctor Freed slumped in the chair and looked down at her hands in her lap. "Lisa called yesterday to check up on me after all this time. I told her I wasn't feeling well and she suggested I go visit my daughter in Switzerland."

"Detectives, I have a warrant for Mallory McDonald's arrest, and one to bring in Dingo Withers for questioning. They're on my desk. Arrest Doctor Freed. And the two of you may execute the warrants." The lieutenant escorted Frank, whose fists were ready to beat someone to a pulp, out of the room.

∽∾∽

Nick, Sam, and Frank followed behind the ESU truck in Nick's SUV. Two patrol cars followed behind them. Dingo Wither's garden apartment in the Belle Harbor section of Queens, a block away from the beach, was on the third floor of a three-story walkup recently renovated, thanks to Hurricane Sandy.

Sam patted Frank's hand. "What did you say to Loo to convince him to let you come?"

He placed his other hand on top of hers and squeezed, appreciating her compassion. "Nothing, really. He must have seen the torment in my eyes and he just nodded as he saw you getting ready to leave. I bolted out the door."

Nick cleared his throat. "Frank, I know you're fuming, but you have to think. We have no evidence that Dingo pulled the trigger. Maybe Lisa was having an affair, who knows? All I know is their marriage has been on real shaky ground since about the time of Jen's murder."

"Nick, wake up," Frank growled. "Who had the most opportunity to conceal evidence? Our lead homicide detective. Who had the opportunity to steer the detectives in the opposite direction? Who had the power to access any evidence room in the city?"

Sam nodded. "You told me yesterday, Nick, that Dingo slept at the Brooklyn precinct. Maybe it wasn't because he wanted to investigate. Maybe he wanted to divert evidence they put into files," she added. "Oh my God! I just thought of something. Remind me to ask Loo a question when he calls for an update."

"What, Sam?"

"Not saying until I have definitive proof."

Nick pulled into a spot. "Anyway, that's a lot of ifs. We have to stay clear thinking. That's all I'm saying."

They waited.

ESU officers entered the building. Thirty minutes seemed like an eternity to Frank. The sergeant exited, looked around, and approached the car. "No one's home. No suitcases out, clothes still in closet, medications still in medicine cabinet in bathroom. So basically no sign of them being runners."

"All right. Let's at least execute the search warrant." Nick's cell rang. "Yes, Loo?…Seriously?…Oh, man. I don't know whether to be relieved or pissed…Yes, sir…At the apartment now. Will search. Hold on, Loo, Sam wants to ask you a question." He put the phone on speaker.

"Lieutenant, please do me a favor and look again in Hemming's file. It's on the conference table in your office."

"What do you need?"

"They day of his arrest."

"Hold on…October first." Sam exhaled a deep breath. "Can

you please find out if Withers was in the 053 that day?"

"I'll get back to you." Loo disconnected.

"Looks like Dingo is high on the triggerman list now. His daughter is actually well and not in the hospital. Loo called to check. Dingo figured out that we're getting close and wanted to make himself and his wife scarce. Loo sounded like crap. And if Withers was in the precinct that day, he swiped the phone, not Hemming's wife. You holding it together, Frank?"

Frank squeezed Sam's hand. "Yeah. Have to."

"All right, let's do a search." Nicked yelled to the sergeant, "Hey, Sarg. We need cover. Get your men up there." He tossed vests and helmets to Sam and Frank.

The sergeant nodded and his team entered the adjacent buildings. About five minutes later, there were three sharpshooters, one on each of the surrounding rooftops.

Nick, Sam, and Frank exited the SUV, looked around, and sprinted into the building. They dashed up the three flights, where an officer had been guarding the door. They entered the two-bedroom, modestly furnished apartment, and removed their helmets, placing them on the couch.

After they all put on gloves, Sam entered the short and narrow galley kitchen. The walls were painted in a mint green with plain sand-colored wood cabinets. The granite counter tops were a veined multi-shades of green. Frank took the bedrooms and Nick the bathroom. Sam opened the cabinets. Pot's in cabinets on either side of the stove.

She pulled them out and onto the floor. She opened the fridge. It was stocked. So was the freezer, with packaged meats. There were the usual flour and sugar canisters on the counter. Sam opened the sugar canister and tilted it.

"In the kitchen, guys!"

Frank approached with a frown. Sugar was his number one enemy. "What, Sam?"

She poured the sugar canister over and into the sink. Out poured rolls of hundred-dollar bills.

"Don't touch the bills." Nick spoke into his earwig. "Need packaging."

Sam picked up the flour container. It was half filled. With flour. She sniffed. "Ew. It stinks."

Nick took a whiff. "That wet newspaper smell. Yeah, like bills have that been in here for a long time. All right. I'm calling this in. They could possibly track this. I'm clueless as to where they'd go."

"Okay, let's go back to the precinct so we can figure this out." Frank opened the door and addressed the officer standing guard. "Crime Scene's coming."

The officer nodded.

Sam propped her hands on her hips. "Hey. I'm not done, yet. And it's too late, anyway. All sorts of stuff could be hidden in a kitchen." She opened all of the cabinets above the stove. Nothing but plates and stoneware. She couldn't reach the cabinets above the fridge. She pulled over a step ladder, climbed to the top, and opened the cupboards.

Frank re-entered the apartment. When he saw her up there, he stopped, putting his hands on his hips. "Hey. Why didn't you call me?"

"I'm on a mission." Stretching her arm to the back of the cabinet, she tapped on a box. They heard the sound of her fingernail against metal. She pulled the metal box forward, her eyes widening.

"What?"

"Here, Frank, take this." She handed him an eight-by-twelve-inch box that was about four inches deep.

He put in on the counter, then put his hands around her waist, and brought her down. His mind was reeling from what he was guessing was in the box. He waited a moment, took a deep breath. Nick put his hand on Frank's shoulder. With the tip of his index finger, Frank opened the box.

Inside the box was a Smith and Wesson .38 caliber revolver.

The same type of revolver that had killed Jen.

CHAPTER 38

The following morning, Loo shouted to get their attention, when he saw Frank, Sam, and Nick walk into the main room of the precinct. "In here. The three of you."

They entered his office and sat around the conference table.

Loo scanned their faces. "Okay. You did great yesterday. Our lab will find out if that's the weapon, Frank. We have to verify it. But you have to keep it together."

Frank nodded, but his jaw was so tight with gritted teeth, he couldn't get a word out. He sat, not giving anyone eye contact, punching his thighs with his closed fists.

As the lieutenant spoke, he focused on Frank. "That being said, I had to call the bureau office. With interstate finances and big institution embezzlement, it becomes the FBI's jurisdiction. They'll be able to trace the money you recovered. And find out how far back their scheme went."

Sam rolled her eyes. "Lieutenant, does that mean Doctor Freed gets turned over? And McDonald and Withers?"

"Yes. In all honesty, you should be relieved. Takes the prosecution out of our hands. You don't know yet, Sam, how hard it is to take down one of our own. The FBI won't care, nor will they have any emotion invested. They're sending agents over to pick up all these files and Jen's computer. You'll sign the exchange of evidence over to them. By then, we should have an ID on the weapon."

Sam looked at him with her mouth open, then forced the words out. "What if Withers or Lisa pulled the trigger? Murder usurps embezzlement."

Loo glanced at Frank before he spoke. "We keep the trigger-man or woman. The Brooklyn DA will prosecute, since it happened there. In that event, we clean up our own."

Frank nodded. "That's all I care about. And Sam and Nick can still make the arrest."

Everyone murmured their agreement.

"But what about finding Withers and his wife?" Frank demanded.

"Again, FBI. All we have now is the embezzlement. Until we get an ID on the weapon."

Sam sat back in the chair with arms folded across her chest.

"You don't know that much about him, anyway." Frank said.

She stood her ground. "But Nick and you do. Okay, I'm not just sitting here and waiting for them. Brainstorming time. Where did he like to go?"

"Okay, I'll bite." The lieutenant sat at the conference table. "Nick, did he talk to you about personal stuff?"

"Only when Melinda was ill. When they sold the house. He wasn't sociable to begin with. The way he treated people alienated them. Now I know that during the last couple of years, that was purposeful on his part."

"Anyone call the daughter? Ask her to come in?" Sam asked, as if they were dumb not to.

Nick tapped Melinda's number on his smartphone. She answered on the fourth ring. "Hey, Melinda. It's Nick Valatutti. Is your dad around? I've been trying to reach him. Have some forensics I need to run by him." He put the phone on speaker.

"Oh, Nick, they're finally getting away for a few days. Can't you let him relax?"

Nick laughed. "Actually, I can't, hon. We've all been up round the clock on this case."

"Yes, I know he told me. Seven something murders and that new little detective, what's her name?"

"Samantha Wright."

"Yeah, he finds her to be a pain in the butt. He told me she reminds him of me and says she whines and thinks she knows it all. And he despises that pout." She laughed. "I do the same thing. It gets him every time."

Sam crinkled her face. Frank patted her back.

"Yeah, she is a pip." Nick raised an index finger at Sam. "But do you know where they went?"

"Yeah. The new hotel that just opened up in Atlantic City, near the big ones, uh, the smoke free one. Lisa's trying to get him to quit smoking. Yeah, the Calgary. Lisa loves the slots and she doesn't care that she loses. They tell us they're spending our inheritance."

"Okay, thanks. When are they coming back?"

"Actually, tomorrow afternoon. So can't you wait?"

"Till tomorrow, yeah. Thanks, Melinda. Be well."

"Bye, Nick."

He disconnected the call. After a quick Google search for the hotel and a phone call, Nick found out Dingo and Lisa were indeed there, but they had checked out a few hours ago. "Okay, get a team around their apartment, a BOLO out for his car on the Verrazano and the Marine Park Bridge. I believe he gets into Belle Harbor that way."

"Yes. The Verrazano. The location of the text. They were probably on their way there last night. Why can't we track the GPS on his phones? Department and personal?" Sam asked.

Frank sure approved of the way this woman thought. On her feet.

There was a knock at Loo's office door.

"Come in."

It was Tom, looking despondent. He rolled his lips together, with his eyes focused on a sheet of paper in his hand. He swallowed, not making eye contact with anyone. "Doctor Khaos, I'm sorry. I don't know how to say this. I wanted to tell you in person, not on the phone."

"Just say it, Tom. I'll be okay."

"That was the weapon that killed your wife, sir. Exact bullet match. Oh, man, I'm sorry. The only fingerprints that were on the weapon were those of Detective Withers. The serial number had been filed down, but I retrieved it. It's all on this printout."

The lieutenant took the document.

The room went silent. Time stood still. Frank slumped in the chair, his fingers over his mouth, and closed his eyes. After two years, one month, three weeks, and three days, he and Frankie were going to have closure. A tear trickled out of the corner of his right eye. "That fucking bastard is mine."

❧

Frank and Sam sat in the rear as Nick eyed the GPS locator on the computer that lay on the passenger seat. They were driving on the Gowanas Parkway, which led into the Prospect Expressway into Ocean Parkway. There was so much traffic here that putting on the siren would have been for naught. According to the GPS map, Withers and his wife were still in New Jersey but were heading back in the direction of the Verrazano Bridge. Their projected route, if they didn't detour, would go over the bridge onto the Belt Parkway to Flatbush Avenue North then onto the Marine Parkway Bridge. Frank wanted to take them down before or after the bridge.

FBI agents still hadn't arrived at the precinct. That was fine with him. He wanted the bust. And he knew Sam was content with that, as well. It would be too painful for her to hand over her long hours of hard work. Loo had let them go, saying he'd take care of the paper work. One thing about Loo, he was a compassionate guy.

Frank spoke to himself the entire drive. He couldn't believe this day was here. In a couple of hours Withers and his wife would be in custody. For over two years he had planned what he'd do the guy who took Jen away from him. After he beat him to a pulp with every martial arts move he knew, and he knew them all, he'd break his neck. The guy deserved to rot in hell. And he would. Frank could kick himself that, no way in hell, in reality, would he be able to do this. He had to remain functioning and out of prison for his son. His whole world revolved around Frankie.

One thing, he had learned through martial arts, was to be humble. To remain clear thinking. To remain mentally balanced. To use brute force only when necessary. He couldn't risk losing his license, his standing in the MMA community, or his gym. Those guys needed him. He had to continue to be their example that violence shouldn't beget violence.

Restraint today would be the greatest personal test of his life.

Nick gave them an update. "They're on the Verrazano, now."

"Something isn't right. Shouldn't be this easy. Could you get a visual? Was it confirmed that it is Withers and his wife in that car?"

"We're following based on the ping on his department-issued phone."

"Any facial features?"

"Just a dot from here, Frank."

"All right. Continue."

Nick headed onto the Prospect Expressway in bumper-to-bumper traffic. He slammed his fist on the steering wheel. "We better make it." He put in a call. "Loo, any updates?"

"Yes. Agents are here now. Very impressed with Detective Wright's analyses."

Frank patted Sam on her thigh and smiled.

"They have your location and Withers's. There are unmarked units on the side of the road at the Belt Parkway entrance. They'll stay back. Don't want a problem with civilians on the road."

On the three-lane Prospect Expressway, an accident caused a merge into two lanes. After the accident, it opened up and, a mile later, Nick merged left, entering onto Ocean Parkway at Church Avenue. His siren went on and he increased speed, running lights, as cars moved over.

Frank became more on edge as adrenalin surged through his system. He couldn't wait to give Jen's parents closure. Their only daughter had been taken from them, stateside. As military parents, and having a daughter in the service as well, they always had to be prepared that there would be a chance Jen wouldn't return to them. But she did. With not so much as a scratch from Iraq. They had truly felt blessed. For eight years.

Twenty minutes later, a voice came through on Nick's speaker. "FBI Special Agent, Brett Case, here. They entered the Belt. I have our other cars on my radar, too. We're following Withers. In a new Lexus."

"When the hell did he get a Lexus?" Nick asked.

"Don't know, Detective."

"Probably got it when he saw the end coming. His last hoorah. Bet it was close to the last two weeks, when this little pip—" Frank patted Sam's thigh again. "—showed up."

She squeezed his hand and smiled.

Nick made it down tree-lined Ocean Parkway in ten minutes. This parkway had three lanes going in each direction, separated by an island, with service lanes on either side. For most of its length, expensive one and two family homes outlined the service lanes. Nick turned left onto Avenue R, all the way through to Fillmore Avenue, around the park and onto Flatbush Avenue.

This commercial avenue was always crammed with trucks and cars. Today was no different. Nick stayed in the left lane and drivers did respect the siren.

About a mile down on Flatbush Avenue, close to the Marine

Park Bridge entrance, Nick spotted Withers's vehicle, with an FBI unmarked staying way back. "There he is, Frank."

Agent Case interjected again. "Detectives, I thought Withers was African American and his wife, Caucasian."

"Yes. What are you saying, Agent?"

"The woman is mixed ethnicity, and the man looks Hawaiian or Asian."

"Take them, now!" Frank yelled.

Sirens rang as three FBI vehicles surrounded the Lexus, forcing it to pull over next to the toll lanes on the bridge. Nick pulled up behind the last car.

The driver of the Lexus rolled down his and the passenger side window as directed by the bellow of the horn from the lead FBI car. Nick, Frank, and Sam exited their car and stayed behind but within hearing distance.

In broken English the driver addressed the agent who came toward his car on the passenger side and flashed his badge. "What? Agent? Why you stop me?"

"Do you have a weapon?"

"No. No weapon."

"Who told you to go this way? Over the bridge.?"

"We live there. In Atlantic Beach."

"Where are you coming from?"

"Hotel Calgary. Atlantic City."

"Let me see your ID. Any receipt from the hotel?"

"Yes. Yes." The man opened the center compartment, took out the hotel receipt, and handed it to the agent who handed it to another agent. Then the driver pulled his ID out of his wallet.

"We were following you because of the signal on your smartphone. Did someone give you a new phone?"

"No. No phone."

Frank lost patience. "We need to search your car. Step out, please."

The man and woman exited the car and were led over to the grassy area, now browned from the late fall weather. Shaking, they held hands.

Nick and Frank each took one side of the car. They overturned the carpets. Opened the glove compartment, checked the middle compartment, the trunk, the compartments on the inside base of the doors, the pockets on the back of the rear seats, the rear cup holders, the middle compartment in the rear.

Each search yielded nothing.

Sam slipped into the driver's seat and pulled down the small compartment above the rear view mirror that was meant to hold sunglasses. Withers's phone fell into her hand.

Frank stood with his hands on his waist. "How the hell did you know that?"

"It was the only place left. Nothing genius."

Frank stormed over to the decoy couple and waved the phone in front of the guy's face. "Who gave you this?"

"Don't know! Don't know!"

The man was so fearful, Frank noticed urine dripping down his pants leg.

Sam looked at the ID the agent held then walked over to the man. "Mr. Chang, did anyone at the hotel look inside your car?"

"What you mean?"

"Well, this is a new car. Did anyone seem to be interested about the model and want to see the inside? Anyone say they wanted to buy one?"

"Yes. Yes. A man. A black man."

"Do you know where this man was going after he looked in your car?"

"No. He didn't say."

"Thank you." She walked away.

"What, Sam?"

"Withers must have looked around, made friends, and planted his phone when pretending to look at the interior. That leaves us nowhere. But I'd bring them in and interrogate."

The FBI man smiled at her. "Detective Wright, you continue to impress. Lieutenant Rojas, told us you're new. Well done, first week."

"Thank you. Second week." Sam smiled. "And you are?"

"FBI SAC, Special Agent in Charge, Brett Case. My men picked up your files, then we got the call to follow."

Frank didn't like how this tall, polished, suited fed was scrutinizing Sam from head to toes. His smile was the same Frank had had when he first met Sam. And that smile had some pretty sensual thoughts behind it. He approached with a distraction. "What now, Agent?"

"Doctor Khaos, we'll find him. We will. Detective Wright, what would be the next step?"

"You want her to do your job?"

"No. She went through the files thoroughly. So what about it, Detective?"

"Brooklyn South Hospital isn't far. I'd like to find out if the staff, Doctor Freed told us about, is there. Do a full sweep. Blow their minds. Really, loud, aggressive. Tie them down until they talk."

Special Agent Case and Frank stared at her like she was nuts. Frank sneered and threw up his hands. *Yeah, that's my Sam.*

"Well, not the last part. But I'd want arrest charges, not only to include embezzlement, but conspiracy to commit murder. Lisa had to talk to at least one of them to warn that we're getting close. She called Dr. Freed. And I bet at least one of them knows where she is. And I'd also bet they'd trample each other to get a deal."

Case nodded in approval. "Okay. Hey, Simpson," he called to his partner.

Simpson approached, pursed his lips, and shot Frank a you-lucky-bastard look. Frank nodded.

"Get into the employee files. See if any of the ones in Detective Wright's notes are on duty now. We'll take what we can get."

In the meantime, an agent had plugged into Withers's phone GPS and found the locations where he had been the past few days. "Detectives. I found an address in Sheepshead Bay, Brooklyn. Seems like a residence. From the activity he leaves around ten a.m. and returns around nine p.m."

Sam nodded. "That could be where's he's staying to throw us off. He had to make a mistake, eventually. This was it. We have a few hours till nine. I'd still like to take down that hospital."

"Brett, the supervisor Murielle Langston and an employee, Paul McCulla, are there," Simpson yelled from the car.

"Okay, Detectives. Let's do this."

The entourage of three FBI cars, followed by Nick's SUV, parked illegally on a side street outside the ER entrance.

The sign said *no parking except for emergency vehicles from six a.m. to seven p.m.* Frank would never had parked there, even with his MD plates, when he visited Jen. But, for the first time, he didn't give a shit.

As the hospital was surrounded by private homes, finding a parking space took a while. Unlike in Manhattan, there was no lot to scoot into. All hell was about to be break loose. No more Mr.

Nice Guy. Now he planned to vent.

He held Sam's hand against his leg. She must have felt his tension, his coldness. "Frank, we'll get them. We'll get all of them. What can I do to help you, right now?"

"Oh, man, Sam, you're something else. You know that? Okay. If I get ready to break someone's neck, come to me and wrap your arms around me."

She looked surprised. "Seriously?"

"Seriously."

"Let's do this." Nick opened the door when he saw six feds walk from their cars onto the handicap ramp to the ER. They walked in pairs, one behind the other. Special Agent Case led.

Nick, Sam, and Frank followed. Case flashed his badge at the paunchy security guard at the door, asked directions to the accounting admin office. The guard pointed. They walked down the corridor at a steady pace. Frank heard military music in his head. He bet a few of those guys were military. He respected that. Special Agent Case looked behind him. He sent eye signals to his team. They knew where to approach. They had found the third woman there who was involved. Karen Horn. The last guy was Teddy Williams. Case told Frank that Williams should be getting surprised at home by an FBI team, right about now. It could be that he was the one Lisa called.

Case raised his palm in the direction of Nick, Sam, and Frank. Frank knew why. Case depended upon Frank's team to support Frank and keep him back, so he wouldn't go berserk or impede the arrests. It was the FBI who had to make them. They had allowed Frank, Sam, and Nick to come along and watch, as a courtesy. Frank didn't even have to beg them. Sam must have seen in his eyes that he was close to bursting. He knew that his brows furrowed and his eyes always became darker, whenever he was livid. Jen had told him she recognized that. Darker eyes. Sam did what Frank had asked of her. She wrapped her arms around his waist and snuggled. Appropriate or not, Frank held her close.

Langston, McCulla, and Horn didn't know what hit them. The teams split up. Case and Simpson went over to fifty year old Mrs. Langston and grabbed her up under her arms as she screamed. As they pulled her up, one of the buttons on her blouse popped open. They didn't care. The agents read her, her rights, handcuffed her hands behind her back. The takedown took less than two minutes. She kept turning her head around to see the others, while trying to wrestle out of their hold on her. The agents just dragged her. Her feet buckled under her. One high heel slipped off. The agents left it on the floor. They carried her, as if through the air. They pulled her past Frank, who was still holding onto Sam. Frank gave Mrs. Langston a long cold stare as she looked at him, pleading. No words came from him. He nodded to the agents, stood straight and strong with Sam supporting him.

Paul McCulla put up a fight at his desk. The second team had to show him who was boss. One of the agents shoved him off his chair to the ground then got on top of him, grabbed his arms behind his back, and handcuffed him. They pulled him up as he continued fighting.

What is he thinking?

McCulla was a scrawny guy, just average height. He didn't look like he had hit a gym in his life. They would add resisting arrest and fighting a federal officer to the charges. Frank couldn't take it. He released Sam and strode up in front of Paul, towering over him. When Paul looked up at this giant, he cowered and started to cry at Frank not to hit him. Frank got close, grimaced, and then backed off. He covered his nose with his hand. The agents had no choice. They had to take this man, who had just defecated on himself, into their vehicle. At that moment, Frank was glad he didn't have the authority to make an arrest.

The other woman, the motorcycle chick, was the youngest, late twenties. She tried to come on to the third team of agents. No luck. She was dressed in skin tight jeans and a low cut sweater. When the agents approached she had been cutting an article for a file. She lunged at one of the agents with a large pair of shears. He moved out of the way, pushed her down over her desk, grabbed her arms in back of her, and handcuffed her.

As one of the agents moved her arms, her sleeves slid up to her elbows. Frank, even from a distance, noticed the needle marks on her forearms. He could guess where her share of the money went. Attacking a federal agent with a weapon would be added to her charges. And an addict still holding her employment in a hospital? Maybe Jen saw that, too. Something else for them to investigate.

Frank stood proud and looked at the other shaken employees, wondering who else was involved. Most of them wouldn't make eye contact with him. He made mental notes of who they were. He was sure these three would rat, fast. More people would turn up. Sam moved to stand by his side. He felt stronger with her there.

The people who had killed Jen and destroyed his family would finally get what they deserved.

The FBI agents took the newly arrested into their vehicles. Case approached Nick, Sam, and Frank. "Glad to see you held it together, Doctor Khaos."

Frank nodded and hugged Sam around her shoulders. "Yeah. Me, too."

"We're taking them to our Manhattan office. The Brooklyn South ESU will give you backup for the other two arrests. Your murder charge trumps ours for embezzlement. You'd keep Withers and we'd get his wife after the arrest, though. We'd charge him with embezzlement added to the murder charge. Good luck, Detectives. Hope now you can move on with your life, Doc."

Frank gave Case a man-tap on his shoulder. "Thanks."

CHAPTER 39

An ESU team was called in to get over to Withers and his wife's Sheepshead Bay apartment to be on call for the detectives when they arrived. Patrol cars from the closest precinct would assist to take Withers and his wife into custody after their arrest, so Frank was confident NYPD had their backs.

The drive was only about ten minutes, but it was an eternity to Frank. Thoughts ran through his mind. Most of all he thought about Withers.

Have they left the state? The country?

It wouldn't be over until they were taken down.

He prayed to God, it would be over. Tonight.

Withers's apartment building was on a side street across the street from a school. There wasn't one parking spot available, even now at night. They found the apartment 6J. Across the street on the main avenue, they spotted Withers's "clonkmobile." That was what Frank had called it. Run down, filthy, it had to have over way one hundred fifty K miles on it. A 2000 model of some kind of Toyota.

Withers certainly kept low key.

Frank didn't know if he could do as well here at controlling himself as he had done at the hospital. Nick parked a block away, out of sight to windows in the apartment. As he reversed to parallel park, Frank jolted back to the present.

ESU had gotten out of their truck. They were the same guys and sergeant that had escorted Frank and Sam to the precinct the night of the text message.

The sergeant jogged to their car about twenty yards farther back from the apartment building, checked the gear Nick had on the floor, and gave them shields.

When Nick opened the door of his SUV, they heard a gunshot coming from a block away.

"Stay in the car, Detectives!" the sergeant shouted, running down the block to his truck.

The streetlights and lights coming from the private houses on the avenue illuminated his path, peeking through the sparse trees. Patrol cars pulled up behind the truck and, immediately, cops went into action, telling homeowners who had come onto their front porches to watch, to go back into their homes.

Leaning forward into the separation between the front seats, Frank and Sam were able to see, through the front windshield, that the ESU and patrol cops had taken cover. Using binoculars, the sergeant looked up. He must have spotted Withers looking out the window. Withers fired another round that hit the armored truck. The bullet ricocheted but, in the darkness, they couldn't see where it landed. All Frank saw were the sparks when it hit the truck. It reminded him of Iraq when he and his men were in a rabbit hole, taking cover, as their vehicle was under attack. You didn't know when it would end.

There had only been two shots fired. God only knew how many more rounds Withers had. Frank was glad ESU had their backs. As good a shot that he knew he was, and Nick was, he had no idea how Sam could fair at long distance.

But he also knew he couldn't just sit in the car much longer. His need to get his hands around Withers's neck grew stronger by the moment. He needed to calm down and balance his equilibrium so, when the time came, and it would be soon, he could keep himself safe and not do anything stupid to hurt his team in the process. Most arrests did not end in a blood bath. Most arrests went smoothly, when the perp was a clear-thinking human being. He didn't know if that applied to Withers and Lisa at the moment.

The blueprint for the building showed that Withers had a corner apartment, with windows on the main avenue and side street. The sergeant pointed to his men, signaling for them to disperse around the line of fire and get into the building. Two men ran to the right, one to the left.

Another shot rang out, and again hit the truck.

Okay, Withers isn't shooting at us. If Withers had made the men the target, they would have been hit. Frank had trained with him at the range. This man was a pro at five hundred yards. He didn't miss any target, even in movement exercises. That was a good sign. *Maybe he isn't prepared to die.*

Three men ran through the front entrance. Withers must have seen them. A few minutes later, Withers and Lisa ran through the garage exit and down the block toward their car. Lisa was in damn good shape. She ran in better form than her husband. In fact, Dingo was slow and gasping for air. Nick, Sam and Frank bolted out of the car, wearing vests, and took cover. Sam edged down a few cars, so she'd have another angle if need be. Frank edged the opposite way so he'd come up behind them.

As soon as they came into view, Nick stood up over the hood of his car. "Freeze, Dingo." His SIG was pointed right at him.

Withers turned toward Nick. "Yeah right, Nick. You don't have the guts." His wheezing was audible. He bent over, hands on his thighs. "Hold on. Gotta get my damn asthma pump."

"Go ahead, but slow. There are shooters on the roof. Make a wrong move. You'll be taken down in a second."

Withers looked up and saw the sharpshooters on the rooftops before he slipped his hand into his pocket. From behind, Frank saw that his pocket didn't protrude enough to hold a weapon, even a small one. Withers pulled out a yellow pump, held it high in two fingers for them to see, before he put the mouthpiece in his mouth and took two puffs. His breathing eased. He panted until his breath normalized. Frank saw his posture, straighten.

"Drop your weapon, Dingo. It's over," Nick repeated.

Lisa clung to her husband's arm. "Dingo, please. Don't listen to him. He won't shoot. Not after twenty years."

Sam stood up tall, in front of them, her weapon held with both hands straight out. "But I sure as hell will. Drop your weapons, both of you. Get on the ground!"

Withers pivoted to face her. "Well, look who's joined the shindig. The little pain in my butt, rookie. You wouldn't shoot, either. We're unarmed."

"Not true, Dingo. We heard the shots you fired," Nick said.

Withers turned toward Nick again. "Yeah well, what do you want, Valatutti? We didn't do anything."

"Then why are you running?"

"Needed a—vacation."

"You just had one. How much money did you lose at the slots, Lisa? And it was a nice trick, stashing your NYPD phone in the Lexus," Sam taunted.

Frank closed his eyes. *Come on, Sam don't provoke them.*

"Get the fuck away from us." Lisa looked around nervously. "For Christ's sake, Dingo, do something!" She turned around and saw the ESU team on guard, two on a rooftop, two approaching.

Four patrol cops, with weapons drawn, started to approach. Frank had put up a hand for the men to stay back. They did.

Lisa slipped her hand into her pocket, retrieved a 9 mm Berretta, and held it down at her side.

Sam shook her head, taking a defensive pose. "I wouldn't do that if I were you, Lisa. We just arrested four of your former colleagues, who look desperate enough to rat on you but good, and we found money and the gun your husband used to kill Doctor Khaos's wife in your Belle Harbor apartment," she said. "It's over. Drop your weapon and hug the ground. I said now! No need to make this end badly, for anyone."

Lisa froze. The Berretta slipped from her grip and fell to the ground. As she bent down to retrieve it, Sam raised her right leg to kick Lisa backward. Lisa grabbed Sam's leg and almost threw her off balance. Sam used her right arm and pushed Lisa sideways and down, jumped on top of her, straddled her thighs, and wouldn't let her move. She pinned Lisa with her arms above her head on the ground. An ESU officer and two patrol officers ran to take over.

While Sam contained Lisa, Frank grabbed Withers from behind, turned him around, and, with his hands glued to his bubble jacket, smashed him back against the hood of Nick's car.

"Why, Dingo! Why did you have to kill my wife?"

He lifted Withers, straight as a plank, and rammed him into the car two more times. He didn't care, at the moment, how many dents he put in Nick's car. The two ESU officers let him have Withers. So did Nick and the two patrol officers. Frank needed his time.

Withers groaned. "I'd do anything for my daughter. Needed the money for hospital bills. All the overtime in the world wouldn't cut it. God forbid if anything happened to your son."

"No excuse for murder, Dingo! How did you get the phone?"

"I was in the precinct when they brought that scum in. Went to where they put his stuff. Slipped it off the table and into my pocket. Didn't know what I was going to do with it, then."

Frank raised his fist, intending to bring it down on Withers's face.

"Go ahead, Frank. They won't put me in the cage. It'll be too much trouble. Between me being a cop and the emphysema, and it'll be a longer trial. And every perp I ever investigated who's now behind bars, will want a retrial. Nah, Frank. They're gonna let this slide."

Frank paused with his fist in the air. Slowly he lowered it to grab the collar of Withers's jacket. "They have asthma meds in lockup. And where you're going, they'll protect you, real good."

Nick patted Frank on the back, signaling for him to release Withers. Frank did. Nick turned Withers around, cuffed him, read him his rights. Sam cuffed Lisa, and read her hers, without further incident.

ↄﾟↄ

Nick and Sam escorted Withers and Lisa, handcuffed, into the Brooklyn South Precinct, with the ESU team and Frank following. Withers had been hacking and wheezing the entire trip there. Everyone stood, shocked that one of their own had done the unthinkable and thought that they could get away with it. Then they looked at Frank. Standing tall. Proud. They knew the torment he had gone through over the past two years. He saw them looking at him. Pity in their eyes changed to hope. Some smiled. Many nodded.

Frank would never wish ill on anyone, but Withers suffering with emphysema, and having to give up smoking cold turkey, would be more payback than the five-minute beat down Frank would have given him.

At the moment he had raised his fist, even before Withers told him, Frankie came into his mind.

What kind of a role model for my son would I be if I came home with bloody knuckles?

FBI Special Agents Case and Simpson were in the lieutenant's office. Lieutenant Rojas was there, as well, for support. Nick handed Lisa over to the federal agents without saying a word. Then he put Withers's ID and badge on the lieutenant's desk.

They all stared at the detective's symbol of honor. One that he had held for twenty years.

Lieutenant Rojas only spoke five words. "Get them out of here."

The agents pushed Lisa out of his office with ESU following them. Patrol officers from the precinct took Withers out to book him.

"You three okay?"

Nick nodded. 'Yeah. I'm okay."

"Sam? Frank?"

Sam sniffled. "I'm okay."

Frank blew out a deep breath. "I'm okay."

"Go home. The three of you."

Nick patted Frank on the shoulder, nodded, and started to leave the office. There were no words. Then, his cell rang. "Hello, Valatutti."

"Hey, Nick, John Trenton."

Sam turned to Nick with a smile. They all yelled into the phone with their voices, tripping over the top of each other.

"Hi, Doctor Trenton."

"Well, did it happen yet?

"What did she have?"

Trenton laughed. "Yes. They're here. A boy and a girl."

"Ooh, ooh, ooh! How sweet! Congratulations!" Sam yelled into the phone.

"Names yet?" Frank asked.

"Yes, Khaos, Alexi Summer and Zachary Lance."

"Congratulations to you, both!" Loo said.

"Thanks, guys. Have to run. Speak with you soon."

"Send pictures. Send pictures!" Sam yelled again.

"Will do." Trenton laughed and disconnected.

"I'm going to the men's room. Give you two some time to talk." Loo said as he followed Nick.

Frank took Sam in his arms, as she slipped hers around his neck. He looked down at her, tears trickling down his cheek. "It's over, princess."

She wiped his tears away with her thumbs as her hands caressed his face. "Yes. It's over." She paused. "I made a decision."

"What decision?"

"I've earned the right to be a detective. I belong working here as a detective—with you."

He held her tight, kissed the top of her head, and rested his lips there.

❧❧❧

Frank's first stop was his in-laws house on a tree-lined block in Mill Basin, Brooklyn. He always teased Sam that her parents lived so close to her. He'd soon have to tell her his in-laws lived closer, around the corner from him. They had been the only babysitters Frankie had known. To Frank, they were Mom and Dad. Like him, they had been waiting for closure for over two years. He sat in the car, contemplating how he would tell them that their daughter's killer had been taken into custody.

Do they need to know the entire story? No. But they deserve to know.

He didn't know why he had felt so pained now. Relief hadn't kicked in, yet. The reality that he could now move on with his life hadn't kicked in. He knew he was falling in love with Sam. Probably already there.

Am I ready?

Doubt riddled him.

Am I using Jen's open murder case just as an excuse not to move on? To close myself down from relationships?

He was getting too old for just a whirlwind of casual sexual flings. He was getting tired of going to women's homes and even having his secret place.

Why should I be secret?

He knew why. He didn't want Frankie to grow up to be the kind of man who hopped from woman to woman. Frank swallowed hard.

He had a lot of psychoanalysis to do. On himself.

Okay, Frank. The time has come to make a major upheaval in your life, no matter how frightening.

As he exited the car, security strobe lighting came on, illuminating the driveway and area leading up to the front door. He knew his in-laws would be asleep at this hour and the lights would wake them. He used his key to open the front door. As he entered, his mother-in-law appeared at the top of the steps. His father-in-law appeared a moment later. Frank greeted them with a huge smile as they came down the steps.

"Frank, what's wrong? Frankie's sleeping."

"Nothing's wrong, Mom. Come on, sit down."

He sat on the dark burgundy couch and they sat on the adjacent love seat. He didn't waste time. Their anxiety had been high enough with him coming over unannounced at such a late hour. He told them that Jen's killer had been apprehended. Tears ran from both of them as his in-law's hugged each other. They didn't let go. He saw that the love they had for each other was the same he and Jen had shared. That undying spiritual love. The unconditional love that grew stronger every day and through each hardship, each tragedy. He hoped he could move on and find the same kind of love.

With Sam.

He gave them time to compose themselves and then he went on to tell them the entire story of the embezzlement plan and that Jen's murder was to cover it up. They sat squeezing each other's hand the entire time he spoke. They hadn't asked any questions. Frank had told him all they needed to know. They embraced him in love and gratitude. Gratitude for him not giving up.

Their talking woke up Frankie who stumbled down the stairs, rubbing his eyes. "Dad, it's the middle of the night." He looked at his grandparents. "Why are Grandma and Grandpa crying?"

"Come here, champ." Frank scooped him up into his lap and hugged him. It took him a moment to think about how to phrase it. "We caught the man who hurt Mommy."

"Did you hurt him?"

"No."

Frankie stared up at him, clearly bewildered. "Why not?"

"Because that wouldn't have been the right thing to do. But he's going to be in jail for the rest of his life."

"Good."

Frank kissed and hugged him for a few minutes. "Okay, go back upstairs to bed. See you tomorrow after school." He needed to go home and get some sleep.

Maybe for the first time in two years, he'd be able to fall asleep in less than a few hours.

ᏒᎧᏒᎧ

Refreshed from a good night's sleep, and thanking God that his torment had ended, Frank strode down the hall to AriellaRose's secure hospital room. He had gotten minimal tests back from the psychologists he had sent in to examine her. Mainly because of her lack of cooperation. He had already decided not to release her into police custody, yet.

For one, the X-rays still showed signs of pneumonia in her right lung. It had only been two weeks and, for a woman who didn't take care of herself, that wasn't unusual. Without the psych tests, he wouldn't be able to diagnose if she was mentally able to stand trial. More importantly, he doubted if she could get along within the regular population in a prison environment. The decision would be his. He had made that clear enough to his department.

He hadn't been here the last couple of days, with trying to apprehend Withers, so he doubted he'd get a warm reception from Miss Larcon.

He straightened his tie as he reached her door. Even though he hated it, for this young lady, he wanted to come across as more formal, rather than a tough guy she'd think she could jerk around.

Yeah, it's all in the approach.

He unlocked the door with the key hanging amongst a bunch on his belt. As soon as he opened the door, AriellaRose greeted him with a closed-lip smirk.

"That happy to see me? Huh, AriellaRose?"

"I hate it when you come in here with that suit and tie."

He approached the bed and pulled over a chair. "How come?"

"Ugh, you plan on staying?"

At least her voice went back to adulthood. Frank paused before he spoke. "Certainly do. Have a lot to talk about."

"I knew it. When you wear that, you're all business."

"Good. You read me well. That's a plus."

She folded her arms across her chest. "What do you want, now?"

"For one, why haven't you been cooperative with the staff I'm sending in to talk with you?"

"Yeah, that sucks. Why are you doing that?"

"To get an idea of how you think. Why you've done what you did."

She rolled her eyes.

He put his lips together. "Well the grand jury indicted you."

"Yeah. My shit lawyer told me. Well, you can all fuck off."

"Do you want to know what's going to happen?"

"When can I go home?"

"To your brownstone?"

"Duh! Yeah, no shit Sherlock, my brownstone."

He frowned, not quite understanding her delusional thinking at this point. "That's not happening."

"Like, hell, it's not."

"Why do you think that? After everything you've been told?"

She stared straight into his eyes, blank expression, giving no clue as to her thinking. "I don't know why you're giving me a hard way to go."

"Do you remember what you told me a couple of days ago? You just about admitted everything."

"You're stressing me out. You know that?"

Denial like this was a symptom of something quite serious. And he didn't get the impression that AriellaRose was playing games. He took a chance. "AriellaRose who do you think would know about what you've done?"

"I don't know what the fuck you're talking about."

"Who's BlackRam?"

She blinked repeatedly. "What? What kind of name is that?"

"It's a Wiccan name. Emma was BlackFlower, Rachel was BlackCloud, and Meredith was BlackMoon. We deduced from the evidence in your ritual room at the brownstone you were BlackRam."

He noticed a transformation in her facial expressions. Her eyebrows straightened. She paled. Evil spewed from her hardened, glacier eyes, again. She contorted her face, twitching her nose, her body writhing on the bed as if something had taken over.

He didn't believe in entities taking over, far from it, but something was retching from deep within her soul at that moment.

Her tone of voice changed to more aggressive, stronger, more confident. More fluent. More sophisticated. "BlackRam will never be defeated. BlackRam will haunt you forever, Tattooman! BlackRam will kill you in your sleep. You and your detective, Samantha. No one can undo BlackRam's spells. BlackRam's energy is powerful. All encompassing. BlackRam will get away with everything she's done. BlackRam will put you in a grave, just like she has done with the others."

He listened intently, showing no emotion, even though thoughts were rambling through his brain.

"Yeah. You'll never find them if you spend the rest of your career looking. She will not talk to you again. No one will put AriellaRose in prison. I'll make her kill anyone she meets." She gazed at the wall in front of her. Hypnotized.

Frank had enough information to make a decision. He snapped his fingers in front of her.

She jumped. "What the fuck did you do that for?"

"Welcome back, AriellaRose. Where did you go?"

"I was having a daydream and you woke me up. What the fuck?"

"What were you dreaming about?"

"You mentioned BlackRam and I just went off. I don't remember. I never remember my dreams."

"All right, take it easy. You need to talk to the doctors I send in to ask you questions."

"Why? Give me one good reason why."

"If you don't, you're going to be in this hospital a very, very long time." He patted her hand and left the room without further explanation.

He wasn't sure if he had unraveled a split personality or what. He wasn't jumping to conclusions. Not until many more tests, researching, for at least another month. But one thing for sure, he was not handing AriellaRose Larcon over to the authorities for a long time.

❧❧❧

Frank cuddled with Sam under the sheets. In his bedroom. In his house. They embraced, kissing, and he rolled on top of her. She yanked the blanket down to his waist. Good. it was getting hot under there. Both their bodies glistened from beads of perspiration. He kissed her face, down to her neck. He treasured her. Appreciated her. He wanted to show her in the most primal way.

They had already gone one round. Oh, man! Did this woman have a strong libido. One that he'd satisfy again and again, and forever, if he had his way.

He pecked her nose with his lips. "Thanks, princess."

She tapped his nose. "For what?"

"For bringing me closure."

She smiled and her lips met his. He reciprocated and there was no more talking for a while.

He rolled over onto his back. "You know? You're the only woman who's been in this bed other than Jen."

Sam rolled over and leaned half on him, half on the bed. "Then I'm honored, King Khaos. And I look forward to many more nights in your bed, and nights you feel you don't have to ship Frankie off to Grandma and Grandpa."

He smiled. A tear trickled from his eye. Sam lay her head on his chest. He looked up toward the ceiling.

Thanks, Jen, for bringing Sam into our lives.

The End

About the Author

Ronnie Allen is a New York City native, born and bred in Brooklyn New York, where she was a teacher in the New York City Department of Education for 33 years. As a New York State licensed School Psychologist, she was given the opportunity to be one of three educators to create a unit in her school for emotionally needy students. Her various roles included classroom teacher, staff developer, crisis intervention specialist, and mentor for teachers who were struggling. Always an advocate for the child, Allen carries this through in the need to understand children with deeply rooted emotional traumas—as the young adult characters in Aries. In the early 1990s Allen began a journey into holistic healing and alternative therapies. She actually completed her PhD in Parapsychic Sciences in 2001, writing the dissertation when she was home for four months recuperating from being in a coma for twelve days. Medical science had given up on her and told her husband and son that she had less than a two percent chance of survival. Well surprise, surprise! Here she is! Definitely the survivor. And so are her characters! Hence, the dedication for Aries.

Along the way, Allen has picked up many certifications. She is a Board Certified Holistic Health Practitioner as well as a crystal therapist, Reiki practitioner, metaphysician, dream analyst, and Tarot Master Instructor. She has taught workshops in New York City and in Central Florida where she now lives in all of these mediums both in person and online, with the goal being to teach people how to make the mind-body connection for their healing and personal growth. Combining a love of the crime genre and her psychology background, with her alternative therapies experience, writing psychological and paranormal thrillers is the perfect venue for her.